THE LAST DAWN

THE LAST
DAWN

Book Three of The Last War

Peter Bostrom

www.authorpeterbostrom.com

Summary: Fear ripples through human galactic society. Another ship travels from humanity's bleak future, targets a populated planet ... and lays it waste in a fiery apocalypse. Nothing survives, and the ship disappears. In the midst of the recovery, Admiral Jack Mattis finds more questions than answers as he tracks down the dreadfully powerful enemy ship. But the most pressing question: why are these mutated humans from the future relentlessly attacking us? What do they want? And at what cost? And are these the same creatures created by the genetic research corporation exposed by Mattis on the planet Chrysalis? The answers lie at the root of a deep conspiracy that goes beyond governments, beyond corporations. A conspiracy that will stop at nothing to succeed, and achieve ultimate power over humanity. And as the deadly ship prepares for its final catastrophic strike, Admiral Jack Mattis and the crew of the Midway are the last defense between us, and our last dawn.

Text set in Garamond

Cover art by Tom Edwards

http://tomedwardsdesign.com

ISBN-10: 1977922643
ISBN-13: 978-1977922649

Printed in the United States of America

For my three favorite admirals: Kirk, Adama, and
Ackbar

Prologue

Tonatiuh System
Planet Zenith
City of New Bristol
Admiral Jack Mattis Air And Space Port
Landing Pad 9

"Aww now, come on ladies, you wouldn't wanna kill a handsome guy like me ... would you?"

Harry Reardon, smuggler extraordinaire, smiled his award-winning smile as he stared down the barrel of a pair of high powered pistols, hands at the level of his eyes. His ship, the *Aerostar*, hummed behind him on the landing pad, a drone refueling its O2 and nitrogen tanks. Nearby, his assailant's ship was similarly being restocked. A logo that looked remarkably like an octopus was half-peeled back from the hatch window. Weird. Just like the Weird Sisters.

"Cute," said Jasmine—or was this one Carolynn? He could never keep track. "You see, we were thinking we would take the cargo *and* the money." She pulled back the hammer. "It just seems simpler that way. Doesn't it?"

"Simpler," echoed Reardon, eyes flicking to the green crate on the mechanical pallet jack he'd transported from Chrysalis to Zenith, all the while taking *great* care to avoid the law. His supplier was quite insistent on that point. "Do you even know what's in that thing?"

"I know it's worth about two million dollars to our buyer," said Jasmine … or Carolynn … or Whichever, her finger tapping on the trigger. "That's enough for me."

Reardon blew out a low whistle, reaching over and pushing his aviator glasses up his nose. "And you're only paying me twenty-five. Jeez. I was getting robbed *before* you fine ladies pulled out your pieces. Weird Sisters indeed."

One of them sneered at him. "Poor, poor Harry Reardon, joke of the galaxy. With your *I'm compensating for something* black leather jacket, cringe-worthy haircut, your ridiculous pink ship, and your crippled brother … everyone laughs at you behind your back"

"Hold on. That's just not fair," he said, frowning in annoyance, tilting his head forward so he could look at her over the rim of his shades. "My ship's not pink." His beloved *Aerostar* was a *very* manly salmon colored. Or, as the salesman had referred to it, *blood in the water*.

"Whatever," said one of the contacts. She gestured with her spare hand. "Hand over the money, and the cargo, and *maybe* we'll let you go."

There was *no* way they were going to let him go. It would be bad for business; easier to just shoot him and and say *he* was the one who double-crossed them, killed in the subsequent shootout. How could he say otherwise if he was dead?

"Sure," he lied, keeping his hands up. "Pallet jack key first.

It's in my breast pocket. Lemme just get it."

"Okay," said Whichever. "But if you make any sudden moves…"

He grinned widely. "You think I've never been robbed before? I know the deal, sweetheart."

Her expression instantly soured. "Don't call me sweetheart."

"Sorry, honey."

"Or that."

"Sorry, darl'n."

She snarled and jabbed her gun toward him. "You just *really* wanna die, don't you, you piece of—"

Just close enough. Reardon snatched the pistol out of her hand, spun it around, and squeezed the trigger.

Click.

The gun had a biolock on it. The woman in front of him —he arbitrarily designated her Babe Number One—slowly drew another pistol. A bigger one, with an extended barrel. And loaded.

"Awkward," he said, and then flung the weapon at her. She ducked, spoiling the shot.

Crack. A bullet whizzed past his head, close enough to almost clip his ear. Babe Number Two fired again, the bullet screaming as it ricocheted off the ground, flying away farther on into the spaceport docking bay.

He dove behind a slightly-too-small crate. Another round screamed past. "Sammy!" said Reardon into his earpiece. His brother was always so slow when it mattered most. "Now would be a good time!"

The ship—still powered on due to the resupply—hummed

with energy. A heavy, twin-barreled machine gun on a ball-turret thrust out of the underside of the ship, spinning angrily as it turned to face the two assailants.

"Wait," said one, dropping her gun. "Wait, wait!"

Nah. "Do it, kid," he said. "It's either them or us."

With a loud rip-saw of a few hundred rounds being sent downrange, Jasmine and Carolynn got turned to chunky salsa.

His ears rang and the air smelled of cordite. "Waste of ammunition," said Reardon, groaning as he grabbed the heavy box's handle and began dragging it toward the ship. Bullets cost so damn much. He stepped over a body part. "Jesus, did you have to get their bits *everywhere*?"

"That was your fault," said Sammy. "You're the one who insisted on installing the 75-caliber guns. Those things are designed to shoot, like, *tanks*. Not people."

That was the great thing about guns that worked on tanks. They worked equally well on people. "Why didn't you shoot 'em earlier?" he asked. "They had guns on me for, like, a minute."

"I was taking a dump."

"Ah," said Reardon, "so kind of you to pinch it off just for me. Anyway, if they were stupid enough to try and mug me in full view of my ship—didn't pay off for the dumb-fuck sisters, that's for sure—that means that whatever we were delivering was *super* valuable. Possibly even super *duper*. I'm sure someone else will be interested in our cargo. Whatever it is."

"Yeah," said Sammy in his ear, his brother's voice high pitched and nervous. "But we should get off-world. Fast. Firing heavy weapons like this is going to attract a *lot* of attention. The cops are probably already on their way."

"Probably," agreed Reardon, dragging the heavy box on the pallet jack up to the loading ramp, straining his arms as he pulled it aboard. He'd totally lied to Babe Number One about the pallet jack—it wasn't motorized and therefore didn't need a key. Why didn't they have a robot for this….

Well, because robots cost money, and I ain't got none of that.

Although that wasn't strictly true. He'd gotten paid for the job and got to keep the merchandise to boot. And now he knew how much it was worth. Time to go get paid … assuming he could find a buyer.

And what the hell could be in that box that was so damn heavy? Oh well—he'd never know. The supplier was insistent that if he opened it, he not only wouldn't get paid, but he'd also be hunted down and turned into even chunkier salsa than the dumb-fuck sisters painted all over the deck outside.

Reardon slammed his fist on the button to raise the ramp. "Sammy, the cargo's aboard. Get us off-world."

"You got it," said Sammy.

Reardon took out his earpiece and made his way up to the flight deck. Why did they call it a flight deck? Probably because *cockpit* sounded funny. He sauntered up to the ladder and put his hand on the first rung.

The whole ship shook as a massive shockwave passed over it.

"Sammy?" he asked, then realized he'd taken off his earpiece. Damn it. He climbed up the rungs of the ladder, pushing open the hatchway. Sammy's wheelchair was parked where the co-pilot's seat normally was, its occupant staring out the cockpit. "Hey Sammy, what the hell is going—"

Out the front of the cockpit canopy, the city of New

Bristol was on fire.

"What did you do?" asked Sammy, glancing over his shoulder, his face pale.

"*Me?*" Reardon stared at the cityscape as one of the tall buildings—some finance headquarters or something—toppled over, crushing several smaller buildings and sending up a huge cloud of concrete dust that enveloped the streets in brown, billowing clouds.

"Yes, you!"

Reardon felt his face go as white as Sammy's, and slid into the pilot's seat. "We have to get out of here," he said, powering on the engines.

Another building toppled over, as though shaken apart at the foundations. "What the hell is that?" asked Sammy. He pointed up into the sky. "What's happening?"

"Doesn't matter," said Reardon, as the engine power built to a high-pitched hum. "This is the perfect distraction for us to get out of here."

The *Aerostar* rose up through the air. Another shockwave raced toward them, engulfing them in a cloud of dust. The ship tumbled, then rightened itself, slowly sinking back down toward the surface of Zenith. Reardon increased the thrust; the ship continued to drop, wobbling in the turbulent air.

"Why aren't we gaining altitude?" he asked, opening the throttle to maximum. The ground slowly drifted up toward them as the *Aerostar*'s engines, at maximum burn, fought to push them away.

"We are," said Sammy, pointing at the altimeter with a shaking finger. It showed them at two thousand feet above the ground which was almost within stones-throwing distance.

"We're going up all right ... but ... the ground is coming up with us."

"That's impossible," said Reardon, but as he watched, the ground got closer and closer and the altimeter climbed higher and higher. "Nope. Guess it's really possible. This is happening. Hold on...."

One of the buildings nearby, the control tower, toppled over. Debris rained all around them, plinking off the hull.

Sammy flailed around. "Do something, Harry!"

He wasn't sure what more he *could* do. Except....

No. It was too dangerous.

But then again, what was the purpose of having an emergency anti-matter engine booster if he never used it when he needed it? The ground was coming up awfully quick, and if he did nothing, they would *definitely* die.

With a soft groan Harry reached over to the switches to his left and turned the knob labelled *Do Not Ever Turn*. The emergency booster-thruster. His own, personal addition. A micro-pellet of anti-matter that, injected into the reaction stream, would essentially quadruple the engine power for several seconds. Or was it a factor of forty? He could never remember.

The *Aerostar* shook angrily as the reactor pumped the surge of power into the engines, thrusters moving beyond normal—safe—levels of thrust into the wildly *unsafe*. The altimeter spun angrily as he continued to climb, and finally, the crust of Zenith beneath began to fall away, breaking up and tumbling in pieces as it did so.

The thruster burned out, and the ship continued to climb up into the atmosphere. He maneuvered the external cameras to see the planet's surface. A section of it had broken into a million pieces, little more than a fragmented debris field.

"What happened?" asked Sammy, aghast.

For probably the first time in his life, Harry Reardon had no answer.

The *Aerostar* broke the upper atmosphere and crossed the threshold into space. He tilted the ship forward, turning the cockpit toward the planet's surface.

A massive explosion had blown a whole continent of Zenith to dust and ashes. The exact nature of the blast eluded him—he wasn't an explosion-analyst or … whatever you called someone who studied explode-y things … but to his untrained eye it looked like the crust of the planet had been lifted up several miles … and then dropped.

"Wow." There wasn't anything else he could say.

"Yeah," said Sammy. "Guess we don't have to worry about not having take-off clearance."

The ship drifted again, giving a view of space, a black blanket full of twinkling white stars.

"What does the radar show?" asked Reardon, unable to hide a little tremor in his voice.

Sammy glanced at it, his face ghostly. "There's … there's a ship," he said. "A big one."

He aligned an external hull camera toward the contact. It was a giant steel wall, a very regular geometric shape—not cubical, but more like a brick floating in space, with a massive protrusion below it like a jousting knight's lance. It glowed a fierce, angry red, lines of power running along it, similarly lit up.

It had to be the military. Chinese, American, it didn't

matter. Could even be one of the smaller space powers. Brazilian, or Indian, or Indonesian. Again, didn't matter. All governments were different faces of one tyrant … and they all offered the same choice. A hand up your arse, or a boot up the same. But he was nobody's puppet. Neither was New London, or Chrysalis.

Or Zenith. What was left of it. Which, at a glance, didn't seem to be much. He remembered that last year this planet had figured prominently in the news, but he couldn't remember for the life of him why.

"ID on the ship?" asked Reardon, touching his Z-drive engine switch. "If we gotta get out of here in a hurry I wanna know who's chasing us. The Chinese are faster but the Americans have bigger guns, so, you know." He diverted extra power away from non-essential systems. "If our Z-space translator fails again, like last time, it'll be good to know exactly how we're going to die."

"No idea," said Sammy. "It's not showing up anything the *Aerostar* can recognize. Just a bunch of jibberish. Like they scrambled it or something, and we don't have the key."

The ship's radar wailed at them. Reardon stared at his system in bewilderment.

"They're launching fighters," said Sammy. He snapped his fingers in front of Reardon's face. "Hey! Bro, they're launching fighters!"

How long had he been staring at nothing? "Shit," he said, flicking the Z-space drive to jump mode, and grabbing the custom joystick that he had labeled, *Zoom Zoom Zoom!* "Sorry. Let's get the hell out of here."

The Z-space drive whined in complaint and, for a

9

moment, he really did think it would fail. He whacked the Z-space control panel with a fist. Then the black sea of regular space faded out around them, a cloud of bright hues enveloping their ship as it moved from real space into the strange, multicolored reality of Z-space, navigating away from Zenith as fast as it could.

"Well," said Reardon, slumping back in his seat. "I guess we don't have to worry about retaliation for taking that cargo. Or legal trouble for killing those two babes."

"Guess not," said Sammy, running his hands through his hair. "Jesus … what was that ship? Did it cause the blast down there on Zenith?"

"Dunno," said Reardon. "It wasn't military. Maybe it was … the aliens."

"Those things that attacked Earth last year?" Sammy shuddered visibly, reaching down and fiddling with the brakes on his wheelchair. "You think they're back?"

He let silence be his answer as the *Aerostar* flew onward through the kaleidescope of color.

"Where are we going?" asked Sammy.

The answer was clear. "To tell the universe what happened," said Reardon. "And the only person who'll listen."

CHAPTER ONE

Earth
Lower Manhattan
GBC News Building

Meanwhile

"Okay, miss Ramirez. We're on air in three, two…"

One. Martha Ramirez smiled at camera two. She'd done this a million times, to the point it was almost routine. "Good evening, this is GBC News Talkback Time with Martha. I'm Martha Ramirez and I'm joined here today by two very important guests." She gestured to her left. "The first is US Admiral Caroline Fischer, Chief of Galactic Operations for the United States Military." She gestured to her right. "The second is Professor Tuyen Vo from University of California at Berkeley's Sociology Department. Thank you both for coming here." She made a show of glancing down at and adjusting her notes, even though the sheets of paper were blank and merely props. "Mister Vo, perhaps you'd like to start us off. Why are we here today?"

"Well," said Vo, his brown tweedy jacket patched in a way Ramirez could only assume was a deliberate fashion statement that said, *I am a Professor and oh so smart!*, "regarding the alien creatures who attacked Earth almost a year ago … Admiral Mattis has made some *bold* claims regarding their nature and origins, that they come from the future—which frankly I find ludicrous, as I'm sure you do as well. His wild accusations, made guerilla-style from his very own ship with you goading him on, have inspired academic discussion from around the globe and in all parts of the colonized galaxy. The question, of course, on everyone's lips is … how much *truth* is there in them?"

"It's interesting you mentioned truth," said Admiral Fischer, her tone clipped and frustrated. "As you are well aware, Admiral Mattis is a coworker of mine, and he went against Department of Defense orders when he spoke to Miss Ramirez as he did. Yes, he *did* claim that the aliens who attacked Earth were not extraterrestrial beings, but humans who had come, somehow, from the future. And so far the evidence we've collected suggests he may be right."

"What, like *Terminator*?" sneered Vo. "Preposterous. Did they arrive naked in a ball of lightning? Did they hit 88 miles an hour? Life is not a campy science fiction movie from hundreds of years ago, Admiral. In real life, we're bound by pesky things like *physics*. And *reality*."

"No," said Admiral Fischer, putting her hands together. "Not like a movie. From what little we've been able to gather

… and as long as we're on the subject of ancient campy science fiction movies … their method of time travel more accurately resembles that from *Star Trek: First Contact*. Some kind of rift in the fabric of space-time, which allows them to journey into the past, but one which can only be used from certain locations and subject to certain, unclear limitations."

"You mean they want to steal our whales?" asked Vo, incredulously.

Admiral Fischer rolled her eyes. "Professor, you're thinking of *Star Trek IV: The Voyage Home*. The other *Star Trek* film with time travel."

"Wait. You mean, the aliens came through a black hole?"

"*No.*" Admiral Fischer scowled. "That's the first reboot film where they destroyed Vulcan." She closed her eyes and took a deep breath, probably regretting that she was arguing details of three-hundred-year-old movies on galactic television. "Look. We don't know how they got here, and frankly, it doesn't matter. All we know is that they're here. What we need to do now is figure out what they want, and how to stop them."

"Right, right," said Vo, waving his hand dismissively. "So it's more like *Austin Powers* and the giant *laser*," he said, forming air quotes with his fingers around the word laser. "Well, you're correct, Admiral Fischer, in that how this alleged technology works simply doesn't matter. Time travel is a ludicrous prospect. The fundamental laws of physics state that time can only flow in one direction. It can speed up, or slow down, or it can be manipulated by things like Z-space—but even in Z-space, the conservation of energy laws and physics apply. That space is simply … shaped differently than our own, allowing seemingly faster navigation without actually bypassing the natural laws."

"Like taking the freeway instead of traveling through backstreets," said Ramirez, her knowledge of the underlying science shaky at best. But, as the face of the news, she had to fake it convincingly. "You still have to obey the speed limit, but you can travel in a way that's much more efficient."

"That's right," said Vo, snapping his fingers. "Admiral Mattis simply doesn't have the educational background to understand these things."

"Excuse me," said Admiral Fischer, leaning forward in her chair slightly, "that is utterly ludicrous. Admiral Mattis has been commanding US warships for decades now, he understands Z-space travel far better than *you* do. Aren't you a Professor of *Art?*"

"Sociology is not fine arts," protested Vo, seemingly quite offended. "It is the study of humans and, now, humanoid creatures of all descriptions. Including the MaxGainz mutants and creatures who attacked Earth. Incidentally, our findings are that they are quite different."

"Indeed," said Admiral Fischer, impassively. "Quite impressive that you, a team of college professors from a university, have been able to determine concrete answers to questions we, in the military, with all our resources and first-hand exposure to the attackers, their bodies, and their technology, have been unable to fully understand."

"It is, isn't it?" he said, smiling widely and reaching behind him, withdrawing a sheet of paper attached to a clipboard. "This is why we're here. UC Berkley's Sociology Department would like to present a list of our twenty demands for civilian research and interaction with the alien creature or creatures. However many there may be."

Ramirez felt her chest tighten. Demands? This hadn't been on the program schedule … she kept her smile going, her reporter's instincts fighting the urge to clobber the professor with his own clipboard.

"Demands?" asked Admiral Fischer, her voice painted with skepticism.

"Yes. You see, humans have always struggled with our urge to destroy that which we don't understand. However, in this century we're a more enlightened people, and accordingly, we at the university would like to open dialogue with the alien creatures." Vo turned to face camera one. "If you're listening, otherworldly citizens, it's our *polite* request that the military not interfere with this. This is citizen's diplomacy."

Ramirez made sure none of the cameras were looking at her and then casually ran her palm along her face. Admiral Fischer looked at her angrily. Ramirez simply shrugged back.

"Well," said Ramirez, trying desperately to bring the conversation back under her control, "that's all very well and I wish you the best with that. However, there's also the matter of the Ark Project. Admiral Mattis made other accusations, too, Mister Vo, including that Senator Pitt was deeply involved in a conspiracy, and that there exists a *deep state* within the US government and all other world governments that is planning some unspecified scheme, and that President Schuyler is part of it and did nothing. I'd imagine tracking down any of them would be easier than tracking down aliens."

Vo went to speak up, but before he could, Admiral Fischer received a message on her communicator.

She stood up immediately. "Miss Ramirez, this interview is over."

Ramirez frowned darkly. "I was under the impression these matters *could* be discussed—"

"It's not that," said Admiral Fischer, tapping away on her communicator before putting it away. "I must return to my duties. Planet Zenith has been attacked."

Ramirez stood as well, leaving a slack-jawed Vo waving his clipboard and shouting something inane as the cameras continued to roll.

CHAPTER TWO

Earth
United States of America
Georgetown, MD
Victory Park

It was good to be back on Earth. Admiral Jack Mattis stretched out on the grass, taking in a deep breath of that natural Earth oxygen, and let it out slowly. The park was crowded and a little noisy, but *oh*, the air was fresh and clean and good, the breeze comforting, and the sun warm and gentle on his skin.

This is what made visiting Earth all worthwhile. Not just the weather; watching baby Jack Mattis—Chuck's son, his grandson—roll around on the grass, squealing happily.

"I think he's getting the hang of it," said Chuck, holding out his hands and letting Jack crawl toward him. "He'll be walking before we know it."

"*Then* you'll be in trouble," said Mattis, unable to fight back a massive grin. "I remember when you started. You used to get into everything … always so inquisitive." He fell silent for a moment, aware that his son hadn't changed at all. He was *still* getting into things he shouldn't and being overly inquisitive. Into dangerous matters. He finally continued. "If Jack gives you the same trouble you gave me, well, you're in for quite a ride."

"Mmm," said Chuck, grinning like a kid himself. "Well, maybe now that things have quieted down, you'll be around to help out more."

The notion was actually pleasing to him. "I've got a few more weeks leave saved up," he said. "Now that the *Midway* is in for a refit on her engines, we're all able to stretch our legs. Turns out these long distance patrols are really great at racking up time off." He watched as baby Jack squirmed and kicked, gurgling happily. "Which, you know, I'm starting to appreciate more and more. How's his condition?"

Chuck nodded confidently. "The doc says he's fine now. Had that weird heart murmur, and his hormonal profile was off a bit, but they gave him a shot of something and now he's fine."

"Good. That's good. Sick babies aren't fun." He smiled as baby Jack spotted a butterfly nearby and crawled towards it, babbling delightfully. "Besides, healthy babies are enough of a handful already."

"Well," said Chuck, his tone suggesting this was something he had been thinking about for some while, "Elroy and I could really use you being here more often, especially in this economy. Have you considered … you know. The R word?"

The R word. Mattis's happiness evaporated. "I'm sure that

I *don't* want to retire. Not yet." He frowned. "And besides, you don't need me. Don't you have Elroy to help you out with the kid these days? I'd imagine since you're not working anymore, finding time for parenting wouldn't be hard...."

Chuck grimaced, looking away. "Yeah. There *is* that, I guess."

Mattis propped himself up on his elbows. "I've been meaning to ask you about that. What were you *thinking*, son? Breaking into Senator Pitt's old office? You're lucky I was able to bail you out ... and that you had a great lawyer."

Chuck managed a smile. "Without Khalid I'd be screwed, I tell you what. He could sell a thing to a person who ... already has access to a very large quantity of that thing."

"No kidding." Mattis reached out and gently touched Jack's nose, who gurgled happily. "Still. You're not exactly out of the woods yet." He wanted to add, *stop sticking your nose into things that don't concern you,* but thought better of it.

"I know, I know." Chuck groaned. "I can't leave the state, I had to sell that old pistol, and of course, I got fired. This won't look good on my resume."

"And I thought Elroy was going to be the unemployed delinquent between you two," said Mattis, a little too teasingly.

Chuck didn't seem to appreciate the humor. "He's working hard, Dad," he said, an edge of pain creeping into his tone. "Two jobs. He feels like he's gotta support us now. Give up all his dreams, you know? Just to make ends meet."

"You need money?" asked Mattis, "Because—"

"Nope. We have plenty." Chuck idly twirled a blade of grass between his fingers. "He's just ... worried, that's all. He feels that everything's resting on his shoulders. Like if he slips up, or has any kind of fun at all, we're all going to be out on the streets starving."

It was an entirely normal reaction to have, even with the generous public assistance that most governments of the world—including the USA—offered their citizens. It was a feeling he'd often had early in his career, with Caroline and Chuck at home and him on some ship halfway across the galaxy, irrationally worrying that one slip-up would send them all to the poorhouse. Supporting a family was a heavy burden. "It won't come to that," promised Mattis. "You know it won't."

"It's not me you have to convince," said Chuck. "That's ... kind of why we were hoping you'd come live with us. Help look after Jack. I mean, after you stepped down from command of the *Midway* the first time…"

"This time it's different," said Mattis, firmly. "After what happened at Chrysalis I can't walk away ... after what I saw, after what I know, it's not possible. Not now. Too much depends on it."

"I know," said Chuck. "I just think it's something worth considering. You've had your turn, dad. Maybe … maybe it's time to let others have theirs?"

The wind picked up, blowing the grass in waves across the field. Mattis's communicator chirped. He'd set it to priority only.

It was tempting—if only for a moment—to just ignore it anyway, but he knew if someone was bothering him during his *very* limited time off, it would have to be important. But with the *Midway* in for a refit, something important deserved his attention.

He flicked open his communicator and stared at the

display.

Lynch: Admiral, we've been advised that there's a top brass meeting happening real soon and they want you there. Apparently something serious is going down.

His XO wasn't known for overstatement. Mattis tapped out a response.

Mattis: How soon is real soon? I'd prefer Wednesday, or tomorrow if it's urgent.

Lynch responded almost instantly.

Lynch: I was thinking more like within the next hour. We've sent a transport to pick you up. We have your location, ETA 4 minutes.

Well … so much for leave. Mattis sighed and stared up at the sky, drinking in the last of that blue, rich sky. "Sorry," he said, genuinely apologetic. "I don't think I'll be retiring today."

Overhead, the shadow of a shuttle passed, descending out of the sky with a faint howl, its engines flaring as it hovered over the park. The crowd, sensing its obvious intentions, parted to let it land; the ship positioned itself in the gap, drifting down toward the recently vacated grass.

"That bad, huh?" said Chuck, obviously a little disappointed, but seemingly becoming used to these kinds of things happening.

"Yeah," said Mattis, giving Jack a playful pat on the head before pulling himself up to his feet. "I'll see you later, son."

"Okay, Dad," said Chuck, scooping up Jack and cradling him comfortingly. "Talk to you soon."

Admiral Mattis started to turn to walk towards the shuttle, but stopped. "Chuck, watch yourself. I know you want to be involved. It's who you are. You've always wanted to be the hero. Like me, I guess. But you've got *him* now," he pointed to baby Jack. "Just … be careful, ok?"

Chuck nodded after a moment, and after several more, finally said, "You too. I mean it. You've had your turn. You've been the hero. Isn't it time to pass the baton?"

He was about to say, *not yet*. But he nodded a goodbye and turned to the dropship as its loading ramp extended. Aboard, flanked by two guards, was a face he hadn't seen in a while.

Admiral Caroline Fischer, her hands folded behind her back, a stern look on her normally jovial, media-friendly face.

He gave baby Jack another wave, then approached up the ramp. "How bad?" he asked.

"Best we wait until the meeting to discuss it properly," said Fischer, diplomatically.

"So, pretty bad," said Mattis, watching as the loading ramp closed and sealed shut.

CHAPTER THREE

Earth
United States of America
Georgetown, MD
Victory Park

Chuck had really enjoyed spending the afternoon with his dad. Too bad that couldn't have lasted. He watched, along with the whole crowd, as the shuttle which had so abruptly landed in the middle of a crowded park just as abruptly departed, leaving a few dozen civilians standing around murmuring to each other in confusion.

Such was life, being the son of a famous war hero. The fact that the shuttle's passenger had walked away from him drew more than a few eyes his way, but he ignored them and, after giving Jack a little bounce to keep him quiet, turned and walked to his car.

The vehicle's charge was running low. Recharging was cheaper if done at home, but if traffic picked up, the vehicle might not make it. Unemployment brought these kinds of concerns to the forefront of his mind; in the past, the pittance for a bit of electricity would have never even crossed his mind. Only a dollar's difference in truth. Now it was a legitimate decision he had to make. Elroy was right to worry about money.

He'd have to find a job, but where? The government sector was built on trust—trust he had violated—and painfully incestuous. Everyone knew everyone. Everyone talked.

Everyone knew what he'd done.

As he got close to his car, out of the corner of his eye, he saw a figure moving toward him, wearing a ratty grey coat and military boots. Another veteran, probably. He instinctively avoided eye contact, holding out his hand. "Sorry," he said, firmly. Dealing with homeless people was just another skill one learned in big cities. Not even universal basic income could take away that.

"Chuck Mattis? Son of Admiral Mattis?" asked the stranger, his English heavily accented. Chinese?

Chuck stopped, turning to face him. An old guy, definitely Asian, frazzled and harried-looking. If it wasn't for his thick foreign accent he would have been just another veteran from the Sino-American war. "Yes," he said, carefully. "But I don't have any money."

"That's good, because I don't want any." The man held out his hand, clutched around something small. "Give this to your father."

Chuck laughed. "I'm not taking anything to my dad without at *least* knowing your name. What, do you think I'm crazy?"

The guy glanced around, conspiratorially, and then lowered his voice. "I'm Admiral Yim."

Chuck *almost* laughed again, but the name triggered a memory within him. Something his dad had mentioned…

"Wait," said Chuck. "Admiral … *Yim?* You … you killed my uncle." Suddenly, he felt all his muscles tighten, his breath coming quicker. "If you're here to kill me too, then I'm going to kick your fucking ass, you—"

"No!" hissed Yim, angrily. "I mean … yes. I did. But that was in war, a long time ago—"

"Get away from me!" Chuck backed away. It was tempting to raise his voice and shout out to the crowd, but something caught the words in his throat.

Yim held up his hands, including the one that was still holding something. "I'm—" he paused. "I'm Smith's chess piece. I think you know what that means."

Smith. The CIA agent he had met during the break-in at Pitt's office—met because the guy was *also* breaking into the same place. He'd mentioned contacting one of his 'chess pieces' which would help him….

Deep breath, calm down. "Okay," said Chuck. "What do you want?"

Yim extended his hand and opened it, revealing a tiny data drive within. "Just to implore you to pass along this to your father. He'll trust me." A pause. "I hope."

Chuck narrowed his eyes skeptically. "What's on it?"

Yim hesitated, but Chuck met his gaze, glaring angrily. "It's a top-secret gravity-wave engine," he said. "The full schematic. And documentation about some of the strange, unexplained effects it can generate. Including quantum dislocation, which…" Yim groaned. "Blah blah blah, mumbo jumbo, it allows very short term time travel for small particles and … possibly more. The notes within will explain it *much* better than I ever could. Tell your father: This is why Captain Shao's ship exploded."

"But—" said Chuck.

"Your father *has* to have this. In payment, for his trust in me at Chrysalis, with Goalkeeper. Without that trust, both he and I would be dead." He offered the tiny drive again. "The password is the name of the man he sent into that place, to infiltrate the facility. He'll know what I mean."

"Funny, since you could have almost asked him yourself, but he just left," protested Chuck, pointing to the sky in the vague direction the ship had left. "If you'd been just a few minutes earlier.…"

Yim glanced over his shoulder, as though looking for some unseen enemy lurking in the shadows, then back to Chuck. "Just get that to him, will you? I have to be going."

"Wait! Why not just give it him yourself?"

"Too many people watching," said Yim. "Any one of them could be … well, it's not important for you to know. Just get it to him. As soon as humanly possible. For all our sakes." He turned abruptly and moved toward the crowd in the park, and in moments he was gone.

CHAPTER FOUR

Earth
Washington, D.C.
Pentagon

Mattis had been to the Pentagon a handful of times, but each time was always impressive. Heavily damaged in the Sino-American war, and rebuilt almost twice as large with an emphasis on security and safety, the building was the throbbing heart of the American interstellar war engine.

Having checked in his sidearm at the heliport façade, he followed Admiral Fischer deeper into the structure. She hadn't said a word since she picked him up. Whatever was going on must be big.

Further and further they descended into the pentagonal structure, taking some stairs down under the ground. Soon they came to an armored door, reinforced steel with hinges on the other side, flanked by two guards. Above them, built into the ceiling, was a ball-turret with a pair of prominent barrels projecting out. From the gauge in the barrels, and the size of the shell-casing ejection ports, these weapons were not here for show. Were they expecting someone to, possibly, drive a *car* down the stairs? Or an APC?

"This is new," said Mattis, eyeing the construction.

"Actually, it was built after the Sino-American war. It's only recently been declassified."

That drew his attention. "Declassified? At what level?" Despite the curiosity of it, he made a joke. "Hiding stuff from your fellow Admirals, Fischer?"

She didn't smile. Odd—Fischer normally loved a joke. "You have no idea," she said, handing her lanyard to the guard to her left.

The man checked it, then checked Mattis's. Both were subject to an inordinate amount of scrutiny; the holographic images were examined, tilted this way and that, and the magnetic strips read three times and verified through a computer whose purpose was not entirely clear. Finally, seemingly satisfied, the guard nodded respectfully and stepped back.

And then the door opened.

Beyond was a tri-forked corridor that lead to a series of doors, each one wooden and simple in design, and each bearing a brass number. *1. 2. 3.*

"This way," said Fischer, pushing open door labeled 1, revealing a round room with an oval table, at which were seated many senior officers, some familiar to him.

The Joint Chiefs of Staff occupied one half of the table, most of whom he knew by reputation only, and at the other side of the table were his XO, Commander Stewart Lynch, and his chief of engineering, Commander Oliver Modi.

They did not look happy.

"So," said Mattis, taking a spare seat beside Lynch, "I came as fast as I could."

"Yeah," said Lynch, his tone gilded with frustration. It was only then Mattis noticed he was out of uniform, wearing suspenders and a dark grey T-shirt. "Me too. Dragged me away from a lovely day's fishing the Red River down in Texas. Not that I could say no; the engine noise scared away damn near every fish in the water."

"I was asleep," confessed Modi. "Fortunately I was given time to shower and dress appropriately."

"It's three o'clock in the afternoon," said Mattis, confused.

Modi simply shrugged. "I adapt my sleeping patterns to the requirements of the job, but if left to my own devices, I inevitably become nocturnal, especially when working on my personal projects. I'd only been asleep for six hours, twenty minutes."

"Damn gremlin," muttered Lynch. "Living in darkness and playing with circuit boards."

Fischer cleared her throat pointedly. "As interesting as this is, shall we move on from our leave-based sleeping habits? We *do* have a lot of ground to cover, ladies and gentlemen. The sooner we begin, the sooner we can take action."

"I concur," said Modi.

"Me too," said Lynch.

Mattis made three. "What can you tell us about what's going on, Admiral Fischer?" he asked. "We're all in the dark here. Is this about my ship?"

"No," said Fischer, reaching under the table and

withdrawing a stack of tablets. She passed them around the table. "But indulge my curiosity; have any of you visited the world of Zenith?"

"I'm afraid not," said Mattis. "But the name came up in our investigations of the—" he almost said *the deep state conspiracy* which, given the high ranking military officers he was surrounded by, would almost certainly be an unpopular topic to broach. "uh, recent unpleasantness at Chrysalis."

"That's a shame," said Fischer, touching the screen of her tablet, lighting up Mattis's and the others as she did so. "Because as of six hours ago, every city, every building, every human being on its surface is gone."

The image on his screen was obviously taken from high orbit and showed the churned, black-brown land typically found in a terraformed but uncolonized world. Soil turned over by aerators, but with nothing planted in it; just raw earth, dirt, featureless and plain like muddy clouds.

Only the smallest thing, faint red embers occasionally dotting the landscape, belied the truth. As he zoomed in, each of the embers became a roaring sea of fire the size of cities. Mattis scrolled around. Whole areas had been churned up, mixed in like cake ingredients.

"My god," said Modi, utterly baffled. "The damage is … not consistent with nuclear strikes, or neutron bombs, or any of the weapons we might have at our disposal. It is almost as though the *entire crust of the planet* were lifted up a kilometer of more, and then dropped—repeatedly. Mixed up the whole surface of the planet." He pulled the tablet close to his face, as though a more rigorous inspection would show him some piece he'd missed. "But it's impossible. The energy requirements are simply *staggering*, beyond any of our capabilities," he paused slightly before adding, the recent brushes with the possibility of time-travel apparently on his mind, "or even our *projected* capabilities, for hundreds and hundreds of years." He looked up, dark skin noticeably paler than normal. "What kind of thing did this?"

Lynch leaned over toward him. "If it scares the engineers," he whispered, a wobble in his tone, "you know it's *gotta* be bad."

Mattis couldn't help but agree.

"We are unsure as to the nature of the device which caused this devastation," said Fischer, flicking her finger across the screen, obviously viewing other images. "But sufficient enough to say, we are extremely alarmed. Commander Modi, your initial assessment does, in fact, seem to be accurate; based on the information given to us by our source, it does, in fact, appear that Zenith's crust was lifted away from the planet."

"Who?" asked Mattis, doing as she did, inspecting other images. They showed the same bleak, churned up landscape, pulverized into bland emptiness by incomprehensibly destructive energy. "What source is this? Another government? Did someone claim responsibility for this?" That didn't make any sense at all. "Who in the hell would attack *Zenith* of all places? It's a backwater."

Fischer tapped on her tablet in rapid succession, and Mattis's screen changed. "This," she said, as the image of a somewhat disheveled, roguish-looking man appeared, wearing a light pink shirt under a black leather jacket and sporting an almost ridiculous set of antique aviator glasses, "is Harry Reardon. At least, that's who he claims to be. He's a … ahem, *private courier* who regularly hops between New London, Zenith, and Chrysalis. He and his younger brother, Sammy Reardon, claim to be witnesses to the attack on Zenith." She paused a moment, letting her words sink in. "They say it was, and I quote, *the aliens.*"

If it wasn't for the images he was holding, showing a ruined planet destroyed by some kind of weapon Modi couldn't even *understand*, let alone theoretically accept, Mattis would have laughed. "You know that the DOD gets a thousand tips like that every day," said Mattis, cautiously. "People from all over the galaxy, trying to cash in on potential reward money, swearing black and blue they got abducted by aliens, or alien mind control made them divorce their husbands, or … whatever."

"We feel this one is genuine," said Fischer. "If only because Harry Reardon has an arrest record as long as your arm—and he hasn't once tried to claim any kind of reward."

"What *has* he asked for then?" asked Mattis, dubiously. "I doubt an … enterprising young man with his own, ahem, *courier business* that only seems to go to the disreputable places in the galaxy is willing to talk to the US Department of Defense for free."

"He isn't," said Fischer, nodding understandingly. "He only wants to talk—" she turned to directly face him, "to you."

"Me." Mattis blinked. "What?"

"By name. You're quite the media *celebrity* these days." Fischer smiled. "Normally we'd dismiss him, but excerpts from his ship's sensor logs did raise a few eyebrows down at Intel. We want the complete logs, and an interview."

"Is there anyone else?" asked Mattis. "I can't believe that

only a single—albeit talented—young pair of brothers with a ship managed to escape planetary devastation on this scale."

"Not as of yet," said Fischer. "He's the only one we've located so far. If Reardon doesn't show up to the meeting, go to Zenith itself. There might be more information there, in satellites or surviving installations if nothing else."

At least they had a backup plan. That was better than he was given in most crisis situations. "Okay," said Mattis, breathing out a low, long sigh. "I'll go talk to the smugger." He glanced to Lynch. "Cancel all outstanding leave and get the crew back to the ship."

"One thing you should know," said Admiral Fischer, her voice suddenly firming. "Regarding the command of the *Midway*."

His chest tightened and he straightened his back. Somehow, he knew this wasn't going to be good. "Yes, Admiral?"

Fischer's voice was a mixture of uncompromising firmness and genuine sympathy. "You know as well as I do," she paused, meeting his eyes before continuing. "Command of the *Midway* was never, truly, meant to be yours after the attack on Friendship Station. Your expertise with the ship's systems and configuration was extremely useful after Captain Malmsteen's untimely passing, and I don't want to diminish that, but…" *wait for it, here it comes…* "Ultimately, command of the Midway will be reassigned after this mission. We'll be monitoring your progress until then, and evaluating you as we go, but you should know this going in."

Lynch practically spat out his own tongue. "You can't be serious," he said. "Admiral, there's *nobody* in this galaxy who's more capable than Admiral Mattis. Nobody."

"Funny words," said Fischer, "from the man we're looking to take command."

Mattis and Lynch exchanged a brief glance.

"Admiral, I—" Lynch sputtered.

"It's fine," said Mattis, keeping his voice even with sheer force of will. "All good things come to an end. We'll discuss it after this mission."

"Aye aye," said Lynch. "I'll go get a uniform on."

"Step on it," said Mattis, grimly. "Harry Reardon sounds like the kind of guy who one might label a *flight risk*. And who knows where that allegedly *alien* ship is going to pop up next. Modi, how's the refit coming?"

"Well, sir," said Modi, hesitantly. "There's something about that you need to know."

"Good news? Bad news?"

"I'm honestly not quite sure, sir."

CHAPTER FIVE

Chrysalis
Rand City
Spectre's Apartment

"Oh," said Spectre as he casually tapped his pen on the surface of his wooden writing desk, "what tangled and messy creations we have birthed."

Birthed. He hadn't planned on using that word, but, considering the mere *existence* of their new, grotesque creations where before they had been simply *human*, the word *birthed* was apt.

He let his eyes drift over the surface of the paper, prosthetics scanning the words and highlighting important bits of information. This report on the mutants was just like the last one but, fortunately, contained the hopeful glimmer of incremental progress; an entirely unexciting notion to be sure, but one for which he knew he should be, at least, a little grateful.

This was, after all, how true science was achieved. Through the rigorous and pragmatic application of experimentation.

It did seem to be a waste that this batch of mutants, although more tame and seemingly more susceptible to control than any previous attempts, ultimately had to be destroyed.

But what was trial without a little bit of error? Error was the lifeblood of science.

Spectre had his prosthetic eyes store the relevant numbers —chemical traces, hormone levels, dosages—and focused on the broad-brush strokes. Remembering precise facts was something that computers were very good at, and interpreting results was something humans were very good at, so he tried to leverage as much of his advantages as possible.

Still, eventually, all the report's words just started to blur together and he switched off the tablet.

"What should we do now, sir?" asked the scientist who stood opposite his desk. Doctor Janet Sizemore, a mousy-haired woman who had earned, somehow, the title of lead researcher into their mutant 'problem.'

"Just keep working on it," he said. "You know what to do. You know what the goal is."

"I understand," said Sizemore, creasing her brow ever so slightly. "I just … I thought you'd be pleased at our progress, and I was wondering if you had any guidelines for the next steps we might take."

Spectre had no time for a lecture, nor the inclination to issue comforting compliments and inspiration. "Half a success is a failure," he said. "The goals remain unchanged." He reached up and rubbed his temples. "Out."

Fortunately, she didn't seem to want to argue and, without

a word, turned to leave.

"Actually," said Spectre before she made it out the door, a light flicking on in his head. "Send in my secretary, if you wouldn't mind."

She nodded, and left, and moments later his secretary leaned through the door. "Sir?" he said.

"Prepare my ship."

"Sir?" asked the man again, clearly bewildered. "You're … leaving?"

"Temporarily," he said, pushing back his chair and standing up. "I have to go talk to a new friend."

"A … friend?" the secretary said, curiously. "Should I pack you a change of clothes?"

"Oh no," said Spectre, giving his best smile. "No need to change. I'm sure Admiral Mattis has prison garments in my size."

"Ah, speaking of Mattis, we've just received a report that the Midway is off to inspect the damage at Zenith and track down the enemy fleet—"

Specter nodded, arranging his desktop for his absence. "As we expected, yes?"

"But first they're going to rendezvous with the only known survivor of the attack, one Harry Reardon."

Spectre glanced up. "Well that won't do at all." He considered. "Location?"

"Deep space. Halfway between Sol system and Sirius."

"Away from prying eyes and ears. I won't get there in time. Send in a distraction. I have far more important business to discuss with Mattis than some random smuggler."

"Lethal?"

"Surprise me."

CHAPTER SIX

Earth
Washington, D.C.
Pentagon
US Naval Ops Situation Room

"Modi," asked Mattis, a little frustration creeping into his tone, "what don't you want to tell me about my ship?"

"It's about the refit," said Modi, twiddling his thumbs. "The new engines have been installed, but that was literally only just yesterday according to the daily reports—nobody's had any time to test them and work out the kinks. And, of course, they will require a few tweaks before they're *truly* operational. But how they were able to install them so quickly —they must be either very simple engines, mechanically, or … they're actually not done and the report was in error."

Mattis swore under his breath, instantly regretting it as he suddenly reminded himself he was surrounded by the highest ranking military offers in the US Department of Defense. He turned to Fischer. "Well, that puts a damper on that. Can we take another ship?"

"Not possible," said Fischer, shaking her head. "Harry Reardon's ... well, as you've correctly inferred, he's something of a nefarious character, and one thing these types have in common is that they're paranoid. He was *very* specific. It *has* to be Admiral Jack Mattis, and Admiral Jack Mattis's ship, the USS *Midway*." A light clicked on in his head. That would be why she had let him keep command ... one more time. "There's simply no time to fully test the new upgrades, and there's no way we can arrange alternate transportation. If Reardon sees you approaching and you're *not* aboard the *Midway*, he's likely to just Z-space translate out of there and we'll lose our best, and only, lead."

"That may be so, Admiral," said Modi, clicking his tongue, "but these engine upgrades were developed by our contractor in the People's Republic of China. There's a *lot* of assumptions Fleet engineering had to make to even *install* the equipment, let alone integrate it with our systems. In *theory* the math checks out, but..."

"I understand," said Fischer.

Mattis squinted, narrowing his eyes at Fischer, glancing briefly around the room to see if she had the Joint Chief's support. She seemed to. "I understand what you're getting at, Admiral, but you're asking me to risk what is still *my* ship on entirely unproven technology, provided by a contractor from a foreign country with whom relations are best described as *strained*, that we haven't even tested yet?"

"That's correct," said Fischer. "I understand that even if Bob Ross was painting this picture, you wouldn't like it, but that's just the way it goes. And it hasn't been *untested*. Plenty of testing was observed on-site in Chinese airspace by our representatives. In any event, our best engineers have taken it apart and put it back together, and we've performed several tests on the ground as best we can. It all checks out. There's no need to be concerned."

"Which engineers Admiral?" pressed Modi.

"Pardon?" asked Fischer, obviously confused.

"Which engineers conducted the inspection?" he asked. "I am familiar with most senior engineers who would have this kind of access. Some I would trust with this inspection and some I would not."

Fischer's eyes narrowed slightly, and rather than address him specifically, she turned to Mattis. "Reardon is waiting. I don't want to blow this chance. And given that the whole of Zenith has been wiped clean … it's worth the risk. Fleet engineering assures me that engines will work."

"Easy to say when you aren't the one taking the risk," muttered Lynch.

If Modi *and* Lynch were agreeing on something, it was probably an issue he should keep in mind. "I understand," said Mattis, straightening his back. "I've tendered my advisement on this matter. That's all I can do. Mister Modi, your concerns aside, are you absolutely certain that the work to the *Midway* is actually complete?"

"Complete enough, without doing a full technical audit," said Modi. "There's a small number of tasks remaining which can be accomplished once we're up there. Small things— realignments, baseline normalizations, nothing fancy, and yes— we *might* even be able to squeeze in some tests before we fire it up." He sighed dejectedly. "I doubt very much my sleep schedule—nor the deficit recently acquired—will be treated with any great kindness, but that's a concern for later. Simply put: the *Midway* is *technically* space-worthy, Admiral. Barely."

He nodded. "Good. Get ready to launch the ship, I'll see you both in orbit."

Everyone disbanded to do their jobs. Mattis answered a few questions from the rest of the Joint Chiefs—mainly promising to avoid any media attention and potential scandals as best he could—and then he was shown back up to the Pentagon's main levels, where he retrieved his sidearm and began to arrange a lift up to the *Midway*.

The whole time, he couldn't help but fight a profound sense of dread. Not just about the mission—what in the hell was going on? What kind of weapon could utterly destroy a planet?—but also about his ship.

This would be his last mission as CO of the *Midway*.

Again.

He'd been down this route before. Given up command of the *Midway* to younger Captains, and … and it hadn't turned out well. He'd played the game. Done his duty. People had died.

Maybe Chuck was right. His turn was over. Maybe it was time to pass the baton?

A shuttle carried him up, away from the Pentagon and D.C. and toward Earth's outer atmosphere, up past the blue sky and into the comforting, familiar black. He glanced out the porthole, watching the continental United States shrink away below him, and the curvature of the Earth grew more pronounced as the planet grew smaller.

Up ahead, the sun reflected off the steel scaffolding surrounding the *USS Midway*, held in place as the work crews tended to her. The long-serving ship had seen many battles in the years Mattis had been in command, and too many systems had been pushed to their limit. Even though hasty repairs had been effected, the scars of too many recent battles still remained. Scorch marks from The Forgotten's cannon shells and future-human weapons alike hadn't even been painted over.

It wasn't just the engines. Every system on board was about to be field-tested. A lot could go wrong. The *Midway* was a fine ship, there was no doubt, but as he drew closer he couldn't help but remember an old, sarcastic witticism.

50,000 moving parts, all supplied by the lowest bidder.

The shuttle docked, and Mattis—his thoughts focused inward, to the task ahead—made his way to the bridge, passing through the newly repaired armored casemate. Intruders had cut their way through it on the way to the ship's command center during the confrontation with The Forgotten over New London. Finally it had been repaired. Only one of the many thousands of fixes scattered throughout the vessel.

"Admiral on deck," said Commander Lynch as Mattis entered.

"As you were," he said, taking the captain's chair, sinking into it slowly and deeply, a human personification of the growing feeling inside him. "Report status."

Lynch arched his back until it cracked. "Well, sir, the good news is, that damn fool Modi was right. The new engines are in and, bonus, they're actually plugged in and talking to the rest of the ship. Apparently. So maybe this hare-brained scheme will actually work out after all. The gantries are standing by to disengage when we're ready; supplies have been loaded, and most of the crew have been located and embarked. The detaching process will take several hours; we're all good to make a start on that, when you're ready."

That was good. "No time like the present," he said. "Get ready to disengage the ship. Hopefully the rest of the crew will be along shortly."

Lynch glanced at his instrument panel briefly, then back up. "Actually, sir, there's ... something else, it looks like. We've received a request to come aboard."

"Stragglers from leave?" asked Mattis, frustration building, even as he tried to keep it in check. *He'd* managed to get back in time, although he understood that, for some crew members, finding them and bringing them here in a timely manner at such short notice was not going to be possible.

"Uh, no sir," said Lynch, eyes widening as he read further. "This request came directly from the office of the Chief of Naval Personnel. We have a tag-along. Orders from Fischer herself."

He frowned. "Fischer wants to put a man on my ship?"

Lynch snorted playfully. "Not unless you want to go to sickbay," he said, turning the monitor around to show him a man he didn't recognize embarking with Admiral Fischer's clearance code. A doctor.

"Does she think I'm crazy?" asked Mattis, and then he remembered.

She said she'd be keeping an eye on him.

CHAPTER SEVEN

Earth, Low Orbit
USS Midway
Pilot's Exercise Room

96. 97. 98. 99…

Patricia "Guano" Corrick's arms shook slightly as she tried for that last pushup. Her arms burned and her chest ached, but Major Muhammad "Roadie" Yousuf, her CAG and the man who would decide if she would return to the flight roster or not, was watching.

… 100.

Did it. She slumped on the mat, body covered in sweat, her forearms aching. She clenched her fists to keep her fingers from shaking.

"You okay there, Guano?" said Roadie, crouching beside her. "Was that a hundred?"

"Yeah," she said, propping herself up into a seated position. She grabbed her water bottle, splashing her face, getting at least some of it into her mouth. "I got 'em."

That seemed to relieve some of his concerns. Or, at least, she hoped so. Roadie clapped her on the back. "A'right, well that's the physical out of the way."

"Like I said." Guano climbed up to her feet, shaking her hair dry. "It was just a cold."

Roadie wasn't buying it. "Colds don't make people just pass out like that," he said. "They had to haul you off to the medbay on a stretcher like a bag of rocks. That's not normal."

She'd been practicing this part of her little … speech … ever since she'd woken up in the infirmary. "The doctors told me it was just a cold," she said. "One that caused dehydration. Couple that with, well, the somewhat *lax* attention to bodily maintenance that some of the pilots, including me, tend to display—" Roadie's face soured but she pushed on anyway. "And the stress of a prolonged combat engagement in deep space, where God knows *what* could have happened to my oxygen supply, and there you have it. Dehydration plus stress plus no O2 equals a sick piece of bat shit."

Roadie groaned slightly. "Yeah, well, Doctor Wright wouldn't know sick if it landed on his *boots*. I'm still worried. I've got half a mind to ship you back to Earth."

"You've got half a mind, period," said Guano, trying to keep her temper in check. "You can't seriously be thinking about sending me back *now*. You've seen the news. You've seen what happened at Zenith. We can't be down our best pilot—"

"Our *third* best pilot," corrected Roadie. "Like, maybe. Boracho is creeping up on you, to be honest."

"Our *best scoring* pilot on the ship," said Guano, a lot more defensively than she probably should have been. "And besides.

Flatline's basically a lost, dumb, idiotic child. If you ship me home you might as well do it to him, too."

Roadie pushed open the door to the gym. "You say it like I wouldn't do it."

"You wouldn't," said Guano confidently. "I know you. You're way too attached to us to do something like that."

Roadie grabbed her arm as she stepped through the door, pulling her back. His face was stern and uncompromising. "You're right," he said, his faces inches away from hers. "I *am* attached to my pilots. You foolish, moronic, stupid, block-headed, cretinous, dimwitted, imbecilic, ignoramus simpletons are basically why I do this job. Including Flatline and Frost and all the other gunners. You're all my family. All of you. But understand this: I won't endanger my family to accommodate one ferret-brained pilot with a problem in her head."

Guano tugged her arm free. "Nothing wrong with me or my brain," she said. "Doctors confirmed it."

Roadie didn't seem convinced but he let her go. "Back to bed with you," he said.

More time in bed doing nothing. Guano groaned and headed back to sickbay.

CHAPTER EIGHT

Earth, Low Orbit
USS Midway
Bridge

Well, ain't that a kick in the teeth. Mattis glowered as the final stages of the ship's launch were undertaken and, soon, the ship would hopefully be ready to head out and find the smuggler, Rearden.

Or fight.

The idea of losing his command after this mission was buried under the more immediate insult: an uninvited 'guest' aboard his ship. The prospect rankled him more than he cared to admit. To soothe the burn of these thoughts, he dove into the details, reviewing the personnel file of the stranger; one Doctor Jacoby Brooks, a medical doctor with twenty-five years of service to the day, with a specialization in dietary nutrition.

Nutrition. That finding actually mollified him somewhat. Perhaps it was simply for the crew's needs. Some fleet-wide change he was unaware of. Why else would they need a dietitian aboard?

Quite the mystery, but one that did not lend itself a great deal of urgency. Whatever Admiral Fischer's reasoning for bringing aboard the good doctor would be revealed in the fullness of time. No doubt.

Still, worries tugged at him. He knew his biases—people tended to think *everything* was about them, but he couldn't help it. Was he under some kind of undisclosed probation? Was the doctor here to spy on him?

Or was he just being paranoid? It wasn't unreasonable to think that—

"Sir?" asked Lynch, with a tone which suggested that he had asked more than once.

The bridge crew were staring. "Sorry," Mattis said, apologetically. How crazy he must have looked in those brief moments. "What was the question?"

"Not a question," said Lynch. "Doctor Brooks would like permission to enter the bridge."

At the main doorway to the *Midway*'s central core, its beating heart of operations, was a tall, rakishly thin man with dark skin and a wide, genuine smile. "Apologies for the intrusion, Admiral Mattis," he said, a vague Chicagoan accent overlaying an educated British, leading to quite a pleasant cadence. "I thought I should introduce myself to you properly."

"Of course," said Mattis, standing and gesturing to his ready room. "Permission granted. Let's have a chat."

The two of them walked to Mattis's ready room. Mattis sat behind his desk, gesturing toward the spare seat. "Please."

Doctor Brooks sat. "Thank you once again, Admiral, for having me aboard."

"Of course." Mattis folded his hands in front of him and leaned forward slightly. "My question, of course, is why. Is there a problem with my medical staff that I should know about?"

Doctor Brooks's confusion seemed genuine. "No, sir. None that I've been made aware of."

"Okay," said Mattis, "then forgive me, Doctor, because I'm not sure exactly why you're here."

Doctor Brooks seemed to visibly stiffen slightly, his face tightening. "Well, as you know, meals aboard Navy assets are provided by various subcontractors and private corporations. These include not just your standard rations, but also dietary supplements and various other nutritional aids. There's been a … *concern* about some of these supplements, so I'm simply here to verify that there's no widespread issue." Doctor Brooks smiled widely, a huge smile like a half-moon. "I was supposed to conduct this survey aboard the USS *Alexander Hamilton* but your arrival signaled the perfect chance for me to get started a month earlier. I won't get in your way, Admiral. I promise."

Any danger to the ship's food was a danger to the crew. Mattis's eyes narrowed. "What's the nature of this concern?"

Doctor Brooks's smile faded completely, his levity replaced by a dour seriousness. "Some time ago, one of your pilots, Lieutenant Corrick, reported that she passed out after a combat operation." He'd heard as much himself, and ordered his CAG to get to the bottom of it. "And yet, weeks later, she remains off the flight roster but is still part of the crew. Current theory about the incident is that it was hypoxia caused by a faulty oxygen supply unit in her ship, but Admiral Fischer feels that it is prudent to investigate all possible angles. Given that I was partially responsible for the initial formulas for the supplements, nobody in the galaxy is in a better position to rule out some kind of allergic or biochemical reaction than I. I'm not here to prove any working theory, Admiral, simply to exclude potential causes, as unlikely as they might be."

That seemed *almost* reasonable. "Still," said Mattis, "I would have appreciated a little more notice."

"Of course." Doctor Brooks shook his head. "And for that, Admiral, you're entirely justified in being slightly miffed. Your ship is your home, and unexpected guests are always a problem. The chaotic nature of recent developments has … necessitated these actions; believe me, my recommendation was to conduct my business aboard the *Alexander Hamilton*, but both your timely arrival and Lieutenant Corrick's potential reaction presented an opportunity too great to ignore."

He mulled over Doctor Brooks's explanation but was unable to find anything directly objectionable.

Silence reigned for a time.

"Admiral," asked Doctor Brooks, "with respect, I'm uncertain as to the source of your obvious discomfort. Is it the implication that your crew might be receiving potentially harmful food, or … is it something else?"

Whenever anyone said *with respect*, Mattis couldn't help but feel that there was very little respect intended at all. "The *Midway* is my ship," he said, but then firmly nodded his head. "You've made your case, and I accept. Welcome aboard, Doctor Brooks."

"Thank you, Admiral Mattis." They both stood, shook

hands with palpable forced politeness, and then left back to the bridge. "Oh, one more thing, before I forget. Something that Admiral Fischer said. She made a joke to me about your … how did she put it? Your *Kirk-like* tendencies? I'm not quite sure what she meant by that."

Mattis wanted to groan. "Admiral Fischer has a thing for old science fiction movies. We'll just leave it at that. Welcome aboard, Mr. Brooks." He indicated to the elevator, and Brooks climbed aboard, leaving Mattis to enter the bridge down the hall, saluting to the marines at the entrance.

After the door closed and Mattis was alone with his bridge crew, he turned to Lynch. "Mister Lynch?"

"Yes, sir?"

"Have security occasionally check in with Mister…" he caught himself. "*Doctor* Brooks. I want to make sure that he's … comfortable as he conducts his business here."

"Aye aye," said Lynch, and went to work making it happen.

Mattis watched him work, and wondered when Lynch himself would be sitting in the CO's chair.

"Sir?" asked Lynch. "We are ready to launch."

CHAPTER NINE

Earth, Low Orbit
USS Midway
Bridge

The *Midway* slipped its berthings and soared out into space. To Mattis, the ship seemed entirely ... *normal.* Smoother, even, as though the quiet hum of her engines and the beeping of the machines on the bridge were somehow more muted, softer, gentler.

"How's she sailing, Modi?" he asked. He'd specifically asked for the engineer to be on the bridge for this.

"The *Midway*'s engines are performing above expectations," he said, an edge of pride in his voice. "Beyond what even I anticipated."

Mattis had been waiting for the modifications to explode, or redirect them into the sun, or in some other way screw them all over, but nothing happened. No big explosion. No massive betrayal. The ship didn't immediately turn and sail toward a star, or implode, or blast them all to atoms. Nothing.

"Very well," said Mattis. "Initiate Z-space translation."

With barely a whisper, the *Midway* was engulfed in a wave of flashing lights and vibrant hues, slipping effortlessly into Z-space; the strange un-reality that allowed ships to move between the stars at much faster rates than traditional space travel.

An anti-climactic launch, but Mattis was honestly relieved, and for the first time since he had returned to duty, actually allowed himself to relax. Anti-climactic wasn't something to be mourned.

"Just a short test," said Lynch. "We're meeting Reardon at an … undisclosed location."

"Is it a bar?" asked Mattis, rhetorically.

Lynch's face showed him it might be more than rhetorical. "He just said, an undisclosed location. Gave us coordinates. It's not far. About fifteen minutes travel. Looks like it's in the middle of empty space, out towards Sirius."

Fifteen minutes—couldn't be farther than a few light years out of the solar system. "Thoughts?"

"Surveys show just an empty point in space," said Lynch. "To be perfectly honest, that'd be where I'd want to meet the military, if I was a paranoid criminal. You can see whoever's coming for lightyears around, and if you need to make a quick getaway, you can head out in basically any direction, turn off your power, and no one will find you in a million years. Like a needle in a … galactic needle stack."

That did make sense. "Very well. Get ready to drop out of Z-space when we're close, and have the ship come to general quarters. Hails on open frequencies. Be here, loud and proud. I don't want to spook him."

"Aye aye sir," said Lynch.

Minutes later, the *Midway* slid out of Z-space, quiet and smooth, like a ghost. The real world reappeared in a flash of color, revealing a dark, inky black void full of un-twinkling stars.

"Z-space translation complete," said Modi, his tone a mixture of relief and excitement. "Extremely smooth translation, sir."

Good. "Any sign of our contact?" asked Mattis.

"Yes sir," said Lynch, after a moment's consideration of their instruments. "We have a PJ-95 mark II transport showing up on long range radar."

Mattis had not even *heard* of that type of craft. "What the hell is that?"

Modi spoke up. "It's a rare ship these days. One of the early fourth-generation transports. Strong and tough, fast, and easily modified. They are a favorite of disreputable types, ironically because many of the first production run were modified into being personal ships for wealthy travelers. After all, if one doesn't want to be seen as a smuggler, one shouldn't look like a smuggler, right?"

"Okay," said Mattis. "Get ready to hail him. If that's Reardon, I want to speak to him. While I'm on the subject— are there any other ships around?"

Lynch's eyes flicked to one side. "There's also the USS *Alexander Hamilton* standing by, ready to execute an emergency Z-space translation if we need them. They can be here in two minutes."

"Okay," said Mattis. "Patch me into Captain Katarina

Abramova. Let her hear what we're doing. Then open the hail."

The connection went through almost immediately. On the main monitor the image of a dark skinned, aviator-glasses clad man wearing a thick jacket appeared. His copilot was a skinny-looking guy with longer hair who looked a lot younger—boyish, almost—who seemed to be sitting in a wheelchair rather than an actual seat. The kid looked like a surfer with shoulder-length hair and thick eyebrows that scrunched up into a shape that suggested he thought he was far too important to have to deal with a United States Space Navy admiral.

"Harry Reardon, I presume," said Mattis, keeping his tone polite.

"You Admiral Mattis?" asked the guy, reaching up and fiddling with his dark glasses. "The guy from the news?"

"I am." He took a breath and leaned forward slightly. "I've heard you've seen some extraordinary things, Mister Reardon, and that you might be able to assist us with our investigations."

"Maybe," said Reardon, dragging out the syllables of his words. "M-ay-be. A'right? It all depends. It all … depends."

There was something in the man's voice which belied his tough, suspicious exterior. Something that actually made Mattis believe he really had seen something.

Fear.

"Okay," said Mattis, putting on his best diplomatic voice. "Let's work this out. What kind of conditions are you talking about?"

"Well," said Reardon, but then glanced off camera for a moment. His eyes widened slightly. "You came alone, right?"

"As we agreed," said Mattis, patiently. "Just me and the *Midway.*"

Reardon shook his head. "Nope. Nope, you aren't alone. I got a contact coming in *fast*. Someone followed you here."

Lynch spoke up. "Sir, it's true. Contact on long range sensors, coming in very fast. They'll be at us in two minutes."

"Two minutes?" asked Mattis, incredulously. Some kind of civilian craft? It was too fast for that. Too stealthy. He made a *mute* signal with his hand. "*Hamilton*, stop that craft from interfering. Intercept. Hail them. Do every damn thing you can do to stop them from messing this up for us."

He let Lynch deal with it and unmuted the connection. "We're doing what we can to keep that ship away from us," said Mattis. "We can protect us."

"They destroyed Zenith," said Reardon, plainly. "What hope do you have of defeating them?"

That was a very good question that he didn't have an immediate answer to. Mattis made the *mute* gesture again. "Why didn't we see them before?"

"Must be small," said Lynch, hands flying over his console. "Fast, too. Strike craft possibly, equipped with Z-space engines. Or ... a long range boarding crew." His tone shifted. "No transponders. No identifying signals of any kind."

Was it the future-humans? No way to know. "USS *Midway* to USS *Alexander Hamilton*, this is *Midway* actual. Report status on intercept."

"We're coming in hot," said Abramova, her thick Russian accent charged with energy. "Frigates are fast, Admiral. We can get to them in moments, but we're detecting a surge of energy from Reardon's vessel."

He motioned for the comm officer to unmute the smuggler. "Reardon," said Mattis, standing up out of his command chair. "Listen to me very carefully. I need you to—"

With a bright white flash, Reardon's ship vanished into Z-space.

Shit.

The contact came out of Z-space. At the range it was at, all Mattis could see was a dot. With a similar flash, the *Hamilton* appeared behind it. "Mister Lynch," he said, his tone dark. "Identify that ship."

"No joy," said Lynch, voice charged with energy. "But they're not ours. And they're not Chinese. Or … anything that I can recognize. No response to hails, and it looks like they're charging weapons and moving into engagement range with the *Hamilton*."

That made the decision easy. "Engage that ship," he ordered. "Forward guns only. Let's see if they have any fight in them. Abramova, you are free to engage at will."

The *Midway*, already on a combat footing, shook slightly as a barrage of fire flew out toward the hostile ship. Even for a craft of its size, the opening barrage would likely only rattle them, even if it hit at all.

The shots flew true, white dots on the radar merging with the hostile signal. Then it abruptly vanished, replaced by an explosion as it blew itself to pieces.

"What?" asked Mattis, stunned.

"I think it self-destructed," said Lynch, glancing at the spectrometer. "I'm not seeing any escaping gasses—just debris. It might have been a drone craft. No crew."

It could have dodged and jumped away after Reardon. But it didn't. It blew itself up … why? Was it there just to delay them? Didn't make any sense. They would have tried to drag out the engagement as long as possible. Then…

The truth drifted into his mind. *Because remaining undiscovered was more important to its owners than being successful.*

"Initiate salvage operations," said Lynch to Modi. "See what we can discover out there."

He knew there would be nothing. "Belay that. They self-destructed—there's not going to be anything worth recovering." Mattis settled back into his chair. "That … was damned peculiar. Get us to Zenith. We'll have to find our answers there."

"Good hunting, Admiral," said Abramova, her tone sincerely regretful. "I wish we could come with you, but we have our own mission. And we've got to stop for a resupply at the Jovian Logistics depot. Farewell."

"Good hunting, *Hamilton*," said Mattis, as the ship began to charge its Z-space engine for its trip to Zenith. And yet he still could not shake the strange feeling, the strange episode from his head. What the hell was with that ship? Out of nowhere, no identification, and yet somehow it knew exactly where he'd be, and yet … it did nothing.

Except scare off Harry Reardon.

CHAPTER TEN

Z-Space
The Aerostar

Mattis was still talking. "Listen to me very carefully. I need you to—"

Nope. Reardon hit the switch that jumped the *Aerostar* into Z-space, and the inky void of space was replaced by a kalliadesaope of colors.

Slowly, gradually, he lowered his guard. He cracked a smile and then, snorting, a little nervous laugh.

"You okay?" asked Sammy, his voice high pitched and stressed. Not entirely unsurprising really. He hadn't exactly been keen on seeing Mattis.

Reardon slumped back into his seat as the adrenaline faded. "Yeah. You?"

"Yeah."

Seconds ticked away. The ship sailed on, slipping through Z-space smoothly and evenly. "Where you taking us?" asked

Reardon, adjusting his glasses.

"Uhh … I just picked a random direction," said Sammy, glancing out the window to the multicolored spectacle outside. "I wasn't really thinking. Sorry bro."

It was understandable. *Anywhere* was better than where they had been; with the alien thingies in pursuit. That was what the little ship must have been, for Mattis to have taken it so seriously. But what in the world could those aliens want with *him*? He was just a no-good smuggler. Well, a pretty-good smuggler. Emphasis on pretty.

The seconds turned into minutes.

"Where should we go?" asked Sammy, his voice edged with just a little plaintiveness. "We can't just keep sailing in Z-space forever."

Well … they kind of could. Kind of. They would have to stop off occasionally for supplies and things—just food and things, nothing *too* important—but suddenly the idea of just sailing on forever and pretending like they hadn't seen a thing was quite appealing.

There were plenty of places in the galaxy a guy like him could go and disappear. Some of them were even comfortable, with amenities and resources he could draw upon. His Indian citizenship would grant him a unique advantage. India had plenty of small colonies all throughout the galaxy. Nothing as big as the Americans or Chinese, of course, but still there.

Heaps of places a handsome guy like him could just disappear into a crowd.

But Sammy…

Sammy would never fit in. The colonies were remote and not exactly wheelchair accessible. A floating model would be too expensive, and would still attract far too much attention. They'd be recognized. No matter what they did, no matter where they ran, the eyes of passers-by would notice his brother. And where passers-by noticed, the government soon noticed as well.

No. It wasn't even an option. Not even for one second did Harry Reardon ever consider leaving his brother.

Besides. Nobody in sexy aviator glasses ever looked cool constantly running away.

"We're going," said Reardon, with what he hoped was suitable dramatic flourish. "To see the only *other* person in the galaxy who will listen."

CHAPTER ELEVEN

Earth
United States
Baltimore, Maryland
John Smith's Apartment

John Smith flicked through the intel dispatches with something approaching boredom mixed with mild disgust.

Everything these days was so sterilized and boring. Drones and technology did most of his work for him, and most of what was left over was sorted through by neural networks and advanced data gathering algorithms.

The rest was just scraps. Why did they even keep humans around in this line of work anymore, anyway?

In the background, the news was playing something about a catastrophe on some far away world. Zenith. Same world where that oaf of a scientist, Steve Bratta, had shot his video of the mutant humans. Same world that was one of the premier genetic research facilities of the now-defunct

MaxGainz corporation. Definitely his circus, definitely his monkeys.

But what was the connection?

He opened the next dispatch. Something about someone posting hate crime advocacy on the 'net. He forwarded it to local law enforcement who, no doubt, would ignore it. Next.

Something about a woman being arrested with bomb making supplies on the tiny colony of New Nebraska, known to the locals as "Newbraska." Domestic issue, one outside of the CIA's jurisdiction. Forwarded to the FBI. Next.

Ahh, now, *this* one was interesting. An analysis of yet another video taken by one Steve X. Bratta on Chrysalis; a shaky recording of the guy practically running through a genetic experimentation lab disguised as a steroid factory. What was it with this guy and bombshell videos?

One of the still images taken from the footage was flagged important.

A blurry, tilted, out-of-focus image of a man labeled *SPECTRE*.

Oh, hello, my old friend. Fancy seeing you here.

Smith leaned forward, tapping a few keys on his tablet. The computing resources of the CIA were significant; somewhere, far far away, a datacenter sprung to life, passing every imaginable algorithm over the image, trying to clean it up.

After a few minutes, the result came back. Smoother but not too much different from before.

Ah well, couldn't get something from nothing. Garbage in garbage out. There simply wasn't enough data to get a good, clean, crisp image ... but it was a lead. A clue. A piece of a much bigger, much more complicated puzzle that, if solved, would be worth the effort.

And definitely Spectre. He knew that face anywhere.

"What are you doing at Chrysalis, my busy little friend?"

Something caught his ear on the news. Zenith ... his eyes followed, finding an image of the rescue effort on that far away world. Flashing sirens and excavator equipment. A quick glance told him it was hopeless. Those people were looking for bodies, not survivors.

But this was the second incident involving Zenith in just a few months. First the MazGainz 'alien' attack, and now this....

Worth a look. He thumbed through the very last of his dispatches, and the last one made him smile.

Harry Reardon wanted to meet with him and had just flown in from the remains of Zenith.

Definitely a meeting worth taking. Just a good chat, from one spook to another. Former spook, that is—Harry unceremoniously took an early retirement years ago, and if it wasn't for Smith, he'd be in jail.

Definitely worth a meeting, and possibly call in some long-overdue favors.

CHAPTER TWELVE

Earth
United States
Baltimore, Maryland
Snapper's Bar

Mistakes had been made.

No, thought Reardon as he upended his glass and forced the last of his drink down his throat. *Mistakes were currently being made. Currently. At this exact moment.* His contact, Smith, hadn't shown up yet. Maybe it was a ruse. Some kind of trick. They might have been friends for years, but ... c'mon. John-freaking-Smith. That *still* sounded like a fake name.

He shouldn't have come. Zenith was gone, there was just no point in messing about with trying to report what he'd seen. It wasn't going to bring people back to life. They were dead. Super, super dead and nothing he could say or do could change it.

So why was he even here?

"Long time no see," said a familiar voice as Smith slid into the seat beside him. "Still drinking those girly drinks you like so much?"

"Excuse me, that is *vodka*," said Reardon, swiveling in his seat.

Smith casually leaned in and sniffed his glass. "That is a pink raspberry cosmo."

"Raspberry cosmos are a manly drink," said Reardon, a little more defensively than he probably should have.

Smith's eyebrow shot up to the ceiling. "Please. Please explain that one. I would love to hear it. I would just *love* to hear how Harry Reardon, space vagabond, gun fighter, smuggler, and all around tough guy thinks *pink raspberry cosmos* are manly."

"Because it's *made from vodka*. The nectar of Mother Russia. That shit is what fueled the Soviets as they, you know, drunkenly stumbled across the Urals. The kind of drink that puts hairs on the chests of your women. It doesn't just separate the boys from the men, it *converts* them." He swirled his finger. "In that direction. From little boys to big strong men."

"It's a cocktail."

"A cocktail … which is mostly vodka," protested Reardon.

Smith ran his finger around the edge of the glass, then licked it clean. "Vodka ceases to be manly when you add raspberry liqueur and raspberry juice, pinch of lime juice, and some syrup. It becomes a pink raspberry cosmo, and that, my friend, is not in any way a masculine thing."

Reardon scratched the stubble on his chin, glaring at his counterpart. First Smith was *late*, then he insulted his strong, manly choice of drinks. "It's still vodka."

"Fair enough," said Smith. "You want another?"

Reardon glowered into his empty glass. "Yeah, definitely. Kind of feeling the need to get wasted after what happened."

"I can imagine," said Smith, tapping on the tablet embedded in the bar to order another round. Reardon got the distinct impression that Smith had been leading him toward that subject and was almost out of patience. "Right. Well, I'm here, we have more drinks on the way, so let's talk. Tell me what happened out there, Harry."

Where to begin, where to begin … Reardon tried to get his thoughts in order, tried to arrange the events into temporal sequence but they kind of stuck in his mind like cold honey in a bottle. The smuggler, and the box, and the planet's crust just *lifting right up off.…*

"Is Sammy okay?" asked Smith, softly.

"Oh yeah." Reardon exhaled a breath he didn't even realize he was holding. "No, the kid's fine. He's fine. A little shook up, a little rattled, but he's fine."

Smith waited patiently.

"They … they blew up Zenith."

"They?" asked Smith. "Who are we talking about, Harry? Be specific."

"I can't. Barely caught a glimpse of them," he said, clenching his fist as tightly as he could. "I … I only saw what I saw." He took a deep breath. "It was those aliens. The … mutants. Future-humans. Whatever. The ones from the news, from the MaxGainz facility, the ones that old army vet guy was ranting about on GBC News. I didn't really believe it at first, but … well. You know the *liberal media* and their lies."

"You're sitting there drinking a fruity pink sugar-drink,

wearing an outfit that makes you look like a gay space trucker, talking about the *liberal media*." Smith casually sipped his drink, then made a disgusted face. Some people just couldn't handle their sugar. "You really need a new outfit. Between your clothes, your ship, and your questionable choice in alcoholic beverages I am struggling to take you seriously."

There was nothing wrong with his outfit. Space mercenaries often wore leather. And he rode a motorcycle. Once. "Any*way*," said Reardon, "it was … *them*. I know it was. I saw their ship."

Any hint of levity, teasing, evaporated from Smith's voice. "Zenith was hit by an orbital strike?"

"An orbital *something*," said Reardon. "It was just one ship, a big one. Like a giant metal brick. And it had a massive…" he held out his arm. "Like a beam on it. Some kind of energy projector, possibly. I don't know. It was a big thing and it caused the whole surface of the planet to ripple, to heave, to lift up and drop back down like it was a fat guy at a wave pool. Obviously, though, being thrown up and dropped like that wasn't good for the people on the surface."

Smith was quiet for a moment. "No," he said, slowly putting down his drink, "I imagine it was not. Did you get a positive ID?"

"No," said Reardon, throwing back the raspberry-sweet contents of his drink and relishing in the faint burning alcoholic aftertaste. "Even the *Aerostar*'s systems couldn't ping it. It was as though its transponder was scrambled, or built from some kind of entirely non-standard architecture all together. Familiar, but different."

"Like it was made by future-humans," said Smith,

"showing us primitives a tablet screen that we think is a moving piece of paper."

Not an *entirely* bad way of describing the ship. Sammy had said it looked like nothing he'd ever seen before. That would make sense if it was alien.

"Seems right," said Reardon. *Definitely* shouldn't have come. Definitely. "What do you want from me, then?"

Smith touched the side of his face, pressing a finger to his temple. Reardon knew that the guy had significant cybernetic enhancements—an eye at least, possibly a kidney that also functioned as a hard drive, and maybe other things—but just seeing him interface with them directly was a strange, unsettling sight. He looked away.

"I'll need your ship's image records," said Smith. "Whatever you have."

Reardon grimaced apologetically. "You know I'm a *smuggler*, right? Smugglers tend to be involved in stuff which is —" he coughed politely. "Ambiguously legal. Keeping logs of what I see and what I do would *really* undermine my business model if I ever got arrested. You know what I'm saying?"

"Of course," said Smith, not missing a beat. "But if you *ambiguously legal* types didn't keep records of the deliveries you made, including what was delivered to whom, where, when, and in what condition, then I doubt very much you would be a very profitable..." he stressed the word. "Smuggler at all."

Damn. He knew. It was true enough; Sammy knew to purge the logs after every job, but because of the chaotic nature of their escape, he probably hadn't gotten around to doing it. *Probably*. He often forgot.

"Uhh..." Reardon touched his radio. "Hey Sammy, did

you purge the logs after we landed?"

There was the very slightest pause. "Uh … of course, Harry," came the answer through his earpiece.

Reardon gritted his teeth. "Are you *very* sure? The answer I want is: no, I forgot, because that way I can prove to my contact what I'm saying is true."

The relief through the line was almost palpable. "N-no, I forgot. They're here. Sorry." There was the slightest pause. "Wait, if we were going to see you-know-who, why would you want the logs erased anyway?"

In truth, he had forgotten to tell Sammy to do it. So they had both forgotten and it had all turned out okay.

Like usual.

"It doesn't matter," said Reardon, in what he hoped was a firm, commanding tone. "Just … don't erase them. I'll log in remotely in a moment and transmit them to the contact." He cut the line.

"Sammy knows who I am, you know," said Smith.

"I know. But … smuggler protocols. Never say names over an open line."

Smith smiled a little. "Okay. That's one thing we can cross off right now. When we're done here, I'll come with you to collect whatever you have; my systems can process it faster than whatever's aboard that pink rust bucket you're flying around in these days."

"It's *not* pink." Reardon narrowed his eyes suspiciously. "You don't want me to just transmit the data to you?"

"Of course not." Smith finished his drink. "I'll analyze it on the way."

"On the way," Reardon echoed, glaring angrily at him.

"You mind telling me what this is about?"

Smith smiled enigmatically. "Congratulations, Captain Reardon. I need a ride and your ship is perfect for it."

"Kind of rude to not tell a ship's captain that they're taking on passengers. Or where they're going, how much they're going to get paid, or you know, *ask permission*."

Smith shrugged. "That's how things used to work back in the day, wasn't it? Good ole' Military Intelligence. *We don't ask, we tell.* Might as well have been our motto."

He wrinkled his nose and, with an annoyed grunt, tapped on the bar and ordered another round of sugary drinks. "I left that life behind for a reason, John."

"I know. But times change, don't they."

Sammy's voice chirped in his ear. "Hey, bro? Uhh ... I went to back up the logs like you said, and the ship's computer's saying something weird."

Reardon touched his radio. "Weird?"

"Yeah. Says there's a docking clamp on the ship—it's been there since we arrived, but there's a law enforcement override preventing it from being actively registered on the ship's computers. I only saw it because I did a full diagnostic."

Their new set of drinks arrived. Reardon stared at the twin glasses. "Mind telling me why you grounded my ship, Smith?"

Out of the corner of his eye, he could see Smith's reaction as genuine surprise. "Wasn't me," he said, tapping the skin on his wrist. "Hang on."

"Hang on," said Sammy. "Lemme just tap into the network here ... jump a few firewalls ... dodge a few fireballs ... aaaaand ... There. We're outta here, boys."

Slowly, Reardon swiveled on his stool, turning to face his

old friend. "Ominous coincidence," he said, carefully. "I was just chased away from the USS *Midway* by what must have been a little alien ship, and before that, a bigger alien ship just blew away the planet I was standing on not two minutes previously. And now someone just tried to ground the *Aerostar*. Wanna tell me what the hell is going on?"

"Just come with me."

"If I said no, you would *persuade* me?"

"I told you. Wasn't me," said Smith, again, and pushed himself off his seat. "C'mon. We have to get to Ganymede."

"Ganymede?" echoed Reardon. Maybe he shouldn't have had so much to drink. "What the hell's there that's worth anything?"

"Nothing anymore," said Smith, "but there's a destroyed colony there that might have a few more answers for us. And right now I've got a troubling surplus of questions and not enough answers to go around. Starting with one of our old friends back at Intel. Guy by the name of Spectre."

Harry shrugged. "I don't remember a Spectre—"

"You wouldn't. Not his real name. But if my suspicions are correct, you're going to be hearing a lot more of him. You, and … well, everyone, frankly. But first, to Ganymede. The puzzle starts there."

"Why there?"

"Because," he stood, and finished his drink, "that was the very first target of that first future-human fleet. Let's move."

CHAPTER THIRTEEN

Four Lightyears from Earth
USS Midway
Captain's Ready Room

Mattis let the warm water wash over his body, and he closed his eyes. Steam rose up all around him, softening his skin and gently washing away his anger. It felt good to be clean, luxurious even, but a nice long shower couldn't hide the fact that, on what would be his final mission as CO of the *Midway*, he had already suffered a serious loss.

Reardon had gone.

The wreckage of Zenith was a long way away and it was going to be difficult to find answers there anyway. But he'd have to see. Hopefully they'd find a clue there about where the enemy fleet was heading next.

That fact crept in the background of his mind. Somewhere out there, a devastatingly powerful future-human ship, or ships, was lurking, waiting to strike their next target.

How many more millions would die next? How many more worlds, and lives, shattered?

Mattis turned off the water and stepped out of his shower when the chime sounded at the door.

"Just a moment," he said, toweling off the last few stubborn damp areas and then, as quickly as he could, pulling on his uniform. When he was satisfied, he called out. "Come in."

Modi stepped through the threshold, stopping when he saw him. "Is this a bad time, Admiral?" he asked, cautiously, eyes falling on Mattis's uniform.

"No," said Mattis. "Not at all. I'll shave when you're gone. What's on your mind, Modi?"

"Well sir, it's the ship's engine upgrades."

Mattis's teeth ground together. "Sure," he said, "give me the bad news."

Modi seemed taken aback, blinking rapidly. "I don't recall saying there was any."

Dealing with Modi always seemed to be a frustration. He was a gifted engineer and a master of everything that beeped or whistled, but he had an extraordinary ability to take almost *anything* and only act upon its most literal interpretation. "It was … implied." He pinched the bridge of his nose and rubbed beneath his eyes in frustration. "Just tell me what the situation with the engines is."

"Well, sir, we're expecting them to be completed ahead of time and well under anticipated manpower cost, and with no issues at all, major or minor. In all ways engine performance is expected to be superior to our previous systems with a reduced power cost, heat production, and operating with additional safety measure."

That was not at all what he was expecting. "You're saying that the integration of a foreign, untested, modification to our classified military propulsion systems is going perfectly?"

"Not going, sir, *gone*. The upgrade is complete."

Well. Would wonders never cease. "Very good, Mister Modi. Is there anything else?"

"Yes, sir. That's why I'm here in person." Modi shifted uncomfortably. "The *reason* the system integration has gone so perfectly was due to us being given the … well, what I can only describe as a complete schematic and installation guide—one much more detailed and complete than the Chinese one we were provided—which dramatically lowered the installation time for the whole system."

Mattis frowned slightly—they hadn't been given the full schematic originally? Why would fleet brass have accepted that? "What was missing from the original schematics they gave us?"

"Oh, nothing *missing*, at least from a mechanical viewpoint. We had the full schematic already. It would be madness to install new engines and not give the chief engineer the full schematics."

Mattis felt like they were talking in circles, and rubbed the bridge of his nose again. To his credit, Modi actually seemed to pick up on his frustration.

"But these new files go far more into quantum and graviton theory than the purely mechanical schematics. And alternate configurations and software setup files and hardware drivers. Apparently, these engines are capable of far more than just propulsion."

"Oh?"

Modi nodded. "Remember the comet fragment that the original intruder ship was trying to push towards Earth last year? And how we were able to stop it with the experimental anti-gravity emitters on those Chinese ships? Well, it appears that these engines may ... have that ability inherently built into them."

"And they gave that to us willingly?"

Modi's eyes darted to the side in confusion, then back to him. "Um, sir?"

"What, Modi?" He took a breath. "And speak plainly."

He seemed unwilling to answer. "I ... thought you knew." A pause. "The plans came from Chuck."

That made absolutely no sense. "From Chuck Mattis? From my son?"

"That is correct, sir. I just assumed that you were aware of them—perhaps he was relaying them for you, or perhaps his contacts in—"

"Chuck hasn't got a job, he doesn't *have* any contacts, and all the diplomatic cred he had he burned when he broke into Senator Pitt's office like an absolute idiot." Mattis took a deep, long breath. "So, before we left Earth, he passed them to you. Probably not to me since I was stuck in that Pentagon meeting at the time. Did he say anything else?"

"Yes sir," said Modi. "He said ... this is why Captain Shao's ship exploded. They were trying to protect this technology."

So. Shao had died for this information. To protect it. To prevent the US from obtaining it, or ... to prevent *someone* from obtaining it. That was a sobering thought, but more pressing ones pushed their way to the surface. "How did Chuck know about that?"

"He said he met with Admiral Yim," said Modi. "I suggest you ask him about it. He also said that Yim referred to your trust in him regarding the Goalkeeper command codes over New London. He said Yim is, in his own words, returning the favor."

That made some sense. "I'll be sure to thank Yim for his kindness when next I speak to him."

"Right," said Modi. He frowned ever so slightly, the furrows on his brow tightening. "I don't like this, sir. Any of it."

Mattis wished he could disagree. "We'll just have to do what we always do, Mister Modi. Wing it. And please feel free to research what else our new engines can do in your spare time." He flashed a small grin. "Just think of it as extended leave." He watched Modi's face for a reaction, but the joke seemed to fall flat. "You should probably head back to work."

"Aye aye sir," said Modi, and departed as awkwardly as he had arrived.

Mattis clipped on his earpiece, took a deep breath, and pulled out his communicator. "Connect me to Chuck."

The device chirped. *Call failure: target unable to be located. Device powered off.*

Dammit. Mattis tried again and again, but nothing came through. He logged this incident in the back of his mind, resolving to chase it up later, and then switched mental tracks to another order of business. This time he selected another number. Admiral Fischer.

This time, the woman answered instantly. "Fischer here.

What can I do for you, Admiral?"

He had kind of hoped for a few seconds to gather his thoughts but pressed on anyway. "I wanted to talk to you for a moment."

She paused. "Regarding?"

Mattis took a shallow breath. "Frankly, your man's presence on my ship, Admiral. I've already spoken to Doctor Brooks about this supplement issue, but you *could* have mentioned that he was coming along too when we met—I would have approved him being here directly. As it stands I'm a little put out that you didn't ask. And frankly, I'm not entirely convinced he's only here to investigate our ... supplements."

"I know," she said. "Do you want the diplomatic lie, or the blunt truth?"

Mattis couldn't resist a little snort. "You're asking me that because you *know* I'm going to ask for the latter."

"Right you are. Well, Admiral Mattis, the problem is, you're old enough to be a literal grandfather and yet you still need a babysitter. You're the commanding officer of the USS *Midway*; your job is to command the ship, *not* to go out on adventures yourself and put yourself directly in harm's way like some swashbuckling starship captain from old-fashioned campy science fiction shows. You're not a Mal Reynolds. You're not a Kirk. You're definitely no Han Solo. Marching down to that embassy like you owned the place, going to that hellhole New London with your senior staff, taking little side trips to Chrysalis—granted that last one was more justified than the others—are way out of line, especially given your fondness for taking your XO with you. Now, I want to be clear about this: the US Navy grants a high amount of authority and autonomy to its COs, but ultimately, even the captain is simply a link in the chain of command. No more adventures. Period. This one is by the book. More Adama, less Kirk. Understood?"

He said nothing. Half because he was far less versed in old science fiction shows that she was, but in spite of that her meaning was clear. And he didn't like the implication for Doctor Brooks's true mission.

"Admiral," said Fischer, "you asked me for the blunt truth."

True. "I suppose I just wasn't expecting it to be so … blunt."

He could sense her smile down the line. "Look. I understand. Doctor Brooks is here to oversee Lieutenant Corrick, but also to keep an eye on *you*, Jack. Medically speaking that is. If you try to pull any bullshit, he can keep you on the ship and doing your job, and not out on your … swashbuckling trips. He has the authority of the Admiralty's office—I've given him a special dispensation just for this, so I would suggest buttering him up with platitudes and trying to stay on his good side."

He ran his hand through his hair. "Mmm. Well, I already screwed that up. He didn't like me asking too many questions about the nature of him being here."

"Well, unscrew it." A tiny playful edge crept into her tone. "Apparently you're quite good at that. It worked on Miss Ramirez, didn't it?"

That was *not* where he was expecting this conversation to go. "Uhh…."

"Yeah. Anyway," said Fischer. "Anyway. Talk to Doctor Brooks again when you have a moment, and this time make good. And Admiral, I've given him direct authority to countermand any of your decisions that jeopardize your own personal bodily safety." Her tone softened. "Jack, listen to me. This is your last mission on the *Midway*. It's past your time. It's past hers. Hell, I had to fight for you to keep her for the six months after Friendship Station. *An Admiral! Commanding a starship! Heresy!* That's all I've heard from the top brass. I can't tell you how annoying it's getting. Anyway. That's all. Just … be safe, and enjoy it while it lasts." She stood up from her desk. "Anything else?"

"No," said Mattis, and closed the link.

He sat there in the quiet, considering everything he had learned, which was at once a lot to take in and, ironically, just too little.

What was going on aboard his ship, and why did he feel like he wasn't being told the whole story?

CHAPTER FOURTEEN

Four Lightyears from Earth
USS Midway
Bridge

With suspicious thoughts churning through his head, Mattis sat back in his CO's chair, taking in a deep breath and letting it out slowly. They had seen a strange ship, blown it up, but he couldn't put the puzzle pieces together yet. There was something missing. Something…

Something external to the ship, or within it?

You're being paranoid, old man.

Admiral Fischer was just doing her job, putting her man onboard. Doctor Brooks was just doing *his* job. He should focus on his own.

"Sir," asked Lynch, a little hesitantly, perhaps sensing Mattis was deep in his thoughts again, "a report about the new engines."

Finally. Something simple at least. Easy to understand. "Sure. Let's hear it."

"Well sir, Commander Modi reports that the integration is going smoothly. He's on his way up from Engineering to report his findings on Z-space translation."

Welcome news. Mattis nodded appreciatively. "Good."

"It is good, Admiral," said Modi from the entrance to the bridge.

Mattis beckoned him on. "Good to see you, Commander. How's my ship's legs?"

"Its landing struts are entirely functional, Admiral."

Lynch glared at Modi. "You spinning me, Commander? He was talking about the engines!"

"Then why did he ask about the landing struts?"

Mattis bit his lower lip. "Commander Modi. Please present your findings about the integration between the Chinese and American engine systems, and disregard any information about the ship's landing struts."

Modi considered. "Well, so far, as anticipated, the engines have been able to get thirty-six percent more power while consuming eleven percent less energy. Couple that with smoother operations and I'm quite happy. There *remains* a slight issue with the way the graviton emitters function. Still trying to understand the significance of it all."

"Graviton emitters?"

"Yes sir," said Modi. "The new engines employ a new form of gravitational lensing. They emit gravitons, which shape Z-space around the ship as it moves, like a giant snow plough in front of a train."

Lynch snorted out a dismissive laugh, accent drawling.

"And here I thought you were *utterly incapable* of using metaphors, Modi. You shock the life out of me."

"I concur," said Modi. "Do you need medical attention?"

Lynch groaned loudly and looked away.

"Modi," asked Mattis, "I need you to stay focused. So it's a graviton engine. Yes?"

"Yes sir."

"And it's not dangerous in any way? It's functioning fine? No issues?"

"Only that I simply have not figured out the precise method by which the graviton emitters form the necessary conical shape yet, but I will. The science in the new files your son passed to me is well documented but … extensive. Exhaustively so. I am only one man, Admiral."

He didn't want to push his chief of engineering too hard. That would be asking for trouble. "At your own pace, Commander Modi. I trust you'll have the system's mysteries well understood in no time."

Modi raised an eyebrow. "I think it will require more than *no time*. Theoretically, that would be less than a planck-second, which less than the amount of time it takes light to travel a planck-length, which itself is quadrillions of times smaller than an atom's nucleus, though I suppose it—"

Lynch snorted. "Good God, you socially-dysfunctional robot ferret, just take the damn compliment and run."

Modi glanced Lynch's way. "You don't give me enough credit, Commander. The culmination of my … joke, was that it would take at least five plank-seconds to complete my research. But as the saying goes, if you have to explain the joke, it simply was not humorous to begin with."

Lynch folded his arms. "Clearly."

Mattis held up a finger to silence the inevitable squabbling. "Is that all?"

"Yes, Admiral."

Mattis straightened his back. "Very well. Get on it. I have a feeling we're going to need that extra power sooner rather than later."

CHAPTER FIFTEEN

Sol System
Ganymede
The Aerostar

The inside of the *Aerostar* had proved itself to be everything Smith expected, and less. Although, that wasn't entirely fair—there were a few places where the decor actually approached sensible, and some of the equipment at least looked like it was in working order, despite some of the outlandish paper labels taped on most of them. *Pew Pew!* Or, *Do not press unless the shitter is full.* For the fluid exchange coupler —the ductwork that channeled in clean water and pumped out waste water when they were docked, he'd labeled, *Sexy Fluid Exchange Bow Chicka Bow Wow.* And for the locking clamps used for docking with a port, *Hanky-Panky clanky thang.*

And for the Z-space controls, *Vroom!.* He chose to credit the younger brother for that one. He'd always been less … blatantly obnoxious than his sibling.

"Exiting Z-space in five!" Sammy called from the co-pilot's space, tapping buttons on the *Vroom!* panel.

"Thank you, Sammy," Smith replied as he unfolded himself from the comfortable, but embarrassingly leopard-printed armchair Reardon had insisted on manhandling into the cockpit and moved to stand behind the pilot's chair.

"Hey! That's my job," Reardon complained. "*I* acknowledge status reports from my minions, because *I* am the captain. That, my friend, is how the chain of command works."

"Because ships that follow actual command structures use phrases like 'in five' to refer to—minutes? Seconds?—Of course," Smith said evenly as Sammy muttered a few choice words about 'minions' and what he thought of Reardon's ability to survive alone.

"Wow, rude," said Reardon, turning to glare at him. "I'll have you know this ship is a professional commercial enterprise, and—"

"Sure, sure, whatever you say," Smith said. "Now, are you ready to go dirtside? Sammy, I'll need you to stay with the ship —this shouldn't be dangerous, but if it is, we'll need a quick getaway, and if I find anything urgent, I might need to send it on to you. Be ready for my transmission. And Reardon—you have a couple of spacesuits? The station is working on a fairly tight budget, so it's faster to get docking permission if we don't need them to wheel out an air bridge."

"Wheel out?" Sammy whistled, tapping his wheelchair. "Oh, I guess I didn't tell you I retro-fitted this baby with zero-g thrusters."

Smith smiled to himself. "No kidding?"

"Low tech is best tech, you know," said Sammy. "A lot can go wrong with high tech stuff ... but older models? They built them to last. It's simple. Rugged. Easier to attach things like, for example, thrusters."

That made sense to him. Kind of. "Right you are. Anyway. Stay here and track our progress—I'm sure we'll need some backup. Preferably with big guns. Right up your alley, kid. Reardon. Suits?"

"Yeah, I got some spacesuits," Reardon said. "I modded them myself, too. Won't find a more stylish kit this side of space, baby. You'll love them."

He doubted that. "As long as they work."

"They always do," the smuggler continued, making for the ladder. "All my things do. And while I'm on the subject ... no touchy, Smith. Stay away from my lady." He twisted around and jabbed a finger at the console.

Smith looked at the control panel, dizzyingly arrayed with bizarrely colored buttons, dials, levers and knobs marked things like *Bad Idea* and *Super-Speedy* and *Pew Pew Two: Electric Boogaloo*, and shuddered. "No, thanks. I don't think I'll take my chances on scattering us across Z-space today."

"That's the spirit!" Reardon's voice was muffled as he disappeared to a lower deck. Smith noticed Sammy looking confusedly after his brother.

"Everything OK?"

"Huh? Uh, sure," Sammy shook himself. Maybe he was cold. "He's just being weird."

"Your brother is usually weird."

"Mmm."

A brief, vaguely uncomfortable silence. "It wasn't because

of the thing I said?" asked Smith. "The thing about …
wheeling out stuff?"

Sammy reached down and turned his chair, his face a half-
grin, half-grimace. "Nah." He paused. "I mean, yeah. Sort of.
But it's not your fault." Sammy leaned forward slightly. Smith's
eyes were drawn down to Sammy's legs—impossibly thin twigs,
basically bones with no muscles on them at all.

"After I got hurt, after the accident, you know, everyone
was so supportive … they were all like, 'don't worry, the docs
will fix it.' And when they couldn't, that changed to, 'this isn't
going to affect anything at all, your life is basically going to be
exactly as it was before, and this doesn't change anything.'
That's the kind of thing people who aren't disabled say.
Because they don't know that it really *does* change everything.
Some people try to hide it, get all offended when it's brought
up. Other people go overboard the other direction and own it.
Call themselves a *crip* or whatever. Regardless of their position,
it changes them. Can't avoid that. Getting offended about
things won't change it. Getting annoyed that I can't go on a
mission with my brother and have to stay with the ship won't
change the fact that it's … the best decision anyone could
make given my capabilities. Still…."

Smith waited a moment. "It's still hard?"

Sammy looked at him as if he'd said the understatement
of the year. "It sucks dick."

Ahh, so *that* was the issue. "I would say I don't understand,
but you know that already." Smith tapped the side of his head,
right beside his cybernetic eye. "Although technically, this is a
prosthesis. And I didn't choose it; it was put in after…" he
smiled. "A complicated series of events."

"Sure," said Sammy. "And you didn't choose it, but does it change how you identify. Are you a cyber-person, or just John Smith?"

"Just John Smith," he said. "But still. An eye ain't a pair of legs. I still get to go on missions."

"Hah, true," the kid conceded, half-grin becoming a full smirk. "You get to go out and get shot at. Lucky you. Me, I have a bunch of guns and inches of hull armor protecting me."

True, although a ship was big, valuable target. "So he gets all weird when he's being protective of you?"

"Nailed it."

A new feeling of respect for Harry Reardon surged through Smith. It couldn't be easy basically raising his younger brother after their mother died, and then, when the younger brother was finally old enough to technically live on his own, keep the kid with him not as a burdensome tag-along, but recognizing him for the brave little genius he was. Beyond capable, where another person would have only seen a wheelchair holding a warm body. And even recognizing all that, Harry still was as protective of the kid as a mother black bear and her cub.

"If it helps," said Smith, nodding to the ladder. "It's more than just being weird. He's still drunk."

"You can tell?" Sammy asked, his face a mixture of skepticism and genuine impression.

It didn't take a highly sensitive prosthetic eye to see it. "Yes."

"Wow. Remind me never to play poker with you."

"You say that every time I see you."

Sammy shot him a dirty look and turned back to his console. "Only because it's true." He leaned over to a mic. "Coming out now, bro!"

Brilliant veils of rainbow light washed over the viewport as they reverted to normal space. Over the space of a few seconds they faded into a spectacular view of Jupiter's titanic marbled storms and Ganymede's crater-dappled surface.

"Civilian craft *Aerostar*, what is your business on Ganymede?" a voice crackled through the a speaker among the pilot's controls mere moments after reversion.

Sammy glanced at Smith, and replied. "Ganymede Station, we are here on classified US government business. Requesting permission to dock, no air bridge required."

Just as they'd rehearsed. Good.

"*Aerostar*, you are aware this is a restricted area?"

The boy seemed suspiciously untroubled by the line of conversation. "We are, Ganymede Station. Sending through permission codes now."

He'd learned to lie well. Not that anything different could have been expected of Harry Reardon's brother.

"Sorry sir," the voice said. Smith could practically hear their eyes widening. "There's a bay clear for you right now. Transmitting a flight path."

"Received." Sammy grinned. "Thank you, Ganymede Station." He cut off the mic. "Must be nice, having people call you sir all the time."

Smith considered mentioning the hours of tedium and short and senseless bursts of danger his job entailed, before simply nodding. "It's a perk."

Then he headed down the ladder and began making his

way through the *Aerostar*'s debatably-organized lower decks in search of Reardon.

Time to suit up.

CHAPTER SIXTEEN

Four Lightyears from Earth
USS Midway
Sickbay
Lieutenant Patricia "Guano" Corrick's bed

Guano hated being in this bed almost as much as she hated the faint sound of music from the bed on the other side of the bulkhead behind her.

It was possibly the worst kind of music she had ever heard. Her taste was eclectic, even totally bizarre, but whatever that guy was playing was just *awful*. It was just noise. Noise that came through with something that resembled a beat, accompanied by untuned violins.

She thumped her fists against the bulkhead. "Hey!" she roared. "Turn it down!"

"The nurse said I can listen to the music at a reasonable volume," replied the man, like clockwork, his voice muffled by the steel wall between them.

"You—you just increased it!"

"No, I didn't."

"Yes, you did!"

"No, I did *not*."

Guano groaned and jammed her pillow over her face. "Just kill me now," she muttered. "Please. Just do it. Just put a bullet in me. I don't want to live anymore."

"Hmm," said a strange, deep voice she hadn't heard before. "Should I note down *suicidal intentions* on your chart now?"

Slowly, Guano peeled the pillow off her face. Some thin, almost gaunt-looking guy was there, wearing a doctor's uniform and carrying a briefcase which swelled slightly as though packed full of junk. "Unless you think it'll get me discharged faster," she said. "Who are you?"

"I'm Doctor Jacoby Brooks," he said, moving up to her bed and folding his hands behind his back. "I'm a medical doctor assigned to your case by the Department of Defense."

Guano grimaced slightly and propped herself up on her elbows. "I told Roadie—I mean, Major Yousuf—and everyone," she said. "I feel fine."

"I think I'll be the judge of that," said Doctor Brooks, with obvious patience. "I understand my presence here is an unwelcome disruption, but trust me when I say, I only want what's best for you and the crew."

Guano, in a manner she *knew* would be seen as pouty, slumped back in her bed. "Right."

Doctor Brooks seemed to consider a moment, looking her up and down. "So you're not feeling any different than usual?"

"Apart from a case of *being in bed too long*, no. I'm feeling fine. Itching to get spaceborn again if you know what I mean." She folded her arms and glared at the wall. "I'm a pilot, Doctor. A bird. I'm not meant to be caged."

"I actually do know what you mean," said Brooks, "I used to race civvie snubs before I went to medical school. One time I broke my leg after a bad landing, and I was out for a year. That was what got me interested in medicine."

Oh yeah. Sure. Guano made a face. "Nice bed-side manner, doc. Mmm. I'm guessing this is where you lie to me to try and bond with me, because we have a shared common interest?"

Brooks raised an eyebrow, looking down at her with genuine surprise. "You know," he said, idly tapping his finger on his forearm, "it doesn't really work that way. See, if I wanted to lie to you, I wouldn't pick something so easy to disprove. What would a doctor know about racing snubs? Well, they might know, for starters, that if you deploy your flaps too late as you come in for a skid after a six point lap, well, you hit the ground real hard and break your legs … but if you deploy them too early, well, you stall, hit the ground, and break your legs. This much is pretty self explanatory, really." He casually put his leg up on the side of her bed and started rolling up his pants, revealing a lighter patch of skin—scar tissue—running up his leg. "But there's a lot they *won't* know, and simply *can't* know, because it's not openly publicized information and it generally takes a fair bit of experience before you discover it on your own. For example, that if you have a surgical pin in your leg, as one might *do* when they have a serious break in their leg, then when you reach higher altitude, they tend to ache a bit. Why? Well, scar tissue is a lot less elastic than regular tissue, so as the pressure changes, scar tissue balloons while normal resists, causing soreness. They call it—"

"The Reminder," said Guano, saying the words before he could. "To always put your flaps down."

"A little pain you can ever get rid of." Brooks put his leg down. "Guess that means you have to trust me now, right?"

Sulking, Guano didn't answer right away. "I guess," she said, finally.

"Okay." Brooks clicked his tongue. "So, Lieutenant Corrick … tell me about what happened to you."

"Just like that, huh?" asked Guano, suspicion building within her again. "You just want me to open up to you about this … thing?"

"No need to rush it," said Brooks, casually pulling out a tablet and tapping it a few times—no doubt turning on the voice-to-text transcription. "How about an easier question. Why don't you tell me about your childhood." He held up a finger. "And, full disclosure, I'm choosing this question because it's stereotypical and you expect it. No other reason."

No way. "How about *you*?" she asked, pointedly. "What don't you tell *me* about *your* childhood?"

"Sure," said Brooks, beaming. He reached over and pulled up a chair. "Well, I was born and raised in New Orleans. The French quarter is a lovely place to grow up, if you don't mind the occasional mugging and gang beat-down, which I guess you could say gave me a thicker skin when it came to recalcitrant patients who won't talk to me."

Guano snorted. "Mmm."

There was a brief moment of silence. Brooks kept smiling, looking away, as though recalling a fond memory. "Did you know I went to West Point?"

"No," said Guano, blinking. "You were a cross-commission?"

"That's right. Straight out of the Army academy into the Navy. Not exactly a standard career path, but it was very … illuminating." His tone became wistful. "Lots of good memories there. I loved the academy. The whole place is seeped in the history of America, just soaked in it … in the grand ballroom there is a series of portraits of generals of The American Revolution. Among them is Benedict Arnold—turned face inward. Arnold is no longer publicly acknowledged as a former Commandant of West Point due to his plan to surrender the fort to the British during the American Revolution."

"Bit harsh," said Guano. "I mean … he *was* the Commandant, like it or not."

"More toward the *not* than anything else. Arnold planned to sell the fort to the British, and when he fully defected, was inducted into the British army under the rank of Brigadier General."

Guano laughed. "Well, okay. Guess he was a bit of a bastard then."

Brooks chuckled, low and genuinely. "Fine way of putting it." He cleared his throat. "But I'm not here to talk to you about ancient history."

"I guess not," said Guano, and she settled back in her bed once again. "I … I just know that this is difficult to talk about, yeah? I haven't even spoken to Flatline about it. Not properly. I mean, he *knows*, but I just … I just don't know what to say about it. I feel like a real freak, you know?"

Brooks cocked an eyebrow. "Well, I'm a half-Puerto Rican, half-Scottish medical doctor, West Point graduate in the Navy, born and raised in Chicago but now living in space, with a series of titanium pins in my legs from a wildly misspent youth. Hardly compares to your strange fugue state, but … I mean, I think there's a bit of common ground there."

Guano stared. "How did you know about that?"

"Major Yousuf reached out to me." Brooks smiled. "Don't worry, your secret's safe with me."

The guy genuinely reminded her of Flatline, her gunner and battle buddy for years. That stupid grin he had, the weird smile—maybe that was why they picked him to talk to her? Did it really matter? Slowly, her suspicions melted away, and she started talking.

"I described it once like listening to Celtic music while stoned. It's like … it's like when you've been running on adrenaline for, say, a full day and just don't care anymore. Time seems to slow down, like I'm *feeling* things before my senses can even process them. It's 'being in the zone' more than anything I've *ever* felt, and I've been a pilot for my whole life—my dad let me take the controls of his freighter when I was five. Anyway, fear shuts down, worries melt away, and everything moves on autopilot. My hands adjust the controls, my feet brush the pedals, I do about a thousand things a second and I barely even remember them."

Brooks considered. "Sounds like Highway Hypnosis," he said. "It's a well documented medical phenomenon. Back before most cars were self-driving, piloting them long distances caused the drivers go into autopilot and just kind of *act* without thinking, and when they arrive at their destination they don't remember how they got there."

"Sounds similar to what happens to me," said Guano. "I *do* remember things, but it's like someone else did it. Like I'm being guided by … *something*."

"Mmm." Brooks looked down to his tablet, considering a moment. "You wanna know a fun fact about Highway Hypnosis?"

"Yeah?"

"It was the leading cause of falling asleep at the wheel, and automobile accidents." The levity slowly evaporated from his voice. "It kills."

Damn. "Well," said Guano, "you better fix me, doc. I like living. It's basically all I do."

"Looking at your piloting record, you do seem to have a fine track record of not dying."

"Not dying is what any good pilot does." She reached out and grabbed his elbow. "Fix me, Doc. I'd like to go on not dying."

"I'll do my best," said Brooks, tapping his tablet. "Anyway. I've arranged a little surprise for you." A wide smile returned to his face as he lifted his briefcase up onto the edge of his bed. "Here's a flight suit. Helmet's in the corridor. Go get changed out of your hospital gown and let's go and see your abilities first hand, shall we?"

CHAPTER SEVENTEEN

Sol System
Ganymede Station
Former site of the Ark Project

Smith stared with both organic and mechanical eyes at the perfectly normal, standard-issue white spacesuits, and actually sighed. "Look, I'll be honest, I'm surprised you actually got me out here on this bucket of bolts without any explosions or Z-space mishaps. But ... these look far too ... normal for Harry Reardon."

"See? That's the trick. The normal-looking suits are a distraction. They'll be expecting something outlandish from old Harry Reardon, and when confronted with *normal*, they'll choke, and that's when I shoot."

"Really?"

Reardon pulled a smile that he probably thought of as roguish and shot finger-guns at him. "Gotcha!"

Smith didn't bother emoting. "Brilliant."

The smuggler laughed. "You know what else is brilliant?"

"Mmm?"

"Your mom last night."

He shook his head. "Reardon, we don't have time for this. Your brother is bringing us in to land as we speak."

Reardon's eyes narrowed. "*You* don't have time for this. I, on the other, hand have all the time in the world, because I work for no one and have no deadlines to meet."

Smith raised an eyebrow. "How does the imminent destruction of everything humanity knows and loves sound for a deadline to you?"

"Overblown," he replied. "But … actually probably, uh, accurate. Oh, shit, that's right, I was trying not to think about the dead planet. Thanks."

"No problem," Smith said as he stepped gingerly into one of the suits, still examining them for some trick or upgrade or abnormality.

"Shit, it's just a vacuum suit, man," Reardon said, laughing. "Also," he continued, the laugh suddenly gone, "just so you know, I'm not doing this because you asked and certainly not because you threatened me."

"I didn't threat—"

"I'm here because I want to be. Because I choose to be."

Smith rolled his eyes. "I believe you."

"Seriously, end of the world? I couldn't care less, as long as there's somewhere left with fuel and food."

"And medical supplies for Sammy?" Smith asked, less than half paying attention.

"Yeah. That." That seemed to steal some of the bluster from Reardon, whose tone changed to something surprisingly

… serious. "I mean, the kid spends his life in that damn chair, and … you know, those things cause pressure sores. Ulcers. Normally pain is the body's way of telling us that something's wrong, but if he can't feel it, then he doesn't know, you know? So you gotta get meds for it. And most places … most places don't stock that kind of shit. Especially the further out from Earth you go."

There was a short time of surprisingly blissful silence as Reardon seemed to mentally check himself. He'd been complaining of boredom, not just a few days ago. Now boredom was preferable….

"But," Reardon began again. "You hearing me? All that shit aside, Harry Reardon does *nothing* for free. Those meds ain't cheap."

Smith sealed on his helmet. "You're a strong, independent criminal who don't need no authority, yes."

"Entrepreneur," Reardon replied with all the integrity of a used-car salesman. "Whereas all in all, you my friend, are just another brick in the wall."

Smith was in the middle of pointedly linking the hideously dated reference to the hideously dated decor when Sammy's voice rang out through the intercom. "Touchdown in three, bro!"

Could Sammy sound *more* like an archetypical surfer from Hawaii? Smith had never been to Hawaii but the kid sounded, to his ear, just like what they *would* sound like. "Helmet, Reardon."

"Two!"

"Harry Reardon *laughs* at the vacuum of space!" said Reardon, hands on hips.

"One!"

"Hard to laugh while you asphyxiate," said Smith, dryly.

"Aaand zero!" Sammy's countdown cut off Reardon's undoubtedly stellar comeback.

"Thank you, Sammy," Smith said into the mic pinned under his collar.

"We good to go?" Reardon's voice came through his helmet's speakers, for the moment. "Can we go?"

"Airlock is cycling. Good luck!"

Smith was glad to be aboard, but as he stepped out of the airlock and onto Ganymede, he realized the truth.

Reardon was talking so much because he was nervous.

Not much made the guy nervous.

Something about sifting through the ruins of a devastating alien-not-alien attack for clues left by a criminal mastermind with influence in nearly all major world governments was getting to him. And frankly, as he surveyed the ruined landscape, it was unsettling to Smith too.

With that thought rattling in his head, they made their way out to what remained of Ganymede Station.

CHAPTER EIGHTEEN

Four Lightyears from Earth
USS Midway
Bridge

"Mister Lynch, set course for Zenith."

The hours ticked by as the *Midway* sailed effortlessly through Z-space, her newly augmented engines purring like a happy, warm kitten. Mattis received frequent updates from Modi, at first every ten minutes and transitioning to hourly, but as time came and went, nothing seemed to go wrong.

It was nice to have a win every now and again. A new system which didn't play up and merely enhanced their combat capabilities significantly with no downsides. Mattis and the bridge crew started to chat as their shift dragged on.

Modi and Lynch were bickering about something so inane and stupid that he could barely even bring himself to follow along, drifting in and out of the conversation as they went back and forth.

"No no no," said Lynch. "I'm telling you. I don't *care* if you're a vegetarian. Southern smoked ribs transcend the labels of mortal men. They just melt in your mouth. Juicy and delicious. They are joy personified in food."

"I told you I'm not vegetarian," said Modi, defensively. "I just don't each much meat."

"That's being a dang vegetarian."

"That's *not eating a lot of meat*. It's not strictly vegetarian. And I eat fish sometimes. And ... boiled eggs."

"Boiled eggs? Aww, hell no." Lynch, unmoved, continued to press his point. "Trust me. When we head back—Smokey Joes in San Antonio. The best place to eat in the whole of the South. So good you will *literally* die. And the live band...."

"It is clear that you *literally* do not know the definition of the word literally." Modi scowled. "And a live band? That sounds like a bar. I do not enjoy bars."

Lynch tapped a few buttons on the engineering console to make a few minor adjustments to the Z-drive. "It serves bar *food*," he clarified. "And alcohol. And has a band. But it's not a bar."

"That is the definition of a bar, my vocabulary-challenged friend."

Mattis tuned out the argument for a bit, and then, finally, he sent Modi down to the engine room for no other reason other than to get him out of their collective hair.

"So sir," asked Lynch, leaning back against his console casually, "I was meaning to ask you. This whole thing with, uhh..." he suddenly seemed a bit flustered. "Your son. Chuck."

He felt the smallest little twinge of mild frustration

building within him, for reasons he could not adequately explain. "Sure," he said. "What about him?"

"Well," said Lynch, "I'm big into whistleblower protection. Think the law should be watching out for people like him, more than it already does. The fact he's back to living on basic income isn't great, you know? The guy did what he felt was right, and because of that, he and his family are being made to suffer. That just ain't right. Gets me all riled up whenever I think about it…" His Texan accent suddenly came on so strong Mattis could barely understand him. "Seeming like most of those laws were all hat, no cattle."

It wasn't something he was entirely comfortable discussing at the best of times, but Lynch's supporting attitude grated on him slightly. "I understand," he said. "And, yes, I feel that whistleblower protection should be nice and comprehensive. Unfortunately … Chuck got himself caught breaking into a Senator's office. No matter how you slice it, that's just something people shouldn't do. It's a serious crime."

"I know," said Lynch, obviously struggling to stay respectful. "And I get that. Really. But it's just that—you know. He thought Pitt was dirty. He had good reason for doing what he did. He wasn't malicious, he didn't steal anything, he just wanted to see the full picture. To serve his country in the best way he knew how. By making sure its politicians were on the level. And he paid for it—losing his job and all, losing his diplomatic credentials, losing … *everything* 'cept his family. That makes him a patriot. A hero."

"It makes him an idiot," said Mattis, but he held up his hand to stave off the inevitable return. "But most truly patriotic people I know are that as well. Including Chuck. I can't condone what he did, but I can admire him for it. I know that might seem like a contradictory position, but it's what I got."

Lynch nodded understandingly. "Yeah, I know how that might seem. I always got contradictory thoughts 'bout ribs you know—" *Oh god, please no, not the smoked ribs again....* "Because a lot of folks have a pretty messed up understanding of what good food is and the way one prepares it. Lemme tell you what my father told me...."

Mattis coughed. Loudly. "You told me," he said, patiently. "I was here too you know. Smokey Joes does it right, all other forms of smoked ribs are inferior."

Lynch looked like he wanted to add something more, but thought better of it. Mattis settled back into his seat, and then, with a chirp, the computer announced it was coming up on the translation point for Zenith.

"That was fast," said Mattis, somewhat disbelievingly. Z-space was a tricky mistress ... its layout didn't match perfectly to real-space. If they had miscalculated, they could come out anywhere. In the middle of a star, inside a planet, or far, far more likely, somewhere in the infinite void of space, possibly even in another galactic quadrant. Or another galaxy. Or galactic cluster. Or—

The ship translated out of Z-space, and the silhouette of Zenith's star appeared on the ship's monitors. Mattis switched the view to the planet but the cameras didn't move. He almost bought up a change in topic, to check that the ship's first exit of Z-space had indeed been flawless, but it was changed for him.

Lynch glanced at his instruments. "Z-space translation..."

his voice trailed off, becoming almost a whisper. "Complete."

He hadn't been looking at Zenith's star. He'd been looking at the southern half of Zenith itself. A whole quarter of the planet was a glowing mass of angry yellow and orange, like a kaleidoscope of fire-colors. The flames covered a continent, lapping hungrily at the oceans, from which large vats of steam rose. A black carpet of smoke blanketed everything, lit up orange from the light below, expanding out to cover fully half of the planet.

"What the fuck?" asked Lynch, mouth agape, voicing Mattis's thoughts perfectly.

"Admiral Mattis," said Modi into his ear, "priority alert; I think the new engines *are* having some kind of effect. As we exited Z-space, the sensor readings from Zenith—they just don't make sense, sir. I think the sensors are being affected by the engine's graviton flux, since I'm detecting *massive* levels of carbon dioxide on Zenith's surface, far more than should be there. The thermal cameras are all out of whack, showing—"

"Showing that everything's on fire," said Mattis, flatly watching the viewscreen of the maelstrom below. "Because it is. The instruments are correct, Commander Modi."

"But sir, nothing could live down there."

"You're correct," said Mattis, gravely.

Modi said nothing for a moment, the silence almost deafening. "My God. I'll try and find out what's the cause of this … is it a weapon?"

"I don't know," said Mattis. "Tell me when you know anything."

Modi didn't answer and shut off the link. It took a lot to rattle him, but as Mattis stared at the ball of rock and fire on the ship's monitors, he understood completely. Anyone on that planet was dead. It would be generations before the planet was habitable again … assuming anyone bothered enough to try.

What could cause such a disaster?

"Admiral," said Lynch, his tone shifting from mournful to business-like, "we're detecting a strange reading in low orbit of the planet."

What *wasn't* strange at this time? Mattis, however, forced down the snappy remark. "What kind of reading?"

Lynch's face seemed to lose a bit of its color. He tapped some more on his console, saying nothing.

"Lynch?"

"It's … a small ship. Unidentified. Not much bigger than a shuttle, but…." He looked up. "This is a quarantine zone. It shouldn't be here, whoever, or whatever, it is."

Mattis stared. "Sound general quarters," he said, sitting up in his chair. "Get everyone to their stations. Let me know when we're ready to engage."

"Aye aye, sir." The room was flooded with red light. "Arming weapons, spinning up the sub-Z engines."

There was a brief moment where nothing happened, and then Lynch spoke again. "Sir? That ship—you're receiving a transmission from it."

Mattis squinted. "Me?"

"Yes sir, directed to *you*."

Mattis stood out of his chair and walked toward his ready room. "You have the conn, Mister Lynch. If that ship moves, or does anything other than keep slowly spinning around Zenith, shoot it."

"With pleasure, sir," said Lynch, as the doors slid closed

behind him.

Mattis power-walked over to his desk and tapped on a few keys. The incoming transmission was encrypted. Audio only. He set up a handshake, piped it through to his earpiece.

"Good morning, Admiral Mattis," said a heavily modulated voice, seeming female but with a strange edge to it, almost synthetic. "Do you know who I am?"

"Should I?" asked Mattis, evenly. "You should be aware that we are currently staring down your vessel, looking for an *extremely* good reason not to turn it into scrap. I'm hoping you can give me that reason."

"I can," said the voice, robotic but seemingly possessed of a certain human flair that was unmistakable. "You haven't met me yet—haven't had the chance—but my name is Spectre."

Spectre. The one who had given them the access code to the gravity pulse weapon during the Battle of Earth.

CHAPTER NINETEEN

Sol System
Ganymede Station
Former site of the Ark Project

The moment they left the *Aerostar*, Reardon kicked off the ground and started bouncing in either an extremely poor dance, or a private game of hopscotch—Smith couldn't really tell.

"You do know it's not that easy to embarrass me?" Smith asked.

"Embarrass? I'm making them underestimate us!"

"You do tend to do that naturally. I assume you're aware."

Sammy spoke up through their earpieces. "No. No, he isn't, actually."

"It's *tactical.*" Reardon's voice was hurt.

The walk to the station's airlock couldn't be over quickly enough.

It wasn't ramshackle—well, not much in space could

afford to be truly ramshackle, the *Aerostar*'s questionable interior decorating notwithstanding—but the entrance was far from state-of-the-art. An array of glorified dusters flanked the door, a primitive but modestly effective method of keeping the dust content in the mechanisms minimal, and the path between the landing zone and the airlock was tidy and even.

A woman in a fairly clean construction uniform met them at the door. "Hello … sirs?"

Oil stain, dandruff—human origin, dust matching chemical composition of Ganymede's crust, hair: human and feline. Smith's cybernetic eye analyzed the dirt on her suit, and found it entirely nonthreatening.

"Good afternoon, ma'am. I'm Special Agent Smith, and my … associate," he let the word hang threateningly in the air, because if he couldn't stop the smuggler's idiocy he could at least put an unsettling spin on it, "is Mr. Reardon. I need to speak to the station chief—a Ms. Harp, I believe?"

The woman nodded. "Of course, of course, she's expecting you. Well, after you contacted us, obviously. She's just on her way up from the building site now."

Smith scanned her for telltale signs of dishonesty—his eye would notice the tiniest sweat-drop, the faintest flush, and it was programmed with the best behavioral pattern recognition tech there was—and came up empty. Something going right, that was nice.

"You can leave your suits here," she continued, indicating an alcove, "Call me Tracy, by the way. Uh, Tracy Stanano."

The trip through the station was uneventful, apart from Tracy Stanano gabbing on about the reconstruction process, and how boring life was on Ganymede Station. No visitors apart from the occasional bureaucrat or "mysterious official who's too high-and-mighty to tell us why they're here, um, no offense"; nothing but standard rations for dinner from "here on 'till hell freezes over"; and "a nice view of Jupiter I guess, though the wreckage you see 'round here still gives me the shivers every time. I worked here before the attack too, you know."

Reardon spent the walk bantering with the woman over "those idiot bureaucrats, don't worry about him," and shooting him meaningful glances. She responded eagerly with a steady flow of station gossip—which suggested Reardon hadn't lost as many of his old tricks as he seemed to want Smith to think. He quietly logged the incidents in his eye. It was hardly likely that cross-referencing them with official records would turn up anything, but there was no sense in not being thorough.

"Well, here we are!" Tracy stopped by a plain door and knocked. "Chief Harp, guests have arrived!"

"Come in!"

Inside, the office was sensible and well-maintained. No picture frames anywhere, and very few personal effects to speak of, and none of the telltale bare patches in dust or general office detritus to suggest anything's hasty removal. Smith was impressed; Harp had her sense of—

Reardon. Why.

Smith turned slowly toward the side of the room, where the smuggler was approaching a cat's bed with exaggerated caution. The bed was adorned with a banner reading "Rudolf: Jupiter's Toughest Cat!" and it was indeed occupied by a sleek, well-fed siamese feline. It blinked at them and stretched, then turned over and curled up in a ball, ignoring the visitors entirely. He barely contained his eye roll.

"Ms. Harp, I won't be taking up much of your time," he told the middle-aged woman. She was staring disapprovingly at Reardon, an expression that looked like it sat quite comfortably on her face. He took out his tablet, selected a folder of stills from Dr. Steve X. Bratta's video. Possibly the only pictures of Spectre in existence. "Have you ever encountered the man in these images?"

Harp peered at the screen. "May I?" she reached for the device.

"Of course." Smith let her take her time, and kept his analysis gear—both human and machine— focused firmly on her. Was she really concentrating on the blurry frames? Behavior was well within acceptable statistical margins. No tics to be seen, no particular sign of nerves, nothing to really get a read on at all—not even the customary nerves an unexpected visit from the CIA tended to produce. Damn. Was she hiding something, or was it a customary poker face? Businesspeople and military personnel were often a problem—

"John, this settles it. We need a cat. Just like this." Reardon was grinning, crouching beside what appeared to have turned into a whirling ball of fluffy death, and darting his fingers in far too close to its stomach for safety's sake.

Sammy's voice jumped out from Smith's earpiece. "Just so you know, bro, I'm expecting pictures. Lots of pictures. You made me miss the kitty."

Before his answering silence could truly become meaningful, Harp responded, eyes softening as she turned to the cat. "He survived this station's destruction, you know? The only living creature that did, unless you count the workers who were rotated off at the time."

Tracy nodded once, expression suddenly distant.

Smith did indeed know, but Reardon's almost comically wide eyes were too good a distraction to pass up. He blinked twice in quick succession, the activation sequence for the video recording function on his eye.

"Are you a clever kitty? Are you? Yes you are! Yes you are!" the smuggler demanded of the cat as he narrowly avoided being mauled.

Tracy's face broke into a wide, genuine smile. "You have no idea, Mr. Rearden. Luckiest, cleverest little bastard in the whole solar system."

"We found him on our scanners a day into the rebuilding effort—remarkably un-traumatized, really, he was asleep when we got to him," Harp continued.

Reardon yanked his hand back after getting clawed, but reached out with his other. "What a champ." He gazed into the cat's yellow eyes. "I wish I could sleep through trauma and death and destruction and apocalypse like that. Who's a good sleeper? Who's a good sleeper? Yes you are!" he said in his exaggerated silly voice that normally one would reserve for a cute puppy, not a tornado of teeth and fur. Another claw, drawing a thin line of blood this time. Good God, Rearden was really committed to petting this monster.

Smith cleared his throat. *All right, enough theatre. And possibly enough traumatizing Ms. Stanano,* he thought. "The pictures, Ms. Harp? Have you or have you not encountered this man before?"

The station chief looked back to the pictures and pursed her lips. "I'm afraid I haven't, Agent Smith. Sorry I can't be of more assistance."

He fixed her with an intense stare. "Are you sure?"

She pushed his tablet back towards him. "Your picture quality leaves a lot to be desired, but yes, I'm sure. I can count the number of guests we've had here on my hands, and that man hasn't been one of them, sorry."

Well, if nothing else, the profusion of apologies was a natural speech pattern under stress, and not necessarily one easily mimicked by the unpracticed liar. "Very well, thank you for your time."

"If there's anything else? I do have a station's reconstruction to be overseeing," Harp said, standing.

He went to stand but Reardon was still crouched next to the menacing ball of hissing and fury. "How much?"

"Excuse me?" said Harp and Stanano, almost in unison.

"How much for the cat?" He made one last attempt to get his hand in to rub the furry belly, and came away with another scratch that started beading blood.

Harp eyed the smuggler skeptically. "You've got to be joking."

Reardon finally stood up, holding a hand to his chest in mock offense. "Joke? Me? Come on, Smith, you know we've always wanted a cat on the ship. Fight off any Daleks or Klingons or Wookies that come aboard."

"I'm allergic."

"You're allergic to cats?" Reardon exclaimed.

"No, I'm allergic to wasting time."

Reardon fixed him with an affronted glare, but Smith was already halfway out of the office. "Ms. Stanano, if you'd be able to guide us back to our ship?"

He was silent as they made their way back to the *Aerostar*, sorting through strategies and hypotheses as he walked, although as before, his companion more than made up for his reticence. They made their final approach to the *Aerostar* across the barren moonscape, and Sammy jetted out to meet them. His suit apparently came with tiny maneuvering thrusters, and he sported two canes—he liked to get out in low-g environments whenever possible.

Sammy began chatting energetically with their guide through the comm. Deliberately, Smith fell behind, into step with Reardon as they approached the ship. He fingered his comm over to *private* and keyed in Rearden's headset.

"So," he whispered, dryly. "You like cats? This a new thing?"

"I like," whispered Reardon, with an impish smile, "casually planting listening devices on cats."

Smith stared. "Why?"

Reardon shrugged. "Might not be useful, but it never hurts to be prepared. They last for *months*." He gave a grin, and inspected the long scratches on both hands. "And, good god, I hate cats."

The ramp descended and they climbed up to the airlock to start pulling their suits off.

"Well, bye Tracy!" Reardon winked. "Keep up the good work! And if you change your mind about Rudolf, call me."

She avoided eye contact by the barest of hints.

Interesting. Best let this play out. He pretended not to have noticed, and continued suiting up.

"Um, actually…." Tracy's voice faltered. Smith dropped his hand from the helmet's seal and looked at her. "I think the boss might have forgotten. Or, uh, not … told you. I've seen that guy here before."

CHAPTER TWENTY

Zenith, High Orbit
USS Midway
Admiral Jack Mattis's Ready Room

"Spectre," said Mattis, shrugging helplessly even though the connection was audio only. It helped him sound … detached. Disinterested. "That name supposed to mean something to me?"

"It should," said the modulated voice, with palpable sincerity. "It means something to anyone who's anyone, politically speaking. Politicians and bureaucrats and administrators—and more than a few military personnel. All the keys to power in every corner of humanity's presence in this galaxy know my name." There was some measure of pride in her synthetic tone. "So many names, so many contacts, so many favors owed to and from everyone … everyone except Admiral Jack Mattis."

He snorted dismissively, waving his hand. "That supposed

to scare me, British lady? Lemme tell you something; this ain't the first time I've had someone big-talk me with threats of power and political revenge, okay? You think that—"

"You're referring to Senator Pitt," said Spectre, calmly. "Yes. We are aware of him."

Well, that was … not reassuring. "What do you want me to say to that?" asked Mattis. "That this guy who hates me for—" he bit his tongue, then said it anyway. "Losing his son under my command … he's still mad at me? Still hasn't forgiven me? Well, of course he hasn't. That's just human nature. And if this is one of his plans, then you can forget about me helping you in any way."

"Oh, Admiral," said Spectre. "This isn't about Senator Pitt and his petty little quest to hurt the person who hurt him. This is *so* much more than that. Far, far deeper than you can possibly imagine."

Everyone always did that. Always tried to make themselves more important than they were. "Having realized that we know where your ship is and that it's dramatically, hilariously outgunned," said Mattis, dryly, "I figure maybe your plan is to mystify me to death?"

"Stupid people are prone to believe incredibly stupid things when they perceive it to further their own self interests."

Mattis squinted. "To what incredibly stupid thing do you refer?"

"The idea that my ship is … oh, what did you say, *dramatically, hilariously outgunned*, or that my purpose being here is to do anything other than to bring illumination and knowledge."

Knowledge. Knowledge they could probably use. "Very

well," said Mattis. "How do you propose to share this ... illumination ... with me?"

"Well," said Spectre, almost tonelessly, "my ship will move to dock with yours, and I will come aboard personally. I will tell you what I know in its full and complete entirety, leaving out nothing. There is, of course, a condition to this otherwise very one-sided exchange."

Of course there was. "What condition is that?"

"Take me with you."

Mattis blinked. "Uhh ... say again?"

"The answers to the questions I know you're going to ask, such as what was this weapon, what did it do, and how can we stop it, are not going to be found on Zenith. When you leave Zenith, I wish to come with you."

"You realize," said Mattis, cautiously, "that if I agree to this—and right now I'm honestly more inclined just to shoot you down—I cannot permit you unlimited access to my ship. If you are to come aboard, your movements will be curtailed, you will be carefully watched at all times and if you so much as step out of line, my marines will put a bullet in you without so much as breathing—I don't care which powerful senator you work for. My ship, my rules."

"I understand," said Spectre, in such a way that Mattis could not help but feel they were not in any way threatened at all. "Let me know when you've made your decision. And just so we're clear, Mr. Mattis, I work for no-one. No one man, no one woman. I work for humanity."

He wanted to roll his eyes. "Standby." Mattis muted the link and, for a moment, put his chin in his hands, trying to work through the play-by-play.

Inviting unknown civilians who claimed to have their fingers in the world's governments aboard military vessels engaged in active investigations was against so many policy guidelines that it was almost ludicrous. So-called 'Tiger cruises,' allowing civilians to sail with the military and get a taste for that life, were relatively commonplace and more frequent in these modern times, but they were designed for friends and family of officers, and required an officer to vouch for them. There were even civilians aboard the *Midway* right now.

Obviously, as the CO, he would have ultimate say in this matter—and technically, counted as an officer for this purpose —but it was a risk. There was no vetting. He had not even seen this person's face and they had been quite … nefarious. Unscrupulous even. Mattis could not, in good conscience, accept that risk without some more concrete guarantees, something better than vague promises and hints towards some greater goal. Even if that person had, earlier, given them the access codes to a secret Chinese weapon. He reopened the channel.

"My answer is no."

Even through Spectre's voice modulation, there was some genuine surprise coming through. "Admiral, you are making a mistake."

"Convince me," said Mattis, firmly. "And quickly. You expect me to trust you yet you haven't even given me a single indication that you really know anything more than I do, and frankly, you represent a profound risk to this ship and its crew, beyond that which I feel is acceptable. I'm only willing to shoulder that risk if there really is something you have for me, and at this present time you haven't given me any reason to think that such information even exists."

"Have a little faith, Admiral," said Spectre.

"Faith means not wanting to know what is true. I want to know what is true. Give me a good reason to think you know more than you know, or we're done here."

"I know about the deep state's gene project," said Spectre. "And since your little adventure on Chrysalis, I'm sure you know something of it too, but not all is as it seems. Who you think are good guys and bad guys is upside down, Admiral. The people you were fighting then … they, *we*, are trying to save humanity." There was a short, playful snort down the line which came through strangely as whatever program Spectre was using to mask it mangled it. "Besides. I've got info that you won't believe. Full report at eleven: the attacking ships really *are* from the future, and I can prove it, I can help you prove it to a galaxy who doesn't quite believe what you've been telling them, and more importantly, show you how to *stop* them. *Permanently.* Now let me aboard your ship and I'll give you this, otherwise … squander it. The choice is yours."

Now they were getting somewhere. Spectre had knowledge, this much he was relatively certain of. Information he needed.

"Very well," he said. "Permission granted to dock and come aboard."

CHAPTER TWENTY-ONE

Sol System
Ganymede Station
Former site of the Ark Project

Spectre had been here before? Well, now, that was definitely something.

"Are you sure?" asked Smith, looking over his shoulder. They were right next to the *Aerostar*, about to leave. The engines were whining loudly—perhaps that's why Tracy had not said anything until they'd reached the launchpad. No chance of being overheard. "What can you tell us?"

"Not a lot," said Tracy, hesitating again. "And yes. I'm sure. But I mean ... I don't know. I could lose my job over this."

They needed a place to talk that wasn't so ... exposed. It might be impossible for someone to actually hear over the whine of the engines, but a good smart camera could still read her lips. The *Aerostar* would have to do. "I think," said Smith, a little louder and clearer than he needed to in case there was something recording him, "I might have an issue with my suit. Gimme a hand with the glove?"

Momentarily confused, Tracy obviously got it after a second. "Sure," she said, stepping up to him. He held out his hand, dropping his voice to a whisper.

"You're absolutely sure?" asked Smith.

"Yeah." Tracy nodded as she pretended to jiggle his wrist. "I've definitely seen him here before. Twice. Once just before the attack, and once about ... oh, several months later. I don't know his name—and I'm not even sure that he gave one, really —but I know he was here with some kind of important government official. I could tell because he wore that kind of suit that they all wear. Nice, but not *nice* nice, like what a businessman would wear."

The difference between a five grand suit and a fifty grand suit was generally only visible to the trained eye. Or the cybernetic eye. "Got it," said Smith. He awkwardly pulled out his handheld and brought up a picture. "This is the guy?"

Tracy glanced at the thing only for a moment. "Yup."

"You're sure?"

"Yes."

Smith closed the tablet. "Thank you, we should get going now."

The journey back to the *Aerostar* was brief, but Smith's mind raced at a million miles a minute. As they stood outside the airlock, Reardon fumbled with the control panel labeled *People Hole Opener*.

"Something wrong?" asked Smith, staring at him.

"Oh, you know," said Reardon, grumbling, his fingers stabbing at the control panel, which didn't seem to be responding. "It's just … it's just, you know. This thing is sometimes a bit difficult. You have to treat it nice."

"If it's defective, why don't you replace it?"

"Money," said Reardon, thumping his fist on the thing. "And money's in short supply right now, you know." He groaned. "I read somewhere that the two best days in boat ownership are the day you buy it, and the day you sell it."

"I was always told," said Smith, "if you can afford a boat twice then you can afford a boat."

Sammy's voice came into his ears. "B - O - A - T - Bust Out Another Thousand."

"Hey, shut up!" said Reardon, angrily. "That's our home we're talking about!" He thumped his fist against the control panel some more, and then, with a brief flash of static, it turned green and the outer airlock door slid open.

"See?" said Reardon, obvious pride painting his voice. "I'm like an Indian Han Solo."

"Han Solo was a pilot," said Smith, drifting into the airlock.

"He also fixed things," protested Reardon.

"You're thinking of Chewbacca. Which, honestly, is more appropriate. You certainly are hairy enough to be a Wookie."

Reardon groaned loudly. "Let's just agree never to discuss my body hair, okay? I'm a hairy man. Hairiness is masculine."

Smith just shook his head. The airlock sealed and began to pressurize.

"You okay?" asked Reardon, his tone genuine. "You seem … even less humorless than normal."

"I'm fine," said Smith, depressurizing his helmet when there was finally air to breathe. "I … I don't have time to discuss it in committee," he joked, but the smuggler wasn't smiling.

"So…" Reardon hesitated, clearly wanting to say something that just wouldn't come. "We got what we came for, right?"

"Pardon?" Smith tugged at his gloves, working at pulling off the whole suit arm to save time.

"The answers," said Reardon. "What we came to Ganymede for. You have it, yeah?"

He did. "What are you getting at?"

"Just, you know … well, I'd love to help you on your righteous quest, but I have responsibilities."

Sammy. Of course. "I know you do." Smith wiggled out of the spacesuit pants. "I know you want to just fly off to the stars, and I get why. But we're done done yet. There's a lot more going on here than I know about, and to be perfectly frank with you, I could hire a ship and do this myself, but it's just not going to be the same as this one, you know? Quiet. Covert. Under the radar."

That seemed to pad Reardon's ego enormously. "Exactly like I designed her."

"You didn't design her," said Smith, patiently. "You bought her. At a junkyard."

"And then modified her," protested Reardon.

"Barely."

For a moment, Smith thought he'd actually offended him. "I *do* have responsibilities," Reardon said again. "Sammy's meds don't pay for themselves."

"I know, which is why it sucks that I'm asking you, but I'm asking you. *And* paying you."

Whatever anger was there evaporated. Reardon chuckled. "Yeah, well, can't argue with money." He paused. "So, how much are we talkin'? Like, new jacket? Or new ship?"

"Lunch at a fast food joint," said Smith. "I'm a spook, not a pimp. Let's get going."

He waited. Then, when Reardon left to go do whatever Reardon-stuff he wanted, and Smith was alone in the airlock, he pulled out the tablet again, and opened the last image he'd shown Tracy.

An image of Senator Pitt.

CHAPTER TWENTY_TWO

Zenith, High Orbit
USS Midway
Space Combat Simulator Room

Instead of taking her to the hangar, Doctor Brooks took a left at the Pilot's Ready Room and led her down a corridor to a large room with a perfect replica of a Warbird cockpit surrounded by screens. Junior Lieutenant Deshawn "Flatline" Wiley, her gunner, was waiting for her by the ladder leading to the cockpit.

"Hey," said Flatline, smiling like a dumbass.

"The *simulator*?" whined Guano. "This isn't first hand. This is…"

"This," said Doctor Brooks, annoyingly, "is the best and safest way for us to test your abilities and see what we can find out about them in a completely controlled, limited environment with full medical supervision."

Which was another way of saying *extremely boring.* "I hate

the simulator."

"Hey, it's nice to see you too," said Flatline.

"The simulator's an educational tool," said Doctor Brooks, patiently. "And if you want back on the flight roster, you need me to approve your application. In order to approve your application, I need to see if what's happening to you—your ability—is harmful. In order to see if your ability is harmful … well, I need to see your ability in action."

That all made sense to her, and she kind of liked him referring to her episodes as "an ability"—it made her feel like a superhero—but it was still annoying. "You really care about this, don't you?" she asked.

"Of course," said Doctor Brooks. "That's what I'm here for."

Grumbling loudly, Guano put a foot on the base of the ladder and hauled herself up to the cockpit, wiggling into the firm, uncomfortable, entirely unfamiliar seat. This wasn't *her* ship … it all felt wrong.

Then again, her ship wasn't even her ship. The fighter she'd flown for years had smashed onto the deck of the *Midway* after their first engagement with the future-human ships. She'd barely broken in her new one before she'd ejected from it. Now, she had a whole new ship, which she had flown a grand total of … once. She flicked the ignition button on the simulator, and it put through a fake-sounding recording of the power coming on.

Flatline climbed into his seat behind her, strapping himself in with a *click*. "You ready to kick ass?" he asked, something *weird* in his tone. Like he was talking to a friend he hadn't seen in a while. She'd only been gone like a week.

What bull crap. Guano cycled through the startup sequence grumpily, touching the buttons and switches in completely automatic mode. "Yeah," she said, sarcastically. "I'm ready to fight some computer programs dressed up like bad guys."

The simulation began, the dark screens flickering to life. Her 'ship' was floating through space on a standard patrol.

"Nice of them to skip all the stupid launch sequence bull," she said, casually flicking her thumb across the fire button. It felt at once both familiar and different; it was obviously taken from an earlier model of fighter. It felt smoother, too, as though it had been worn down by hundreds of hands and tens of thousands of hours. Smoothed down to a sheen—the ship even smelled wrong, like the body odor of a hundred pilots all layered over each other, then covered with industrial grade cleaner.

The whole thing just felt *fake*. She couldn't take it seriously.

"Well, this is the scenario that I picked out for you," said Doctor Brooks.

With a bright flash of white light, three large ships appeared as though transitioning from Z-space; their blocky, angular design and glowing red engines all too familiar. Recreations of the future-human ships.

"Contact," said Flatline behind her, and she blinked.

"Wait? Three cap ships?" Guano clicked off the autopilot and jammed the stick into her gut, pulling the nose of her ship up and away, opening the throttle. There was no push, no inertial change crushing her into her seat.

"I wanted to test you," said Brooks, with a coy edge to his voice. "Stress brings out the trance. Can't do that if you're comfortable."

She didn't feel comfortable at all, but neither did she feel stressed. Just ... going through the motions.

The three cap-ships began to launch swarms of fighters. Dozens of them. Guano rolled her eyes. A single Warbird was powerful, but as she counted, any last dangling threads of verisimilitude she had slipped away. There were just too many of them. The solution was to punch it for home and live to fight another day ... but that wasn't what Brooks wanted, so she turned toward them despite the obviously suicidal nature of the action.

"Okay," said Flatline, encouragingly. "Let's go do this! Let's get some!"

Normally he was pissing and shitting himself when they flew into combat, but now he seemed eager to engage these overwhelmingly odds.

More fakeness. More bullshit. *Just focus on the fight, try to bring it out* ... Guano pointed the thin nose of her ship toward the angry red swarm of hostile fighters, and she focused, trying to force herself into the battle trance.

Nothing. She just felt like an idiot sitting in a fake cockpit.

Grunting in frustration, Guano flicked the master arm switch on her missiles and picked out two strong radar returns, locking them up. "Fox three," she said, trying to summon some energy. *Click click. Bzzt.* The computer chirped to let her know the missiles were fired, and as they streaked past her cockpit, she could see the pixels in the exhaust trails.

"Yeah!" said Flatline. "Take that, you shits!"

Guano just vaguely shrugged as the missiles went in. "Two hits," she said. "Splash one, splash two. Good effect on target."

"How are you feeling?" asked Doctor Brooks.

Questions. The questions didn't help. She lazily drifted her fighter out of the way of some return fire. "Normal."

"Is there any indication of intestinal pain?" he asked.

Intestinal pain? What? She squinted, and a dozen red lines bored into the side of her ship with an electronic *chirp chirp*. She dodged again, kicking the rudder thruster pedals. "No," she said, swerving the ship side to side. "Nothing like that. Why would that matter?"

"Well, all crew are given dietary supplements," said Doctor Brooks. "Under stress, sometimes they can cause…" he coughed politely. "Intestinal distress."

"Guano?" Flatline laughed, his gun making a very fake *chirp chirp* as it 'fired' at the distant enemy, fake tracers streaking across space. "Holy hell, did you get explosive shits when you passed out?"

"No."

Flatline tapped her on the back of her helmet. "Truth! Did you? Did you leave skid marks in your flight suit? Oh my god, you did, didn't you?"

"No!"

"Tell me! Tell me you did!"

She hadn't and the taunting just pushed her to the edge. She squirmed around in her seat, trying to slap his hand away, and in the distraction, her ship was damaged by blast after blast from the virtual alien fighters. "Shut up," she said, shaking her head and pulling the ejection handle, which ended the simulation.

"What?" asked Flatline, reaching around and tapping the back of her head. "What happened? You feeling okay?"

"I'm *fine*," she said, with a lot more frustration than she truly intended. "And that's the fucking problem!" She sighed and ran her hands through her hair. "Look, look. I can't consciously summon this thing at the *best* of times ... let alone in a simulator. It just doesn't work that way."

"Okay," said Doctor Brooks, seeming to understand. "That's fine. Look, obviously the simulator isn't going to bring this out of you."

"*Clearly*," said Guano, casually swinging a leg out of the cockpit. "And no. I didn't shit myself. I'm fine."

"Well, thank you for your honesty," said Doctor Brooks, smiling a little. "The truth is—and this is just between you and your gunner—apart from regular health and physical benefits, the supplements are supposed to also be stress relievers. They're biochemically engineered to activate during times of great stress and produce a profound calm in the person instead. Just ... well, not *quite* so serious as what you're experiencing."

What the *hell* were they feeding them? She didn't like being ... experimented on. It might not, in truth, have been a real experiment but it felt like it.

Flatline leaned out of the fake cockpit. "I don't feel anything," he said.

"I know," said Brooks. "The effect is supposed to be minor. Subtle. Just to take the edge off—which is why I'm looking into why it's affecting Lieutenant Corrick so much." He shook his head. "Lieutenant, I'm going to look into your medical file again and see what I can find. You just rest, relax, and I'll talk to you soon."

She wasn't sure how she could do that having just learned

the pills she'd been swallowing for months were in some way a little more than vitamins, but she resolved to put that out of her mind and never think about it, just like so many of her problems.

"Your hospital gown is in the bathroom," said Brooks, and then he left. And then she was alone with Flatline.

"You wanna go again?" he asked. "I got time enough for another go before the next briefing, if you want to give it another shot."

No. It was time to get out of there. "Thanks, but hard-pass. I gotta go lay in bed and listen to the most annoying music in the universe from some dickhead on the other side of the wall."

"Okay," said Flatline. Way, way too casually. Like he was trying really hard to be supportive, but it just came across as insincere, pissing her off even more. "Whatever you need."

Bah. Guano climbed down and stormed off toward the simulator room bathroom, shoving open the door and angrily began peeling off her flight suit. She shoved it into a corner and pulled on the gown.

But then a thought occurred, something that made her smile.

The very good doctor never *actually* ordered her back to sickbay. Just to *relax and rest*.

Clad only in the off-white gown, Guano slid the door open a crack. Flatline was gone.

She slipped out of the simulator room, heading towards the pilot's lounge.

Time to hang out with her buddies and get drunk. Wearing only her open-backed hospital gown. She was sure in about half an hour she'd be too plastered to care.

CHAPTER TWENTY-THREE

Zenith, High Orbit
USS Midway
Hangar Bay

Mattis and two teams of marines—including the full squad of the infamous armored suit-clad Rhinos—stood by the threshold of the hangar bay as the small ship, really no larger than a shuttle, sailed silently through, leaving an expanding red trail behind it, just like the future-human fighters. The ship had the same blocky, aggressive architecture the hostile ships had, with the same unclean, angular lines.

If it was a disguise, it was a damn good one.

The shuttle silently drifted toward the centre of the hangar bay and touched down. The armored hangar bay doors closed. Jets of gas streaked out of the deck as the whole area pressurized, and then the door to the shuttle began to open, bathing the area in a dim red glow.

"When we're done here," said Mattis to Lynch, "make sure

Modi and his engineering nerds take that ship apart. I want to know *exactly* what's inside it."

"Aye sir," said Lynch.

"And Lynch?" asked Mattis, his tone serious. "Make sure that ship gets put on a launcher. The kind we use for heavy bombers. Keep that thing primed and divert emergency power to it; if that ship so much as *squeaks* I want it ejected out of my ship at once."

Lynch nodded firmly. "That would be my pleasure, sir."

A man appeared at the loading ramp. Mattis was expecting a tall, strong woman with strong hands and a warrior's outfit. Instead, he got a short, pasty-looking man with an antiquated British suit and a wide, nervous smile, and an obvious earpiece clipped into his ear. His balding head was covered with flop-sweat. If this was an intergovernmental intelligence mastermind, the disguise was perfect—Mattis would have never guessed.

He ground his teeth and touched his radio. "One person, Spectre. No bodyguards. No hangers-on."

The man held up a device to his throat. "I'm afraid this is me," said Spectre, the man's lips matching her words. "Just a formality, you see. To throw people off-balance. To challenge their preconceptions and … well, to be perfectly frank with you, see the stupid looks on their faces when they find out they're adversary—or ally—is just an out-of-shape bald guy in a bad suit."

"Off-balance is not what I want to be right now." Mattis took a deep breath, held it, then let it out slowly. "No more tricks. Formalities or otherwise. Leave your little voice changer thing on your ship."

With a playful smile, Spectre tossed the thing over his shoulder, and then slowly raised his hands above his head. "Okay," he said, in his natural voice, a polite, clipped, British accent. "Let's talk."

Mattis gestured forward. "Rhinos," he said, his tone conveying an edge of caution, "search him, but don't break him."

"Roger," said the nearest one, and the five of them stomped out toward the ship. With steel-clad hands they roughly patted down Spectre, searching him all over for anything big and metal. Then they waved a metal scanner over his body—did those muscle heads even know how to use that? —and, apparently they were satisfied.

"Looks clear," said the lead Rhino, waving one of her massive steel hands. "No sign of weapons or explosives."

Hardly a ringing endorsement. As though sharing his thoughts, one of the marines standing by glanced at him. "Admiral," whispered the guy, "you know, one of the Rhinos shot themselves in the head last month, playing Russian roulette in some dingy dive bar on New London."

Mattis grimaced. The Rhinos had a somewhat less-than-stellar reputation. One of his marines had once said, *it takes a special kind of person to want to crew something that's designed to get shot at ... much less enjoy it.* The Rhinos were a necessary part of shipboard defenses—the kind that said, essentially, bring heavy weapons or go home—but it was true. They weren't exactly recruited for their brainpower or ability to solve complex problems.

Fortunately, the scanner wouldn't lie and it was simple enough to use. "Good," said Mattis. "Walk him in."

Spectre, flanked by Rhinos, walked back toward the doorway that lead away from the hangar bay and toward the rest of the ship. It seemed almost a comical picture to him; a short, pudgy man in a suit being escorted by giant armored suits of metal brimming with weapons.

Again, Mattis expected treachery. Bombs. Tricks. Every little nasty piece of work human minds could conjure, but it was all for nothing. Spectre made his way over to the hatchway and one of Mattis's marines pulled it open.

"Welcome aboard," said Mattis. *Definitely getting paranoid, old man. Not everything that can go wrong, will go wrong. Murphy was an idiot sometimes.*

"Glad to be here," said Spectre. "Those metal hands are cold."

Mattis flashed an equally cool smile. "Just a formality," he said, beckoning for Spectre to follow.

Flanked by armed guards, the two of them marched to the bridge. The journey happened in silence, apart from the marines occasionally checking in and giving reports. They came to the bridge, and Mattis escorted Spectre inside, past the armored casement and the secondary door, inside the ship's beating heart, then to his ready room.

"You're letting me into our own private little study?" asked Spectre, smiling as he came into the ready room. "This is more than I expected."

"Because you expected the brig?" said Mattis, sitting behind his desk.

"Mmm." Spectre tapped his foot on the deck. "Yes, frankly. This is a surprising amount of trust you're putting in a complete stranger."

"We need the workspace," said Mattis, sweeping everything off his desk with a clatter and tapping on it, lighting up the screen embedded within. "You're no use to me sitting in a cell, breathing our air and eating our food while we try and make absolute certain that you're not a threat. So here's what I'm thinking: if you *are* here to cause mischief, I'm giving you the perfect time to play your hand so you might as well do it now and get it over with, otherwise…" he folded his fingers. "Start talking."

Spectre smiled a whimsical half-smile and sat in the chair opposite. "Well." He took a deep breath. "The first thing you should know is, we can track the craft that attacked Zenith. Or at least I can tell you how to track it. It's very complicated; I'll pass along the schematics to your engineers."

"If it's a device you're building, I'm not putting any of your technology aboard my ship. End of story."

Spectre nodded understandingly. "Well, there are other ways. Less good ways. But they'll work. Again, I'll need to speak to your chief of engineering to make the modifications we need."

Mattis tapped his earpiece. "Mister Modi. I have someone here who needs to speak to you."

"Aye sir," said Modi. "Our visitor, I presume?"

"Exactly." Mattis transferred the call to the speakers and indicated to Spectre to speak. "Happy for you to talk."

Spectre immediately began talking in what Mattis could only suppose was some form of derivative English comprised entirely of techno-gibberish. He genuinely tried to follow along with the conversation but simply could not; it was a torrent, a stream of words that he understood the base meaning of but, put together, meant nothing. The only pause was when Spectre listened and, after what seemed like too short a time to him, gave his answers.

Back and forth, back and forth. *C'mon Modi*, he thought to himself. *If there's bullshit here, I need you to smell it out. Find what he's doing. Where the trick is.*

After several minutes, Spectre looked at him. "I like him," he said, brightly.

Mattis glowered and clipped his earpiece back in to talk semi-privately. "You there, Modi?"

"Absolutely," said Modi, his tone positively aglow. "I like him."

Mattis suppressed his frustration. "What are you two planning to do to my ship?"

"Well," said Modi into his ear, "it turns out the ship that we're trying to find emits a form of radiation which we can easily track if we're looking for it."

"I'm aware," said Mattis. "Lynch himself worked on an early, primitive version of their cloaking technology. If you recall, he was able to use this information to track the fleet that was heading to Ganymede, and then on to Earth."

"Of course," said Modi, a slight shift in his tone suggesting something similar to talking to a child. "That's not what I'm concerned about. Since that discovery our passive sensor suite has been upgraded, fleet-wide, to deal with that version of the cloaking technology. The ship which attacked Zenith appears to be carrying a different model."

That, in and of itself, was worrying. The idea that their enemy was adapting to their technological advances. Countering their every move.

Which would make sense, since he'd assumed their enemy was the powerful, secretive interests scattered across the power centers of the United States and China, buried so deeply that he wondered if they'd ever have any hope of uprooting them. Of *course* they'd have been apprised of the military's upgraded abilities to detect their ships, and would have adapted.

But so it always was in war. One side would develop powerful armor, another side, a new weapon, spurring the development of even newer armor. Or active countermeasures. Or some other fantastic, brand new technology which would make previous generations of tech obsolete instantly.

Unless … unless what Spectre had mentioned was true. Unless their enemy truly was from the future.

Which was … ludicrous. Even though he'd proclaimed as much on Martha's broadcast, it didn't make it any less ludicrous.

"Okay," said Mattis, thoughtfully. "So what has Spectre given us?"

"It's … complicated," said Modi, to his complete and utter *shock*. Modi never said anything was *complicated*. The closest he ever came was *interesting*. "But the gist of it is—we can now track the graviton-based residue left by this radiation, which lasts a lot longer … hours, days, months. The future-human ships are leaving a trail for us to follow. Their cloaking device has, ironically, become a locating beacon."

That was useful. "When can you have it working?"

"It's working now," said Modi. "The path the ship has taken is clear as day."

Complicated my ass.

"Send it to my desk." Mattis closed the link, removing his

earpiece.

Spectre smiled across his desk at him, inclining his head respectfully. "The first of many gifts," he said.

Not a gift. A gift was given with no expectation of return. This was a trade.

And Mattis didn't know what he was expected to give away.

His desk lit up with a star chart, which Modi had helpfully drawn a bright red line through, showing the ship's projected path through Z-space as translated into real space. The line ended in the vast void between stars … its path and destination unclear. Just a blank area of space. Nothing for lightyears around.

"Fascinating," said Spectre, nodding as though this brought great understanding. "Well, now we know where they're going at least."

Mattis blinked at the red line. It seemed to lead nowhere. "We do?"

Spectre tapped on the desk and drew with his finger a series of numbers. "Head to these coordinates," he said. "We might be in time to stop them."

CHAPTER TWENTY-FOUR

Earth
United States
Georgetown, Maryland
Chuck Mattis's Apartment

03:01 hours

Chuck was fast asleep when his phone jingled and jangled, playing the theme song to some antiquated tv show he'd watched a few years ago with dragons and swords and icy undead armies. His favorite kind of entertainment, lightyears away from his actual work—babysitting politicians.

He blindly groped for it, picked it up and, stifling a yawn, clicked the answer button without looking at the screen—his eyes were too bleary to have a chance of seeing who was calling him. "Hello?"

"Sorry to get you out of bed," said Smith, a voice Chuck

had hoped to *not* hear again for the foreseeable future. "But I need you to find something out for me."

Something. Always something. Chuck dragged his legs out from under the covers and sat up, feeling the cool night air quickly begin to steal away the precious warmth from his body. "Is this something going to get me put into jail?" He rubbed his eyes with his spare hand. "Again?"

"You did that on your own," said Smith, a point Chuck couldn't contest.

"Fair enough. What do you want?"

The line buzzed slightly, indicating a long distance. Possibly lightyears. "I need to talk to a mutual *friend* about a problem I have. I think you have the best chance of locating this particular *friend*, seeing how you've … visited his office before. Can you help me out?"

Chuck knew, instantly, Smith was talking about Senator Pitt. "Are you fucking high?" he said, standing out of bed and moving over to the window, keeping his voice low to not wake up Elroy. Fortunately the guy was a heavy sleeper. "I can't get involved in this shit again. I already lost my job and spent a night in a filthy cell thinking I was going to get shanked at every moment, I can't get involved in Pitt again. I just can't. You know that as well as I do."

"I *do* know," said Smith, "but I can't do this on my own, and it's important. I wouldn't be asking if I could do it by myself. I need your help, Chuck."

Chuck debated all the various ways he could get out of doing this, including simply hanging up, insisting that Smith try something or someone else, or just … lying. But instead, he sighed long and loud into the microphone and, moving out of his bedroom and into the living room, tried to forget that what he was doing was a breach of his bail conditions.

"Fine," said Chuck, grimacing internally *and* externally. "I'll call you back."

He hung up and then spent a few minutes pacing about his living room, trying to find some kind of plan. He couldn't do it in person; everyone knew his face. He'd have to use a friend or an old acquaintance. But which number to call, which number … there was no point calling his office, they would have that monitored. It would have to be a personal number. He scrolled through his list of old work contacts, searching….

And then he found her. Sherry Franco. The secretary who'd joined only a few days before he was fired. Perfect.

Before he realized what he was doing, and forgetting it was three AM, Chuck tapped the call button.

"Hello?" said a tired sounding woman on the end.

Well, fortunately, Chuck had a line fresh for this one. "Terribly sorry to get you out of bed," he said, putting on his best fake accent. "But a jolly good morning to you, old bean! My name is—" he thought of a fake, British-sounding name. "James Pendleton the Third, Esquire, with the British Ministry of Defense, and I'm terribly curious about something of import, my good woman. I need to know where the good American whig, Senator Pitt, is at this moment and I would be just *chuffed to bits* if I could get him on the line. Chop chop."

There was a long, pronounced moment of silence on the other end of the line.

"What?"

Oh God, she wasn't falling for it. No way forward now but to *commit.*

"I'm *James Pendleton the Third, Esquire*. House of Lords. British Parliament. Ministry of Defense." said Chuck, stressing his words to accent perfect British frustration, "and I need to speak to Senator Pitt right now. Can you please tell me where he is?"

The response down the line was slurred and vague. "He's … on vacation. In, uhh, the Losagar system. I can take a message if you like." She paused and he could hear the faint sound of scratching. "Who is this again?"

The Losagar system was a luxurious resort designed to cater only to the mega-rich. It was totally believable. "James Pendleton the Third," said Chuck, now eager to get away from the call without arousing too much suspicion. "Please let him know I called. Thank you for your time, mum. Goodbye." He hung up.

Done. Mission complete. Chuck paced across his living room as he sent Smith a text message.

Losagar system. Holiday.

Never, ever, call me again.

"Chuck!" came an urgent voice from the bedroom.
Now what.
"Elroy?" said Chuck, "What's wrong?"
"It's Jack."
Chuck ran to the nursery. Elroy was sitting in the rocking chair, Jack on his lap. The baby rested against the man's abdomen, eyes open, very pale, but lethargic.
"What's wrong with him?"

"I don't know. When I woke up and heard you talking, I just came in here on a whim to check on him, and found him like this."

"Fever?"

Elroy touched Jack's forehead. "Maybe? But ... look at him."

Jack wasn't crying. Just ... pale, and staring at the wall.

"Ok. If he's not fine by morning, we're going to the hospital."

And as the word *hospital* crossed his lips, he realized he'd far prefer to be back in jail than in a hospital with his kid, sick. "Don't worry," he told Elroy, but more to himself, "he'll be fine. He'll be just fine."

CHAPTER TWENTY-FIVE

Zenith, High Orbit
USS Midway
Admiral Mattis's Ready Room

Mattis examined the set of numbers Spectre had given him with a skeptical, cautious eye, trying to pry out their secrets with sheer force of will. His earpiece chirped but he reached up and turned it off. No time for distractions. Lynch would have to handle it.

"What's at these coordinates?" he asked, trying to mentally map them to the digital map he had displayed on his desk. It was just an empty piece of space; nothing of particular interest. Something had to be there ... but what?

"Does it matter?" asked Spectre, plaintively.

Mattis affixed a firm stare on the portly British man. "Yes," he said, firmly. "Your bargaining position here is extremely dubious. You're aboard this ship, in this room, on my grace alone. You promised me answers. Not more secrets."

"I promised you answers *eventually*," said Spectre, a slow, knowing smile spreading across his face. "Everything will be revealed in due time."

Mattis glowered. "With a word I could have my marines put you out the airlock."

"With a word you would lose any chance, any hope, of finding any solution to the attacker that killed hundreds of thousands of people and then *vanished*. Tell me, Admiral Mattis, do you think whatever power did this is satisfied now, ready to slink into the darkness of space and never return?"

Of course not. And he knew it was true. Spectre was playing games—after being expressly told *not* to play games—but Mattis knew he couldn't afford to let the man go inspect the outer hull without a spacesuit. Not yet, at any rate. "Tell me more about this weapon," he said. "The effect we're seeing—fires raging across a whole planet—are inconsistent with what our witness tells us happened. They reported that the whole crust rippled and lifted up, then was dropped. Not … this."

"A planet is a curious thing," said Spectre, the smile disappearing from his face. "I'm no geologist, but my ship's sensors were studying Zenith as you approached. What we found was this: any planet with indigenous plant life, as Zenith has, typically possesses a thick coal bed. Zenith's stretched across the whole of the southern continent. The staggeringly vast amount of energy required to lift the continental crust of a whole Earth-like planet—one hundred and ninety *billion* tonnes of mass, give or take—immediately ignited this layer of high-energy, flammable material, causing the fires which enveloped that continent.

"The fuel, heat, and air fed through the mutinous cracks in

the surface led to wildfires that will rage there until you and I are long dead." Spectre leaned back in his chair, face somber. "Strangely enough we have seen this kind of thing before. During Earth's early primeval history, trees evolved an organic polymer called lignin, which let them grow tall and high. Yet it could not be broken down by the bacteria and fungi of the time, so when those trees eventually fell over and died, they formed a belt of coal across Earth. During the Permian period, a chain of volcanic eruptions in Siberia triggered the ignition of Siberia's coal belt. Carbon and atmospheric gasses flooded Earth, and in the oceans and on the lands, plants, animals, and almost all forms of life—ninety percent or more —were extinguished. They call this period of time..." Spectre took a sombre breath. "The Great Dying."

"And now," said Mattis, "someone has visited the same upon Zenith."

There was a brief moment of quiet as the two of them digested this news. "It takes a lot," said Spectre, gravely, "to rattle someone like me, Admiral."

"I can see that."

Spectre looked away for a moment and Mattis wondered, for a split second, if he was listening to some radio transmission only he could hear. Then he looked back to Mattis. "I know what they're after," said Spectre, "and I'm happy to guide you towards the next attack, but any further information is for the President's eyes only. You can talk to her if you like, I'll talk to her, we can work something out ... but if we want to stop the next attack, Admiral, we need to get moving."

"How soon?" asked Mattis. "It will take some time to

contact the President and arrange a meeting to discuss this. And fleet command has taken a dim view of my unapproved contacts with the President recently."

"Sooner rather than later would be better," said Spectre, with seemingly genuine sincerity. "Lives hang in the balance."

Mattis took a deep breath and considered, but then the door chimed.

"Excuse me, Admiral," said Modi, from the other side. "You asked to be informed if there was any issue with the engines."

"Come in," said Mattis, his chest tightening. "What do you have for me, Modi?"

Commander Modi poked his head around the corner of the door frame. "Well sir," he said, "we are detecting an issue with the fuel mix. Some kind of strange gravity distortions; we don't quite know what purpose they serve. They're increasing efficiency all right, but it's…" Modi's voice drifted, shrugged away some obviously confusing thought. "It requires more study."

Mattis's eyes flicked to Spectre, then back to Modi. "We'll talk about this later," he said. "So they aren't as perfect as we thought, but they work." He paused. "I'll send you some coordinates. Let's find out what these things can *really* do."

He stood, Spectre stood after him, and then the three of them walked into the bridge. Modi kept going, heading back to Engineering.

"Get the ship ready to execute a Z-space translation," said Mattis, when the bridge was resealed. "Coordinates should be on my desk."

Lynch went straight to work. "Aye sir, no worries." He

paused. "This is nearby. Only a few minutes jump with our new engines."

Mattis moved over behind Lynch. "Modi said—"

"Modi talks too much," grumbled Lynch, tapping away at his console. "The engines are *fine*. They're basically smack bang centre in their operating parameters, but because there's a mite of difference, well, now we all have to *panic*." Lynch groaned softly as though in pain. "That damn robot is a technological hypochondriac who is freaking out because his goddamn mind can't process the idea that there might, very well, be some kind of physics effect he doesn't quite understand right at this moment."

"I did ask him to come to me with anything he had," said Mattis. "It wasn't exactly his fault."

"Still," said Lynch, tapping at keys. "Okay. We're ready to commence Z-space translation."

"Do it," said Mattis.

Once again the ship was bathed in rainbow hues and leapt into the strange unreality that was Z-space. Once again, nothing disastrous happened. The *Midway* sailed smoothly toward its destination, the mysterious coordinates given by Spectre. Mattis slid into the CO's chair and waited.

True to Lynch's word, the ship cruised for only a few minutes, and then the computer signaled they were approaching the Z-space coordinates which would translate them back into real-space.

"Sir," said Lynch, glancing over his shoulder. "We are ready to—" He stopped, eyes widening. "Hey!" he roared, wheeling around, eyes widening. "What the fuck are you doing?"

It took Mattis a second to realize Lynch was looking over his shoulder. At Spectre. Who stood, his hand guiltily positioned over one of the unused terminals.

"Just performing some calculations," said Spectre, smiling sheepishly. His British accent crisp and clean. "Nothing more."

Mattis rose out of his chair in fury, but as he did so, the ship translated out of Z-space and into the real world.

"Contact," shouted someone. "One RCS contact matching the future-human ship, bearing zero-zero-one mark zero-zero-eight. Dead ahead!" The officer stopped. "And … sir. There's a rogue planet here. A planet without a star."

Rogue planets. Whole worlds perpetually shrouded in night, drifting silently through the inky void of space, frozen dead worlds for the most part … occasionally populated by smugglers, illegal and unsavory entertainment establishments, and explorers who liked the idea of claiming their very own world to themselves, one which would be almost impossible for strangers to ever find.

And military black-ops units.

But there was no more time to think about it. "Sound general quarters," said Mattis, and then pointed to one of his marines. "Scramble the alert five fighters and launch all wings. Lynch, get me what we know about that rogue planet. And officer of the deck?" He pointed to Spectre, who was still hovering near the terminal, "if that man touches anything, shoot him in the head."

CHAPTER TWENTY-SIX

Zenith, High Orbit
USS Midway
Pilot's Ready Room

"The conquering queen returns!" laughed Guano as she burst into the ready room, still dressed in her medical gown, bare ass remarkably chilly in the processed atmosphere of a starship.

Stunned silence. Everyone stared at her. They didn't cheer. They didn't react more than the occasional grimace.

Roadie just stared at her, wide eyed. Behind him, projected on the wall, was a massive presentation which boldly proclaimed, in thick letters:

Military Suicide Prevention
"One Loss Hurts Us All"

Pain isn't always obvious, know the S.I.G.N.S:

- S.aying they want to die or to kill oneself
- I.ndicating hopelessness or having no reason to live
- G.etting into excessive drugs or alcohol
- "N.o way out"
- S.leeping too much, or too little

"Uhh," said Guano, blinking as she took in the slide's content. "I didn't realize there was a briefing."

"What are you doing out of bed?" asked Roadie, his tone edged in worry. At that moment he seemed more like a concerned friend than a CO. He took a step toward her. "Are you feeling okay? Do you know where you are?"

"I'm fine," she said, eyes flicking to all the pilots and crew around her. "I just wanted a drink, that's all."

"A *drink*," said Roadie, his concerned tone suddenly slathered over a layer of *really pissed off* as though evaluating her quickly and realizing she was being a dumbass. "No, I think not. Rather, I see you're here to contribute to the lecture today."

Slowly, it began to dawn on her that, perhaps, this might not have been a good idea. "Actually, you know what, I might just head back to sickbay and think about what I've done, yeah?"

"Guano…" groaned Roadie, his teeth grinding together. There was a very brief moment where he seemed to consider, trying to decide if she really was sick or just being a tool so he could either let her go or berate her. He chose the latter option. "I'm actually—no, fuck it. Fuck it! I'm actually *glad* you're here. *Just* the person I wanted to see." He marched up to her, clicking off his laser pointer, his voice transitioning from *polite officer giving a health and safety lecture* to the much less formal *angry CAG berating one of his pilots*. "Dipshit! *You* are the fucking reason people kill themselves, you know that?" He swung his hand over the gathered audience. "Here we all are, having a polite, boring-as-shit mandatory lesson in how you shouldn't hang yourself like a dumb, idiotic, inbred hunk of meat and in waltzes—" he jabbed a finger at her. "You! Got anything to say for yourself, huh?"

"Uhh," said Guano, awkwardly pulling the back of her gown around behind her to try and hide her exposed backside. "No sir."

"You're goddamn right you have nothing to say!" roared Roadie, a vein above his eye pulsing wildly. "You're a comprehensive disgrace, showing up here when you're supposed to be un-fucking yourself in sickbay and interrupting my perfectly boring presentation!"

The CAG only got mad when his people were endangering themselves or not performing to their best. A little guilt flickered through her. She *wasn't* really meant to be here after all. "Sorry sir," said Guano, arms firmly by her sides. "No excuse."

"Good," said Roadie, taking in a few deep breaths and seeming to calm right down. The angry act evaporated and, very briefly, was replaced by a look of concern once more. "Now since you're here … have a seat and listen."

That was Roadie-speak for *you're forgiven, this time*. Guano sheepishly slid into a spare chair.

Roadie paused and then turned back to his presentation. "So," he said, his tone returning to *professional officer* levels. "As I was saying, a profound change in sleeping patterns can be a sign of depression and self-harming thoughts. None of these elements are problematic in the specific case; instead, what we are doing here is looking at the big picture. The whole spectrum of the mental health of one of your fellow pilots. These things are subtle and...."

Guano, slowly but surely, stopped paying attention.

"Fancy seeing you here," whispered Doctor Brooks, right beside her.

"Shit," said Guano, a little too loud.

Roadie affixed a dagger-stare upon her, and she shrank back slightly until he resumed his lecture.

She leaned towards Brooks. "What are *you* doing here?" she hissed. "I thought you went off to check on my medical file. This is for pilots and crew!"

"Well," whispered Doctor Brooks, "I definitely will look into that, but as you know, I'm here to observe the flight crew and make sure that your issues are not systemic in the air group." That made sense. "It requires me to assess how the standard mental health programs are being presented by senior officers."

"Okay, okay," said Guano, waving a hand dismissively. "I get it. I get it." She folded her arms and settled in to listening to the remainder of Roadie's speech. "Jeez. Boring presentations make *me* wanna kill myself."

Brooks snickered quietly under his breath, and went to say something, but then the red light of general quarters flooded through the room, followed by the wail of a klaxon.

"Oh shit," said Roadie, clicking off his laser pointer. "Okay, we're gonna wrap this up real quick: don't kill yourselves. Now get to your ships, come on!"

The pilots and crew scattered, running to their birds. Guano stood up, and in doing so, realized she was still wearing her hospital gown. "Oh boy," she said, grinning at Roadie. "Hey, Daddy, can I go shoot people too? *Please please please.*"

His expression was a sour, annoyed mask as the flight crews bustled all around him. "Hell no. You're not even *dressed* properly, you dumb shit."

"I can change," she said. "Nobody else is wearing their spacesuits. It won't be any slower."

"No." Roadie jabbed his finger towards the door. "Sickbay. *Now.*"

Guano whined loudly, clapping her hands together. "C'mon—"

"Actually," said Doctor Brooks, moving to stand beside her, "I think it would be really helpful to my work to observe her in action."

There was a brief moment where Roadie and Doctor Brooks locked eyes, and she could see that there was a struggle between the two of them. One which ended with Roadie dipping his head ever so slightly.

"Right," he said. "You're the doctor." Roadie looked to her, then flicked his eyes towards the hanger. "Get. I'll make sure Flatline is waiting for you." He held up his finger. "But he's flying this time."

"What?" Guano scowled. "No *way*. He's a gunner. I'm a pilot. It's … *perverse.*"

Roadie's voice rose once more and that vein began to pulse. "He's a fully qualified stick and if you don't fucking take this offer that I'm giving you on a goddamn silver platter, you're never stepping foot in a fighter again. Cross my heart and hope you die."

"Take what you can get," said Doctor Brooks, reassuringly. "I'll observe your vitals from here."

She pursed her lips sourly, but he was right. Any time in space was worth it. "You put the buddy in buddy spike, buddy," said Guano to Roadie, and then hurried off to change back into a borrowed flight suit.

CHAPTER TWENTY-SEVEN

Rogue Planet Serendipity, Low Orbit
USS Midway
Bridge

Mattis watched as the bridge crew leapt into action, the weeks of lethargy and the push of a rushed relaunch and rapid recall from shore leave thrust away in a moment.

"Sir," said Lynch. "Gun crews are standing by for engagement orders. The Alert Five fighters are away."

"Bring up the contact," he said. "I want to see it."

The main monitor lit up. There, hanging in space, was the future-human ship, its blunt, blocky nose pointed straight toward … nothing. A dark hole in space. Not a black hole—although to the untrained eye it might well have been, for a rogue planet had no sun to light it, nothing but the faint illumination of the stars, making the planet's surface visible only by the segment of space that it swallowed.

A red beam, glowing and angry, pulsed as it pumped

energy toward the surface of this strange, dark world, lighting up a patch of frozen rock, a finger of light pointing to the world.

Whatever they were firing on, the fact that they wanted to do it was reason enough to stop them. "All guns, engage that ship," he said. "Have the alert fighters form a screen and engage anything they launch; weapons free. I say again, they are authorized to engage at their discretion."

Lynch relayed his commands. A shudder ran through the ship as her guns spoke, the vibrations of the guns shimmying through her. Bright white streaks, angry hornets leaping across the stars, drifted toward the ship.

It was nearly a minute away from them, but if it was concerned about the incoming barrage, it didn't seem to act like it. The ship didn't maneuver, continuing to fire its weapon at the surface.

The *Midway*'s guns spoke again, and then again, sending three waves of shells toward the invader.

"Prosecuting the target," said Lynch. "We have three barrages coming in … and the contact doesn't seem to be dodging in any way."

"Works for me," said Mattis, trying to project an aura of strength and confidence, but that fact nagged at him too. Why weren't they dodging? "What's on that world?" he asked, pointing to the monitor. "What do we know about it?"

"Not much," said Lynch. "It's a rogue planet, and sensors aren't picking up any significant electromagnetic. Running a topographical analysis…" he paused a moment. "Dammit. It's Serendipity."

"I think you mean coincidence," said Mattis, focused on

the thin streaks as they drew closer and closer to the enemy ship.

"No—the world. It's a gambling hub called Serendipity. Basically a series of casinos all linked to a fusion reactor, lit by floodlights and warmed by heating systems, and not much else."

Good information but not useful at the moment. On the main monitor, the bright streaks that were the first wave of the *Midway*'s gunfire screamed towards their target, veering slightly to the left.

Veering? Were the dumb explosive shells changing course? No. The target must be maneuvering. Mattis smiled a little bit to himself. "I guess they noticed us," he said. "Draw us closer and have the subsequent barrages adjust for their heading changes."

Lynch, in a very uncharacteristic move for him, stammered slightly as he responded. "S-sir, the … the target ship isn't moving."

Was he really going insane? Mattis watched, incredulously, as the rounds continued to drift, veering off course. They sailed silently past the enemy ship, and out into the black.

The second wave did the same.

"Analysis," said Mattis, his fists balling by his sides. "What the hell is wrong with our guns?"

"It's not our guns," said Spectre. Since the battle had begun Mattis had forgotten he was here. "The future-human vessel is using its gravimetric drive to repulse the rounds as they approach, in lieu of moving."

There was something in the man's voice which suggested that—although he wasn't entirely aware of this, maybe—he might have suspected this was a possibility. "Okay," said Mattis, his patience wearing thinner than an atom. "Tell me how we defeat it."

Spectre shrugged helplessly. "I have not been able to determine a weakness in gravitational lensing; if one exists, I do not know of it."

Well that was helpful as a bag of shit. "Then what good are you?" Mattis spat, and then reigned in his temper. It would not solve anything. "Okay ... okay. Get the fighters in there. We'll soften them up using our strike craft."

"Aye aye," said Lynch. "Alert Five craft moving in, designated Wing Alpha. Other wings to follow."

Mattis watched the swarm of his own fighters fly through space toward the future-human ship, and he wondered what other tricks this new vessel might have up its sleeve.

And how long the ten thousand or so gamblers, casino workers, and other people on the cold surface of Serendipity had to live.

CHAPTER TWENTY-EIGHT

Rogue Planet Serendipity, Low Orbit
USS Midway
Hangar Bay

Guano was the last to arrive at the hangar bay despite sprinting out of the ready room still tugging on her boot. Luckily she remembered to clip it on before stepping into the depressurized area.

The hangar bay doors were already open. Scrambles were always tough; procedure was disregarded, everyone got sloppy, and the main goal in her mind was getting to her ship as fast as humanly possible.

As she ran up to her ship—her movement was more of an awkward waddle given her bulky flight suit—she saw two figures standing by. One had FLATLINE written on their helmet, so no prizes who that was, but the other had their back turned.

"Hey," said Guano, touching her radio as her voice

wouldn't carry in the vacuum of space. "C'mon. You, get to your ship."

The pilot turned around. "This *is* my ship," said Frost. Roadie's gunner.

"You're gunning for Flatline?" she asked, incredulously. No way the CAG's gunner would seat up with *her* gunner … that would be one hell of a demotion. It didn't make sense.

"No, of course not!" said Frost, her chirpy and ever-happy tone grating on her nerves. "Of course not. I'm flying for him."

Guano glared at Flatline who simply lowered the reflective visor on his helmet.

"Wait," she said, eyes widening as the truth dawned. "You … you *replaced me*? With a *gunner*?"

Flatline said nothing, pulled open one of the panels on the side of her ship and pretended, extremely unconvincingly, to be working on some last minute adjustment.

"Hey," said Frost, putting her hands on her hips. "I'm a pilot too, you know! I'm trained to do this."

"You're trained to fly *in an emergency*," said Guano, shaking her head and hoping the gesture could be seen through the thick suit. "Get your own useless bastard. This one's mine. My ship. My gunner."

Frost frowned and checked a display mounted on her wrist. "It says you're not on the flight roster."

"Because *Flatline's* flying and *I'm* gunning for him," she said, even saying the words making her feel dirty. "Just … just go away. We got this one."

"Okay," said Frost, raising up her hands and taking a step away. "Jeez, Guano … what the hell's gotten into you?"

Never, ever, did Guano think she would be *happy* to be getting into the gunner's seat. She swung her leg up over the ladder and practically ran up it to the secondary cockpit.

At first sight of it her smile faded. The thing was *cramped*. Even smaller than her regular cockpit ... and almost bereft of controls. It had just a simple set of screens for instruments, and a twin-handled control column fitted with a smaller screen for the gun. She'd done her training in it, as expected, but she never realized it was so *small*.

Still. Her pride would simply not accept that gunners had anything other than an easy life. She slide into the cramped space, wiggling around to get comfortable.

"Okay," said Flatline, "this ... this is a bit weird."

"Yeah," said Guano, reaching around and thumping him on the back of the helmet. "That's why you were being so *weird* to me, avoiding visiting me in hospital, and—and generally being such a weirdo." She knew that a combat prelaunch sequence was *not* the place to have this argument, but dammit, she was angry. "You could have just told me, you know."

Flatline squirmed in his—or rather, *her*—seat, the pilot's seat. "Let's talk about this later, okay?" he said, a faint whine in his voice. "C'mon. We're missing all the action."

With palpable reluctance, Guano focused on the prelaunch sequence. The ship lifted off, away from the deck, hovering for a moment before zipping out of the open hangar bay.

"Woah," said Guano as Flatline jerked the stick around. "Calm down there, buddy. You're all over the place."

"This is harder than it looks," said Flatline, steering the nose of the ship toward the hostile future-human ship.

"Funny that," said Guano, completely unable to keep the

venom out of her voice. "It's almost like *I told you so* about four hundred billion zillion times: our job is really, really hard."

He didn't answer, seemingly focusing on flying the ship. *My ship!* She had to keep reminding herself. Fortunately, Flatline seemed to get it pretty quickly … and soon they were racing to join the last of the fighters who were well on their way toward the hostile contact.

Guano unlocked the console for the gun and swung the turret around experimentally. She aligned it to the rear of the ship, pointing the barrels into empty space. Now, how to remove the safety….

The gun went off, chattering as it sent a few rounds flying into space. She almost jumped out of her skin.

"Hey, you remembered to check it before you had to use it." Flatline smiled proudly at her over his shoulder. "Nice work."

Guano realized her fingers had been hovering over the firing button. Apparently the twin triggers were *extremely* sensitive. Carefully, and certain she was white as a ghost, she pulled her fingers back. "Yeah," she said with as much strength as she could manage. "No worries. We're all good here."

"A'right," said Flatline, and she felt the ship accelerate. "We're almost back in formation."

Guano let him do the flying and checked her instruments. The ship's computer displayed blue diamonds all around her, friendly fighters, and the big red square of the hostile capital ship. She swung the turret toward it, and as the gun got closer, the square got narrower. Since the ship wasn't moving, all she had to do was point and shoot.

And summon the battle fugue.

She took a deep breath and watched as the first wave of fighters, the Alert Five ships, swarmed around the future-human vessel, and she tried to bring herself into the same mental state she had been in previously. To bring out the calm, the precision, the perfection.

C'mon brain, don't fail me now...

CHAPTER TWENTY-NINE

Rogue Planet Serendipity, Low Orbit
USS Midway
Bridge

The group of fighters, lead by the Alert Five craft, swarmed over the future-human ship. It continued, almost defiantly, to fire its weapon, pulsing as it pumped its beam, crackling with energy, into target planet. The ships were visible only by their navigation lights; with no star in the system, there was no ambient light at all to reveal them.

No doubt the future-humans were doing the same thing to this strange rogue world as it had done to Zenith. Mattis didn't know why, exactly, they were attacking this planet—it couldn't have been a test; they already knew their system worked—but he also didn't care. If they wanted to do it, he wanted to stop it.

"Status on the strike craft?" he asked, watching the swarm shoot at the future-human ship, the streaks of their missiles and flashes of their guns highly visible against the dark backdrop of the unlit world.

"Alpha Wing reports that their weapons are largely ineffective against the target," said Lynch, in a tone which suggested that this was not an entirely unexpected outcome. "Their guns are struggling to penetrate the thick hull, and their missiles … well. Strike craft are typically outfitted to fight other fighters. They're not carrying torpedoes."

Fair enough. Truthfully, Mattis had hoped they would be something of a distraction, if nothing else, but the future-humans seemed fixated on their work.

As he watched, the planet's surface rippled. If they were going to do something, they would have to do it soon.

Think, Mattis, think … there's gotta be some weakness. Some way we can force them to pay attention to us.

"Gravity is a weak force," said Mattis, more thinking out loud than actually giving an order. "Those shells took an awful long time to turn. So let's not give them that time." A plan of action solidified in his head and he gave it voice. "Yeah. Okay. Lynch, let's get in nice and close. I want to see the whites of their eyes. Blast that skunk from point blank range."

"That … would work," said Spectre, tilting his head curiously. That man always seemed to just lurk in the background like some kind of cat, forgotten.

"As Commander Modi might say," said Lynch, "I concur. But the risks of them aiming that thing at us—"

"Do it," said Mattis to Lynch.

"Aye aye, sir," said Lynch, and worked at his console. The image of the hostile ship grew bigger in the main monitor and the image resolution sharpened as it came into focus.

"Pull the fighters back," said Mattis, taking a deep breath. "And ready torpedoes. We're going to nuke that son of a bitch."

CHAPTER THIRTY

Rogue Planet Serendipity, Low Orbit
Deshawn "Flatline" Wiley's Warbird

Guano tried desperately to bring out the battle focus. Or fugue. Or whatever it was. She lined up her gunner's crosshairs on an incoming ship and squeezed the trigger. The gunner's station sounded so much louder from the back; vibrations from the ship's cannons shook her little seat, but the rounds flew true, splashing off a future-human fighter, seemingly to minimal effect.

"Nice shooting," said Flatline, jerking their ship all over space. The fighter she'd hit disappeared into the battle, and she ignored it.

"Keep it steady," said Guano, lining up on a new target. It flew beneath them before she could fire.

"Since when have *you* ever kept it steady?" Flatline pulled the ship up, and Guano squeezed off a few more shots at a new target, missing it completely. "You're always so rough."

Guano scowled and held down the trigger, sending a spray of fire across space, white-hot tracers streaking toward the enemy. The stream of cannon fire blasted one of the future-human ships to pieces and it burst, silently, in the void of space.

A flash of red light half blinded her. A future-human ship darted over her head, strafing them from above. The ship rocked as Flatline tried to avoid the incoming fire.

An alarm shrieked in her ears. "Damn, we're hit," said Flatline, a measurable spike of panic rising in his voice.

"I can fucking see that," said Guano, swinging the turret around wildly. Right near the base, a dozen ominous black holes leaked white gas into space, the outer rings glowing red hot. The closest was only a half-inch away from the turret's canopy. "They nearly got me."

A signal chirped in her ears. "All wings, priority alert. This is Roadie. Withdraw to the *Midway*."

"Confirmed," said Flatline, practically squeaking the words. He swung the ship's nose back toward their home base. "This is Flatline, RTB."

Damn. Guano watched as the battle retreated away. All she had to show for it was a single score and a busted ship, their fighter belching smoke as it leaked away its atmosphere reserves.

No battle fugue. Not even real combat as a gunner could bring it out of her.

Maybe it was gone forever. Just as mysteriously as it had arrived, it had gone, and she was just an ordinary pilot again. Perhaps she'd burned out her head … overloaded whatever *thing* was helping her. Icarus, too, had flown too close to the sun and paid the price.

Guano's eyes drifted to the ammunition counter. Two hundred and eighty rounds remained, barely a breath on the trigger for her. She had dumped almost all her ammunition taking out a single fighter, damaging another, and shooting a whole bunch of space. Flatline usually did much better than her even on his off days—and, here she was, seemingly useless. The numbers didn't lie. A computer could have probably shot better.

She'd always considered herself an ace pilot. This whole mind-*thing* was new to her and she was expected to perform without it. If she couldn't even do a *gunner's* job without it— what good was she?

What was the point in flying?

She slumped into her tiny gunners chair and sulked the whole way home.

CHAPTER THIRTY-ONE

Rogue Planet Serendipity, Low Orbit
USS Midway
Bridge

The minutes ticked away. The future-human ship, its weapon still active, pulsed as it blasted the surface.

It felt so odd to be closing the distance against a stationary target. Weapons in space had essentially infinite range, limited only by the target's ability to maneuver. But this new technology presented new problems. Hopefully getting close would solve it.

The future-human ship grew to be crystal clear on the monitor. The swarm of friendly strike craft, their weapons mostly expended, withdrew back to a safe distance. As each one of them crossed the red line which indicated safety, Mattis felt a little more at ease.

"Torpedoes one and two ready," said Lynch, typing furiously on the keyboard at his console. "The warhead yield is primed for armor penetration, but can be detonated with a proximity fuse if it looks like they're being shunted away. The effect will be a lot less, but heat and radiation in that proximity are never good; close enough for government work. Ready to fire on your command."

No time like the present. "Let them have it," said Mattis. "Fire torpedoes one and two."

The ship shuddered as the heavy missiles flew away from the tubes, each one leaving a rapidly expanding silver exhaust trail behind it, floating lazily in space to mark their path. They seemed so slow, even though Mattis knew they were traveling at hundreds of kilometers per second.

"Torpedoes away," said Lynch. "Good on guidance, both birds tracking the target. Impact in forty-three seconds."

Forty-three seconds seemed to be both a long time and nothing at all. "Any word from the surface?" asked Mattis, casting his eye to Spectre. "What do we know that's down there?"

"A casino," said Spectre, his tone suggesting that he genuinely thought everyone else had figured it out before. "Everyone knows about the Dark Side."

Silence, broken only by the chirping of the computers as they gave their reports.

"Okay," said Spectre, reaching up and pinching the bridge of his nose. "Apparently not *everyone* in the US Military is as familiar with illegal casinos as I am. The Dark Side is a nightclub where you can find anything, buy anything, any*one*, for a price. You can bet on anything and probably lose, and if you can't cover your debts, they saw off your head and use your body as fertilizer for the hydroponics labs. Smugglers love it. Criminals love it. It's not as bad as everyone says; the few hundred miserable souls who make that place their home are certifiable, and the regulars even more so, but birds that are born in a cage think that freedom is a crime." He looked to the main monitor, smiling whimsically. "Guess I won't be going back there again any time soon."

"Not really concerned with your vacation plans at this stage," said Mattis. "Why would these aliens—future-humans —whatever … why would they attack the Dark Side?"

Spectre smiled wryly. "Maybe they gave in to their anger."

"Enough with the joke, Mr. Spectre. Why are they attacking a casino?"

Spectre shrugged. "Your guess is as good as mine, I'm afraid."

Mattis reconsidered flushing the guy out the airlock.

"Torpedo impact imminent," said Lynch, clicking his tongue. "Big pair of missiles, fixing to smack that skunk dead on." His accent always got stronger when he was excited or stressed. "Three, two, one…."

Dual flashes washed out the screen, as the dual nuclear warheads detonated simultaneously, the piercing light flashing on the surface of the dark world, bringing a split-second of daylight to the perpetual darkness which otherwise ensconced it.

"Impact on target," called Lynch. "Dual detonations, straight in. Happier than pigs in mud."

"I'm not really sure they have feelings," said Spectre, watching the light from the explosions fade away. "Or at least … not anymore."

Mattis wanted to press him for more information—how

he could know something like that, but he filed it away for the future. "What's the status on the target?" he asked, as the camera refocused, bringing the future-human ship back into view.

It had ceased its attack, the spire mounted on its bow slowly retracting and sinking back into the armored hull.

And it was turning.

Its whole surface was blackened and marred, and there were small puffs of gas leaking from cracks in the hull, but overall the ship looked combat worthy.

"Looks like we got their attention," said Lynch, grimacing. "The skunk's turning toward us. Torpedo tubes one and two are reloading. Kind of hoping that weapon doesn't work on ships…."

"Fortunately we also have guns," said Mattis. "Let's see if we can finish them before we get a chance to find out."

The *Midway*'s guns spoke up, firing another volley, and the rounds smashed into their target, striking the turning broadside of the future-human ship and bursting into dozens of little flashes that died almost immediately in the cold, oxygen-free vacuum of space. Each left red hot disks at their impact points, superheated penetrations that seemed to at least have some effect. But no precious oxygen poured from them, so … more would be required.

Another volley smacked into the future-human ship, but by then it had completed its turn. The ship hovered there, seeming to almost consider the *Midway* for a moment, then thin cracks spread over its hull, and it opened up like a flower, revealing a massive array of missile tubes. Dozens of them.

"They have more missiles than us," said someone on the

bridge, a sentiment Mattis fully agreed with.

And then they launched.

Dozens of red streaks burst from the missile array, streaking out in one large mass like a star gone nova. They turned, a massive claw of missiles heading straight towards the camera.

"Vampire, vampire, vampire," said their radar operator, using the naval brevity word for incoming missiles. "Missile contact."

"Evasive maneuvers," said Mattis, fighting down the wave of apprehension that came from staring down so many little instruments of death. "Spin up point defense and load flechette rounds in the main guns; prepare to kill with anti-missile burst rounds. Airburst those suckers, cut them down, but make sure we don't hit our fighters. Away decoys, and deploy flares, chaff from all launchers." He checked his instruments. "Fighters are fast enough to engage them. Order any craft close enough to intercept."

"Solid copy on all," said Lynch, and the noise in the bridge picked up as his orders were repeated throughout the cramped metal room. The voices came at once and he struggled to filter them.

"Decoys away. Faux radar signal is strong."

"Gun crews report flechette loaded, airburst coordinates set, eight rounds rapid, firing in ten. Danger close."

"Flares and chaff are deployed, sir."

"Helm reports maneuvers commencing."

Mattis ran everything through a quick mental check. Everything they could do was being done. "Status on torpedo tubes?"

"Loading sir," said Lynch. "Two minutes."

Damn those things were slow. They would be hit long before they had a chance to reload. The newer ships loaded twice as fast, but the *Midway* was not a newer ship. "We should definitely work on speeding that up," he said, glaring at the future-human ship and its exposed rows of missile tubes. "Or, at least, you know … getting more of them."

The *Midway*'s guns spoke again, but this time the streaks that leapt out stopped short of the future-human ship, exploding as they flew through the mass of missiles heading toward them, silently exploding into thousands of finger-sized darts that sprayed out in a wide arc. As they collided with the hostile missiles they shredded them in showers of sparks, slicing through nearly half of the incoming threat.

Which was a charitable way of saying that their best physical defense didn't even get half.

"Vampires six through thirteen are down, killed with guns," said Lynch, reading off his monitor. "And fifteen, nineteen through twenty one, and twenty four."

That still left a lot of missiles active.

"Flares seem ineffective," said Lynch, a little bitterly. "None of those birds are turning even a little bit. Not for the chaff neither."

Well, guess they would have to rely on their point defense, some fancy flying, and a whole lot of luck.

The *Midway* maneuvered valiantly, powered by her new engines, and Mattis almost felt a little vertigo as the ship twisted around, presenting its most armored front to the remaining missiles. Each of them was significantly smaller than the *Midway*'s torpedoes, but he doubted very much if they packed a smaller punch. The ship's point-defense guns chattered, spitting out lines of high velocity explosive shells that criss-crossed, like angry fingers swatting down a swarm of bees.

"Vampires one, two, sixteen are trashed," said Lynch. Mattis watched as the angry red lights that indicated the hostile incoming missiles, one by one, winked out. "Three, seventeen, eighteen, twenty two…"

The main guns fired from point blank range, the explosion of their flechette shells intermingling and creating a billion shards of glinting metal that shot in all directions in a wave that passed over the ship, completely unable to penetrate its armor, but still ruining the new paint job. Two missiles flew through the maelstrom, the lone survivors which the computer helpfully labelled as *5* and *23*.

"All hands," said Mattis, giving the command he hated the most. "Brace for impact."

The first of the missiles soared in, tracked by one of the ship's many external cameras. It struck the hull, bouncing off the thick metal without exploding, shattering into a million pieces.

"A dud," said Lynch, with amazement. "Unbelievable. I guess even future-humans still have quality control issues that —"

Lynch fell silent as the second missile turned at the last minute, avoiding the front of the ship and skirting along its broadside. For a moment Mattis hoped that its guidance systems had been damaged by the explosion, but it turned again and speared into the ship's rear.

The *Midway* shook from stem to stern, the violent pitch of

it throwing the bridge crew off their feet and Mattis out of his command chair. Mattis hit the deck hard, cracking his shoulder on the unforgiving metal, his grunt of pain silenced by the wailing of alarms. In the corner of his eye, he saw Spectre land on all fours like a cat, displaying almost impossible agility for someone so portly.

"Report!" he roared, climbing back up to his feet and dragging himself back into his command chair.

"Damage to the ship's stern," said Lynch. "They put a damn missile right up our tailpipe."

"Status on that skunk?" he asked, squinting at the monitor, trying to find the enemy ship….

"It's gone," said Lynch, simply.

He glanced down at his own tactical readout. He was right. It was gone.

CHAPTER THIRTY-TWO

Rogue Planet Serendipity, Low Orbit
USS Midway
Bridge

The *Midway* slowly rotated, the slight Coriolis force throwing Mattis off balance as he tried to recover his bearings. Maybe the ship was spinning faster than it looked. Maybe it was just his head.

"It can't have just vanished," he said, "especially not when they just got a good hit in on us. That skunk could have fired again and we wouldn't have been able to do anything about it."

"I can confirm that they're no longer on our scopes," said Lynch, rubbing his back ruefully.

"Do you think they jumped away?" he asked, throwing a concerned eye to Lynch. The way he was rubbing his back was a worry.

"I'll have to check the logs to see if they entered Z-space —I was kind of on the floor when they would have."

"Check them. Now."

Lynch hunched over his terminal. "Must have," said Lynch, although the lack of confidence in his voice was telling. "Damn. Those missiles have some horsepower. Maybe that's why they didn't want to engage, and why they left so soon … just one barrage of missiles. Then they have to reload or something."

It made sense, but who would design a weapon with such an obvious limitation? Then again, only two missiles had gotten through, and one had been a dud. Maybe it was a crappy weapon after all.

"Right," said Mattis. "For now, we have to figure out what the hell they just did to us."

"It's fairly obvious, isn't it?" asked Spectre, casually adjusting his suit as though he'd just discovered it was slightly out of place, his clipped British accent almost demure. "They fired a nuclear missile up our bums. Tsk. The least they could do is buy us dinner first."

Mattis thumbed his radio. "Modi," he said. "Tell me good news."

The noise that came through on the other end was laced with static and … something else. Was something burning in the background? "Admiral," said Modi, his voice more flustered than normal. "Standby."

It took a *lot* for even a full Commander to tell an Admiral and CO of a naval warship to standby. Mattis waited patiently, offering his hand to one of the more junior officers who had brained themselves on their chair when the deck had pitched.

Mattis continued to help out the injured, and finally a few corpsmen arrived on the bridge to take care of the most seriously hurt. Medical resources were stretched over the ship; it made sense for someone to not be available right away.

When the injuries were taken care of, Mattis touched his comm again. "Modi. How's that damage report?"

"You didn't ask for a damage report," said Modi, matter-of-factually. "You asked for good news."

"That'll be the same thing, won't it?" asked Mattis.

"No."

Of course. Modi didn't do anything that wasn't literal. "Just tell me," he said.

"Stand by."

Frustrating. Mattis tried to turn his thoughts away from Modi's obvious issues—complaining about them and demanding things wouldn't fix the problems any faster—and just let him work.

"They didn't trash us," said Mattis to the room, although he was talking as much to himself as anyone else. "But we didn't trash them. We both got a few good hits in, and they blew their load trying to stop us … so I guess it's a draw for now." His eyes turned to the dark world beyond where the future-human ship had been floating. "We had better figure out what they wanted down there, and see what's left of that casino. Unless it's just been crushed under a million tonnes of rock, or picked up and dropped until there's nothing left."

"Unlikely," said Spectre, casually taking off his glasses and polishing the lenses. That they had stayed on his face at all was some kind of miracle. "The complex is built into thick underground tunnels buried well below its surface, in order to try and harvest whatever heat the depleted planet's core can muster. It's probably pretty badly shaken up but … well, Dark

Side City residents are survivors. I'm sure they will have a contingency plan."

"Great," said Mattis. "Lynch, get Modi, we're going to head down to the surface of that planet and see what we can find."

Lynch smiled widely. "You got it, sir."

Spectre squinted at him. "Wait, Admiral … you're going down *yourself?*"

"Sure," he said. "Watch me."

CHAPTER THIRTY-THREE

Rogue Planet Serendipity, Low Orbit
USS Midway
Hangar Bay

When Mattis and Lynch arrived at the hangar bay, Modi was there waiting for them, his arm in a sling. Doctor Brooks was checking his bandage.

"Doctor," said Mattis, giving a polite nod. "Good to see you here. I figure you would be kicking around somewhere."

Doctor Brooks gave a little smile. "You guessed correctly," he said. "I may not be a trauma surgeon, but I can bandage a busted arm. Most everyone else is helping out wherever they can."

"That is correct," said Modi, waving away the Doctor. "I am fine."

"You don't look so good," said Doctor Brooks, "Seriously, it was just a needle." And then to Mattis, "nor you. What did you do to your ship? And what are you doing *here*? Is there a problem in the hangar bay?"

Mattis couldn't help but scowl a little. "There's a rogue planet nearby. It was attacked by the future-humans we have been pursuing. Myself, the good Mister Modi, and my XO, Lynch, are going to head down there in a shuttlecraft and see what we can find."

Doctor Brooks chuckled mirthfully, but then his eyes widened. "Wait, you're serious."

"Of course," said Mattis. "Why wouldn't I be?"

Doctor Brooks hesitated, folding his hands in front of him. "Well, where to begin. Your ship has just suffered some kind of serious damage—Mister Modi definitely did not want to leave Engineering, but as a good officer, he goes where he is told, even when it involves horrible scary hypodermic needles. Secondly, Admiral, is there some kind of staffing issue on your vessel? The *Midway* has, last I checked, a full complement of marines who specialize in these kinds of away missions, along with heavily armored, specialist units whose favorite thing, so I hear, is to go to strange, dangerous places and kick ass. I doubt your Rhinos will ever forgive you if you don't send them down to this world. And finally … as a commanding officer, your position should be with the ship and with its crew—not gallivanting off to deal with some unknown element while they are left to patch up the damage. You are a leader. Lead."

Well, that was certainly a lot to take in. Mattis glowered angrily but, on any specific point, he could not refute the Doctor. The issue was, of course, his growing caution regarding … well, everything. These new Chinese engine upgrades. The Deep State. Spectre.

"And, don't forget, this is the main reason why Admiral

Fischer sent me here. To … reign in certain … tendencies of yours."

He wanted to punch the doctor in the nose. How dare he? "You're right," he conceded, avoiding the fight, taking a deep breath and letting it out. "Modi, stay with the ship. Fix the damage. Lynch, get the Rhinos and tell them they are going to probably go die in some really stupid way … make sure they bring their big guns, this place is dangerous enough at the best of times, and they don't like outsiders even when they aren't bombing them from orbit."

They both seemed relieved, in some way, by the change of orders. "Aye sir," said Lynch, and got on the radio to the Rhinos.

"Modi," said Mattis, trying to put the uncomfortable conversation with Doctor Brooks out of his mind. "Engines."

"Yes sir," said Modi, rolling his obviously injured shoulder. "It's very complicated, so I will summarize and only relay the information you need to hear: the engines are damaged and they will require approximately four hours worth of work, at our current manpower strength, in order to make them operational again, and that will only be at approximately eighty percent of operational capacity."

Mattis grunted quietly. "Lynch, you hear that? You have four hours down there on that shit hole. After that, well, I hope you make friendly with the locals … if there are any still alive."

"Right," said Lynch, beaming widely. "And by the way, Modi only told you what you needed to know. He's learning, Admiral. Faster than a scalded cat that one."

"That," said Modi, narrowing his eyes in confusion, "is

animal cruelty."

Knowing exactly how this would transpire—Lynch would get angry, Modi would get confused—Mattis cut them both off. "Get going."

"Aye sir," said Modi. "I should get back to engineering."

"And I should suit up," said Lynch.

Mattis nodded firmly. "Get to it," he said, the ghost of a smile forming on his lips. "Whoever finishes first—fixing the engines, or finding out what can be found on this planet—can have a week's extra shore leave when all this is done."

Lynch blew an appreciative whistle. "A whole damn week?" he said, eyes widening. "Depending on when this trip wraps up, we could be back in time for the Ranches & Rodeos meet this year. I've always wanted to go." The Texan gave Mattis a knowing wink—senior officers, by federal law at the end of the Sino-American War, each got the exact same amount of shore leave, period. But he went along with the joke.

"Maybe this is your chance."

"As for me," said Modi, "I could spend the time examining the ship which Spectre brought aboard. I'm sure its construction is fascinating, and I cannot wait to just … pry it apart and see what's inside."

That sounded suspiciously like *work*, but Mattis had the sneaking suspicion that, perhaps, Modi didn't really have any particular hobbies. "Whatever makes you happy on shore leave."

Lynch went off to go get changed and get ready for his mission, while Modi ambled back to engineering, leaving just Mattis and Doctor Brooks alone.

With a polite chuckle, Doctor Brooks nodded approvingly. "Positive reinforcement, even for your senior staff, game-ifying rewards to encourage friendly competition. You're not half bad at this, Admiral Mattis."

Mattis didn't smile. "This is my boat," he said, firmly. "And while I appreciate your input, and accept that you are here on Admiral Fischer's request, do not ever presume to give me orders when you're standing in these corridors."

The mirth flew from Doctor Brook's face, but he seemed to take it well in stride. "I understand. My apologies, Admiral. It won't happen again."

"It better not," said Mattis, and without further ado, turned and walked back to the bridge.

CHAPTER THIRTY-FOUR

Losagar System
Planet Waywell
Senator Pitt's Vacation Estate

Smith crept forward slowly. Painfully.

"John, freeze. You need to freeze now." Sammy's voice issued low and fast through Smith's earpiece.

For the fifth time in as many minutes, Smith locked his muscles and relied on the imported flora—a sterilized European woodland grown in a terraformed circle exactly as far as the eye could see from the remote estate, and no further —to hide from the guard passing by on a distant wall. Apparently Pitt's ego was stronger than his sense of paranoia, because this was not something Smith would have classified as a defensible location.

"OK, you're good," said Sammy. It was times like this Smith wondered just how old he was. Still a kid, right? Sort of?

"Thanks," he muttered back as he began slipping toward

the compound once more.

Having a smuggler's illegal camouflage and scanning equipment was coming in handy, he had to admit. Not to Reardon's face, though. Still. The stuff worked and it worked well.

How many crimes had Reardon gotten away with using this stuff?

He resolved not to think about it. Combining their skills had payed off; they'd mapped the area, plotted the best route, and downloaded it into his cybernetics. Unfortunately, said 'best route' ended in a crawl through some dense and likely thorny underbrush, but that was the job. He ghosted between trees, moving quickly enough to keep from dangerously open areas, and just slow enough to not catch a human's immediate attention with his motion.

Reardon spoke up. "Drone showing up over your spotlight-hogging ass, Smith. Get it under cover."

"Spotlight-hogging?" he murmured as he slipped under some particularly dense foliage. Overhead, the buzz of tiny motors drew closer. "We both know who's always been better at *stealth* missions. Not the guy in the pink space ship." The unseen device passed overhead and faded away.

"Drone clear," Reardon said by way of reply. "Also, the ship could be a distraction, you know. While I sneak off into the distance."

"Reardon, *you're* a distraction, cut the chatter."

The smuggler ignored him. "And for your information, it is a perfectly respectable salm-"

"*Chatter*, Reardon."

Smith dropped flat beside a cheerfully burbling stream as

another watchman made their way onto the wall. Within moments they had passed, and he was off again.

"Coming up on that hidden wire," Sammy informed him. "Twenty steps out."

Smith smiled. Sammy was learning fast, already an excellent navigator. Although that wasn't exactly surprising, living with Reardon's … *Reardon-ing*, as the kid did. If that wasn't the definition of a trial by fire, Smith didn't know what was.

"A wire as razor-sharp as my wit, and electrifying as my skill!" Reardon crowed. Always with the stupid comments….

"Actually, it's coming up as a sensor wire," Smith commented mildly, running the tiny scanner embedded in his left index finger over the general area. The thing chewed through battery like a hungry goat might chew through a vegetable patch, but it was one of the most useful pieces of equipment he owned. "So yes, sounds about right, Reardon."

"Do people usually call skill 'electrifying?'" Sammy asked as Smith carefully stepped over the ground where the wire was hidden.

"It's often reserved for events involving overly excited hicks and revving motorbikes," Smith replied. He was closing in on the compound now.

"Oh. Explains why Harry's using it." The younger brother sounded very convincingly thoughtful.

"Hey bro. Guess what?"

Smith resigned himself to Reardon's constant blathering as he reached the underbrush. It was definitely prickly, but at least that would keep his mind in the moment, rather than, say, on the brothers' bickering.

Sammy replied even as he crouched, looking for the path of least resistance. "What?"

"Guess who's cleaning out the waste module for the next month?"

"...Is it you?"

"Nope!"

"...Is it John?"

"Hey, that could w-"

"No." Smith cut him off as he shuffled sideways and began his crawl. For a short while, the air support was silent.

Then, "We can see your ass."

"*What?*" he hissed at Reardon.

"Through the scrub, there's a gap above you," Sammy replied, voice urgent. "We're not kidding. Your backside is poking out. Guard on the way, you need to get out of sight."

Move too fast and he'd disturb the brush above and the guard would spot him. Move too slow and the guard would spot his rear anyway.

Not ideal.

He slowly rolled onto his side, curling back towards the nearest roots. Hopefully, minimizing his profile would be enough.

"Head, get your head back," Sammy's voice rose in pitch. "He's getting close."

Smith contorted himself further, getting a face full of thorns for his troubles. He muffled a groan as one of them scraped his organic eye, swearing under his breath.

"Wow," Reardon broke in. "Ease up on the eighteen plus talk, Smith. There's a child listening."

"Hey!" said Sammy. "I'm nineteen!"

Maybe the guard would find him and shoot him. Then he wouldn't have to listen to the Reardon brothers anymore.

Tempting, but no. Smith stayed very silent, and very still.

"Okay," Reardon's voice dropped. "He's about to go past now. Don't move, John."

He didn't.

"He's looking, he's looking!" Sammy gasped.

"He's on his way by, it's going to be fine," Reardon said, the tension in his voice not doing much to allay anyone's concern.

Blood started trickling into his eye from a scratch on his forehead.

"He's moving away," the kid said, elation filling his voice. "Holy hell. That was close."

Years of training kept Smith from so much as breathing a sigh of relief, though he couldn't quite say the same of the Reardon brothers.

"Am I good to go?" he whispered.

"Clear," Reardon responded, and the rest of the crawl passed without incident.

Then, when his two nattering eyes in the sky told him it was safe, he shimmied up a tree to get a better look inside the compound.

And promptly nearly fell out, because under a patio, hidden from any sort of prying aerial sweep, Senator Pitt was indeed home.

So was his blown-up-by-aliens, body-found-and-identified, given-an-actual-state-funeral, incredibly-dead son, who was alive.

And they were talking.

CHAPTER THIRTY-FIVE

Rogue Planet Serendipity
Surface

Lynch wasn't happy.

The shuttle touched down on the surface of the dark world, and the loading ramp slowly—almost mockingly so—began to lower. It had taken far, far too long for the Rhinos in the away team to get suited up. Almost a quarter of their time had elapsed, and Lynch wanted those weeks of leave. At least, he wanted Modi to think he wanted them.

They were too slow and his patience was already running out. The idea of going to the rodeo had ignited an eagerness in him which, bizarrely given all that he and the crew had been through, was motivating him to get the job done and get back to his vacation.

Or maybe it was just beating Modi. That stupid idiot didn't have enough sense to spit downwind when it came to … basically anything that didn't beep or whir or zoom.

Or maybe … thousands of people had just been killed on Zenith and he needed a distraction to remain focused on the job. They all did.

Suddenly, at that very moment, he understood. That was why Admiral Mattis had dangled the seemingly childish offer in front of them. Of course. Not because a few weeks paid vacation would motivate him or Modi any further, or to game-ify their jobs, but if they let themselves dwell on the tragedy and loss of life, they wouldn't get anything done.

Admiral Fischer's words echoed in his mind as the ramp extended fully. He would be CO of the *Midway* at the end of this mission, most likely. Soon these responsibilities would fall on him. He'd remember that little trick in the future.

For now, though, think about the rodeo. And how nice those smoked ribs are going to taste….

Lynch took in the desolate, empty landscape from behind his spacesuit. The surface was jagged and littered with rocks about the size of his head. There was no light; everything he could see was illuminated by the shuttle's landing lights, and the comparably feeble lights on his suit.

"What kind of guy makes this place his home?" he asked, simply.

"Don't know, sir," said the Rhino near him, a Corporal Janice Sampson by the label on her chest. She had a massive, eight barreled rotary gun slung across her back like it was a sword. Their suits gave them strength beyond what normal people could sustain, at the cost of occasionally malfunctioning and twisting the person inside like a pretzel. "But, you know, some people choose to live in France, so I mean … everyone's got a preference."

Lynch smiled. "France is the most amazing place to live, if you take away all the people who live in France."

"Right," said Sampson, unslinging her massive gun and jiggling the ammunition belt nervously.

Obviously the devastation on Zenith had rattled everyone. "You okay?" asked Lynch.

"I don't like the dark," said Sampson. Well, at least she wasn't focusing on the recent loss of life.

Or maybe she was.

"Okay," he said, tapping the side of his helmet to bring himself into focus and banish the thoughts of how the cracked surface stretched out before him must be what Zenith looked like now, and tried to conjure images of cattle and massive hats. "Well … just going to have to suck it up. Based on Spectre's intel—don't trust that snake as far as I can throw him and throwing snakes is really hard because they're all rope-y, so that's not going to be very far—there's an entrance to Dark Side City somewhere near here, in a cave or fissure."

"Hey Sampson," said one of the other Rhinos, jokingly, his name tag obscured by the missile launcher he carried. He shouldered the weapon, revealing the name Baranov. "We're going to the Dark Side." He tweaked a knob on his suit, turning his voice all distorted. "Corporal Sampson, I am your father. Join me, and together, we shall rule the galaxy as Corporal and Private."

"You're going to have your hand cut off if you keep that up," said Sampson, her heavily armored head turning slowly as though scanning the barren rock. "There. A cave. That's probably our entrance."

Just as Spectre had said. "A'right," said Lynch. "Let's move out."

"Aye sir," said Sampson. "We got your back."

Lynch and the Rhinos stepped onto the loading ramp and began walking toward the cave. It was less of a traditional cave and more of a place where the ground had split, exposing a crack in the surface. It looked like it had seen better times; several chunks of the rock face had broken off recently, giving the cave opening a jagged, toothy look.

"Looks like a mouth," said Baranov, skeptically. "Like in that one space movie. Giant asteroid-worm with teeth."

"It's not a mouth." Sampson looked around for a moment, nervously, her helmet mounted light casting a white finger over the barren world. "It's just rocks."

"I know that, you idiot."

"Hey, I am *not* an idiot. I got like 87% on my IQ test. That's basically a B+."

"I only got a B-," said Baranov. "But at least I passed. That's all I care about."

Grimacing, Lynch interjected. "Actually, 100 is average."

"Wow," said Baranov. "That's scary. That means … that means, like, *half* of everyone I've ever met was less than average intelligence."

"Why is that scary?" Sampson kept jamming a finger into the side of her helmet, as if trying to dig out earwax but forgetting about the composite shell.

"Nevermind," said Lynch. He knew that providing commentary into their … insights … would only annoy them. He kept his mouth shut for the rest of the walk to the cave.

His troupe made their way into the wide open maw, walking two abreast with Lynch taking the lead, walking alongside Sampson. He reached down and adjusted the oxygen supply on his suit. Damn thing was always set too low...

An arm from a spacesuit lay on the ground, almost buried in soil and dust, barely protruding from the surface.

"Got a body," said Lynch, crouching down beside it.

Sampson whistled. "Probably buried when this place went rocking."

Curious, Lynch pulled on the fingers. The arm came loose, and for a horrified moment, he thought he had dismembered a body. But it was just a suit. No person inside it.

"Dammit to hell," he said, exhaling a breath he barely realized he was holding. "Jesus."

"Not reading any blood," said Sampson, waving a sensor over the thing. "No tissue residue... it's old, sir. At least twenty years. The plastic is fading, and the paint's been bleached off the metal by the star. It's not a body."

"No," said Lynch, looking upward. Hanging from the inside mouth of the cave were other spacesuits, some with bones inside, others eerily empty, nooses around their necks and signs nailed to their chests.

CHEATERS

"It's a *warning*."

Sampson whistled again. "Cheaters. Wow. They sure take their gambling serious here on Serendipity. Cheating patrons get the shaft."

Lynch examined one of the bodies hanging from the cave's low ceiling. "Patrons were bitten to death by human teeth?"

The signs were unmistakable. And the body inside didn't look like it was dressed as your run-of-the-mill gambler. It was wearing a lab coat—or rather, what was left of it. "This was a scientist."

CHAPTER THIRTY-SIX

Rogue Planet Serendipity
Surface

Lynch couldn't spare the time to cut down the bodies, so left them there, leading the troupe deeper into the cave's mouth, the jagged stalactites above them suddenly a lot more intimidating.

As they walked, Sampson's helmet mounted flashlight jerked around, casting strange shadows which seemed to grow and shrink with alarming speed. The further they got inside, the more nervous she seemed. Sampson clutched her weapon tightly, eyes darting around inside her armored suit.

Lynch switched channels so that he was just talking to her. "You okay there?" he asked, keeping his head straight so that the others wouldn't realize they were talking. She might be dumb as a post, but if she had some kind of issue ... then it was better that he knew about it so he could handle it.

"Yeah," she said, a firm tremor in her voice. "I just ... I

just hate the dark."

That confused him. "Aren't you meant to be trained to fight on a space ship?"

"Spaceships are always lit. Even with emergency lighting."

That was a good point. "If we have a problem … you could watch the entrance."

"Naw," she said. "I ain't going to do that to you. I'll stick with you till we find whatever it is we're looking for here, sir."

"Good to hear." He switched frequencies back to the group, coming into a conversation about a video of a cat eating spaghetti which had done the rounds a few months ago, and some spirited debate about if the cat was inbred or not.

The away team continued down the tunnel, until they came to a thick, reinforced steel door which had fallen off its hinges, the thick metal frame torn and bent. Whatever tumultuous damage the partially activated future-human weapon had wrought on this rogue world, it had obviously damaged the installation significantly. Just beyond it lay another door, similarly destroyed and open.

"Looks like an airlock," said Sampson.

"Hope that's not the only one," said Lynch, "or everyone in there is dead." He shone his light further up, revealing an elevator, its doors open. "Think that's serviceable?"

"Even if it is," said Sampson, "no way I'm trusting that technology. Shit could be booby trapped. Best cut our way through the floor and rappel down."

That seemed simple enough. "Do it," said Lynch.

He expected her to use a blowtorch. Or perhaps explosives. But Sampson, instead, simply pointed the barrel of her massive gun toward the floor and shot out a crude hole—

silent and eerily somber in the lack of atmosphere—then casually slung it back over her shoulder. "Done," she said, reaching to her belt and withdrawing a spool of thick wire. She bolted it to the wall with some kind of advanced nailgun and then, without any further ado, leapt down the hole.

As brave as she was stupid. Lynch hooked his suit onto the wire and followed her down.

The elevator shaft was a crude rectangle into the planet's surface that descended further down than his light could easily penetrate. "Hope you brought plenty of wire," he said.

"Heaps," she said. "Spectre said the main casino was far below the surface. And the earthquake-thing was likely to mess everything up. So, you know, I brought three spares. And I switched out our radio transmitters for lower bandwidth ones optimized for dealing with underground interference, since, you know, big slabs of rock with chunks of iron in them tend to mess with radio waves."

Apparently Sampson wasn't all that dumb after all—most of it was probably an act. To fit in with her grunting, scratching, neanderthal Rhino buddies. As Lynch slowly lowered himself into the crudely cut elevator shaft, he reconsidered his opinions on the Rhinos. They weren't necessarily *stupid*, just … specialized. That was a charitable way of putting it. They could do one thing and do it well.

That was enough.

Down into the ground they went, with Sampson occasionally changing and extending the wire. As they descended, the temperature climbed, but there was still no sign of atmosphere, until finally they arrived at the bottom.

There the lower airlock lay smashed open too, and beyond

that the casino, its light still on and games still active, silently flashed in the dim gloom. Debris littered the floor and gaming tables had been tilted over, machines flattened on the ground, and piles of casino chips lay scattered around like some toddler with anger issues had tossed them in all directions.

"No more bodies," said Sampson. "That's … good?"

"I thought we were looking for things," said Baranov, quietly. "People are the best intel."

"Actually that's computers," said Sampson. "People lie."

"So can computers," said Baranov.

Lynch couldn't help but agree with the sentiment. "People are bastards, but it's a mistake to trust computers too much." He slowly crept into the ruined airlock, stepping between the outer and inner doors, but then noticed something remarkable.

The wall to the left hand side of the airlock, normally just an unremarkable steel sheet, had bent and warped from the geological activity. Beyond he could see a corridor, formerly concealed by the otherwise unremarkable sheet. Lynch reached up and tried to pry the metal open, but it wouldn't budge.

"What's this?" he asked, curiously.

"Eh," said Sampson. "Looks like some kind of hidden passageway. I think the earthquake busted it."

The more Lynch searched the more it seemed to be the case. Normally, the corridor beyond would have been perfectly hidden—it did seem like the warped steel sheet had been some kind of secret door, pre-destruction. The airlock was three-way. "I can't get it open."

"Let me," said Sampson, putting her massive glove on the thing and tearing it out by its hinges.

On the back of the sheet was the symbol of MaxGainz,

the steroid company that had caused them a great deal of misery of late. Just seeing it made him feel hot under the collar. "Well, this is just great," said Lynch, stepping past Sampson into the exposed secret room.

It glowed ominously, a pale green light emanating from row after row of fluid-filled transparent tanks. About half of them had partially decomposed skeletons within, although it looked like the area hadn't been used in a while, with a thick layer of dust covering everything, even after the earthquake.

"Looks like we found a thing," said Baranov.

"It's *definitely* some kind of thing," said Lynch, a little edge of bitterness creeping into his voice. "If only we had Modi down here to sort it out."

"What should we do?" said Sampson.

"Take pictures," he said. "Lots of photos. Videos. Take a few samples, find any computers or data sticks you can, and then get the hell out of here. We're running out of time for the climb back. Fifteen minutes, people, no more."

"Aye aye," said Sampson, and then she and the other Rhinos went to work.

CHAPTER THIRTY-SEVEN

Rogue Planet Serendipity, Low Orbit
USS Midway
Bridge

Mattis quietly fumed in his command chair, doing his best not to let his frustration show. The incident with Doctor Brooks grated on his nerves.

The *Midway* was his command. Outside forces messing with it, apart from the issue of his pride, would only bring problems. Problems they could ill afford at this point.

Fortunately, Lynch's voice came through and broke him out of his thoughts. The transmission was heavily garbled, but definitely understandable.

"Commander Lynch to *Midway*, do you copy?"

Mattis smiled despite himself. "You're coming through loud and clear, Commander Lynch. What did you find down there?"

"Well first," said Lynch, "how's Modi going with the

repairs? He's listening in, right? Lemme tell you, I want that extra week."

"Oh," said Mattis, whimsically. "Yeah, I've piped this down to engineering. He's doing okay from early reports. Quite motivated to get that week's worth of leave, or so I hear. It's causing him to work *extra* fast."

"Well, tell him to shove it up his tailpipe, because believe me, I have cracked this thing wide open. I know why the future-humans were attacking here." He paused, presumably for dramatic affect, although Mattis could hear a winch whining in the background, so it might have been related to that. "There's a goddamn MaxGainz facility here. It's old. Twenty years at least, and abandoned. Just like what that science-nerd guy found. Modi's little buddy. You know, um, Breeman—Freeman? I want to say, um … Christopher?"

"Bratta," said Mattis. "Doctor Steve Bratta." His teeth ground against each other. Steve Bratta had, against Mattis's best judgement, gone 'undercover' on the outlaw world of Chrysalis. There, they had located a human experimentation facility. "Any indications what it's for?"

Lynch snorted over the line. "It could be anything." Another pause, broken only by the faint sound of whirring in the background. "You know, this sounds crazy, but my gut is telling me this is important. Something more than just some scientist's play pen, you know? And some of the scientists, well, they were dead all right. But looks like something tried to bite their heads off. Something … human …-ish."

Mattis had the same this-is-important feeling. "You say it's abandoned?"

"If it's not, they put an awful lot of effort into trying to convince us that it was. I had the Rhinos raid what we could of their computer hardware—" Lynch raised his voice suddenly as though speaking to someone nearby. "Careful with that, it's fragile!" Then, he seemed to refocus once more. "Look, I got their computers, I got heaps of photos and information, I got what I need to prove it to you, or to anyone else, that that's what was down here. It was more than just a casino. A lot more."

"Very good," said Mattis, "get back here as soon as you can." And then he closed the link.

"Well," said Spectre, his voice quite chirpy. "That explains a lot of things."

"It does?" asked Mattis, curiously.

"Isn't it obvious?" asked Spectre, as though it truly were the easiest thing in the galaxy to understand. "When the future-humans attacked the first time, they blew up Friendship Station, obviously, because without it they wouldn't have a way of getting past our defenses without being detected—but they didn't count on the *Midway* being there, so they ended up losing the element of surprise regardless. So they took out the facility there. And where did they go after that? Ganymede, of course, to take out the seed bank for humanity. Then, well, straight to Earth to blast our researchers and technological centers to ashes, and then, presumably, a tour of the sector, winding up in Chrysalis to finish the job."

It all made sense, but something Spectre said leapt out to him in a way that made his whole chest tighten. "There was a MaxGainz human gene research facility on Friendship Station?"

"Of course," said Spectre, blinking in surprise. "I …

thought you would have figured that out by now."

"News to me," grumbled Mattis. Just when he thought he knew it all. "Anyway. While we're waiting for Lynch to come back, we should start tracking that ship." He touched his radio. "Modi, how are my engines looking?"

"We should have them ready momentarily," said Modi, pride in his voice. "Although I see that Commander Lynch has not yet returned from his away mission."

"He's on his way back now," said Mattis, perfectly honestly. "I'd say you don't have more than a few minutes before he does get on board. He's got a theory—a theory with a lot of evidence to it—but until I have that evidence in my hand, the game is still on." His tone betrayed the playful nature of his comment. "First one to solve their problem wins, remember."

"Of course," said Modi, and without further ado, cut the link.

Well, having engines back would be decidedly pleasant, but having the mystery solved would also be good. The whole thing bugged him. But what didn't these days? He was turning into a cautious man; a suspicious man.

An old man.

His earpiece did a very strange thing and chirped twice at the same time, two different tones indicating that both Modi and Lynch were trying to talk to him. He opened both channels, patching the two conversations into each other.

"Engines are operational," said Modi.

Lynch talked over him. "Sir, we're aboard the shuttle, and —damn it!"

"Sorry Lynch," said Mattis, grimacing slightly. He had seemed so eager to win. "I'm a man of my world. Modi solved the situation first." He took a breath. "Okay, Modi, prepare for Z-space translation."

"That won't be possible just yet," said Modi. "I haven't completed the diagnostics to verify the repairs are working."

"Then that doesn't count!" laughed Lynch down the line, with perhaps a little more energy than was *strictly* necessary, for a game, at least. "You goddamned android; tie a quarter to this competition and throw it away, and you can say you lost *two things*." His voice came through, revitalized and charged with a passionate energy. "Sir, our shuttle is burning hell for leather back to the *Midway*. We will be there as soon as we can."

Modi's stammering voice cut over the conversation. "The rules said—"

"The rules," said Mattis, calmly, "said you had to fix the engines. You can't be sure that you have yet."

"There's a high probability—"

"You," said Lynch with a laugh, "are a day late and a dollar short. Sorry, Modi, buddy, you gotta do better than that."

Modi's tone turned sour. "I will perform the diagnostics, and then I shall report back."

Mattis nodded even though neither of them could see it. "Right, well, let me know when you have something *concrete*, both of you. Mattis out." He craned his neck, looking to his tactical officer. "We can't wait for Lynch. Have we figured out where that skunk is making for?"

"Not yet," said the tactical officer, frowning as she consulted her instruments. "There's a lot of interference in the residual signal. It might be a byproduct of the rogue planet, or possibly the result of battle damage inflicted on the future-human ship's engines … or maybe something they did deliberately. Either way it's hard to find their exact heading."

Spectre coughed politely. "What about an *imprecise* heading?"

The officer looked to Mattis for confirmation. He nodded.

"Roughly one-one-nine, mark two-zero-zero. Accurate to a degree doesn't count for much in space, unfortunately."

Spectre smiled. "It's near enough." His face slowly split into a cheeky grin, his British accent intensifying. "Rather than me spoiling it, why don't you ask Admiral Fischer yourself? She certainly knows."

He gently bit the inside of his cheek to keep himself from saying what he really felt, maintaining professionalism in the face of … that.

"I will," said Mattis, straightening his back. "And that's enough out of you, I think. Spectre, your usefulness to me has expired. Marines, take him to the brig."

"Arrest me?" Spectre held up his palms innocently. "On what charge?"

Mattis didn't trust him at all. Spectre presented an unacceptable operational risk; he was only useful when he was providing information, and his supply of that seemed to have run out if he was sending him to Admiral Fischer. "Pissing off the CO of a US naval vessel."

Spectre shrugged happily and didn't resist, holding out his wrists and letting the marines cuff him, then haul him off to the ship's tiny jail.

Leaving Mattis to wonder why he went so easily.

CHAPTER THIRTY-EIGHT

Rogue Planet Serendipity, Low Orbit
USS Midway
Patricia "Guano" Corrick's Quarters

Guano threw herself down onto her bed with an angry growl.

"So," said Doctor Brooks, settling into a chair beside her bed, but not before picking up an armful of clothes and gently pushing them onto the floor. "I'm guessing being a gunner didn't exactly work out for you, in terms of bringing out your fugue state."

"Nope," she said, practically spitting the words. "We flew out there, genuine combat and all. There were pew pews and missiles and an alien ship—but a gunner's cannons couldn't penetrate its hull armor, and we were too far behind to catch the missiles. So basically I just turned a whole bunch of perfectly good fuel and ammunition into a nice pretty bill for the US taxpayer. Then we landed. Debriefed. Now I'm here."

"I can understand your frustration," said Doctor Brooks, sympathetically. "But at least you got out there."

"Yeah. Too bad I was *garbage*." She angrily punched her pillow. "Damn it! This is pissing me off. I just wanna bring this thing out so you can study it and get it over with, but it just … it just seems like everything around me is working to prevent it from coming out, you know?"

Doctor Brooks was quiet for a moment. "Yes, actually, I do. Wanna hear a story?"

Guano groaned and rolled over onto her back. "Is this about your leg?"

"No," said Doctor Brooks, smiling a little. "This happened before that." He crossed his legs, putting his hands on his knee. "There's a mountain in Nepal that, as a young child, I wanted to climb."

"Mount Everest?" She narrowed her eyes. That was a bit … common, for someone like Brooks.

Doctor Brooks laughed. "There are more mountains in Nepal than Mount Everest," he said, shaking his head. "No. Fishtail Mountain … or as its known in the local tongue, Machapuchare. Everest is high, certainly, but Machapuchare is something else. It's steep—basically straight up at points—and it twists. It's brutal, despite being lower than some of the nearby peaks. To the local Hindus, the mountain is sacred to the god Shiva. I gave up on that dream after I screwed up my leg, but the fact is, I was never, ever going to climb that mountain, no matter what I did."

"Sounds like a challenge," she said, nodding understandingly. "But I mean … you could probably buy a tour or something if you *really* wanted to. Hell, just last year I heard some girl with some kind of horrible disability managed to climb Everest solo. People like climbing stuff. What's stopping you?"

"Not the leg, that's for sure. No, unfortunately, Machapuchare has never been successfully climbed before, believe it or not. In the 1960s, two groups tried and failed, and because of the risks on such a steep slope, the Nepalese government banned any further attempts after that. They backed it up by declaring the whole mountain a sacred site. Another team snuck in again in the late twenty-second century, but that's it. They failed too. Spectacularly so—they all died." Doctor Brooks clicked his tongue, sighing a little, although the smile remained on his face. "It's honestly pretty enlightening knowing there is a place on Earth—our homeworld, cradle of our people, the only home we knew for ten thousand years— where no human has ever set foot, and cannot ever set foot."

Guano snorted. "Aww, c'mon. Surely someone's snuck in and done it illegally."

"Can't," said Doctor Brooks, simply. "Machapuchare is not something you can really climb on your own, due to its difficulty, and if it got out a group was trying to make the attempt the Nepalese would absolutely block them from entering the country."

"Still," said Guano, closing her eyes a moment. "What's the point?"

"The point is … sometimes you can commit no errors and still fail. Sometimes you can have everything going right for you, you can tick every box and be the best, most perfect you can be, the absolute pinnacle of perfection in action, and still not get what you want." The edge of his lips turned up in a playful smirk. "But like the song goes … sometimes you just might find, you get what you need."

Guano couldn't help but smile too. "Yeah. I guess."

Brooks picked up one of Guano's shirts, with the blue and white splotched mil-standard camouflage pattern. "I like the Navy's camo," he said, bouncing the shirt in his hand. "I've always sort of thought, where are they hiding on a ship? They should be red, or orange, or yellow while at sea."

The answer was obvious to her, and knew it probably was to him as well being that he, too, was in the navy, but answered anyway. "It's made that way so that, you know, while you're at sea, if you fall overboard you'll blend in with the water so that the SAR craft can't find you."

"That's exactly my point, though. How does it matter in *space*?"

"See, doc'," said Guano, waving her hands around above her like she was painting an invisible picture, "you're not thinking military enough. You have to understand the mindset of government services. Things aren't just stupid, they're *catastrophically* stupid. That's how you train people to do stupid shit like get into fighter aircraft and submarines and space ships; you bombard them with inanity and idiocy so that they don't even question what they're doing." She snorted. "It's how you can differentiate people who *have* served in the military and those who *haven't*. Civvies are like, 'the military is a powerful, fine-tuned engine of destruction and precision carnage,' and vets are like, 'the military is the most stupid people you've ever met given the most high powered weapons money can buy."

The two shared a playful chuckle.

"Seriously, though," said Guano, "with the uniforms? The

idea is that if you get oil or grease on it, then it's not as prominent as on another color scheme. Plus it looks cool. Uniforms are recruiting tools as well as practical ones."

"I actually liked the Air Force uniforms," he said. "Blasphemy coming from a Navy man, I know, but they always looked the best. Totally impractical, of course. All that white would get filthy in the field...."

"Airman? In the field? Unthinkable!" Guano grinned at him. "They don't call it the *chair* force for nothing."

"Sometimes they get lost on their way to the *Glorious Humanity* coffee shops," said Doctor Brooks, and then, nodding as though having come to some kind of conclusion. "You were right, though."

"Mmm? About the coffee shops?"

"About why the military stresses people to ensure that during real combat they can survive and trust their training. True skill only comes through adversity. You weren't challenged in the simulator and based on what you were telling me, you weren't challenged by being a gunner, either." He leaned forward slightly. "So let's head back to the simulator, because I have a special program for you."

"Special program?" Guano scrunched up her face. There was just no way it could match to combat. "What kind of program?"

"Well, have you ever heard of the Kobayashi Maru?"

She propped herself up on her elbows. "What, from that ancient campy space show? Star Wars?"

"No, the other one."

She grimaced. "I've heard of it, what about it?"

"Because," said Doctor Brooks, his tone turning serious,

"that was child's play. You're about to experience a real no-win scenario."

CHAPTER THIRTY-NINE

Losagar System
Planet Waywell, High Orbit
The Aerostar

Smith dabbed a soaked tissue over his bleeding scratches as he rewatched the video he'd taken at Pitt's compound.

Useless.

He scowled. The angles were all wrong for lip-reading, and what words he could even *maybe* make out were too few and far between to piece together a general sense of the conversation. They might as well have been talking about the last night's opera, for all the good it was doing him.

Reardon wandered in, settling on the other side of the table in the ship's tiny living area. "So. What are you doing?"

Smith gestured towards his tablet in disgust. "Hitting my head against a wall."

"Huh." Reardon stared. "Hey, don't you have your own first-aid kit?" he added, pointing to Smith's makeshift wound-cleanser.

"Don't need it for this," he shrugged.

That, and he'd *found* the Reardons' medical supplies—or rather, what passed for them. *Money's in short supply right now* indeed. He wasn't entirely convinced he shouldn't sneak his kit aboard when he left. Just to help them out a bit.

"Sure."

The smuggler was being unusually quiet. Smith looked up, frowning.

"What the actual *hell* is going on?" Reardon burst out before he could so much as open his mouth.

"What do you mean?" the spy asked, voice deliberately neutral.

Reardon scowled. "You know what I mean. I call you to drop some information—already a risk—and instead of just taking it and buggering off, like any *sane* creepy secret agent, you drag Sammy and me halfway across the stars on some mysterious goose chase. Why?"

"Because," Smith took some time to fold his hands, picking his words carefully. "The prey I'm after is … powerful. Dangerous to have on official records, if only because he already has his fingers in those pies, and he'd know I'm coming for him. You know what that means. I need off-grid contacts, and I need them to be trustworthy." He pointed at Reardon. "You."

The other man laughed. "It's going to be dangerous, so you come to *me*? And *Sammy*? Wow, glad to know." Reardon groaned slightly. "You know I have a piece of cargo in my hold, completely unopened, and it's burning a hole in my hull … I haven't had the chance to even *look* at it yet, much less find a buyer and unload it."

Smith raised an eyebrow. "You *are* a career criminal. With an inordinate number of buttons marked 'pew pew' on your dash, so you're no stranger to violence—"

"Yeah," Reardon broke in before he could finish. "I *choose* which butts I'm going to kick. Me, calling the shots. Not you, not anyone else, because I don't do the entire 'beholden to other people' thing, you know? So, spill it. Why should I not dump you at the nearest space port and go back to my *life?* I have a hot cargo to sell."

He nodded slowly. "Do you remember Spectre, Reardon?"

The smuggler gave him a piercing look. "No. Not my problem. Court-martial made sure of that, didn't they?"

"Maybe," Smith shook his head. "I think he wants to make himself everybody's problem. I'm not really interested in seeing that happen—are you?"

"Is that what you were doing down planetside?"

"Sort of." He pushed the tablet forwards. "Looking into his allies."

Reardon stared at him for a long moment. "Ok, fine. Why do I care? You can get your own transport, I don't have to be your taxi driver. And I sure as hell don't have to live next to the target you're painting on your back, either."

Smith returned the gaze evenly. Reardon narrowed his eyes. "You hate the 'system,' right? Well, Spectre *is* the system. Top to bottom. He's the guy pulling all the strings." Not *entirely* accurate, but close enough. "It's the biggest middle finger you'll ever find."

Reardon's moronic grin reappeared. "You know, it's a myth that bigger is better when it comes to body par—"

"Reardon." Smith wasn't in a mood.

"Yeah?"

"Are you in?"

He paused. Then shrugged. "Old time's sake. What could go wrong?"

"Really?" Smith asked, fighting down an edge of frustration. "Why do you *always* have to say that?"

Reardon snorted as he walked around the table, picking up Smith's screen. "Jeez, imagine if your workmates knew how superstitious you are. They'd have to revoke your generic name privileges."

Smith ignored him and cleaned some more blood away from his eye.

"Hey," the smuggler remarked, glancing at the video. "That's not Spectre, is it? Guy's looking pretty fit these days."

"No, that's not him, and as far as I know Spectre is still ... jolly. That's America's Senator Pitt, and his dead son."

Reardon peered at the video. "You just took this, right?"

"Yes."

"And the second guy's the son, right?"

"Yes."

"He doesn't look very dead, Smith. I thought they taught you the difference between living people and dead ones at whatever fancy CIA academy you went to."

"He should be dead," Smith replied. "He died during the first battle with the *aliens*," he made air quotes with his fingers, "at the battle over Earth. Body found, identified, buried."

"A cover-up?"

"Where's the motive? Pitt Jr. was lined up to take command of the USS *Paul Revere*, his father was proud.

Nothing outstanding in his record, other than good service, no known debts—though if his father is working with Spectre, unknown debts are always a possibility, but otherwise he and Pitt Sr. come up pretty … well, not clean, one of them is a politician after all, but hardly dire."

"So whatever it is," Reardon stared at the screen, "the kid and his father have to be in pretty deep, and they're *really* trying to keep it on the down-low."

"Hmm. Yes." Smith contemplated for a moment. "Can you get anything of what they're saying? I can't make head nor tail of it, even with my eye."

"Stand aside technology, and make way for your inevitable betterment by man." Smith waited while Reardon stared at the screen. "Um. Well. From what I can see, you're not going to like this."

"Why?"

"They're literally talking about the weather."

Smith groaned. "Really?"

"Yup. Lip reading is an old smuggler's trait … I can sign, too. Sammy as well. It's always good to communicate in ways people don't expect, and to be able to intercept communications people think are secure."

Fascinating but irrelevant. "OK, well, can you get me a transcript? I have to make a call."

Reardon looked skeptical. "I can't get much from this, you know? I think they're mumbling. But yeah, I'll try."

Smith walked over to the other side of the room, bringing up a contact on his communicator. The phone rang about ten times before it was picked up.

"Chuck Mattis, speaking."

Smith was careful not to say his name. "Hi, it's me, I need —"

"Excuse me?" the voice on the other end of the line cooled abruptly. "I told you to never call me again."

Lover's quarrel? Reardon mouthed from the table.

Shut up, Smith mimed back. "Look, I wouldn't be doing this if it weren't life-or-death, buddy," he explained patiently.

"Great," Pitt's former aide replied. "Not my life, so why don't you just—"

"Jeremy Pitt is alive."

A long, long pause. "What?" His voice dropped to a hushed whisper. "Is this a *joke?* That's impossible."

"Yes. Yes it is impossible, utterly so. And yet I just saw him talking about the weather with his father."

"*What?*"

"Friend, I don't know how this is possible, but—"

"I promise you, I saw him go into the ground myself!" Chuck broke in. "This is … insane. If it's even true."

"We both know it's a risk to even be speaking. Notice the careful lack of me using your name? I wouldn't have called you if I had another option, and if I was lying—well, why would I bother with something so far-fetched?"

"…Shit." A pause. "I shouldn't have said my full name at the beginning."

"Nope, you shouldn't have, but we're going to move past that. All I need from you is Senator Pitt's itinerary for … the last few years. Can you do that for me?"

A pause—Smith suspected the admiral's son had simply forgotten he was on the phone and replied with a gesture. "Sure. Why not. It's only like I'll, you know, *go to prison* if I get caught because it's a violation of my parole. It's only like I have a family to take care of now. It's only like—" he whined loudly, a low, continuous tone which finally stopped. "Fine. It'll take me a bit to drag it up, but sure. What's a felony between friends? How do you want me to get it through to you?"

Smith rattled off a list of instructions, and soon the information was downloading over a secure channel.

Just as he was about to cut off the line, Chuck spoke up again, voice turning strange. "Hey Smith, you might want to know. There's been another attack, happened right now."

"The future-humans?"

Reardon looked up sharply.

"Yeah," Chuck replied. "Rogue planet, Serendipity. They're saying there's no survivors."

CHAPTER FORTY

Rogue Planet Serendipity, Low Orbit
USS Midway
Space Combat Simulator Room

When Doctor Brooks and Guano arrived, Flatline was there waiting for them, already suited up and obviously eager to go.

"So," asked Guano, casually. "How was flying a real, actual fighter instead of being a gunner?"

"I was great!" he said, making little finger guns at her. "I was, like, the Red Baron of fighter pilots. Pew pew pew."

"The Red Baron *was* a fighter pilot, moron."

"Sheesh. If you have to explain the joke … all I'm saying, is that I was *on fire!*"

Something in his tone suggested that he was putting it on. "You sure?" asked Guano, hands on her hips. "You seemed to be having a lot of trouble with, you know, just getting from point A to point B. Let alone actually doing any kind of engagement. You were too slow to get to the target, and too slow to catch the missiles, so … you were basically zero for two back there."

"Yeah," said Flatline, the facade falling away. "Look, I … I know. I wasn't good enough back there. But hey, bonus points —you *suck* at being a gunner."

She laughed, a flood of relief washing over her. "Well, okay, fair enough. We're both fucking awful at … not what we're specialized in. I think that's fair. We can handle that."

"We can definitely handle that," said Flatline, reaching out and giving her a playful clap on the shoulder. "Okay. You better play me some Kenny Loggins, because we are going into the Danger Zone."

"So I hear," she said, hooking her foot onto the ladder that lead up to the simulated cockpit. "Apparently it's a no-win scenario."

"Mmm," said Flatline, climbing up behind her. "Yeah. Problem with those simulations is, they never really take into account thinking laterally. That's how you beat the no-win scenario; you do something the programmers don't expect. Like, you know, say you're supposed to go out and engage a target, but when you get there, your guns jam. So that's it, right? You're done? Well, no. You can always, you know, retreat. Or ram them. Or dump your fuel and then ignite it using your decoy flares. And that's what you're *supposed to do in real life.* Think creatively. Cheat as often and as hard as you can. The best fight isn't fair; it's won before you even fire the first shot. If things go south you aren't supposed to just sit back and go, *oops, well, guess I should die now.*"

"Right," she said, sliding into her seat and clipping herself in. "It takes, like, twenty-four million dollars to train a pilot, gunner, or spaceborn technical specialist *a year*. A spaceworthy fighter craft is worth *two hundred* million dollars. You don't just throw them away. This shit is valuable. Contrary to what people might believe, and it really is dumb that I have to say this, *you aren't supposed to lose them*."

"Although," said Flatline, clipping himself in as well, "before the Battle of Earth we, like, did ditch a whole bunch of fighters overboard. Oopsie daisy."

She snorted and fired up the simulator. "Right," she said. "But that doesn't count. Don't undermine my point, dickhead."

Flatline swung the gun around as the simulator booted up. "So," he said, "did you learn anything about gunner life during your brief stint in the world's most awesome ejection seat?"

"Sure did," she said. "I discovered that on the ground you could power on the ventral turret and, from the gunner's station, swing the guns to them to fuck with the ground crew. I heard over on the USS *Walcott* they actually play baseball with them." She smiled. "We should do that."

"Only if you want an article fifteen," said Flatline, the joke obviously a little too on the nose for him. Not even a smile. "That's just one mistake away from a court martial."

"Yeah, but, think of the laughs." Guano adjusted her straps. "That's what I'm about."

"Huh," said Flatline.

What was *his* problem? She settled in as the various screens around the simulator lit up. The ship was in space, having just launched from a ship identified as the USS *Concord*, a fighter-carrier. She was flying out with eight other Warbirds, a heavy strike package. She tapped on the screens, bringing up her mission objectives.

> *- Depart from USS* Concord *as part of Alpha wing*
> *- Investigate RCS return at Objective Alpha*
> *- Destroy refueling station at Objective Beta*
> *- Return to USS* Concord

"Seems pretty simple," she said, turning the autopilot on and letting the ship steer itself to its objective. Their wingmen formed up around her. She glared at them. "Hopefully those simulated targets can fly good."

"Probably as good as any enemies we're going to face," said Flatline.

That was true enough, but it made her scowl. It was okay to dodge a joke or two, but to no-sell three in a row?

Something was wrong.

"It's idiot proof," she said, testing the waters again. "And fortunately, and I'm a real idiot."

"That's … not a good thing," said Flatline.

Fine. Be that way then.

The autopilot carried them far, far away into deep space. Slowly, as the minutes ticked away, Guano felt annoyance and frustration seep into her. Where was the challenge in this? And why was Flatline being so … flat?

They arrived at Objective Alpha. A blank empty space with a single comet drifting through it, a silent ball of ice with a ferrous core. That would explain the radar blip the *Concord* had seen. "Right," she said. "Onward ho, I suppose."

"So much for the no-win," said Flatline, as the ship turned to Objective Beta. As it did so, a light flashed on her console.

Incoming transmission.

She thumbed the talk key. "This is Alpha one," she said, hoping the computer would acknowledge her. "Send it."

No reply.

"Guano," said Flatline behind her, "behind us!"

She twisted her head around, and saw her wingmen—previously flying behind her in a V-shape—suddenly turned toward her, and she only had a split second.

Guano yanked the control stick downward, kicking out with her left foot. Space spun in front of the monitors as her ship pitched down and the missile-warning klaxon sounded in her ears. "Shit!"

The program had lured her into utterly empty space where there was no cover and no tactical opportunities, almost an hour away from rescue.

Cunning devils.

Virtual bullets darted over her cockpit, drawing silent streaks in space. Flatline's gun chattered behind her, and she flung the stick from left to right, reversing her ship and flying backward, hitting the fire button with her trigger finger and spraying space with bullets.

"Contact portside," said Flatline. "They're firing."

The computer played digital noises—tearing metal, explosions muted by the partial vacuum, and lights flashed on her console. She'd been hit, but how bad, she couldn't know. She lined up one of the fighters and squeezed the trigger. Gunfire slammed into the Warbird, small explosions covering it as the rounds detonated, and then the ship burst into an impressive fireball.

No time to think about it. Guano kicked out her left foot,

to bring her fighter around to the next one.

Her fighter didn't respond. A swift glance at her cockpit showed her why. Lateral thrusters had been damaged; she couldn't turn left. So right it was. She opened the throttle, her ship traveling forward once again, darting out of the line of fire. She rolled a hundred and eighty degrees, and used her thrusters to stop her momentum.

A missile burst beside the ship, spraying her with shrapnel. This would have killed her in a real fight—maybe—but the computer seemed to give her a shot. It, with seemingly cold precision, took away one of her missiles and halved her maneuvering ability.

"I winged one," said Flatline. "Got it good."

"Finish it off," said Guano, taking a deep breath. "There's kids in Africa who don't have any spaceships to shoot at all."

One of the Warbirds flashed in front of her, heading port to starboard. She kicked out her right foot, swinging the ship after it, and the missile lock tone sounded in her ears. She squeezed off a shot—the missile flew in a wide arc, slamming into the fighter and blasting it to pieces.

Interesting. She had expected the program to cheat and have it be a dud or something, but it seemed as though the program was confident.

Guano rolled again, to right her ship, and just as she got it straight, a missile flew straight into her cockpit.

SIMULATION OVER

"Oops." Guano grimaced. "Guess I didn't see that one."

Flatline chuckled behind her. "Life sucks, as is tradition."

Now he laughed.

"So," said Doctor Brooks, somewhat hesitantly. "That doesn't sound like the battle fugue to me."

It hadn't been. She groaned. "Nope. Nothing like that at all. That was just regular fighting and ... regular ole' dying, I guess." She grunted and thumped her fist on the console. "And it wasn't even a real test. What kind of no-win scenario was that? Just ... fly out into the open and die? C'mon. So *what?* You promised me something hardcore; that was just difficult. No different than the ship just exploding after takeoff. No wonder it didn't work." She twisted in her seat. "And you! What the hell is wrong with you?"

The vaguely uncomfortable look on Flatline's face told her nothing except he knew exactly what she was talking about.

"Mmm." Doctor Brooks paused for a moment, obviously considering. "We've tried twice now to make this thing happen in simulators, and judging by your heart rate, you were a *lot* more into this one."

That was true. She wasn't exactly sure why—maybe she wasn't trying to dodge Doctor Brooks's questions anymore, or maybe it was just a change of mood or way of thinking—but she had been a lot more engaged with that simulated fight than the previous one. "Yup," she said. "Didn't really feel anything though. I didn't ... I didn't even *try* to bring it out, dunno why. Either way, nothing happened."

"Maybe," said Doctor Brooks, "you just need to be in a *real* life or death situation."

Guano leaned out of the cockpit and stared at him, bewildered. "What exactly is *that* supposed to mean?"

Doctor Brooks smiled widely. "No more simulators. No

more tests. I'm reinstating you to full duty."

CHAPTER FORTY-ONE

Admiral Jack Mattis's Ready Room
USS Midway

Mattis cast one last look at his desk, making sure everything was neat, tidy and presentable for Admiral Fischer, and then he walked over to his desk, angled up the monitor that was embedded into it, and connected the call.

"Good morning, Jack," said Admiral Fischer, dressed in her full uniform. A brief moment of static came across the line, distorting her image momentarily before it resettled. "To what do I owe the pleasure?"

He put his hands on the edge of the desk, tilting his head. "Two things, I guess. Firstly … you've been awfully quiet since we launched. I almost began to think you weren't actually keeping an eye on me after all."

"I wasn't," she said, leaning back in her chair on the other end of the line. "I know you well enough to understand that if something were truly wrong, you'd just call me." The ghost of a smile came across her face. "Which means this call is somewhat worrying to me."

"It should be. I've been talking to Spectre. Our … *guest* … aboard."

"Spectre," she echoed, skeptically, her voice obviously curious. "Interesting. I … didn't know he was there. You can't honestly believe that's a real name."

"Not even for a second. As a matter of fact, I doubt basically everything that comes out of his mouth—and anything he does. And, I see you know him too. *Interesting*," said Mattis, carefully repeating her wording back at her. "But, you know, he's been right on the money about everything so far. Basically. I don't *want* to trust him—and I don't—but I am relying on him a lot more than I should be."

"Okay," said Fischer. "What does this have to do with me, and why I'm here?" She paused, considering. "Do you want me to talk to him? I can have a whole fleet of frigates come collect him. Just say the word."

That was slightly more than what he was going for. "No," said Mattis. "I'd rather keep Spectre on as short a leash as possible, and with as little contact with the rest of the ship as possible, if that's alright with you, Admiral."

"That's fine with me," she said. "I just want to make sure you're not being sent on a wild goose chase."

Plenty of geese out there. "I understand," he said. "Instead, what I need from you is something a little more … specific." Mattis tapped on his desk, bringing up a schematic of the local area of space and putting it on both his screen and hers. Through it ran a thick red line, intersecting nothing. "This is the future-human ship's projected path. As you can see, its course doesn't seem to make sense to us. Previously, their path lead to Serendipity—the rogue world we are now in orbit of—and that didn't make sense to us either. They're obviously looking for *things*. Things that are off the grid. Secrets that are hidden away from the public eye."

She leaned over toward the camera and studied the image intently, and after a moment, Mattis saw a profound, obvious wave of recognition come over her face.

"Admiral," said Mattis, gently but firmly. "I need to know what you know."

Fischer settled back into her chair, touching her chin with her hand. "And you say that Spectre gave you this information?"

Her deflection was obvious, but Mattis let it slide for now. "That's right."

Fischer tapped her jaw. "I would very much like to talk to him about this."

"And I'm sure we can arrange that," said Mattis, patiently. "But for now ... I need to know where the future-humans are heading. They possess a powerful weapon and a ship with surprising capabilities. They already badly damaged the *Midway* with their toys, and I haven't gotten a full report back from Commander Lynch about what he found down on the surface yet, but I'm guessing it wasn't good. Either way, I don't want to get caught off-guard again. No more than I need to."

"Well, you know as well as I do that senior Naval officers are expected to keep a host of secrets. It's part of the job. Some information needs to be kept on a need-to-know basis."

"I do understand," said Mattis, plainly. "Believe me."

She seemed, for just a moment, to be unwilling to

cooperate, then whatever guard she had put up slowly melted away. "Look, I trust you completely, Mattis. But I can't—I simply *can't*—talk to you about this without direct authorization from the President."

Interesting that she spoke of trust. A vanishing commodity in these times.

"Then get that authorization," he said, firmly. "Make the call." He paused, then added, "and get us some backup. That ship can kick ass. I don't want to be on the back foot when we find it; they won't be escaping from us this time."

Fischer nodded grimly and, with a resolute nod, adjusted her uniform. "I can't make you any promises, but I'll do what I can. Let me make some calls. Stand by for my update…." She reached over to close the link.

And he waited. Surprisingly, he only had to wait five minutes before her message came through. He read it once, then again.

"Dammit, Fischer, this is cutting it kinda close," he said to himself.

CHAPTER FORTY_TWO

Rogue Planet Serendipity, Low Orbit
USS Midway
Bridge

"Congrats, Commander Modi," said Admiral Mattis, grinning slightly as he caught Lynch's sour expression out of the corner of his eye. "Hope you enjoy your *leave*."

Modi's preening voice came through with no small amount of pride. "Of course I will."

"This ain't over," said Lynch, voice dripping with frustration. "The South will rise again."

"They haven't yet," said Modi, his tone matter-of-fact. "And I highly doubt they will in my lifetime. As for my leave … mmm. I haven't decided what to do with it yet; I have a substantial amount of leave saved up as it stands, so … I don't know."

Lynch growled into the communications link. "Are you kidding me?" He paused. "How much do you have?"

"Sixty eight days," said Modi.

"Sixty eight days?!" Lynch roared into the line like a lion. "Are you pulling my chain, Modi?"

"I'm perfectly serious."

Lynch glared at Mattis—how was this *his* fault?—and then hissed into the line. "You're a real sum-bitch, you know that?"

"Perhaps," said Modi evenly, "you should spend your leave more frugally." Mattis could *swear* there was an edge of sarcasm creeping into his voice. "Be more like me."

"More like you—?" Lynch caught himself, took a deep breath, and then laughed. "Okay, okay. You earned it."

"Yes," said Modi. "I did."

There was a brief moment of pause where Modi's completely serious tone threw him. "Uhh," said Mattis, "you *are* aware this … was just a game, yes?"

Modi was quiet for a moment. "I was not. Am I to understand there is no actual leave?"

Lynch stared at him. Mattis stared back.

"There … is," said Mattis, carefully, wondering how he could circumvent federal law and grant the man five extra days. Show him a needle, make him faint, and call it medical leave? "But the goal was to …" he sighed. "Never mind."

"As you wish," said Modi, "I look forward to enjoying those leave days at an appropriate time." Then he closed the link.

Modi. Just … Modi.

"You okay?" asked Mattis, curiously. "I mean, really?"

"Yeah," said Lynch, his smile coming easy. "Modi and I like to compete. In case you hadn't noticed. It's just … something we do. And sometimes the payoff is to watch just how seriously he takes it. Damn robot." He considered for a moment. "Still, pretty damn amazing how fast he got those engines up and running. Can't read between the lines for nothin,' but the man sure can perform miracles when you need them."

"How're the engines holding up?"

Lynch checked the instruments. "Just fine," he said, "but there's a note here from…" he stressed the name slightly. "*Modi* which recommends not traveling beyond sixty-six percent of maximum power. Just because, well, they did just get nuked. Makes sense. Honestly, it's a miracle they got it back up anyway."

"Modi's good at what he does," said Mattis, settling into his chair and watching the colors of the strange unreality of Z-space flitter by. "Can't deny that."

"Never did," said Lynch. Then he seemingly refocused, locking his eyes onto the console. "Okay. The trace shows we're coming up on where the future-human ship dropped out of Z-space." He glanced over his shoulder to Mattis. "Do we even know what's there?"

Mattis didn't know that, but couldn't *say* he didn't know. That wouldn't help anything. "Admiral Fischer's been making a lot of calls. If there's anything more out there we can learn, we're working on it."

That, seemingly, was enough for him. Lynch tapped on some keys. "Here we go," he said. "We should be dropping out of Z-space momentarily. Stand by…."

The light on the bridge monitors began to fade. This time, as the ship slipped out of Z-space, it wasn't smooth. The whole ship rippled as it transitioned, and the movement into real-space was a rough shove.

"Woah," said Mattis, gripping his chair a little harder. Fortunately the inky black field of real space appeared, dark and punctuated by a field of unblinking stars. He touched his radio. "Modi?"

"Everything is fine, Admiral," he said, sounding both harried and relieved. "The damage means things were a bit rough. But we got there."

That would have to do. "Report," said Mattis to Lynch.

"Z-space transition complete," said Lynch, grimacing slightly. "More or less. Scanning for targets." Almost immediately, the computers chirped, signaling a contact. "They're here. RCS, painting the target. They're right in front of us. Designating Skunk Alpha."

"Show me," said Mattis.

The main monitor snapped into focus, showing the hostile ship, battered and scarred from their weapon impacts. It was silhouetted against a huge gas giant, a massive marble floating in space, obscuring everything behind the target. It had its nose pointed toward a moon, the tip of it glowing as energy built up around it.

"They're getting ready to fire," said Lynch, his tone charged. "Looks like they haven't started yet. They probably weren't expecting us to get here so fast—so we got the drop on the sons of bitches." Lynch bought up the tactical section of his command console. "Getting ready to engage."

They could thank their special Chinese engines for that little bit of luck. But they couldn't play their card just yet. "Hold fire," said Mattis. "Ready strike craft for launch and open the hangar bay doors, but don't launch them yet. Prepare torpedoes for launch."

Lynch stared at him over his shoulder, wide-eyed. As did the rest of the bridge crew.

"We aren't shooting?"

"Wait for it," said Mattis, checking his watch. "Hold steady. …"

The future-human ship began to turn. It had felt the sting of their nukes already wouldn't ignore them a second time—Mattis knew that.

He was counting on it.

"Sir?" asked Lynch, worriedly, as the future-human ship continued to slowly spin toward them, its whole body opening up like a flower once more, revealing the ominous rows of missile batteries within.

"Steady," said Mattis. "Steady…"

"Sir," said Lynch, suddenly snapping his attention back to his console. "A ship is moving out from behind the shadow of the gas giant!" He stared at his instruments. "And another, and another. Designating Skunks Beta through Juliet—no, through Kilo." His tone wavered. "That's—that's ten ships, sir. And I'm not reading any transponders on them. No radar, nothing … not even any navigation lights."

"I know," said Mattis, letting the edges of his mouth curl up in a little smile. "If they did that, then the future-human ship would detect them as well." He touched his radio. "Admiral Fischer, please inform your ships to power on and engage at their discretion."

The future-human ship completed its turn, still far too distant away to fire, but it was beginning its slow advance towards them, fixated on the *Midway*. Behind it, a US Naval fleet flickered to life, powering on their systems and moving to engage.

"Mister Lynch," said Mattis, staring intently at the monitor showing the future-human ship. "Fire at will."

CHAPTER FORTY-THREE

Pinegar System
Gas Giant Lyx
USS Midway
Bridge

Gunfire leapt out from the *Midway*, a barrage of streaks against space that lit up the hull with bright lights as they darted toward their target. Though seemingly fast, the projectiles would take some time to reach their target, given the distances between them.

But their trap had been sprung. Mattis watched with grim satisfaction as their fleet powered up, the ship's computers flagging them from Skunk to their actual names: ten frigates, lead by their old battle comrade, USS *Alexander Hamilton*.

"Hail the *Hamilton*," he said. "I want to talk to Captain Katarina Abramova directly."

"*Midway* to *Alexander Hamilton* actual," said their communications officer. "*Midway* actual requesting to speak to

Alexander Hamilton actual on a secure line."

There was a brief pause. As Mattis watched, their first volley of shots went wide; the future-humans were using their device to deflect them, exactly as he had anticipated.

"Abramova here," came the thickly accented Russian, down the line. "What is a nice looking man like you doing in a place like this, mmm?"

Mattis couldn't help but smile. "Good to see you again, Captain. I'd offer to buy you a drink, but you're Russian; I'm afraid you would put me to shame in front of my crew."

"Such is the gift, and the curse, of being Russian." Abramova's voice was lighthearted. "Admiral, we are all Americans here, we can drink together when this is done. I'll go easy on you."

"You'll have to."

A brief pause as another wave of gunfire went out from the *Midway*—they had plenty of shells, might as well try it.

"What can I do for you, Jack?" asked Abramova. "Admiral Fischer was remarkably non-specific about our purpose here. I barely had time to scramble the task force after our resupply at the depot. The Jovian Logistics goons took their merry time on the restock."

That was good. He appreciated her discretion. "Well, you come in at exactly the right time. You see the future-human ship that's just floating between you and me? It's presenting its nice fat backside to you; and while we don't have the specs for that ship on-hand, if know anything about armor, it's always stronger at the front weaker at the rear. I'm giving you a prime shot here, so … if you can, say, blow it up, I'd greatly appreciate it."

"Ahh, Admiral Jack Mattis you really know how to woo a girl." Her tone changed as though speaking to someone else. "Commander Bourne, engage that target and destroy it. Relay the same command to the rest of the fleet."

Their second barrage went wide, just as the first one did, but then the rest of the fleet—all those blue dots—fired simultaneously, and a massive storm of explosives and steel leapt across the stars, streaking unerringly toward the future-human ship.

Exactly as Mattis predicted, the future-humans didn't swerve or in any way attempt to avoid the secondary barrage. It sailed in and then, just like the *Midway*'s rounds, all the shells were deflected.

"Draw the fleet together," said Mattis, drumming his fingers on the arm rest of the command chair. "We want to get this blasted ship between us. Pen them in."

"Aye aye, sir," said Lynch, grinning like a wild man. "I like that plan."

Mattis raised an eyebrow expectedly. "No witty Texas-ism for me to try and unravel?"

"I'm saving them, is all," said Lynch. "Don't you worry."

He wasn't worried about that. But as he turned his attention back to the future-human ship, other concerns of their own came through. "I was kind of hoping they wouldn't chase just us," said Mattis, watching the ship bear straight toward them, unerringly, its missile bays ready to fire. "Prepare to launch strike craft. Ignore the future-human ship; we already know they can't hurt it. Instead, target its missiles. That's their game plan. Let's head it off before it starts."

"Sir," said Lynch, frowning darkly as he looked over his

console, "I … I'm getting some *really* weird readouts from that planet."

"Little busy right now," said Mattis, as another volley of fire went out—with both ships accelerating toward each other, the distance had been closed quite rapidly. The wave of fire didn't *quite* get deflected enough; the shells bounced off the frontal armor of the ship, nearly half exploding in bright flashes before dying in the cold emptiness of vacuum.

Mattis knew that at that angle, they were unlikely to penetrate, but more worrying was how close the ship was getting. They would be in missile range soon… "Switch to flechette anti-missile," he said. "And ready torpedoes."

"They're ready sir," said Lynch. "We're waiting on the fleet."

"*Midway, Hamilton,*" said Abramova. "We are thirty seconds away from torpedo launch."

Thirty seconds. Mattis mentally counted down the seconds. "Fire when ready," he said.

And then the future-human ship fired, a blossom of its missiles bursting out in a wide spray, all of them turning toward the *Midway*, bearing down on them, each missile leaving a fiery red trail behind it.

"Belay that." They needed a better way of dealing with those missiles. "Lynch, adjust the warheads on the torpedoes. Have them detonate in between us and the enemy ship. Use the blast to destroy them."

"But sir," said Lynch, "without an atmosphere, there won't be a shockwave. There'll just be a flash of heat and energy…."

His mind churned at a thousand miles a second. "Doing that last time turned half their missiles into duds, and the two nuke hits *really* hurt them. Maybe the missiles' electronics aren't rad-hardened. It might be a weakness of their technology."

"That might well be it," said Lynch. "Hitting missiles with nukes is crazy, because everyone protects against it, so they didn't protect against it. Firing!"

"Torpedoes away," said Abramova. "Full spread."

The radar screen got extremely cluttered. Ten frigates, each firing two torpedoes, their ordnance a bright blue cloud angrily racing toward the rear of the future-human ship. The *Midway*'s own torpedoes raced out toward the incoming missiles.

Silence, as three sets of ordnance moved in space. "Spin up point defense anyway," said Mattis, his voice quiet. "And fire the main guns at those missiles. Take down as many as we can before our torpedoes get there. We're likely only going to get one volley, so make it count."

"Firing," said Lynch, and the quiet hum of the guns filled the room.

Splashes. Bright lights in space. A billion glinting shards shredded some of the missiles, dooming them to oblivion.

"Impact in thirty seconds," said Abramova. "Twenty nine, twenty eight…"

The *Midway*'s torpedoes intersected with the oncoming missiles, and every camera went white.

"Status report," said Mattis. "Tell me we got 'em."

Lynch spent a second staring at the radar screen. "Yup," he said, a triumphant edge to his voice. "We got 'em. Scope's clean. All vampires are trashed."

Slowly, the external cameras returned their vision, just in time to see the massive barrage of torpedoes, one by one, slam into the rear of the enemy ship. Once again the screen went white, washed out by energy in almost every spectrum.

And then, as it faded, Mattis expected it would be difficult to determine the effect from their front-on perspective. He needn't have worried. The future-human ship was a rapidly expanding cloud of gas, debris, and secondary explosions; little sparks against the black void.

"Skunk Alpha is trashed," said Lynch, proudly. "They are *super* dead. Great plan, sir."

A cheer went up from the bridge as the elated crew watched flaming pieces of debris tumble end over end in the nothingness.

Mattis relaxed into his chair, his back aching. He realized he'd been sitting up straight, ram-rod straight, for … well. For too long. Not as young as he used to be.

"Uhh," said Lynch, blinking in surprise. "Admiral, those readings from the moon…."

Now was a good time. "Give it to me straight, Lynch. What the hell's going on over there?"

Lynch shook his head in bewilderment. "I don't know," he said. "It—it just makes no sense. The amount of energy I'm seeing is *massive* … beyond that which even the future-human ship can use. It's like that but turned up to a billion. Like we were looking at—"

A flash of blue light cut him off, and the strange moon cracked, broke apart as several sections of the crust *lifted up*, just like what had happened at Zenith, and then imploded; pulled into itself by some kind of horrible force, the pieces of it tumbling and fragmenting towards the glowing center.

"Oh my god," said Mattis, staring in horror at the display. "That's…."

"That's impossible," said Lynch. "Fuck me."

The pieces of the moon shrank away to nothing and all that remained was a swirling vortex, barely the size of Earth's Alaska, hovering in space … and behind it, the gas giant, seemingly oblivious to the loss of its moon.

"What the hell just happened?" asked Mattis, but nobody had an answer.

CHAPTER FORTY-FOUR

Losagar System
Planet Waywell, High Orbit
The Aerostar

Harry Reardon washed his hands in the small sink in his quarters, flicked them dry, then made sure he was composed.

Serendipity ... gone.

Some of his best friends had lived there. It was impossible to believe they had all been killed. Smugglers always had a way; they always managed to find some way to survive. Those slimy bastards would have gotten away ... definitely would have gotten away.

For sure.

He opened the door and stepped out into the main area. Smith was there, waiting for him.

"Sorry," he said, "call of nature."

"Well, you should have let it go to voicemail." Smith tapped on his tablet, then turned the device around to show

Reardon. It was a list of system names. "I have that contact of mine on the line. He found us something we can use. Senator Pitt's itinerary for the last five years."

Reardon let out a low whistle, sitting opposite him. "Who's this mysterious contact you keep calling?" he asked.

Smith just gave a wry smile. "Can't reveal that," he said. "The poor guy's in enough trouble already."

"I can hear you, you know," said a voice on the other end of the line. "Just stop talking about me, okay? I'm not exactly thrilled that you got me up in the middle of the night—*again*—to go on one of your errands. I had to find one of Pitt's assistants who *doesn't* know my face and sweet-talk the information out of them. It wasn't easy."

"I know," said Smith. "But just relax, okay? We're going to sort this out."

There was a brief moment of pause, and then the voice dropped to a whisper. "I gotta go." A green light on the tablet's screen turned red.

Smith lay the tablet down. "Sorry," he said. "My contact is a little … skittish right now."

He could see that. "Senator Pitt's a powerful man," he said. "And his son … I guess he's pretty powerful too, although I don't know if zombies are, you know, powerful or not.'

"They are," said Smith. "Typically."

Reardon blinked skeptically. "You … have a lot of experience with zombies?"

"I have a lot of experience with a broad amount of things," he said. "You know that."

"Yeah, but, *zombies*."

"That experience come from old films," said Smith, a little

smile that carried just an edge of shit-eating-ness on his face. "So, you know…."

Reardon groaned. "Okay. Anyway. That aside … what's all this *mean*? Senator Pitt, other Pitt dead but not dead, the alien attacks that aren't alien … what ties them all together?"

Smith opened the timeline of Pitt's travels and, together, the two of them dove into its contents.

As a raw, unfiltered file there was just so much raw *stuff* there that Reardon started to get a headache. It showed every last meeting that he'd been to, every Z-space trip he'd made, every planet and system and asteroid he'd visited and the full list of every settled place he'd put his boots on.

But the more disheartened and overwhelmed Reardon got, the more confident Smith seemed to get. His prosthetic eye darted around, drinking in information from the tablet, seeming eager to acquire more.

Eventually, Reardon went and got coffee for the two of them, and checked in on Sammy. When he got back, Smith was grinning like a triumphant little kid who had just solved the puzzle.

"What?" he asked, sliding into his seat.

"Figured it out," said Smith, showing him the tablet. "Here. Every place Pitt has been, right?" He tapped the tablet. The list shrank considerably. "Now cross-referenced with everywhere that the future-humans have attacked." Smith mockingly waggled a finger. "But we're not done yet, because … some of these places aren't exactly open ports of travel, you know? Like Serendipity."

"Lovely place," said Reardon, forcing his tone to be wistful and almost completely failing. "Ahh, memories of gambling away the earnings from a good job."

"Shame they all died," said Smith.

Reardon grimaced despite himself. "Looks like their luck ran out. Hazards of the gambling life, I suppose."

"Right. Well, unfortunately for Pitt, in order for him to have been there, he could only come at certain times. So we can narrow that down even further. And what do you know…" He tapped again. The list shank down to just a few places. "Pretty much six months before a place gets hit, right on the dot, Pitt visits it. Combined with every place Spectre has been during that time … and I bet he's there too."

"Okay," said Reardon. "So you're saying … we can guess where he's going to hit next?"

"Exactly."

"Where?"

Before he could answer, Sammy's voice cut over the conversation. "Harry! John! The radar's screaming about some fighters who are heading right toward us!"

"Fighters?" Harry stared. "What?"

"There's some kind of black fighters—hard to get a good radar fix. Coming in fast."

Reardon stood, tilting his head up to talk. "What does it matter if they're black?" he asked.

"It doesn't, you idiot! They're just *colored* black!" Sammy groaned. "Fine, fine. They're … ebony."

"Made out of wood?" said Reardon, patiently, but thumbed towards Smith indicating they get down to the two rail gun turrets.

"No, they're just … wait, are you fucking with me?"

"I would never." Reardon pointed down a hatch that had

opened up at the touch of a button that was labeled, 'More Pew Pew'.

"What have I told you about fucking with me?" Sammy was shouting over the comm.

"To not do it." Reardon took a seat in a firing turret, indicating the other to Smith, and flipped power to the controls.

"Listen, *Harold*, I told you—"

"Calm down, cupcake. We're in the turrets. Now let's show these bastards what happens when you go up against the Reardon brothers."

Smith tried to power on his turret electronics. Nothing. "Uh ... Reardon? When's the last time you had these things serviced?"

When was it again? Recently? Reardon pulled at his control stick. Nothing. "Well ... shit."

CHAPTER FORTY-FIVE

Pinegar System
Gas Giant Lyx
USS Midway
Bridge

The vortex spun slowly in space, a two-dimensional rift in the fabric of space where a moon had once been.

"Report," said Mattis, trying to recover his composure, and restore some discipline to the bridge. "What just happened?"

"I … I don't know," said Lynch. The stark confession was as shocking to him as the actual destruction of the planet. "It looks like … it looks like the whole mass of the moon was turned into energy, at once, and then that energy was used to create a *massive* spatial-temporal disturbance. It's … it's unlike anything I've ever even read about."

That much was obvious. There *was* someone who might know something. "Modi?" he asked into the radio. "What the hell is going on out there?"

"S-standby," said Modi, something Mattis was rapidly learning to mean, *I have absolutely no idea.*

He turned to the marines on the deck. "Fetch me Spectre," he said. "Bring him here. Right now. I want answers. I want—"

"Sir!" Lynch almost shouted the words. "Look!"

On the main screen, the vortex shimmered slightly as though being seen through a warped lens. A visible aura of energy extended out from it, rings of light that expanded, contracted, and then drew right into the centre of the maelstrom.

From the heart of the vortex, the bow of a ship emerged, seemingly unconcerned with the massive torrent of energy whirling around it. It was the same dark metal and red lines of power that the vanquished future-human ship bore; but this one, unlike its defeated friend, was undamaged.

"Designate that ship Skunk Bravo," said Mattis, ominously, "and order the rest of the fleet to engage it at once. Ready torpedoes and guns; prepare vector strike craft to engage. See if they can find a weak point."

"Aye aye, sir," said Lynch, and the whole bridge sprung back into action, both the joy of their victory, and their confusion at seeing the moon disappear, gone in an instant.

His command console flashed. He, as the CO, was receiving a private communication; he put it through to his earpiece.

"*Midway, Hamilton* actual," said Abramova, her tone painted with amazement. "Are you seeing this shit, Jack?"

"Regrettably, I am." Mattis stared at the main monitor as the future-human ship pulled completely away from the vortex and began maneuvering, turning toward the *Midway.* "We are getting ready to engage. Spread the fleet out, but maintain formation; I want the *Hamilton* at the tip of the spear when we engage that thing. I don't know where it came from, and I simply don't care; turn it to scrap."

Her tone betrayed her eagerness. "With pleasure, Admiral. USS *Alexander Hamilton* moving to engage."

A glance at the radar screen showed it to be true. The fleet, lead by the *Hamilton*, had turned from the debris-field that was Skunk Alpha and aligned their guns to the new threat. Against the inky blackness of space, bright flashes heralded a wave of fire that raced toward Skunk Bravo. At almost the same time, the *Midway*'s guns spoke, firing their own volley.

"Strike craft away," said Lynch. "Wings Alpha and Bravo are en-route, Charlie launching in twenty seconds. The fleet is also launching strike craft…" his tone became charged. "And Skunk Bravo is *also* launching. Looks like a whole bunch of drone craft. It's going to be one hell of a dogfight over there, sir; suggest we patch in our fighters so that we don't get into a blue-on-blue situation."

"Do it," said Mattis. As he watched, scores of red, angry-looking fighter craft flew out of the enemy ship like a kicked wasp nest.

Lynch blew out a low whistle. "I count nearly two hundred fighters from that thing," he said. "That's nearly ten times what we can put out. And they launched them all almost instantly."

Mattis gripped the armrests of his chair. "Just keep focused," he said.

The first volley of shells flew past the future-human ship. One or two, the outliers, clipped the edges of it, splashing into nothingness. The ship retaliated, firing angry red streaks at the rest of the fleet from turrets that protruded like warts from its otherwise blocky, smooth surface.

"Definitely a different configuration," said Lynch. "Looks like this one doesn't have the planet-shaker weapon … but it does have a mighty amount of guns and strike fighters."

The other one had not been expecting a fight, but this model seemed to be looking for one. "Keep firing," said Mattis. "Lemme know when we get into torpedo range."

"Will do," said Lynch. "We don't want to fire too early, or we risk them countering it."

It was always a waiting game with these kinds of weapons. Missiles simply travelled too slowly to be used outside of close quarters, and *everything* in space was about distance. "As soon as you have a clear shot you take it, understand?"

"Yes sir," said Lynch. "Torpedoes standing by for firing solution. We're closing the distance now."

The *Midway* raced toward the hostile ship. But, unlike last time, their contact seemed to be hanging back; it floated in space, unmoving, near to the vortex that had brought it to the battlefield, although its guns were blazing and its strike craft seemed more than happy to move further out.

But not the ship itself.

"What's it playing at?" asked Mattis, glaring at the monitor. "Surely, if it has missiles like the other ship, it wants to get close too…"

Abramova spoke into his ear. "*Midway, Hamilton* actual, priority alert: we are detecting another energy surge."

Lynch was already showing it on the monitors. The vortex was fluctuating again, surrounded by energy rings, and once more came through a warship, just like the first.

"Designating that ship Skunk Charlie," said Lynch, an edge of frustration to his voice. "Dammit. Now there are two of them."

"I see it," said Mattis. "And I can count too. Get us closer; we need to use our torpedoes on those bastards and finish them off before more arrive."

The second ship formed up beside the first, clearing the way for, presumably, more ships. That wasn't good.

The ships drew closer to the vortex, the *Midway* on one side and the rest of the fleet on the other. From each vessel came waves of fire that splashed off both targets with seemingly minimal effect; the explosions blackened their hulls, and left glowing red penetrations where the shells hit, but they didn't seem to be able to get through the hull completely.

Still, it was something.

"Ten seconds to estimated effective torpedo range," said Lynch, "and forty for the rest of the fleet. Should we delay for a barrage?"

Now that there were two ships, it didn't seem worth it. "No. Just fire as soon as the torpedoes are loaded and primed."

"Aye sir," said Lynch. "Three, two ... firing."

Twin missiles leapt away from the stern of the *Midway*, heavy nuclear-tipped missiles streaking away from the ship toward their target. The rest of the fleet fired shortly afterward, their missiles like the fingers of a dozen giants, jabbing and thrusting toward their enemy.

"The vortex is fluctuating again," said Lynch, "another ship is appearing. Designating Skunk Delta."

Mattis swore under his breath. Space between them was full of gunfire and fighters, all turning and banking and blasting each other with missiles and guns. "They're bringing in more ships and we haven't even managed to do more than piss off the first one," he said, watching the torpedoes draw closer. "But hopefully this will—"

Both ships, Skunk Bravo and Skunk Charlie, vanished in a pair of white flashes.

"Did they just execute a Z-space translation?" asked Lynch, incredulously, and then he corrected himself. "Skunk Bravo and Skunk Charlie emerging from Z-space. They micro-jumped."

Impossible. A ship's Z-drive needed immense power to jump; most ships couldn't keep their Z-space engines charged during a combat footing. But … he'd just seen it happen with his own eyes.

"To where?" asked Mattis, searching at his radar screen. Then he saw.

The future-human ships were right behind them, with the third in front, and a fourth one emerging from the vortex, only seconds away from joining the fight as well.

They were flanked.

CHAPTER FORTY-SIX

Pinegar System
Gas Giant Lyx
USS Midway
Hangar Bay

Back on the flight roster. Guano felt so *good* as she raced toward her Warbird, the scramble klaxon wailing in her ears, the boots of her flight suit clomping on the metal deck.

"Hey," said Roadie into her ear. "Guano. Guano! I see you, what the hell are you doing on my flight deck?"

She laughed and grabbed hold of the ladder that lead up to her cockpit. Even the *ladder* felt so much more real than the simulator. "Doctor Brooks approved me back onto the flight roster," she said, laughing as she started to climb up.

"Bullshit he did!" Roadie's voice sounded strangely distorted, as though he were shouting inside his tiny little helmet. "He's a goddamn fucking dietitian, not a medical doctor, he can't make that decision. It's *my* decision. And you are *so fucking grounded*."

"Jeez, Daddy," she said, swinging herself into the cockpit and settling in. "You're really going to ground me during a red alert?"

Roadie's tone shifted. "Yes." He actually sounded genuinely angry, his yelling replaced by cold, evenly-paced words. "I won't endanger this flight if you're not fit for duty. Lieutenant Corrick, step out of that ship right now."

"He approved me," she said, plaintively. "He did. I swear."

Roadie's voice was completely devoid of any kind of humor. "If you're lying to me, Lieutenant Corrick, this will in end in a dishonorable discharge."

For once she wasn't actually bullshitting him. "It's true."

The silence on the line was *palpable*. She could practically *feel* Roadie trying to see if she was lying. That or give her cancer with sheer, absolute force of will. Finally, he spoke. "Fine. You get to fly. This time. *This time*. But when this is done —"

"Yeah, yeah, yeah." Guano tapped on keys on her cockpit instruments, initializing the power-up sequence. "Yell at me later."

"Ooo," said Flatline into her ears. "You called him Daddy. Heard he likes that."

Guano clipped herself in, making sure the ejection seat was primed and ready to go if she needed it. "And how would you know *that?*" she asked, grinning like an idiot. "You fucking Roadie, Flatline?"

"No. I don't yank the chain of command, if you know what I mean. I would though. Have you seen his abs? That guy works out." Flatline swung the turret around, checking that it was functional. "I mean, I'm straight, but no one's *that* straight."

"True," she said, bringing the engines up to power and tapping the talk key on her radio, indicating that she was good to go. "This is Guano, we are go for launch."

"True?" Flatline chuckled playfully in her ears. "Something you wanna tell me, Guano?"

She felt vaguely odd, sitting there with one hand on the throttle and one hand on the control stick, waiting for the hangar bay doors to finish opening and for launch approval to come. "Huh?"

"Are *you* fucking Roadie?"

Guano hesitated just a fraction of a second but that was long enough.

"Oh. Oh. My. *GOD.*"

Her cheeks flushed. "No."

"Yes!"

"No!"

"Yes! Yes you are! Ohooooo!"

"Stow it!" Guano ground her teeth together. "Flatline, I am definitely not knocking boots with Roadie, okay? I promise you. Absolutely not. I'm *not.*"

"But you hesitated," said Flatline, seemingly more excited than she had *ever* heard him be. "You hesitated!"

"Shut the fuck up!" she hissed, trying to think of a way out of this shit, but nothing came to mind. "Look, it … it-it was a long time ago."

Flatline hollered loudly, kicking at the back of her chair. "Holy shit! Holy shit! Holy *shit!*"

She felt her whole face burn bright red. "Look, it was *one time*, before he was even CAG, a billion years ago—"

"Guano and Roooadie, sitting in a tree! F-U-C-K-I-N-G!"

"One time!"

"F-U-C-K-I-N-G more than one time!"

"You know," she said threateningly, "the pilot's seat has the *option* to simply eject the gunner."

"First comes love, then comes marriage, then comes Guano with a demented baby in the carriage!"

Guano groaned and put her head in her hands. Why the hell did she say anything… why the hell did she *confirm* it…

"You fucked! You guys fucked! You fucked like inbred bunnies! You fucked on the *couch*, you fucked on the *bed*, you fucked in the closet—"

"In the *closet*? What? No! It was just that one time!" She wiggled the control stick to test her systems, sending little puffs of gas in all directions, desperate to not talk about this any more. "A-after the Officers Ball, when we were doing all those shots, we were drunk, it doesn't mean anything—"

"This is the greatest thing in the *world*. I can't believe this. This is going *straight* on the walls of the Ready Room. You guys are going in the Hall of Shame! Hah, man, could this day get any—"

A light flashed on her console. "Oh, look at that," she said, opening the throttle as far as it would go. "Time to go."

Jerking forward, her Warbird darted out into space, almost ramming into the back of the ship in front of her. She pulled back in time, the wild maneuver turning Flatline's gloating into panicked shrieking.

"Guano!" roared Roadie in their ears, "did you forget how to fly? Stay in formation or I'm going to kick your arse so hard you'll be tasting boot polish for a month!'"

"Daddy's mad," said Flatline, his tone teasing. "He going to spank you again?" His voice became high pitched. "Oh Daddy Roadie, *give it to me, ohhh, oooh … lemme see your joystick!*"

Guano groaned audibly. "Sorry," she muttered, and pulled her ship back into formation with Wing Charlie as the three wings of fighters soared out from the *Midway*, racing toward their target; a ship surrounded by blue light, and behind it, a massive brown gas giant.

"Hey," said Flatline, the levity evaporating from his voice. "Wasn't there a moon there just before?"

The observation took all the embarrassment away, replacing it with a strange kind of foreboding. This wasn't a simulator … if they died here, there were no do-overs.

She put those kind of thoughts to the back of her mind and focused on flying in a straight line, the rest of her wing on all sides.

"Contact," said Flatline. "We got a bunch of bandits right ahead."

She checked her radar screen. So many of them. Over a hundred. More like two. They were heavily outnumbered.

Just the way she liked it.

Guano locked up the nearest few fighters and got ready to dump all her missiles at once. There was no point hanging onto them; all around her, her sensors told her that the rest of the strike craft were doing the same thing.

"Fox three," she said, holding down the missile fire trigger. Her ship shook with the force as all her radar-guided missiles flew off their racks and leapt toward the enemy; given the massive amounts of hostiles in the area, she prepared to fire her much shorter range heat-seekers almost immediately. They would find something, even if their main engines burned out, the guidance systems and proximity detonators would take at least one fighter each out with them. "Fox two," she said, dumping the second wave of missiles.

The missiles streaked toward their targets, bursting silently in the black, multiple secondary explosions silhouetted against the gas giant making bright, playful little flashes as the missiles found their mark.

And then, right as the two flights got close to gun range, and a bright red projectile streaked past her cockpit, suddenly, it came.

Utter calm. Focus.

"Hey Flatline," she said, thumbing the master arm on her guns off. "Tally. I'm feeling it."

"You're…" his voice suddenly sounded relieved. "You mean the thing?"

"Yeah," said Guano, locking up her first guns target. "Let's kick some arse."

CHAPTER FORTY-SEVEN

Losagar System
Planet Waywell, High Orbit
The Aerostar

Harry jiggled the control stick of the dorsal rail gun turret of the *Aerostar*, but nothing. The HUD projected on the glass lit up; it was just as Sammy had said. A bunch of little fighter craft, five of them in total and all as black as night, flying directly toward them. A big red cross was painted across his gunsight, along with the words:

SYSTEM OFFLINE

"Sammy, bring the guns online!" said Reardon.

"They are, bro!"

"Mine is off too," said Smith. "Is the ventral gunner position supposed to be on lock down?"

Reardon swore and pounded a fist on the console. The

words flickered and disappeared. "See? Just got to be firm with her."

"Ahh," said Smith. There was a brief pause. "Holy shit, you've installed some serious weapons on this thing since I was last in here. Are these 75-caliber guns?" He whistled loudly. "Oh boy, you've upgraded. And you are going to spend a long time in prison if anyone ever catches you with these things."

He had kind of hoped that Smith wouldn't see them. "That's why," said Reardon, "we house them inside 45-caliber gun barrels with 'big thick coolant sleeves.' Most cops can't tell the difference and don't think to look inside." He swung his turret around. "Anyway, point being, we got fighters incoming. Let's take 'em out. Sammy, charge the Z-space drive, we gotta get the hell out of here."

"Righteo," said Sammy. "Charging." There was a brief pause. "Do you want me to pull the lever marked *in case of missiles?*"

Reardon grimaced. He'd been saving the electronics countermeasures package for a special occasion. A special occasion like fighters with radar-guided missiles getting ready to blow them up. "Why the hell not," he said, grinding his teeth together. "If we get blown up by those fighters, how am I going to get to try out all the other things I've been saving for a rainy day?"

Smith snorted. "You really are something," he said.

A volley of ship-to-ship missiles flew past the *Aerostar*, jerking and turning wildly as they chased phantom RCS returns. The ECM package had not been cheap, but evidently it was worth every little penny he'd paid for it. Still, though….

"Hey Reardon," Smith said, his voice annoying. "How

come you don't have money to fix the airlocks and make them work reliably, but you have money for all the illegal toys in the world?"

"Never question a man about his toys," said Reardon, pointing his turret toward the incoming red dots. "They'll be coming in for gun-runs now, and despite what you might believe, I don't exactly have a nice little trick stored away for that scenario."

"Apart from the 75-calibre guns," said Smith, pointedly.

Reardon whined and squeezed the trigger, sending twin streaks of gunfire toward the incoming craft. "Apart from the 75-calibre guns," he confirmed, watching eagerly as the rounds splashed against the lead fighter, blasting it into fragments.

"Nice shot," said Sammy.

"Damn right it was," he said. "Pay attention kid, you might learn something." He squeezed off another burst, but it flew wide.

"Nice shot," said Sammy, this time sarcastically.

Smith hadn't fired yet. "You okay down there?" asked Reardon, as the fighters broke around them, swarming like a host of predatory hyenas.

"I'm fine," said Smith. "Just … gathering information about them."

A fighter flew in front of his arc of fire. Reardon's turret tracked it, gun chattering as it sprayed death after the bothersome little creature, but he barely scratched it. "How about you shoot first, record later?"

"Fine," said Smith. A faint rumble from below signaled him shooting, and one of the fighters vaporized. "That's one for me, and one for you."

"Great. To quote an old favorite: don't get cocky," said Reardon, grumbling loudly as he tried to line up another shot. A line of gunfire zoomed past the turret, one round bounced off the transparent material, cracking it ominously. "I'm fine," he said.

"Nobody asked," said Smith, his own turret chattering angrily. His chair shook with each shot.

One of the fighters looped around, bearing down on them once more. Reardon lined his gun up with the thing. It was so close he could see the insignia overlaid on the cockpit. Like a hydra, with ten or twelve tentacles coming out, enveloping the composite shell of the cockpit. Where the hell had he seen that before...? No time to think. He squeezed the trigger.

The drone fired as well, twin streams of fire overlapping as they crossed over, his high velocity rounds blasting the thing into debris.

But then the spray of gunfire splashed over the *Aerostar*, and the ship's metal screamed as the stutter of fire raked across the top side.

"Sorry," said Sammy. "I tried to dodge."

Yeah, well ... try harder. Reardon grit his teeth as the spiderweb cracks on the turret glass got thicker, wider, spreading out like angry fingers.

He leaped out of his seat and hopped out of the turret, sealing it. Right as the door hissed closed, the turret blew out, spraying gas and glass into space.

"You okay?" asked Smith, voice nervous.

Reardon deliberately said nothing for a second, then, "Yeah."

"Okay." Smith's gun fired two short bursts, and then, "All

targets destroyed."

"Z-space translation complete," said Sammy, relief painting his voice. "We're safe."

Not that it mattered, since all the fighters were destroyed. Reardon wandered back to the main living area of the ship, whistling playfully. "All in a day's work," he said. "Hey Sammy, did you grab any shots of those things?"

"What, like pictures?"

"Yeah."

"The combat computer took video. I can grab a few stills."

Reardon nodded. "Ok, zoom in on the cockpit and take a good look at that insignia. And run it against records. I swear I've seen that thing before."

"You broke the turret," said Smith, grimacing as he sat down. "And your gunners' seats are super uncomfortable."

"That one's made for Sammy."

Smith raised an eyebrow. "You let him come down here and shoot?"

"Why not?"

"It's just … I don't know. You seem so protective of him, and then at the same time you have him do these incredibly dangerous things—"

Reardon cut him off with a raised finger. "Look. We can handle ourselves. He can handle it. He's handled it since he was fifteen and his mom died and I had to start hauling him all over the galaxy with me so we could feed ourselves and buy his jacked-up-expensive meds. I don't need a lecture from Mr. C. I. A. Spook about endangering minors."

Smith shrugged and held up his hands defensively. "Hey. Sorry. I was just saying."

"Saying what?"

"Nothing. I was saying nothing. Look. I can tell how … I mean … It's clear how much … aw shit."

Reardon dropped the finger and started to chuckle. "Spit it out."

"It's just, I'm impressed, Reardon. I really am. You put on this badass take-no-prisoners cold-hearted facade, uh, I mean other than the pink ship and the fruity girlie drinks. You're this hardened criminal smuggler who shoots up thugs who get in his way, and yet at your core, you're an old softie."

"Softie?!" Reardon looked incensed.

"I mean … a good guy. A real good guy. Not everyone would be so devoted to someone that depends on him as much as Sammy. Color me impressed. It's certainly changed my opinion of you."

"Aw, shucks, Jonny." He tapped his chest and mocked some emotion. "You make me feel it. Right here. You know." The smirk returned. "Look. Sammy is brilliant, and competent, and can look out for himself. He don't need no babysitter. In fact, I'd trust him more than you to pilot a ship and keep me alive."

Smith smiled. "Exactly. Look how far you've brought him. Reflects well on you, Reardon."

An uncomfortable silence, only interrupted by Sammy's voice blaring over the speakers. "Look, guys, I hate to interrupt the love-fest, but I found something."

"What is it, bud?" said Reardon.

"I don't know—I'd like to tell you, but can you too stop smooching and keep your hands off each other for a few minutes?"

"Cut the shit and tell me, kid."

"Right. So remember the babes we tore up on Zenith? The ones who pulled the guns on us and tried to take the cargo *without* paying us?"

That's where he'd remembered the insignia. The Weird Sisters. It was on their ship. "So. Babe number one and babe number two. They were contracting for … what was it? Jovian Industries, or something?"

"Close. Jovian Logistics and Supply."

Smith swore. "You've got to be kidding me."

"What?" both Reardon brothers said at once.

"Jovian. It's one of Spectre's companies. Well, it's not *his*, but he's got considerable influence there. Tell me again, what was up with this cargo?"

Reardon shrugged. "The seller didn't say. I was just supposed to be an untraceable middleman. Seller delivers to me, I deliver to the Weird Sisters, and they transport to the final destination."

"We need to find out what the destination was. And what the cargo is."

"I can cut it open…" began Reardon.

"No. Don't tamper with it yet—we might still want to deliver it and have them think you never peeked, whoever *them* is. There's got to be another way to figure out what's in there, and where it was headed."

Sammy cleared his throat, which, over the comm, came across as terribly scratchy. "Well, fellas, I guess I could look it up in the Weird Sisters' computer."

Reardon rolled his eyes. "Kid, the Weird Sisters are chunky salsa and their ship has been ground into fine dust along with the rest of Zenith."

"Well, yeah. Unless if someone … accidentally of course … hacked into their computer and ran a data-dump. If I recall, I did tell you, but in fairness, you were being shot at at the time."

Smith and Reardon both looked at each other, and Reardon grinned. "Told you he could take care of himself." He cocked his head up toward the comm. "I thought you told me you were *taking* a dump. Fine. Out with it, kid. I can tell by your voice you've already checked.

"Looks like there were lots of different identical cargos. Ours was just one of them. All headed towards … believe it or not, US military ships."

"Huh," said Reardon. "I don't suppose it's just a super-secret-classified piece of military hardware that the top brass can't trust their regular suppliers to deliver?"

Smith glared at him. "Right. Cause *that's* how the US military operates."

"If you only knew." Reardon shook his head. "Ok, kid, does it say what's in the box?"

"Nope. But I've got a destination for *our* box."

"Am I going to like the news?"

"USS *Midway*. Mattis's ship."

Holy shit.

Smith pulled out his communicator. "I need to warn Mattis."

Reardon blinked in surprise. "What? At a time like this?" He glared at Smith. "We just nearly got killed; those things had shitty, weak-sauce guns, yeah, but they had a *lot* of missiles. Where did they come from? Why didn't we detect them sooner? And if they're Spectre's, why the hell is he trying to kill us? We barely know anything, and you want to just call up old Admiral Jack Mattis on the phone and say, hey man, I think there might be a plot to … do … something … bad. *That's* your plan?"

"And why," said Smith, dialing absently on his phone, "does a logistics company have advanced fighters, and the people to pilot those fighters? No. Something big is going down."

Reardon blew a puff of air. "Well, two planets just exploded because of a maybe-alien ship. Understatement of the year."

Smith finished the call initiation and started to wait. "It's all finally starting to come together for me. The specific locations of the attacks. Maxgainz. Spectre. The pattern is undeniable. And we need to figure it out before we're all dead."

"Why the hell do aliens want to kill us?"

"*Aliens.*" said Smith, rolling his eyes at the word. "I have to warn Jack Mattis." He glanced up. "And if there's one thing I'm learning from all this: there's no such thing as aliens."

CHAPTER FORTY-EIGHT

Pinegar System
Gas Giant Lyx
USS Midway
Bridge

A brief moment of stunned silence stole everything on the bridge, finally broken by Mattis.

"We have to get out of here."

The simple command galvanized the bridge from *controlled offense* to *steady defense.*

"Yes sir," said Lynch. "Working on it!"

"Order the strike craft to merge with those of the frigates," said Mattis. "We are pulling back to the rest of the fleet. Regroup with the USS *Alexander Hamilton*, and link up with the rest of the frigates. Present a united front."

Lynch muttered something darkly, and then thumped his fist on his console. "Dammit, sir, another ship is emerging from the vortex. Designating Skunk Foxtrot."

They were eleven to five, possessed the advantage of numbers and of not having to defend a fixed point, but the future-human ships had such great capabilities that Mattis *felt* outnumbered. A swift glance at his radar readout showed the situation was deteriorating rapidly. The five hostile ships were moving to surround them in a sphere.

The *Midway* rocked as a barrage of gunfire struck her stern, and the wailing of alarms rang throughout the bridge.

"Decompression in deck six," said Lynch. "We have a hole in the rear hull."

Dammit. The enemy was attacking their weakest points … the sides and rear. "Coordinate with the fleet," he said. "Focus fire on one ship—Skunk Charlie. Cripple that bastard and blow us a hole to escape from."

"Aye sir," said Lynch, fingers flying over his console.

"*Midway* actual to *Hamilton* actual," said Mattis. "We could use a hand here."

"I was wondering when you were going to ask." Abramova's voice sounded stressed. "Tell us what you need us to do."

"Throw everything the fleet has against Skunk Charlie," he said. "They're presenting their ass to you, so get in there and nail them."

"Aye sir," said Abramova. "Torpedoes away. USS *Hancock*, move into position and engage."

"Aye aye, Captain," said Captain Peter Bowe. Mattis vaguely remembered meeting the CO of the USS *Hancock* at some formal dinner or something. Good guy. "Standing by!"

The *Midway* shook as wave after wave of fire rolled over it, the flash of the explosions on her hull drowning out the view from their cameras. Through the blasts, barely visible, the *Alexander Hamilton*'s torpedoes roared in, spearing into the ship marked Skunk Charlie and—with a bright flare like a miniature sun in front of the gas giant—burst into flaming debris.

But Skunk Foxtrot, the new arrival, pointed its nose toward the *Hancock*, and with a surge of energy, fired its red lance—using the same gravity pulse that had devastated Zenith, Serendipity, and now the former moon below.

"*Midway*," said Bowe, his signal coming through heavy with static. "That weapon … gravity based. Our structural integrity … —ifty-eight perce— … failing. … and we're pulling back —"

But the USS *Hancock* and three nearby frigates crumpled like drinking cans in the hand of a giant, their hull plates cracking and buckling, folding as it was collapsed down under an intense gravimetric force, smashed smaller and smaller, until they were too tiny to track.

Just gone.

"Sir," said Lynch, his tone gilded with horror. "Another ship is emerging from the vortex."

And then Mattis knew they were in *serious* trouble.

"Where the hell is Spectre?" he asked, brow furrowing with anger. "I want him up here. Now."

CHAPTER FORTY-NINE

Pinegar System
Gas Giant Lyx
Patricia "Guano" Corrick's Warbird

Time to kick ass.

The battle fugue washed over her like a high tide and suddenly she was ready. She kicked her foot out and jammed the control stick to the left and back into her gut, squeezing the trigger on her guns in three swift bursts, each one raking along the top of an enemy drone in quick succession, blasting them to oblivion.

"Jesus," said Flatline. "I forgot how intense this was. Contact left! Contact left!"

She let him take care of that one, alternating feet on the rudders, sliding her ship from side to side in space, keeping the throttle open. Red streaks flew past her, the enemy projectiles barely missing her ship and vanishing off into space, or falling down toward the gas giant below them. There was movement everywhere; the ships from the rest of the fleet joined the merge, dozens of friendlies hurtling through the melee, spraying gunfire everywhere. The drones from ever more hostile cap-ships continued to pour in, heedless of their friends' destruction, guns spitting fire and death in every direction. Space was criss-crossed with lines of fire, dotted with burning debris and the occasional missile screaming toward its target.

But to Guano, the world was moving in slow motion.

She carefully selected her next target; a gentle tap of the trigger blew it to oblivion. She *sensed* movement beside her and threw the ship into reverse thrust, slamming her forward into her restraints, as a hostile drone fighter darted in front of her eyes. She opened the throttle forward again, sliding sideways and spraying the ship in the tail, sending it spiraling toward the gas giant, trailing flame and smoke.

For every one she killed, six more joined the fray.

"I got one on us!" said Frost, Roadie's gunner. "He's right behind us! Shit!"

With barely a glance, she saw Roadie's ship amongst the massive dogfight, a bright blue dot in a sea of green fleet-ships and red hostiles.

"Hold tight, Charlie-1." Calmly, easily, Guano tilted her ship forward, giving her gunner a perfect shot. "Flatline, waste them." She took the opportunity to blast the fighter in front of her with gunfire.

Her Warbird's gun turret chattered, the sound muted as it travelled through the hull of her ship, and then Frost's voice came through, infinitely relieved.

"Thanks, Flatline! You're the best!"

As though some other force guided her, Guano navigated the battle like a fish through a bubbling stream; she turned, shot, turned again, making sure to give Flatline a clean shot at their enemies, always keeping the craft steady whenever he needed to shoot. She zipped around debris and incoming gunfire, barely saying a word, as calm as if she were reading the weekly newspaper.

It was a dance amongst the drones, a ballet in the dark, a symphony of flame and gunfire.

And then it all went wrong.

The missile alarm warning screamed in her ears, something she didn't expect. At all. And it jolted her out of the fugue.

"Look out," shouted Flatline. "Two of them, right behind us! They're painting us with their targeting radar!"

And then, right behind them, one of the enemy fighters loosed a missile and her whole cockpit lit up with warnings.

CHAPTER FIFTY

Earth
United States
Georgetown, Maryland
Presbyterian Hospital

Chuck just couldn't quite look at his phone as it rang. He told Smith never to call him. And yet he had, twice in two days.

He was tempted—sorely, sorely tempted—to just ignore it. To be a man of his word and make a stand, here and now, about this issue.

Being in a hospital with his sick kid was bad enough. Especially when the triage nurse gave a shrug when he asked her what could be wrong with pale little Jack.

But try as he might, he just couldn't let the phone ring out. He answered it with a click.

"*What?*" he snapped into the line.

"I'm sorry."

Anger got the better of him. "Yeah, well, you *better* be

sorry," said Chuck. "I told you not to call me at home; you called me twice now. I tell you leave me alone, you won't leave me alone. You ask me to break the law. *Even when I told you that I'm already in deep trouble*, and you know it, and you ask anyway. I have half a mind to just hang up right now!"

"I know, and I'm sorry."

Chuck took a long, deep breath and slowly, slowly let it out. A trick he'd learnt from his dad. "Okay," he said finally. "Lay it on me."

"Okay." Smith, similarly, took a long breath. "Here's the thing. There's this guy. A British guy. His name is Spectre. He's got his hands on everything; in corporations and governments and probably even smaller businesses and organizations all around the galaxy. Powerful guy, always hiding in the shadows. And he has it in for your dad. The problem is … we think— and we think this with pretty good reason—that the … *things* … from the future are actually trying to kill him. *Him*, Spectre, personally. Not all of us. Him. And that's why they're here."

"That's why they're here?" Chuck stared out the window of the hospital waiting room in bewilderment. "To … kill some Brit?"

"It's … difficult to overstate how powerful this guy is."

"Clearly." Chuck grimaced and fidgeted with the lint in his pocket. "Right, so, what you want from me?"

"Nothing illegal, and nothing even challenging. We just need you to call your dad and let him know. Let him know not to trust Spectre. Let him know that it's *him* they're after … and, you know, maybe to do with that what he will."

He paused, waiting for the *but* or the *and* which he knew would have to follow, but it didn't. "That's it?"

"That's it."

Chuck smiled despite it all. "Sure. I can do that."

"Okay," said Smith. "Let me know me when you're done."

Chuck hung up, then selected his dad's number in his phone and dialed.

It rang for almost a minute and then stopped.

Huh. Well, an Admiral was a busy guy. And probably hundreds of lightyears away. Chuck tried again. And again, it rang out.

And again.

And again.

And again.

Chuck stared down at his phone in bewilderment. Normally the device would have alerted him that someone was trying to get through, and his dad would have picked up, even if he was in a meeting or asleep or something.

What in the devil was the old man *doing*?

The door opened. The doctor walked in.

His face was grave.

"Mr. Mattis? Please come with me. We need to talk about your son."

CHAPTER FIFTY-ONE

Pinegar System
Gas Giant Lyx
USS Midway
Brig

Spectre casually hummed a tune. The ship rocked all around him, and muted explosions found his way to his ears. The marines on guard stood impassively, resolute in their duty, although he could sense their unease. How they felt powerless standing guard during a time of war.

So, instead, he hummed. Not for any particular reason but because he wanted to. Something quintessentially British. Stout and brave.

It was all about painting a picture. He added a few words to the humming.

"It's a long way to Tipperary,
It's a long way to go.

It's a long way to little Mary
To the sweetest girl I know!
Goodbye, Piccadilly,
Farewell, Leicester Square!
It's a long long way—"

"No singing," said one of the marines. The *Midway* shook again to accent his point.

"That's a bit unsporting," said Spectre. "Especially since we're all going to die and all."

"No talking," said the marine, a little more forcefully.

Oh, fine. Spectre just sat there on the cell's cot, swinging his legs idly. Any minute now his people would be contacting him—being in the brig was, ironically, the best place for him to be at that very instant.

And there it came. A faint chime in his ear, as though from far away bells. It was the implant signaling him.

Casually, as though scratching an itch, Spectre rubbed his arm, tapping out a quick signal.

You've finally had some success.

"Hey," said the marine, looking directly at him. "What are you doing?"

"Itchy." Spectre gestured to his seemingly bare arm, confident that the prosthetic skin wouldn't be visible to even a trained eye, let alone a grunt on a ship.

The marine glared.

"I have a question," said Spectre. "If I tried to escape, would you shoot me in the leg?"

"No," said the marine, his eyes narrowing in frustration. "Centre of mass only."

"That's not very sporting," said Spectre, just trying to get a rise out of him. "Sounds like excessive use of force to me."

The marine's obvious frustration grew. "There's a reason why aiming for the arms, legs, etc isn't taught in any military, police academy, self defense class, or paramilitary school … *ever*. Because it is essentially impossible to reliably hit the extremities of a human in such a way as to disable them, and that's at a gun range against a static target. Not in a volatile, real-world situation where if you fuck up, you will be turned into chunks of meat and given a state funeral. So I'll be putting my sights on your centre of mass."

"I wouldn't count on it," said Spectre.

The guard shouldered his weapon. "You *want* to die?" he hissed, jabbing the weapon at him. Obvious stress reaction to the combat raging around them.

For a moment, Spectre thought he might *actually* do it, and so accordingly shut up, but then the marine seemed to receive some kind of transmission. "The Admiral wants to see you on the bridge," he said. "Now. C'mon! Move!"

The door swung open.

Spectre casually stood, brushed off his suit, and extended his palm to the two marines. A hum filled the air and then the implant in his hand discharged, shocking the two of them and throwing them back against the bulkhead. Their crumpled bodies twitched as they lay there.

"I told you not to count on it," he said, reaching up and brushing back his hair.

Now he had a few minutes quiet before people started to ask questions as to where he was.

Perfect.

He wandered over to the small locker that held his personal belongings and withdrew his tablet, tapping on it furiously. Only a few minutes.

That would be time enough for what he needed.

When he was done, he sauntered up to the bridge, finding it engulfed in endless, bothersome shouting back and forth, back and forth, as people gave reports about various things.

Rather than waste time with anything, Spectre just walked right up to the one called Commander Lynch, and handed him his tablet.

"Here," he said, smiling a polite smile. "You're going to want to see this."

CHAPTER FIFTY-TWO

Pinegar System
Gas Giant Lyx
USS Midway
Bridge

Mattis stared intently at the radar display monitor, steeping his fingers. Every ship was a chess piece … every decision a move which would bring either deliverance or ruin.

The door to the bridge opened and Spectre walked right in like he owned the place, handing over a device to Lynch. Where the hell were the marines?

Mattis blocked out the transaction. Spectre had taken his time getting here and he obviously had something for Lynch, something so important he didn't even ask for permission to enter.

His command console flashed with another piece of flash traffic. "Admiral Mattis," said an unfamiliar, panicked voice. "This is Captain Fiona Bassi of the USS *Lafayette*. We're losing atmospheric integrity, and our reactor is heavily damaged. Torpedoes offline, most of our guns are dead and what we have, we'll slave to your firing computers so they can be operated by remote. I'm giving the order to abandon ship. Don't forget to pick up our escape pods when you win."

If we win, he wanted to say, but kept such remarks to himself. "We won't forget about you, *Lafayette*. Godspeed."

The link closed. Mattis hoped to meet Captain Bassi after all of this. He flicked his monitor to show her ship, battered and broken from too many weapon hits, its hull lit up from within, obviously on fire. Escape pods drifted away from the vessel, their computers guiding them into an orbit around the gas giant.

"Lynch?" he asked, glancing his way. The guy was busy reading Spectre's tablet.

"It'll have to wait," said Lynch to Spectre. Then he turned his attention back to Mattis. "Sir, another ship is emerging. Designating Skunk India."

The future-humans had continued to increase in number, and now were up to the letter *I*. And while they had blown two of the enemy ships to atoms, with two more ships floated awkwardly in space, listing aimlessly with fires on multiple decks, they themselves were down three ships, four including the *Lafayette*, and the *Midway*'s hull armor was starting to wear away in places. Most of the remaining frigates had some kind of damage to them, some of them critical.

The *Lafayette* wouldn't be the only ship whose crew would be recovered from escape pods.

"Fire torpedoes," Mattis said. "Full spread, target that new ship—Skunk India. I don't want them joining the fight fresh.

They don't seem to be able to maneuver or redirect our attacks with their gravity weapon when they're emerging, so let's use that to our advantage."

"Yes sir," said Lynch, tapping in the commands. "Torpedoes away."

Skunk India, a fortunately immobile target, just sat there as the torpedoes plowed into its topside, bursting it like an overripe fruit.

"Nice call, sir," said Lynch, grinning like a wild jackal. "I think we should get all of them like that."

"First," said Mattis, cautious and not too eager to celebrate a victory too early, "we have to make sure to get rid of the ones we already have. My space is a little crowded right now, Mister Lynch. Reload those torpedoes as quickly as you can. Secondly—" he pointed to Spectre. "You. We need a weakness. Something we can exploit."

"You could give me my ship," said Spectre. "It's still in your hangar bay after all. I might be able to—"

"No. Not going to happen."

Spectre smiled friendly-like. "Then I'm afraid I can't help you."

"Great. Then stay out of the way."

"Certainly," he said. "Please don't get the ship blown up while I'm on it."

As if to accentuate his point, another ripple of fire ran up the length of the ship. "We're taking too much damage," said Lynch, "and the frigates are starting to lose damn combat effectiveness. The *Lafayette* is evacuating, the *Dawes* isn't responding to hails and isn't shooting anything … I don't know how much longer we can hold out."

"Tell me some good news," said Mattis, glaring at Spectre for just a moment, infuriated by the man's playful smile.

"I think the vortex is shrinking," said Lynch. "And it looks like ships are coming out at a slower pace. Maybe they're running out … or maybe they can't keep the vortex open indefinitely."

Well, now, that was good news. "Okay. Now we just have to figure out how to get out of here before there isn't a ship left to do it."

CHAPTER FIFTY-THREE

Pinegar System
Gas Giant Lyx
Patricia "Guano" Corrick's Warbird

The missile alarm tone screamed in her ears. Stunned, and with the fugue disrupted, she didn't know what to do. A yellow light flashed on her HUD, urgently informing her:

MASTER CAUTION

"F-flares!" Guano stammered, her training kicking in suddenly. "Flatline, pop flares, chaff, activate broad spectrum ECM!" She flung open the throttle and jerked the control stick back against her gut, the force crushing her back into her seat. She had to outmaneuver the missile. It was a bright yellow dot on her scope, flashing angrily. Her craft vibrated angrily, almost humming with energy as she flung it around.

"No joy," said Flatline. "Flares ineffective! Chaff deployed

—Guano, punch it right now!"

She risked a glance in the rear view screen. Her ship accelerated away from a sea of bright red flares, and twinkling puffs of chaff, but there, streaking directly toward her ship, was the missile, a thin red exhaust plume behind it.

The thing seemed to ignore their flares, their chaff, and the ECM suite in turn. Worse, it seemed almost supernaturally maneuverable, twisting and turning to keep up with her, its engine flaring whenever it needed more power, and cutting out when it needed to turn, preserving fuel.

Shit. Shit shit shit.

"Flatline, shoot it. Shoot it!"

His guns chattered behind her, but the shots went wide. "It's not exactly that easy!"

The missile closed the distance with frightening speed, seeming to almost feed upon her fear. She fishtailed, swerving her ship from left to right, but the evil thing's tracking seemed perfect. All around her the battle raged—a piece of debris the size of her fist slammed through one of her ship's stubby wings, tearing a jagged hole in her ship. A shot from an enemy fighter—red and angry—slammed into the underside of her ship, doing who-knew-what damage.

Distractions. Too many distractions. She felt panic rise up in her, threatening to freeze her limbs solid. All she could do was kick out wildly, jerking the ship from side to side, hoping to shake it.

"Guano, it's gaining, Guano—"

"I know, I know!"

"Slice left, hard left, go!"

She already was, the stick hard over. The Warbird spun as

she fought to shake the thing.

"If you kill us, Patricia, I'm going to be fucking *pissed!*" Flatline let off another burst. "Scoop it. Get the nose away from the flight path!"

Options. She needed options. Her head swung around as though on a swivel, trying to find something—anything—that might help.

Then she saw one of the future-human cap-ships, closing into the melee, probably to provide fire support for their fighters.

"I have a crazy idea," she said, and banked the fighter toward the cap-ship.

"No," said Flatline, and she could see him shaking his head at the edge of her vision. "No, no, no, no, no, no, *no, no, no, no, no, no!*"

"Yes, yes, yes." She zig-zagged toward the cap ship, then powered directly toward it, the missile in hot pursuit. Around her, alarms screamed out their warnings.

Flatline pounded on the back of her seat. "Vector away from the cap-ship, Guano! They're going to blow the hell out of us!"

No way that was going to happen. Guano felt cold all over. She knew her little fighter was more maneuverable than any missile. It would suck—suck a lot—but … it was the only option.

She waited until the very last split-second, when the missile was almost on top of them, and she disabled the grav-safety and jammed the stick back into her leg.

The crushing weight of inertia mushed her into her seat. The human body could only sustain 9g sustained turns, but it could survive much more than that for brief periods. 15g … 17g.

Guano was gambling on the turn being brief.

Her vision swam, and a black curtain rapidly descended over her face. *BLACKOUT WARNING* flashed in bold red letters in front of her HUD, but she didn't relent. If she passed out, she would die. Her flight suit squeezed her legs, forcing blood into her upper body, an uncomfortable, painful sensation designed to keep her awake.

"Unnnggghh…" Flatline moaned behind her, similarly incapacitated.

The wall of metal that was the enemy cap-ship raced close to her, her vision fading…

Then the fighter crested the bow of the ship, and the missile behind her smashed into the future-human ship, as Guano almost passed out.

"-ey," said Flatline, his voice groggy. "Gu- … Guano … wake up."

She struggled through the fog. "I don't wanna go to school today," she murmured, then snapped back to her senses.

They were drifting in space, well away from the dogfight, their momentum having carried them away from the battle.

"Report," she said, checking her instruments. They were okay … everything was okay.

"We're good," said Flatline, laughing with relief. "We shook the missile, and we even gave it a little *return to sender*, if you know what I mean." He thumped the back of her chair with his fist, cackling like a moron. "This battle fugue is great."

"Hah," said Guano, her hands shaking just a little from the effects of oxygen deprivation to the brain. "That one was all me."

"Okay," said Flatline. "We're getting an order to recall. We gotta get back to the *Midway*, stat."

"Righteo," said Guano, turning her nose back to their mothership and, with a flick of her wrist, turned on the autopilot, letting the fighter's computers take her home.

"You okay?" asked Flatline.

"Yeah," said Guano, "but I don't think we're done yet."

CHAPTER FIFTY-FOUR

Pinegar System
Gas Giant Lyx
USS Midway
Bridge

Mattis gripped the armrests of his command chair tightly. "We need to break out. Lynch, can we charge the Z-space drive if we adopt a purely defensive posture?"

He shook his head. "It'd take twenty damn minutes, Admiral, or longer. You know damn well that ain't an option."

He *did* know damn well. "Modi," he said, touching his radio. "I need your magic up here."

"What do you need? I am … overwhelmingly busy down here."

"I'm sure you are," said Mattis. "But we're encircled, and I need a way to get the hell out of it."

Modi's voice conveyed hesitation. "That is beyond my area of expertise. I do not even know why you're asking me."

"Well, I've heard it said that you should never make an engineer mad. They tend to get explosive."

"I'm not that sort of engineer," said Modi.

Damn.

"Actually sir," said Lynch, curiously, "I do have something." He held up the tablet Spectre had given him. "The gravity pulse from our new engines. Apparently—" he shot Spectre an annoyed glare. "It can be used to repel objects at a distance, in a much smaller, much more restrictive manner similar to the gravity pulse weapon the future-humans use."

He'd left the line open. "Modi? Did you catch that?"

"Certainly did," said Modi, "and I'm working on it. I might very well be that kind of engineer after all."

"I'll take what you can give me," he said.

Spectre chimed in. "It *will* work," he said, "you just have to be careful of hitting your, ahem, *remaining* ships. Get them to form up with you and punch a way out." The *Midway* shuddered again as it was repeatedly hit. "It will work."

Mattis really, *really* did not want to trust Spectre in any way at this particular juncture, but he knew he had no choice. "Make it happen," he said. "Lynch?"

"Yes sir," he said. "I'm working on it now. It'll require extra power from the engines, which I'm sure Modi won't be happy about given their state—"

"Given the state of the engines—" said Modi, but Lynch cut him off.

"I know damn well the state of the engines! Just do it you damn robot!"

Mattis risked a glance at the radar screen. Only two ships were reporting combat ready; the rest were silent—blown to debris, or too badly damaged to even move. "*Midway* actual to USS *Hamilton*, USS *Gage*, priority alert: we have an option to get out of this mess. Stand by for instructions."

"Aye aye, Admiral," said Abramova, her voice laced with fire, Russian accent coming through thick. "We have all the survivors from the *Hancock* that we're going to be able to get."

Mattis grimaced as another wave of fire hit them, followed by the wailing of alarms and the ominous creak-groan of stressed metal.

"Hope this works," muttered Lynch.

"It had better," said Mattis. Or they were all dead.

"Ready down here," said Modi.

Mattis took a deep breath to steady his nerves, then touched his radio. "*Midway* actual to USS *Alexander Hamilton*, USS *Gage*, form up with me; make a wedge. "

"Confirmed," said Abramova. "*Hamilton* on your port."

"*Gage* on your starboard," said the captain of the USS *Gage*, whose name he did not recall.

"Then let's get the *hell* out of this kill zone." Mattis glanced to Lynch. "Activate the gravity drive. Push those bastards out of the way, and clear the road."

The screens on the bridge shook and shimmied as power was diverted away from various systems, and emergency batteries struggled to keep up the load.

A noise he had never heard before spread throughout the ship. A low, pained groan, like a beast in agony, reverberating from the walls, and a shudder ran through the decks, deep and ominous, signaling something dire which he did not truly understand. Everything seemed to bend and warp, as though the ship itself were being squashed, twisted, flexed.

But it worked. The future-human ships tilted as they were shoved violently out of the way, clearing a hemisphere around the blockade. The *Midway*, with the *Hamilton* and the *Gage* fast behind them, tore out of the gap, heading to the horizon of the gas giant. If they could get behind it, they could be safe … for a time, at least.

Closer and closer it came, with the *Midway*'s engines straining under the load. The ship fired its guns off the stern, rear torpedo tubes loosing another volley, and the future-human ships—disorientated by the gravity push—seemed unwilling to pursue.

For a second he thought they might, actually, make it.

Then a lone torpedo, a single missile, drifted out toward the USS *Gage*, lazily, like a fat wasp coming in to sting. Point defense shells exploded all around it, but heedless of the maelstrom it tore through, dug into the ship's aft, and detonated.

When the light of the explosion cleared, the *Gage* was gone.

The *Midway* and the *Hamilton* sailed on, around the horizon of the gas giant, and finally, everything was quiet.

CHAPTER FIFTY-FIVE

Pinegar System
Gas Giant Lyx
USS Midway
Ready Room

With the gas giant interposed between them and the vortex—and the future-human fleet seemingly content to lick their wounds, regroup, and try and recover their damaged ships —they had a break in the battle which Mattis was infinitely grateful for.

The ship's shifts were changed, the significant damage the ship had taken throughout patched up as best they could, and a stocktake was made of their ammunition.

Plenty of torpedoes left. That wasn't the problem, however. They didn't have enough shells for the main guns to have another sustained engagement, especially with the anti-missile flechette rounds, and the USS *Hamilton* was almost completely dry on everything, plus their forward hull plating was cracked and weakened.

Then came the bad news. Modi was requesting to see him in person. Modi finally arrived in his ready room looking forlorn, and even Lynch didn't say much.

"Sir," said Modi, saluting crisply—something Mattis realized he had rarely seen him do, except where necessary. "There's an issue with the repairs."

Whenever Modi said there was an issue, it tended to be either tiny, or huge. "What's the problem?" asked Mattis.

"The issue is … systemic," said Modi, his tone conveying the most sincere apologetic tone Mattis had every heard in a person. "A warship is more than simply a collection of plates. It has a framework. It has a skeleton. A skeleton made out of metal. The stress of using the damaged engines in the way we did, along with the ship's numerous battles … the metal superstructure of the ship is riddled with micro-fractures. Almost the whole ship. Down to her bones. She's an old woman with osteoporosis, brittle."

Weren't they all. Mattis considered a moment. "How do we fix it?"

"At some point," said Modi, heavily, "you can't fix a thing. The process required to cut out the pieces of damaged superstructure and replace them with new ones will, by sheer necessity, create more weak spots. The ship's not engineered that way nor, really, can it be. The Ship of Thesus is a myth; some parts of a boat simply can't be replaced. Engines, yes. Computers, yes. Even the wiring and hull plates. But not her skeleton. This kind of metal fatigue is why airframes get retired, why cars eventually become unroadworthy, and why ships eventually get drydocked." He winced, visibly, as though in great pain. "This isn't something we'll be able to work our way out of, sir."

He didn't accept that. "But—"

Modi shook his head. "Sir, all the faith in gods or overengineering can't keep physics at bay. I've seen the damage myself. It is real."

"It's real," echoed Lynch, somberly. "He brought me down to show me before we brought this to you. The superstructure's … sir, it's like frayed wood. Splintered everywhere. If we were an ocean-going vessel we would be floundering, but because there's no gravity outside, and *only* because there's no gravity outside, we're holding it together. Push the ship too far and she'll break."

Mattis put his chin in his folded hands. "What do you suggest we do?"

"Retreat," said Modi, simply. "Initiate Z-space translation, and head back to Earth. It'll take us months to get there at the speeds we'll need to travel at, in order to not tear the ship apart, but we'll get there. Dock at the shipyard, and have the *Midway* stripped for parts and salvage."

"Or," said Lynch, a fire creeping into his tone, "come around the other side of the gas giant, and let those future-human mother fuckers have whatever we've got in the tank. Take out as many of them as we can, with our nukes, with our guns, with our everything, until there's nothing left."

"I can't just withdraw and let our adversary build up strength," he said, shaking his head firmly. "If we let more and more of them come through—let them establish a defensive line, maybe even manufacture space-gun-platforms or otherwise fortify the vortex they've made, then we're only

making problems for ourselves and our people in the future."
He looked to Lynch. "But I also cannot take this ship on a
blaze-of-glory run with unclear objectives, limited resources,
and accordingly, no real chance of success. The *Midway* and her
crew deserve better."

"A'right," said Lynch, "what do you suggest we do then,
sir?"

He considered. "Modi, this damage to the superstructure.
How does it affect our combat capabilities?"

"Ironically," said Modi, curiosity gilding his words, "the
hull plating—that which absorbs the majority of weapons
impacts—was largely undamaged by the gravity drive, and still
remains effective. The issue is with maneuvering. If we push
the engines beyond about forty percent, for a short Z-space
translation, that should be fine; we'll slowly be worsening the
damage, which will, eventually, cause the ship's hull integrity to
fail and she'll break up, but as long as we don't push it beyond
sixty percent … it should be okay for a short stint. Above sixty
percent, in a *limited* burst—no more than an hour—would be
very unwise."

"How unwise?"

Lynch grimaced. "Sir, my gran used to say … *sometimes the
juice ain't worth the squeeze.*"

"I concur," said Modi. "Let's just say, that I do not wish to
remain aboard if that's the case, given the alternative."

He considered. "So you're telling me that we can make a
short quick burn, or a long, slow burn?"

"Precisely. Also a short, slow burn, but I'm not sure why
you would want to do that."

Mattis closed his eyes a moment. Options … they needed

options. "Okay. Dismissed, gentlemen. Do what you can. I'll send for you when I have something."

Lynch and Modi saluted crisply, then left, leaving Mattis alone in his ready room.

He ran his hands through his hair. Time to report to Fleet Command.

He picked up his communicator and saw that he had many missed calls from Chuck. There was no time to answer them, but as he went to connect to the military channels relayed through the ship, it started vibrating, still set to silent.

On a wild impulse, he clicked the answer key.

"Chuck," he said, a slight waiver in his voice. "This isn't a good time."

"I know," said Chuck, urgency in his. "But listen. I got something big for you, and you *have* to hear it."

CHAPTER FIFTY-SIX

Earth
United States
Georgetown, Maryland
Presbyterian Hospital

Chuck *finally* had his father on the phone. The connection they had was bad, static-y and full of distortions from the vast distances involved, and he knew, on some level, that he had to be quick.

Besides, the doctor had delivered the news: a new heart murmur, worst than the last. He'd abruptly left, and something told Chuck that he wasn't telling him the whole story yet. He wanted to be done with this conversation before the doc came back.

"Listen dad," he said, speaking quickly. "I know you don't want to hear this, but I've been doing some digging around here—me and a guy named…" he almost said the name but didn't. "Doesn't matter. Look. Me and this *guy*. A CIA officer.

He's connected to Harry Reardon. You remember him?"

"Of course," said Mattis, his tone distracted. "I barely got to exchange any more than a handful of words with him, but he left an impression. What did you find out?"

"Well, I know what the future humans are after."

A long pause. "How in hell did you figure that out?"

"It's Spectre," said Chuck, his tone energized. "It's Spectre in a very literal, real way. The future humans ... all the places they've attacked. All the worlds they've been to. They're all chasing after Spectre. They want ... him."

His dad frowned in confusion. "They ... they want *Spectre*? As in, they want to kidnap him? Why?"

"I don't know. My CIA contact thinks so, but ... I don't think it's kidnapping," said Chuck, stressing his tone to get his point across. "I think it's more ... returning him. Or retrieving him." Chuck hated speculating but this was all he had. "There's *something* about him that is connected to all this. And the alien-future-people want him badly. If you ask me ... I think he's one of *them*. I could be wrong, but...."

Rain began to fall outside the hospital window, a grey sheet that pitter-pattered on the glass. His son was sick, and he was speculating about the motives of mutant humans from the future. Where the hell was that doctor?

"That doesn't make any sense," said Mattis. "The mutated future-humans we've seen didn't have any resemblance to humans that exist now. Spectre is—"

"Spectre might be something like a variant of them," he said. "Maybe. I have no evidence of this, but there's more to him than we could know. The exact truth ... I don't know. That's what I've been trying to work out. What the people I'm working with have been trying to work out. What exactly he is. And we're not certain, but what I *do* know is that everywhere Spectre has been, the future-humans, just like clockwork, have shown up and attacked. And not just in any random order—systematically. Planet by planet by planet, moon by moon by moon, all the places Spectre went, they went—within six months. They want him."

"But that can't be true," said Mattis, shaking his head at the tiny communications device. "Spectre came to us for protection. With information. He's a rat, but he isn't—"

"Wait," said Chuck. That bought a surprised scowl to his face. "Spectre is … aboard your ship? Right now?"

"Yes," said his dad. "He's been aboard for some time." He paused. "Listen, son, do you have *proof* of what you're telling me?"

Of course he would ask for that. "Sending through what I have," said Chuck. "It's not much, so prepare to be underwhelmed. Just hold tight."

He swiped on his phone, selected all the files that Smith had sent through, and uploaded them. The connection seemed slow, almost as though the signal strength were poor wherever he was. He watched the progress bar lengthen, planning to deliver one last piece of bad news before they hung up. Though … perhaps he shouldn't. Perhaps old Jack shouldn't be distracted with something like….

His grandson being sick with some mysterious … something. Dammit, of course he had to tell him.

Just as the upload finished, Mattis swore softly down the line and, after a brief squeal of static, the line went dead.

CHAPTER FIFTY-SEVEN

Pinegar System
Gas Giant Lyx
USS Midway
Ready Room

Mattis barely had to scroll through Chuck's information to see that what he was telling him was true. The more that came through, the more he saw it all lined up.

Everywhere Spectre had been, the future-humans had followed.

They were after *him*.

Spectre had been playing him the whole time.

He should have seen this.

Should have predicted this.

Should have protected his crew from ... from all this.

Mattis almost hurled his phone against the wall. The tiny device dug into his palm as his fingers tightened around it, flexing the metal and plastic. He could just so easily crush it, or break it, but he knew from experience that this wouldn't make him feel any better.

Slowly, gently, Mattis put the device back into his pocket. He took several deep, long breaths, fighting to control his anger, and when finally he had let his rage play out, his emotions settled into cold, cold fury.

With careful, measured steps he walked out of his ready room onto the bridge. "Lynch," he said, gesturing for him to follow. "Walk with me. And you too," he said, to one of the marines on the bridge.

Obviously confused, Lynch and the marine fell into step with him.

"Sir?" he asked. "Where are we going?"

"To the brig," he said. "To find out if Spectre is really there."

"Uhh … okay. And then?"

Mattis didn't say a word, but marched, grimly, down through the corridors of the *Midway*—busy, bustling corridors full of crewmen moving to effect repairs throughout the ship —towards the ship's cramped, uncomfortable, small brig.

He had been so paranoid about everything that he hadn't seen it right in front of him. *The thing to remember about crying wolf is that, in the end, there really was a wolf.*

When he got there, the presence of the two guards laying sprawled out, their bodies shocked and burned, almost made him think he wouldn't find Spectre there at all. But, sitting on his cot as though nothing was wrong, the door closed, was the man himself, quietly humming some kind of tune.

"Ahh, Admiral," said Spectre, smiling widely. "I see the information I gave you was of some use. Given that we are alive." His gaze turned to the two dead marines. "Not so for these men, unfortunately. Electrical fault. Terrible bother. At least they went quickly…."

Mattis glared at him angrily. "Give me one good reason why I shouldn't kill you."

Both of Spectre's eyebrows shot up in surprise as he looked back toward Mattis. "That's a mighty fine way to talk to the person who just saved your ship and your life, Admiral, eh?"

"Mmm," said Mattis. "Yes. How thoughtful of you to save us from the fight that we were only in because you were being hunted."

"Me?" asked Spectre, innocently. "Whatever do you mean?"

He had no mood for games. "I mean," said Mattis, "that we've figured out the truth. That the future-humans that we've been fighting this whole time … were after *you*."

Spectre just shrugged absently, like it was no big deal.

Lynch glowered beside him. "As my good old Pa used to say, some people would look good with bullet wounds on them."

"All those lives spent," hissed Mattis. "Those ships destroyed. You came to us ostensibly with information, but that wasn't it at all. You were just using the US Navy, using me and my ship, to protect yourself. You *coward!*"

"It's not cowardice to want to live," said Spectre.

"Your actions," said Mattis. "Have left many US citizens— people under my command—injured or dead."

"They would have died anyway," said Spectre evenly. "Nobody lives forever. All I did is move the temporal location of their demise."

What kind of a justification was that? Spectre was baiting him. "Do not play with me." said Mattis, evenly. "As someone who wants to live so badly, you won't like what I'm going to do to you. It's a popular misconception that humans explode when thrown out an airlock. They don't. Nor do they boil. They say we just kind of … pass out from lack of oxygen and die. It's well established scientific fact, but you know what?" He smiled grimly. "I've always wanted to see for myself."

Spectre just smiled despite it all. "You can be better than that, Admiral. Marcus Aurelius once said, *The best revenge is to be unlike him who performed the injury.*"

"Fuck that shit," spat Mattis. "Marcus Aurelius didn't have nukes. Or firing squads. And believe me: you won't like them either. The shooters in the firing squad aboard this ship are so accurate they ejaculate exactly one sperm."

Spectre rolled his eyes. "Make up your mind, my dear Admiral. Are you going to shoot me, or throw me out an airlock?"

"I haven't decided, to be honest," said Mattis, "although I did like that you didn't bring up option three: turning you over to your own people."

Spectre squinted, tilting his head. "The … British government?"

"No," said Mattis. "The growing future-human fleet on the other side of that gas giant."

"You wouldn't dare," said Spectre, shaking his head. "You're the kind of man who doesn't go back on his word. We had a deal."

"Deals are made to be broken."

"So are necks," said Spectre, all pretense of British jovialness about him instantly evaporating. For a moment—for just a brief moment—Mattis could see the *real* Spectre. A dark, manipulative, sociopathic maniac with no concern for anyone but himself.

Mattis stood by his initial assessment. A nasty piece of work. "Do you know what happens to a body when it dies?" he asked. "Sometimes, under the right circumstances, it shits itself. The same thing is happening to your little web of lies, Spectre. But your shit is your lies, your schemes, your manipulations … all spilling out everywhere, stinking the place up. Luckily it all ends soon."

"All an asshole can talk about is shit," said Spectre, playfully.

Mattis wasn't amused. "Triple the guard here," he said, "and instruct the marines that if this piece of space garbage so much as opens his mouth, fill his body full of lead."

"Don't threaten me," said Spectre, ominously. "You won't like me when I'm feeling threatened."

"I don't threaten. I act. Don't make me act." said Mattis, and then turned and left.

CHAPTER FIFTY-EIGHT

Pinegar System
Gas Giant Lyx
USS Midway
Bridge

On the way back to the bridge, Mattis gave his report to Fleet Command. It was brief, detailing the losses they had suffered, and that the USS *Hamilton* was the only ship to survive beyond their own. He advised them to send whatever resources they had in the area as quickly as they could, but he knew it wouldn't be much.

And wouldn't be enough.

Lynch opened the door to the the armored casement onto the bridge, and as Mattis stepped through, Lynch spoke up.

"Sir, we've dispatched a probe to the other side of the gas giant. We now have eyes on the vortex."

"Good," said Mattis, moving over to his command console. With a tap of a key he bought it up. The image was somewhat grainy and pixellated—the probes didn't have a great resolution—but it was there. There were now fourteen enemy future-human ships, including the damaged ones.

And it was just the *Midway* and the *Hamilton* to oppose them.

"Admiral," said Lynch, "I have Captain Abramova of the USS *Hamilton* on the line for you."

Speak of the devil. The only surviving ship to get out of that cluster-fuck with them. Mattis clipped on his earpiece. "*Hamilton*, this is *Midway* actual. Send it."

"Sir," said Abramova, jumping straight into business. "I've been talking to your XO about the ammunition situation, as well as the damage to our respective ships … nothing we can do about the latter, without a dry dock, but I think we might have a solution to the former."

That conjured a faint smile. "If you have the means to conjure ammunition out of nowhere, I'm all ears, Captain."

"That," said Abramova, "is exactly what I plan to do. Do you know of a small, little, entirely reputable, libertarian outpost called Chrysalis?"

He'd been there. Hadn't exactly been a great memory. "Lots of space mines that automatically destroy any ship that approaches unless their transponder code is on an approved list, lots of assholes who hate the government, and a lot of actually quite nice coffee now that I think about it. Why? Do you need a java hit?"

"Actually I wouldn't mind," she said. "But there is more there than just coffee. My XO … well, she used to be a bit of a wild child, you might say, and she's got a contact there who's prepared to sell us some shells for the standard Mark 22's we both carry, and *might* even be able to acquire us a new barrel for one we had damaged in the battle."

That surprised Mattis greatly. "Criminal elements at Chrysalis are able to get hold of *ammunition for state-of-the-art navy guns?* And replacement parts too?"

"You'd be surprised what people can buy on the black market," she said. "Or, more correctly, trade for. And Admiral —while we're there, I suggest, diplomatically speaking, *not* referring to it as a criminal element. Riley tells me it's an, and I quote, 'entrepreneurial free-enterprise unburdened by heavy-handed government regulation, and supplied by creative logistical solutions aimed at undermining the capitalist hegemony of multinational corporations.'"

"Of course it is," said Mattis, flatly. "So they're tax-dodgers who steal weapons from the US taxpayer and sell them."

"It's all in the interpretation."

Naturally. "Fine," said Mattis. "Give me a moment to decide."

He didn't want to go back to Chrysalis, but as he sat there, trying to think of a better option, Lynch spoke up, his voice charged with energy.

"Sir," he said, "the probe is detecting another *massive* energy surge."

"A second vortex?" Mattis asked, grimacing. How many of them could there be...?

"No sir," said Lynch, his tone curious, "I ... I think they overextended themselves. The vortex is collapsing."

The future-human ships sped away from the vortex, leaving their damaged, still burning companions behind. They were obviously afraid, and it was tempting to order the *Midway* to reengage, but it would take hours for them to round the gas giant—they simply couldn't.

So he watched as the vortex shimmered, shook, and then winked out of existence—replaced, ever so briefly, by a strange sight. The burned-out, partially consumed husk of the moon which had been there previously—it looked like a crescent moon on a cool Montana night, missing a big chunk of itself, glowing red hot as though the process used to open the vortex had consumed some great piece of it, converting it to energy.

The broken husk of the moon exploded, and from it came a massive turbulent blast front of energy and mass, traveling outward in an ever-expanding sphere.

Lynch stared at his console, wide eyed. "Sir," he said, "that blast front—the gas giant isn't going to stop it. We need to get into Z-space."

"Modi," said Mattis, touching his radio, "get us the fuck out of here. Emergency Z-space translation. Now."

"Sir, the engines will take an hour to charge at their current capacity—"

An *hour*. "Time until that energy pulse passes through the gas giant and gets to us?" asked Mattis.

"Thirty seconds," said Lynch. "Possibly less. That damn front's moving almost as fast as light."

Which meant if they were observing it using optical cameras, it was *substantially* further ahead than they were seeing. That didn't leave them much time at all. "I need a Z-space translation in twenty seconds, Modi," he said.

"But the engines—"

"Can you do it?" asked Mattis.

A brief, agonizing pause, and then … "Yes."

"Do it!"

All around them, the ship began to prepare for Z-space translation. Normally the process was gentle and quiet, but this time, the whole ship vibrated angrily, like an old man protesting being hustled out of bed. The *Midway* groaned again, just like it had before, and on his monitors, the glowing, writhing surge of energy got closer and closer.

"Hurry, Modi!" hissed Mattis.

The energy front touched the outer atmosphere of the gas giant. It was like a wall—it pushed the gasses along with them, as though it were some kind of impenetrable field, completely unlike anything he'd ever seen before. It smashed into the gas giant at what must have been a ludicrous speed, splattering its atmosphere out wide. Wide. Wide.

Then the roiling gasses engulfed the probe, and the video feed winked out.

"Now, Modi," said Lynch, gripping his communicator tightly.

"Standby," said Modi. "Charging."

"No!" Mattis almost shouted. "Now, now, *now!*"

The roiling wall of gas leapt towards them as the gas giant behind them disintegrated, squashed into nothing, the sheer amount of energy involved turning the gasses to a white hot stream of plasma that licked hungrily as it advanced toward them, the white light of it blocking out their cameras.

"Now, now, now, now, now, now, now—"

Then all was replaced by the bright, multi-hued pattern of Z-space, and the ship leapt away from the area towards Chrysalis.

CHAPTER FIFTY-NINE

Chrysalis, Low Orbit
USS Midway
Bridge

Mattis slumped back in his seat. "*Midway* actual to USS *Hamilton*," he said, his heart pounding in his chest. "Report."

"Do you think they made it?" asked Lynch, quietly.

There was a brief pause, and then Captain Abramova's voice came on the line. "This is *Hamilton* actual, we made it."

Mattis smiled widely as a cheer went up on the bridge. "Good to hear your voice."

"Same," said Abramova. "Listen, we're heading to Chrysalis ... figured that blast made up your mind for you."

"Sure did," said Mattis. "There's no way that fleet all got vaporized; most of them probably slipped away into Z-space like we did. Let's make for Chrysalis, rearm, do whatever repairs we can, and get going." He paused, considering. "Um, how are we going to pay for the shells?"

"Don't worry about that," said Abramova, "I got a plan."

"Fill me in on the way," said Mattis. "Hold please." Then he changed frequencies. "Modi, status on engines?"

"Well," said Modi, "They're holding. Thanks to some wizardry from me. I had considered simply letting them blow up, but then I wouldn't be able to spend those leave days you owe me … and I want to see the look on Lynch's face when he finds out I am going to spend them attending the rodeo he wants to go to. After, of course, I've finished disassembling Spectre's ship. Especially since I have *just so many leave days available* that I can, easily, do both!"

Lynch's dark scowl made it all worthwhile. "Good to hear," said Mattis. "Now, we're going to be pulling into Chrysalis soon, to rearm. The good Captain Abramova has a plan to get us some currency—or the local equivalent—to spend while we're there, so make sure that you have a shopping list ready."

"Will do," said Modi, and cut the link.

Mattis's communicator chirped. An incoming signal from the *Hamilton*.

"Admiral Mattis," said Abramova, her tone betraying a tiredness that he knew was from a lack of adrenaline. "How are you doing?"

It was strange to hear such a request from one so obviously drained. "I'm fine," said Mattis. "Combat keeps me up."

"I wish I could say the same," she said, stifling a yawn. "I'm going to switch out for a few hours sleep. You'd be wise to do the same, sir, if you don't mind my recommendation."

It would be wise, but he had so much to do and so much

nervous energy he doubted very much he would be able to anything more than simply lay there waiting for time to pass. "Maybe," he said. "Call me when you get there. We'll talk shop."

"Of course," said Abramova, a slight edge of humor dripping through her thick Russian accent. "You promised me coffee, sir. Do not forget."

The notion of something so refreshingly genuine made him smile. "I won't."

There was a slight pause, where the only noise down the line was a faint hissing. "Maybe something stronger," she said, her tone softening. "We lost a lot of good people today, Admiral."

"We did," said Mattis, soberly. "But we're going to avenge them. Our job isn't done yet. We have a lot to do; I've been to Chrysalis before, they aren't exactly the most friendly type, especially to the military. They have a pretty nasty minefield which we'll have to talk our way past. If we piss them off, they'll crunch us. Gravity bombs. Nasty little pieces of work. And they're hard-coded to lock onto military ships that get too close."

"I know, sir. I'm hoping Riley can charm them until the bad guys show up." Something came into Abramova's voice. A kind of casual whimsy that made him smile. "You know they're right behind us, yeah? The hostiles. Even though we can't see them on sensors … they're there."

"Bound to be," he said, as certain of it as he'd ever been of anything. "They won't let us go. Not after that. They may be humans from the future, but if they're anything like us, they're going to want revenge."

"Let's give them some revenge first. Let's give them …
pre-venge."

Amused, Mattis shook his head. "Go get some sleep, I'll
talk with you when we arrive."

"*Hamilton* actual out," said Abramova and closed the link.

The Z-space journey to Chrysalis was a short one, even on
reduced power, and Abramova was right. There was no sign of
pursuit but he could feel them out there, watching his ship.
Watching *him*.

When they arrived, all seemed quiet.

As they had planned, Abramova's XO—one Commander
Jessica Riley—negotiated with the Chrysalians. She seemed to
be almost a local, even sharing their accent.

When Mattis found out what they were expecting to trade,
however, he was less than impressed. Due to the losses
incurred during the battle, many of the strike craft no longer
had frigates to return to. While they had escaped in the
Hamilton's hangar bay, they had no way of repairing, refueling,
or rearming them, so their plan was to trade top-of-the-line US
military space supremacy for what they needed.

This, Mattis reasoned, was one of those things that the
history books would never record and that the US taxpayer
would never find out about. Those craft would be classified as
'lost.'

He just had to hope that they didn't find their way into the
wrong hands.

The notion put him in a slightly foul mood as the *Midway*
and the *Hamilton* sailed through Chrysalis's gravity-weapon
minefield, a relic of the last war with the Chinese, but as it had
been before, the *Midway* was permitted passage without a fight.

Or being blown up by the devilish things. Even so, it was disconcerting to have his ship orbit Chrysalis, drifting alongside the repurposed mines. Any moment they could light up, attach themselves to the hull, and crush the ship into tiny pieces.

Best not to think about it.

The trades were done. Spacecraft for ammo, armor plating, and even a new forward gun for the *Hamilton*. Modi's 'shopping list' came to much less stuff—mostly just circuits and electronics, a large amount of reinforced titanium plating, along with some raw materials and things that seemed inconsequential to him—and all for the low, low price of a single Warbird worth hundreds of millions of dollars.

He knew they were being ripped-off, but there was nothing they could do. For hours, engineers on the *Midway* and *Hamilton* worked to patch things up as best they could; even to the point of simply bolting armor plates over any battle-damaged areas. It was crude and ugly but it worked.

Tons of ammunition were bought aboard in what were clearly stolen, converted cargo freighters, and unceremoniously dumped in the hangar bay in a massive, entirely unsafe, pile. Modi would have pitched a fit if he had seen it, but at least it was aboard. Bringing it to the guns would be the next job.

Then, nearly six hours after their last contact, before they could move the ammunition, and just as Mattis was starting to think they could actually get this all done in time, a simple text message came through from Chrysalis station.

The future-human fleet had arrived.

CHAPTER SIXTY

Earth
United States
Baltimore
Public Spaceport
Dock 57A

Smith took one last look around the *Aerostar* and smiled. "Hey, thanks, guys."

Sammy smiled back, and Reardon nodded. "Always a pleasure," the older brother replied. "You're a problem, Smith, but not too much of a problem, you know?"

"I don't, bro," Sammy shifted in his wheelchair, feigning mild puzzlement.

Smith chuckled. "Look after each other, okay? And ... just don't touch that box for now. I'll contact you in a few days and tell you what to do with it."

"Sure, mum," Reardon laughed. In a flash, a thought bloomed across the smuggler's face. Rare sight. "You too, okay? Don't do anything … *too* stupid."

"Of course. Drop by some time. I'll take you to the awesome kebab place around the corner. You'll love it."

Sammy's expression brightened. "Wait, free food?"

Smith shook his head. "I guess so, Sammy."

"I do like food," the younger brother said. "We're taking him up on that."

Reardon shrugged, expression shuttering a little. "Next time we're all in the same system, maybe. Get me a nice jumper, Smith. You don't want to be caught without."

The spy let his laughter continue as he backed down the ramp. "All right, I'll buy a suitably awful pattern on the way home."

"*Two* patterns! You'll buy *two* suitably awful patterns on the way home!" Reardon called out after him.

"I'm not wearing the same thing as Harry!" Sammy added.

Smith waved lazily over his shoulder as he walked toward the dock's exit.

He set his eye to *lookout* function, and sorted files as he made his way back towards the underground carpark where he'd been storing his vehicle. All of his evidence was saved on his tablet, and his handheld, but he could work on the copy in his cybernetics and download the changes when he got to his car. After that, it was a quick transmission to the folks in Langley, and all his work would be backed up in HQ. There was a lot to sort, honestly. Most of the work had already been done in Z-space, but there were a few things that could be better-organized.

As he was walking down to the first level of the carpark, his eye beeped. *Suspicious activity.* Wasn't that strange to get a false alarm for that, but still. *Keep looking*, he instructed it as he began moving his latest changes onto his absolute last-resort backup device, a data storage chip implanted deep in the bone of his ankle.

The first level didn't have many people in it, but then, it wasn't time for most workers to knock off yet.

Apart from the cars, the second level was deserted.

Uh-oh.

Smith made a show of looking around in confusion and winked, activating a distress signal from his phone. He started dialing Reardon, turning to go back up the ramp. And almost ran into a black-clad man looming right behind him.

He really needed to get those tracking algorithms looked at.

He smiled tightly, looking for all the world like a stressed businessman, and tried to step past. "Sorry, sorry...."

The man in black blocked him.

Ah well. They were doing this, then.

Smith feinted right and side-stepped, trying to get a little higher up the slope. His opponent matched him step for step, drawing a shock-stick as he moved in closer.

Great. Smith retreated, staying on the balls of his feet.

A split second before the attacker fired his eyes narrowed, and Smith dove down the ramp, tumbling out of the way of the prongs. The thing probably had a second shot, but he'd have to be in range first.

Something scraped on the concrete behind him. More attackers. *Shit.* He used his momentum to keep rolling, bursting out of a circle of black-clad legs just before they could close in.

All in black? Seriously? What did they think they were, ninjas? That, or whoever hadn't liked his digging was *really* hell-bent on a color scheme. He skidded behind a car, narrowly avoiding a fist to the face. They regrouped quickly, rounding the car to cut him off.

Too slow. He slammed the head of the first pursuer into a window as they came round the corner and bolted as they slumped, stunned. That was the problem with ambushes in covered carparks like this. Heaps of places to hide, but then, heaps of cover if you didn't take out your target fast. And if said target could activate a sensor that saw into the infra-red, well...

Someone behind the next car. Alright. Instead of dealing with them directly, he leaped, narrowly avoiding a hand grabbing for his ankle. The pursuer behind him reached again and the hidden one reared up, but he was already over the windshield, on the roof, leaping between cars.

This would have been a really bad idea, he reflected, *if I hadn't spent a large part of my life training for basically this exact scenario.*

He cleared the aggressors quickly and slid back down, racing to another row of cars. God, ninjas swarming a spy in an underground carpark, it was something straight out of some gritty comic-book adaptation. *Pity I'm not that kind of hero,* he thought, flicking his handgun's safety off.

Crack! Some idiot dumb enough to show his face went down.

Crack! One of his ninja-friends followed.

They started hanging back. A heat-signature started tracking around the aisles of cars, obviously looking to get in a flank.

Nice try, buddy. Smith slipped around a few cars, staying low. The guy kept looping around. He leveled his gun. *You're going to have to give me a clear shot eventually.* They were level with him now. *Come on, come on...*

An arm appeared over a bonnet and lobbed something at him. Thin and cylindrical.

Grenade. *Shit shit* shit—

He snapped off a shot at the arm, at the body that must have been behind it, and moved for cover but it was too late. The device flashed three times, pulsing with purple light.

His stomach lurched in a profound way he hadn't ever expected, as though being tossed around on a rollercoaster. His prosthetic eye stopped working, as did various other implants.

Some kind of tech wizardry had taken them out. He fired in a moment of shock, emptying the last of his magazine.

Smith shook his head, suddenly half-blind, and tried to plan. Making a target of himself was bad, getting trapped would be worse. The gun was next to useless, now that his depth perception was significantly affected.

He put his blind side to the car and stayed very still, drawing his own shockstick. With any luck, he might pick up anyone's approach from a blind spot with good old-fashioned hearing.

Indeed, he heard a scraping sound from the blind spot, on the side where most of the enemies were. He whirled and met the probably-not-actually-a-ninja's charge with 50,000 volts to the chest. That stopped her. He gave her a solid kick as she went down and then moved back a step, because there was another one just *begging* for a shock to the face and—

Something very solid and *very* fast connected with the back of his head.

He staggered. His remaining vision spun.

There was a sickening *thud* as the second blow landed.

And agent John Smith dropped like a sack of potatoes.

The black-clad figure who had launched the implant-disabling device hunkered down beside the fallen spy, looking for a pulse.

They nodded and pulled out a communicator. "Alright boss, target subdued. Still breathing. Let's get him back to base."

And that was all he remembered.

CHAPTER SIXTY-ONE

Earth
United States
Baltimore
Public Spaceport
Dock 57A

"This is it," said Reardon, flicking on the blowtorch and adjusting the flame until it was a hot blue. "You ready for this, Sammy?"

"Yeah," said Sammy, leaning forward in his wheelchair excitedly. "Come on. Open the box. I wanna see what we got."

"Even though Jonny-boy told us not to?"

"*Because* he told us no to."

He smiled. Fair enough. With careful deliberation, Reardon put the blowtorch to the box's lock, heating it until it glowed a faint, angry rose color. Then, holding the torch with one hand and a pair of hydraulic bolt cutters in the other, he snipped the bar and the hot metal fell to the deck.

"There we go," said Reardon, grinning over his shoulder. "Just had to ask nicely."

"Do you think it's gold?" asked Sammy, curiously. "Data drives? Maybe even something more valuable."

Reardon turned off the torch and set it down, rubbing his hands together gleefully as he reached up for the lid. "Hey presto," he said, lifting off the lid triumphantly. A rush of cold air washed out, chilling his hands. "It's a—"

A dead body.

Crammed inside the small box was the withered, almost rotten creature, its flesh a sickly green color, limbs warped and gnarled like the branches of a wasted tree. It didn't smell— either it had been preserved in some fashion, or the body had deteriorated to the point it no longer reeked.

"Well?" asked Sammy, grinning from ear to ear. "What is it?"

"Nothing," said Reardon, grimly, as he slowly, almost reverently, put the lid back on the box.

Sammy wheeled closer. "Come on," he said, a slight whine to his voice. "I wanna see it. What is it?"

"It's nothing," said Reardon, his voice hardening slightly. "Believe me, you don't need to see this. It's not valuable. It's just—"

"It's a body, isn't it?" asked Sammy.

Reardon didn't like lying to his brother. He often had, to protect him, but he never liked it. "Y … uh, no." And he was never any good at it either.

"I want to see it," said Sammy, his hands resting on the wheels of his chair. "I'm not a kid any more, Reardon. I might not have made the call to shoot those people back on Zenith

… but I was the one who turned on the guns. I aimed. I pulled the trigger. It might as well have been me who made the decision. I was in this job from the start, I want to be there for the end." He paused, eyes flicking to Reardon. "I want to see it."

"Not like this," said Reardon, hands balling by his sides. "Not like this. Sammy, come on."

"I'm not a kid," said Sammy, gently, but with an underlying firmness that could not be denied.

Dammit. He was right. He could trust his little brother to fly him through a deadly firefight, talk Smith through a dangerous infiltration of a senator's high-security vacation estate. He could trust him to shoot thugs off his back. But he wanted to protect him from seeing a dead body?

Time to let go, Reardon. He's all grown up.

So, carefully, he lifted the lid and set it aside.

Sammy stared impassively down at the body, eyes occasionally drifting over its form. Reardon hated seeing it … hated doing this to his brother. Why did he want to see so badly?

"Hey bro," said Sammy, nodding down to the body. "Check it out."

He didn't want to look. "What?"

Sammy nodded again, insistently. "Look. I think it's still breathing."

Nah. That guy was green and dead. There was no way. Reardon kept his eyes averted for a moment but, quickly, curiosity took hold. He looked.

"Holy shit," he said, as he watched the body's chest gently rise and fall. It seemed impossible to him, completely impossible, but there it was … gentle, slow breathing, as though artificially induced.

"It's … it's *alive*."

Reardon babbled something in a frightened stammer, half falling back. But rather than attack them, the creature just lay there, its chest rising and falling. Below the body was another box, and from the label on the top, it was very clear what it was.

High explosives.

"Okay," said Sammy, "what are we going to do with this thing?"

He had *absolutely no idea*. Slavery—buying and selling people—wasn't exactly what he was in the game for. "I'm not sure," he said, hesitating.

"I got an idea," said Sammy, considering. "Why don't we just take it to the last person Spectre would expect us to deliver it to?"

CHAPTER SIXTY-TWO

Chrysalis, Low Orbit
USS Midway
Bridge

Right on the edge of the minefield, ten future-human ships—Lynch had helpfully re-designated them Skunks Alpha through Juliet—transitioned out of Z-space at the same time.

"Sound general quarters throughout the ship," he said, as the ship's lighting switched from the standard to the ominous red of battle.

Lynch assessed the radar output screen with a critical eye. "Looks like that bizarre shockwave took care of most of the damaged ones," he said, nodding with grim satisfaction. "And it might have roasted a few others, too, before they got away."

"I'd like to think they're coming into this battle as soft as we are," said Mattis, although he knew it was, in many ways, a forlorn hope. Still, nothing wrong with hoping for the best and preparing for the worst.

Without seeming to waste any time at all, the hostile ships began steaming straight towards Chrysalis, the forming up into an aggressive attack formation, their weapons glowing with eager energy.

"How long do we have?" asked Mattis.

"Not long at all," said Lynch. "They exited Z-space real close to Chrysalis—way closer than we could ever try. Based on how fast they can move, they'll be in effective firing range in five minutes. More or less. Enough time to finish what we're working on, then get everyone back in place and ready to fight."

Five minutes. It seemed both far too long to wait, and yet, just barely any time at all. Mattis watched as the enemy fleet drew closer and closer. With the tap of a key, he called up the *Hamilton*. "How are those repairs coming?" he asked into his radio.

"Admiral, we're coming along well," said Abramova, "but if you could ask the enemy to *politely* hold off their attack for a moment, we could really use the extra time."

Lynch glanced at him. "I don't think they're really much for talking."

Mattis clicked his tongue thoughtfully. "As much as that is my preference … neither am I. Get ready to engage. Are they close enough for a firing solution yet?"

"Almost," said Lynch. "Give the gunners a moment to calculate the initial firing solution. Stand by."

Combat in space using projectiles meant that the effective range of their weapons was only what they could see, and what they could hit before their target dodged. Inevitably these kinds of things turned into knife fights.

"Firing," said Lynch, and the ship shook slightly as the *Midway*'s guns spoke.

A thought flashed through his mind. "Captain Abramova, the mines around Chrysalis … the last time we were here, they were programmed to destroy any ship without a valid transponder ID. Does Commander Riley know if that's their standard configuration?"

"That's my understanding," said Abramova, and there was a brief pause, presumably as she conferred with Commander Riley. "Yes. That's correct."

Mattis smiled grimly. "What's the bet these fuckers don't have clearance?"

"They aren't really much for talking," said Lynch, echoing his earlier words.

The ship fired again, another wave of shots flying out toward the encroaching future-human ships. "They haven't fired back yet," mused Mattis. "Almost like they're hesitating…"

"Maybe they don't want to hit Chrysalis," said Abramova. From one of his screens on the command console he could see her frigate firing too, white hot streaks of cannon fire leaping into the void. "Our orbit currently puts us between the asteroid and them. If they miss us, they'll hit the surface."

The memory of Zenith's scoured surface, fire and smoke and ruin, flashed into his mind. "Since when have they shown a reluctance to endanger civilians?"

"Unknown," said Abramova, "but they aren't shooting."

The enemy ships continued to advance, the first wave of fire striking their armored front, sparks and flame flying as they absorbed the impacts. She was right; their weapons lay silent, still, not even tracking them.

"Whatever the reason," he said, "let's use this to our advantage. Adjust our orbits … switch from low to stationary relative to that fleet. Put us between the asteroid and them, permanently. It'll buy us more time, and if they want to engage us at close range, they're going to have to contest that minefield."

"Aye aye, Admiral," said Abramova.

"Executing orbital shift," said Lynch, fingers working at his console.

The *Midway* and the *Hamilton* began to drift, their engines flaring in the cold dark of space. Slowly they gained distance from Chrysalis, firing their guns as the two ships moved to keep the rough, jagged disk of the asteroid behind them and the enemy ship ahead.

"Keep firing," said Mattis. "We're throwing our shells at their strongest point, but hell. We just reloaded. Might as well spend what we got."

So it went. The *Midway* and the *Hamilton* fired their weapons until finally the hostile ships drew close enough for some of the spherical mines to light up and begin to move toward them.

If the future-humans had any fear of the mines, they didn't show it at all. They steamed on ahead, sailing straight toward the approaching gravity mines. Right as the two signals merged, the attacking fleet fired volleys of their strange red gun toward the mines, striking them straight on. But the Chinese had apparently built the things to last. They absorbed the gunfire handily, the blasts seeming to only make them angry, accelerating on toward their target.

The lead enemy ship collided with a mine. There was a flash of some kind of energy in the high ultraviolet spectrum, and then a powerful, invisible force crushed the ship as though a giant had stepped on it from behind, leaving it a broken, crumpled hulk.

That seemed to get their attention. The remaining ships halted, blasting away at the approaching mines, slowly cutting their way through the encroaching swarm.

"That should stall them for a bit," said Mattis. "But keep shooting. Whittle them down as much as we can."

Nearly ten minutes later, three more of the ten future-human ships had been crushed like aluminum cans, and another had been heavily damaged, and the remaining five ships pulled out, seemingly unsure of what to do.

Would they retreat?

Unlikely. But if they didn't retreat, fighting was all they had, and five to two was still no contest.

Time to give them what they came for.

"Hail the lead ship," said Mattis. "Open channel, all frequencies, no encryption. Just send it out to all listeners."

"Aye aye, sir," said Lynch. "Channel open."

Mattis cleared his throat. "Attention enemy fleet, this is Admiral Jack Mattis of the USS *Midway*." He paused for emphasis. "You want Spectre? He's all yours."

Slowly, inexorably, the future-human fleet stopped where they were, guns pointed menacingly toward them. That, he figured, was what would have to pass for a *yes*.

"Put that annoying British shit in a shuttle," said Mattis to Lynch. "Go with him to the hangar bay. Make *certain* he gets onboard—automated pilot. No humans, no risk. Let's finish this once and for all."

CHAPTER SIXTY-THREE

Chrysalis, Low Orbit
USS Midway
Corridor

Spectre walked, dressed in a spacesuit, his legs draped in heavy chains. Marines and Commander Lynch lead him toward the hangar bay.

"Hey," said Lynch, glaring at him. "You really are a peace of shit, bless your heart, ain't you?"

He said nothing, just continued to stare down at his hands.

"I've always wondered about this," said Lynch. "It seems some people are born right out of Satan's asshole. They just … come out wrong, you know? You strike me as one of those people."

Again, Spectre said nothing for a moment, then finally he spoke up. "You know they're going to kill me, right?"

Lynch snorted. "You looking for sympathy from me, boy? You ain't getting none. You caused everyone a great deal of trouble, and a lot of people—good people—died because of it. If I had my way I would have just shot you, but it's nice that we had you as a bargaining chip."

They had arrived at the shuttle, and the marines shoved him up the ramp.

"Yes," said Spectre, glumly. "I suppose that is true." He sat down on the bench outside the cockpit. Lynch stood over him. "If you know it, and I know it, can I have a final request?"

Lynch narrowed his eyes. "I'm not about to whip you up a steak, if that's what you mean."

"No final meals for me, thank you. No. There is one small detail which I believe you've overlooked."

Lynch eyed him disbelievingly. "And that would be…?"

"My datapad. You really think those things out there are tracking *me*? As in, bodily? My person?"

Lynch demurred. "Well…."

"Fine. Believe what you will. Good day, Mr. Lynch." He closed his eyes and leaned back against the bulkhead.

He heard Lynch swear, and moments later, he heard a thud from the floor.

"Burn in hell, you freak," said Lynch, walking out the hatch. It closed behind him.

Specter cracked an eyelid and glanced at the floor.

The datapad.

"Thank you, Mr. Lynch." He picked it up, and checked for any final messages from his research assistant, Janet Sizemore. There it was, and just in time.

Latest test more promising. Code attached.

He looked up from the message, and out the front viewport towards the advanced ship the autopilot was taking him to.

And smiled.

The shuttle groaned slightly as, presumably, the future-human ship's gravity beam caught it and began dragging it in.

Finally, the slight tremor stopped and everything was still.

"We have arrived at our destination," said the ship's computer, in its smooth, polite, masculine voice. "Please disembark through the forward loading ramp."

Spectre stood up, straightening his back. "Well, old chum, this is goodbye." He reached out and touched the ship's hull. "Thanks for the lift."

A speaker mounted on the wall crackled. "This is good riddance to bad garbage," came Lynch's voice. "Adios, amigo."

"Ta ta," said Spectre, as the loading ramp at the back of the shuttle opened. "Goodbye, automated shuttle."

The machine, somewhat predictably, said nothing. It just sat there waiting for him to leave.

So leave he did.

The hangar bay of the future-human ship was pressurized, as he expected, and there, waiting for him, were a pair of them. They were so ... beautiful, in their own grotesque way; the pinnacle of human evolution, the absolute peak of humanity's genetic potential. So strong and deceptively cunning.

"Ugly mother fuckers, ain't they?" came Lynch's voice from the tiny speaker. Obviously he could see ... somehow.

"Haven't I taught you anything?" said Spectre, over his shoulder, as he walked down toward the creatures. "Appearances aren't everything."

He walked down the ramp. Behind him, it rose up and sealed, and then the shuttle lifted off, engines roaring as it slid out of the hangar bay—the atmosphere being held in by artificial gravity, giving the automated US Navy shuttle a clear run out to the stars.

"Hello," he said.

Almost as though on cue, the future-humans advanced on him, hands outstretched, their faces distorted in fury.

Spectre only smiled. He carefully turned the tablet around so it rested on his palm—a difficult task with his shacked hands—and then, swiping left a few times with his thumb, bought up the menu.

The future-humans, hissing loudly, stepped up to him, their faces enraged and twisted with fury. Hatred.

"Shh, shh," said Spectre, touching the button labelled *override*. "No need for such incivility."

The creatures stopped, frozen completely. For a brief moment they just stood there, then the anger left their faces and, suddenly calm, they relaxed completely.

He held up the shackles. "Remove these without harming me."

The creature, obediently, reached toward him, took hold of the chain, and snapped it. A few links fell off, tinkering onto the ground.

"Stand aside," said Spectre.

The creatures did so, moving away from him without complaint.

It actually *worked*. "Well now," said Spectre, tapping idly at the buttons on his device as he wandered off toward the airlock that lead toward the ship's bridge, "that was worth all the trouble it took to get here, wasn't it?"

CHAPTER SIXTY-FOUR

Chrysalis, Low Orbit
USS Midway
Bridge

Mattis watched the shuttle return with a grim sense of satisfaction.

"And they definitely took him?" he asked Lynch, for the second time, as the tiny ship pulled into the hangar bay.

"Absolutely sure. They didn't look too pleased to see the guy, either—like they were going to just tear him to pieces the moment the shuttle left. Which it did. In a big hurry. Guess even computers get rattled sometimes."

Well, that was something at least. "They haven't left yet," said Mattis, an air of caution creeping into his voice. "The hostile ships. They're just … sitting there."

"Sir," said their communications officer. "We're receiving a transmission from the enemy fleet. Audio *and* visual."

Visual? This might be a chance to see *inside* the enemy

vessels. He nodded his head. "Put it through. And patch in Abramova, too; I want her informed about what's going on." He paused. "And Modi, too, so we have his eyes on the internals. I want him to absorb as much as he can from what little, I'm sure, they'll show us."

The main monitor flickered and, upon it, appeared Spectre, flanked from behind by two future-humans. Immediately, his smug, arrogant face dashed any hope that he was genuinely a prisoner there.

"Good morning, Admiral Mattis," he said, cheerfully.

Mattis frowned slightly despite himself. "You don't look like you're much of a prisoner over there," he said. "They must be treating you *very* well."

"Oh yes," said Spectre. He raised up his hands to the camera, showing they had no shackles on them. "Very well."

Anger built up inside him, threatening to spill over. A niggling worm whispered in his ear that he had been played, manipulated into standing in this very place and in this very situation. "Very well," said Mattis, forcing himself to keep as calm as possible. "You're obviously free. Why are you calling me? Just to gloat?"

Spectre shrugged playfully. "Oh, nothing so distasteful as that. Just a few loose ends to tidy up." He clicked his tongue several times, as though thinking about some difficult problem. "Admiral, I'll be frank with you; I want your ship. Hand it over to me, or I will destroy it."

Matters raised an eyebrow. "Your bargaining posture seems fairly weak," he said, "despite the lack of handcuffs. Assuming you have full control of the hostile fleet—well. We have our guns. We have the mines. The rest of the US Fleet knows we're here—reinforcements are only a matter of time. Every second you spend here your position decays and mine strengthens. So ... no."

Spectre almost seemed to genuinely consider that, eyes flicking to something off screen for a moment, then back to the camera. "Tell me, Mister Mattis, is Mister Lynch listening to this conversation?"

Mattis and Lynch exchanged a brief glance. "You know he is."

"And what, pray tell, did I say to him right before I stepped off his quaint little shuttle?"

There was a brief pause, and then Lynch spoke up, his voice strangely curious. "Appearances can be deceiving?"

"Exactly," said Spectre, snapping his fingers. He casually drew a pistol, showing it to the camera, then he put it to the head of the grotesque mutant creature beside him. The creature—vaguely human—didn't move, just stood there, and Spectre pulled the trigger.

Messy. Mattis didn't blink. "So I'm guessing you're running the show over there. What is this designed to prove? That you have total control of those ... *things*?"

"You *are* a good guesser," said Spectre, beaming widely. "In fact, this whole fleet is now mine. You see, in the future, the governments of the world decided that humans having free will was ... inconvenient. A design flaw in the schematic of the species. So they fixed it. Biological impulse within all of them, a kind of natural computer if you will, turning them all into fearless, obedient, perfect puppets. And now I control the strings."

Mattis wasn't sure he believed even a single word of that,

but Spectre's display was … disturbing.

Modi's voice came through his earpiece, static-y and tinny, as though the microphone was some distance away from his mouth. "Sir, I am receiving a *very* faint signal emanating from outside this system. It's coming through on a military frequency, but it's … low powered. Almost deliberately so. It doesn't even have a message, just a faint pulse."

He knew what it was. They called it a *flashlight*; an extremely weak signal focused in a narrow beam, designed to evade enemy detection disguised as background radiation. It could be used to send rudimentary Morse Code, but was more commonly used as a simple signal: *We are here.*

They had reinforcements en route. Nearby. What exactly they were… he couldn't say. But it was something. Something reassuring.

Mattis had to stall them. "Why do you want my ship?" he asked. "You surely must be aware that this is a US Navy asset and quite expensive. I'm not going to turn it over to you because you say so."

"Actually," said Spectre, absently, "I could care less about your rusted, ancient, beaten-up piece of shit you call a ship. All I *really* want is the Chinese engine upgrade you so carelessly managed to mention, several times, when you were in my presence. If you could turn *that* over, I'm certain we could arrange for you and *most* of your crew to go free. Except Commander Lynch, of course. He and I … well." Spectre chortled. "I have taken a personal dislike to him and I would greatly enjoy some private time with him to resolve our differences, if you'd be so obliged."

Mattis snorted dismissively. "That isn't going to be

possible. I'll never turn Lynch over to you, or any of my crew. I would rather die."

"Oh come now," said Spectre, smiling knowingly. "You and I are both aware that your ship is heavily damaged. I also know that your other ship is also heavily damaged. I know that you considered turning me over to your enemies to be your absolute last resort. And it has failed. Now you face the full might of this advanced fleet with me at its head, and I … well. I know too much about you. I'm too smart. I'm too, frankly, brilliant. You and I both know that there is only *one* way that this ends. I will have your ship. Your guns will damage my ships, your mines will whittle us down … but your advantage before was that the former crew of this ship did not want to harm Chrysalis. I, personally, don't care much for that rock. In fact, I'll more than happily bombard it from afar, well out of the reach of your guns, and your mines—mines which will just as surely attack any reinforcements you conjure up.

"Interesting, isn't it, that your first line of defense would also be your undoing. A wall that keeps attackers *out* also keeps the defenders *in*. You're not keeping me away with your Chinese-made relics … you're keeping yourself exactly where I want you."

Stall him. Keep stalling him. "Is that so?"

"Correct. You see, Admiral Jack Mattis, you may be able to dodge incoming fire easily enough, but an asteroid… well. They aren't known for their agility, shall we say." Spectre extended a hand, hovering it over some unseen console. "Do you need a demonstration of my willingness to do this?"

"No," said Mattis, genuinely. "I believe you on that front."

"Good," said Spectre. "So it comes down to this. No

tricks. There is nothing you can do about what is about to transpire, so let's just … avoid all the bloodshed, yes? You give me what I want, and I will promise you—swear on my life— that I will let you and your crew, including Commander Lynch, free."

"And what is that?" asked Mattis, glaring at the screen. "The new engines?"

"Specifically, yes," said Spectre. "I would like them now … but, as discussed, I will allow you and your crew to disembark to Chrysalis before I take it."

"No."

Spectre smiled just a little. "Are you sure that's wise?" There was a slight pause. "Is Captain Abramova of the *Hamilton* listening? Lovely little Russian thing, I'm sure you know who I mean. First generation immigrant—a pure patriot. So rare these days. I want to know if she can hear me."

Something about the way Spectre was … *describing* … the XO of the *Alexander Hamilton* sent a cold chill down his spine. "No," said Mattis, his tone guarded as he lied. "She is not."

"Good," said Spectre. "Because if she was, I'd ask her if she'd managed to stop for her scheduled resupply at the Jovian Logistics and Supply depot in the Aussie System. Let me just check if she did…." he tapped a button on his device.

For a second, nothing happened. Then, a wail of alarms, including the proximity alarm, filled the bridge. The radar operator's voice shouted over the din. "Admiral Mattis, the USS *Hamilton* just … exploded."

A wave of debris pelted the port side of the *Midway*, pieces of the former warship clanging off the armor plating and bashing against the side of the ship, digging in deep. The ship rocked violently from the impact, then settled down to an ominous quiet.

Spectre's finger hovered ominously over his device. "One of the advantages of being the kind of person that I am is that things often work out the way I want them to. Because I plan. I think ahead. More than you could ever, ever know. And consider, Admiral, there are two buttons on my little toy here. One was for the Hamilton. Care to guess which the other is for?" Spectre's finger did a little wiggle.

Snarling, Mattis balled his fists and then, slowly, let them relax. Spectre was insane. A madman—he was many things, and a liar was not one of them.

There was no point sacrificing everything. Not yet. He just needed to buy them more time … something he couldn't do if his ship was in pieces.

Mattis ran through a mental calculation. How long it would take to evacuate the ship versus engage Spectre's fleet, potentially damaged or crippled….

It was too much of a risk.

"No," he said. "We accept your terms. Give us time to evacuate, and the *Midway* is yours."

CHAPTER SIXTY-FIVE

Chrysalis, Low Orbit
USS Midway
Bridge

"All hands, all hands, this is the Captain speaking. Abandon ship. I say again, all hands, abandon ship. This is not a drill."

Mattis gave the command he, and every other commander, hoped to never give. The most dreaded, the most hated, command in the US Navy. "Commence evacuation proceedings immediately. All shuttles in the main hangar bay, prepare for emergency launch, and to receive personnel from sickbay and command staff. Escape pods and shuttles are to make their way to Chrysalis, where we will rendezvous and await pickup. I say again, this is Admiral Jack Mattis, CO of the USS *Midway*. All hands, abandon ship."

He looked around the bridge, to the crew gathered there, and nodded firmly. "Take an escape pod," he said. "Lynch, let's head down to the shuttles."

"Good thing I'm still wearing my spacesuit," said Lynch, obviously trying to make light of the situation.

"Yeah," said Mattis, and stood out of his command chair … for what he suddenly realized might be the last time. Admiral Fischer had gotten her wish after all; for the second time, Admiral Jack Mattis was stepping down from the command of the USS *Midway*, although he had to admit, not even she would have anticipated him going out like this.

Then again, if she had wanted the ship back at the end of the mission, she should have been more clear about that. He couldn't help the little smile that crept over his face and, in amongst the realization that this, really, was the end, he was in some way relieved that the *Midway* was his ship to the last.

"You okay there, Admiral?" said Lynch, his voice soft.

"Yeah."

"You sure?"

"Yeah." Mattis took a deep breath and pushed everything else out of his mind. "Let's get going."

The long, slow walk down to the main hangar bay was made in silence. Mattis felt numb; the processed air of the warship felt suddenly cold to him, as though it were stealing the warmth from his bones, stiffening his joints in a painful, physical way, almost as if the ship itself was trying to discourage him from leaving it. Around them, the crew made their way to the escape pods, and Mattis made sure to fall behind anyone he saw. He would get off last.

Half-way to the hangar bay, Modi met up with them, a pair of senior engineers in tow. "For what it's worth," he said, his tone even as he fell into step with Mattis and Lynch, "I think this is the right course of action. Sorting through the ammunition we loaded would have taken far too long."

It would. Mattis nodded grimly. "Thank you, Commander. Even if Spectre was bluffing us—and I simply don't think that's in his nature—there was just no way we could take on all the remaining ships on our own. We couldn't win. But…" he let just a little bit of a smile play over his lips. "We can force a draw."

Modi inclined his head slightly as they rounded the final corridor toward the hangar bay. "What do you mean, Admiral?"

His mind played over the possibilities, slowly putting together … something. Not quite a plan, but an idea. A start. "Modi," he asked, "have you had a chance to inspect the ship Spectre came aboard with?"

"I have only performed a customary evaluation of its capabilities," he said, curiously, "it seems to be of a standard construction, none too dissimilar to our own, if significantly more advanced in most ways. But this is hardly the time to discuss its capabilities."

"Actually," said Mattis, his grin turning positively Cheshire-like, "now is *exactly* the time." He stopped outside the airlock to the hangar bay and pulled out a spacesuit from a nearby locker. "What can you tell me about its engines?"

Modi's face fell. "If you are seriously considering taking that ship's engines and giving them to Spectre, I can tell you that will take *far* too long, and … why would he fall for that? He *came aboard* on that ship, there's just no way he'd be fooled by anything we could do to it. If we try to blow it up, he'll know."

"Of course," said Mattis, matter-of-factually. "I can't expect anything else." He paused, pulling on a glove. "What about the ship's other systems?"

"Other … systems?" Modi stared blankly at him. "Well, they're … they're basically just the ones that come on a standard shuttle. Nothing special." Modi squinted. "You think Spectre left something in the shuttle's computer that would let us, I don't know, hack into those ships out there? That won't work, because—"

"That's not what I'm planning," said Mattis, pulling on the legs of his suit. "Listen. Here's what I want you to do.…"

CHAPTER SIXTY-SIX

Chrysalis, Low Orbit
USS Midway
Pilot's Ready Room

Guano had barely trundled into the Ready Room, still clad in her flight suit, when the evacuation alarm sounded, followed almost immediately by Admiral Mattis's voice.

"All hands, all hands, this is the Captain speaking. Abandon ship. I say again, all hands, abandon ship. This is not a drill."

There was a brief moment where the fifty pilots and gunners crammed into the ready room all looked at each other, as though sizing up if the sound was real or not. If they should act or ignore it. Remain seated and wait for orders or follow protocol and get to the escape pods. The lighting flickered and turned red.

It wasn't a joke.

Roadie's booming voice broke the spell. "Go! Go! Go!" he

shouted, making a dramatic shooing motion with both hands. "What the hell are you waiting for, a signed invitation? You heard the Captain! Get to your coffins, now!"

Coffins. The pilot's slang for escape pods. Because they were small, fit one, and were notoriously unsafe.

A slightly-less-than-totally-disorganized stampede of flight-suit clad aircrew flowed out through the door to the ready room and spilled out into the corridor. Roadie followed up the rear, shooing everyone along like some kind of angry mother hen, shouting over the constant drone of the evacuation alarm.

"What the hell?" asked Flatline, his voice pitching upward. "Did we get hit? Hit in the reactor? We didn't even get to launch again!"

"I don't know," said Guano. Someone tripped and crashed into her from behind; she grabbed Flatline, instinctively, and nearly pulled him over too, but the three of them kept their footing.

"Sorry," said Frost, her dark skin several shades lighter than normal. "Oh my god, I can't believe this."

"Just stay calm," said Guano. Someone else jostled her and she fell against the bulkhead, and then with a groan, pushed herself back up to her feet.

A sudden surge of panic leapt through her. An instinctive fear. Things were getting out of hand, and fast. There were people all around her, pushing and being pushed, and the corridor suddenly got a lot tighter.

Stampede.

"Stop!" roared Roadie, which bought everyone to a screeching halt in the middle of the corridor.

For a moment she thought he was going to yell at them all, but, instead, his finger pointed to the pressure doors embedded in the bulkheads. The escape pods.

Not a second too soon.

"Everyone aboard," she said, taking in a deep breath to steady her nerves, shaking off just how close they had come to disaster. "C'mon, c'mon."

She and Roadie, working together, managed to corral most of the flight crew into the cramped, uncomfortable pods, a situation made worse by their flight suits. One on hand, some seemed glad for the extra protection. On the other, it made an already uncomfortable fit distinctly claustrophobic.

With her heart still racing and images of being crushed to death by her fellow pilots flashing through her head, Guano waited until the crowd had thinned out and then, hurriedly, began peeling off her flight suit. No way she was getting into one of those things without maximum room, air be damned.

"What the hell are you doing?" asked Roadie, shaking his head as he saw her yank off her gloves. "No, come on. Put your suit back on."

Guano shook her head. "Nope."

"You can't be serious," said Flatline, still dressed in his.

Roadie's voice became soft. "Guano … you know those things aren't exactly robust."

Guano wiggled out of the suit pants. "I know. But if I'm going to asphyxiate, I want it to be because there's a hole in my coffin, not because my own flight suit gave me the ole' hug of death." She kicked her feet, shoving the thick leggings away. "Besides," she said to Roadie, grinning like an idiot. "If I die, I won't be around to bother you anymore."

Roadie's face was a somber mask. "Patricia, don't even say that."

The use of her first name knocked the goofiness out of her. "What," she said, managing to crack a little smile. "The ship's evacuation siren means we're now on a first name basis?" She twisted in a little teasing tone. "Mo?"

"Something like that, I suppose." Roadie smiled a light, pleasant smile that, if just for a moment, reminded her of that night they had all drunk *way* too much tequila. "You be careful, a'right?" he said, briefly reaching out a hand and touching her cheek.

"Yeah," said Guano, closing her eyes a moment and leaning in to the touch. His hands were so warm, and after nearly getting trampled to death, she ... suddenly felt like she needed a little touch that wasn't threatening at all, wasn't dangerous, and was ... almost very nice.

There was a brief silence as they stood there, the only sound the wailing of the klaxon.

"*Oh baby, mmm..., oh baby, yeah baby,*" said Flatline, grinning at the two of them like the infantile moron he was, then ducked into his pod.

Any semblance of there being a *mood* utterly vanished. Roadie put his hand down, and then, in a moment, the CAG-attitude was back. "Into the coffin, Lieutenant," he said. "I'll see you on the other side."

"See you on the other side," said Guano, hesitantly stepping into the tiny little pod. A thick metal sheet sealed her in with a hiss, and through the tiny window she could see Roadie.

The two exchanged a look, and then she touched the

bright red *launch* button and her tiny craft shot away from the *Midway* and into space.

CHAPTER SIXTY-SEVEN

12,449 km from Chrysalis
Future-human Vessel S-84
Command Center

Spectre watched with eager satisfaction as the first of the escape pods flew away from the *Midway* toward Chrysalis, their automated pilots doing exactly what he thought they would do —make for the nearest source of human habitation and land.

He scanned each one, carefully, using the advanced ship's sensors. They showed, very clearly, that there were humans aboard ... living people. Not decoys. Not false heat signatures. The resolution on the future-human ship's scanners was extremely fine—it could watch the thermal readings of the people inside just like a black and white movie.

None of them were Admiral Jack Mattis, however, but there were just so many that perhaps he'd missed him.

No matter. If Mattis decided to go down with his ship, that would be fine. Otherwise he would die on the surface of

Chrysalis. Either way suited him just swimmingly.

The future-humans standing around him, like impassive golems, didn't move or react to the chaotic scenes taking place on the holographic displays all around them, just as they hadn't reacted to their friend having her brains blown out right in front of them.

So perfect.

"Take away the body," he commanded one of them, absently, his gaze fixated on the *Midway*. His minions grabbed the arms of the dead one and dragged it away.

He used his handheld to link his implants to the ship's command codes. A series of impulses directed through his implants brought the fleet closer, and closer, cautiously advancing, wary of any tricks.

Spectre was prepared. He scanned the *Midway* constantly, an eye on their reactors. The standard tactic to secure a ship being abandoned was destroy it; damage their reactors in a catastrophic explosion using well-placed high explosives. Not dissimilar to what he'd done to the *Hamilton*. Now that he could control those mutant ... things, a simply command to the green monster inside that box on the *Hamilton* was enough to get it to spark the explosives it was sitting on. Poor bastards wouldn't have even had time to cry for their mothers before they died.

But the *Midway*'s reactors looked totally normal to him, humming away at low power mode, typical for a ship at rest. Even a high resolution scan indicated no high-explosive anywhere in the vicinity of the reactors. Everything seemed so ... safe.

Yet he couldn't trust them. Couldn't begin to think that

Mattis didn't have a plan for just abandoning his ship like this.

"You," he said, pointing his finger toward a random future-human. "I'm making you my assistant."

"As you wish," the creature hissed, its voice a combination of wet leather and sandpaper. That immediately bought a frown to his face. Why would anyone build one of these beautiful creations with such an unpleasant cadence to them? Was it an error in its DNA? Some kind of manufacturing defect?

"What's your name?" asked Spectre, barely able to keep the disgust from his voice.

The creature didn't answer. So perfect, so obedient, even the *concept* of names was alien to them.

"I'll call you Lurch," he said, nodding resolutely. Lurch was a good name for such a malformed shadow of perfection. Or possibly Grue, for gruesome? No, Lurch was better. "Lurch, I imagine you're good with starships since you've been piloting one. In your evaluation, is the *Midway* in any danger of exploding?"

The creature, Lurch, ducked its head and consulted the readouts. "No," it said, dragging out the words roughly. "Reactor temperature, stable. Hull integrity, stable. No signs of —" a thick glob of drool descended down from its quivering lower lip, splashing on the console with a wet, disgusting splatter, "elevated system use."

Spectre tapped his foot impatiently. "How goes the evacuation?"

"Eighty-five percent of their escape pods have been launched." Lurch, slightly too slowly, craned its head around, looking at the various displays and screens. "Based on tactical evaluations of the *Midway*'s crew, and given that they are currently executing a well-ordered evacuation which is not under duress, this would likely be a full complement of their enlisted crewmen, and most of their officers."

It was difficult to listen to that thing's rasping any more. If Spectre knew Mattis at all, the crotchety old bastard would want to wait to be the last man off the ship. And since he was, well, old … he'd want to take a shuttle. Not a rickety escape pod.

Using the high-res thermal camera, Spectre scanned over the *Midway*, looking for people. He moved from face to face to face, scanning them, taking them in … searching.

And then he saw him. Admiral Jack Mattis, climbing aboard a shuttle, the last man to leave the USS *Midway*. The shuttle sealed, then took off, flying out of the hangar bay and banking toward Chrysalis.

Now the ship's engines would be his—and with their gravitational lensing ability, he could create his *own* vortex. And leap forward into the future … where the next phase of his plan would take place.

Time travel was a fun game. And Mattis had given him the tools to play.

"Lurch, come with me," he said, triumphantly. "Wipe that silly drool off your face. We're going to that ship. Bring a security detail just in case; sweep the ship, kill anyone you find. Alert me immediately if there are any stragglers."

"Yes, Christopher," said Lurch.

Spectre glared at him. "Never call me that name again," he said, and made his way down to the shuttle bay.

CHAPTER SIXTY-EIGHT

Chrysalis, Low Orbit
USS Midway
Shuttlebay
Shuttle Zulu-1

Mattis took one last look at the hangar bay of the USS *Midway*—it seemed like a lifetime ago he'd taken command of her again, following Captain Malmsteen's death—and then stepped aboard shuttle *Zulu-1*, waiting as the hatchway sealed with a hiss.

The craft took off, leaving the hangar bay and the ship far behind.

"You okay?" asked Lynch, carefully.

"I will be," said Mattis, resolutely staring out the window at the slowly receding sight. "It's just a ship."

"Jack," said Lynch, hesitantly. His drawl softened, which Mattis had come to recognize as Lynch taking a matter very, very seriously. "She's not just a ship. You know that."

It was too true to confront. Not yet. There would be time later.

"I know, dammit. I know."

Mattis pulled out his communicator, searched through the various frequencies, and patched it through to the one Spectre had used to contact them.

"You won, goddammit," he said, completely unable to keep the absolutely genuine anger out of his voice. "Take my ship and *never* show your face around here again."

"Thank you very kindly," said Spectre, a distinctly superior, mocking tone in his voice. "I assume the keys are under the sun visor?"

Mattis glowered. "The president going to hear about this. You can't just steal a US Navy warship and expect to get away with it."

"My dear Admiral Mattis," said Spectre, "I already have." And then he cut the link.

"Jack," said Lynch, smiling nervously as the shuttle drifted away from the *Midway*, "he's not going to fall for it."

"I'm counting on it," said Mattis, smiling a little bit, too.

CHAPTER SIXTY-NINE

Chrysalis, Low Orbit
USS Midway
Hangar Bay

Spectre stepped off the shuttle like Julius Caesar coming to inspect his latest conquest.

It was tempting to think to himself that it had all been too easy. In truth, not everything had been smooth. There had been hiccups. Mistakes. Minor errors. But now … now it was okay. Everything had worked out in the end, and now, his hard work was finally about to bear very sweet fruit indeed.

Spectre walked through the hallways and corridors of the ship, admiring how *empty* it was. He kept checking, again and again, the reactor levels, but if Mattis had done something to sabotage it, whatever he had done was so minor that not even the incredibly advanced future-human tech could detect it.

Maybe he had really, truly, given up. Checkmate was checkmate, after all.

Spectre took his time walking all the way to the bridge. Upon arrival, he discovered Mattis had, very helpfully, left the armored casement open; invitingly, almost mockingly so.

"Lurch," said Spectre into the strange device the future-humans used in lieu of radio. "Sweep the ship from stem to stern. Make sure you check *everywhere*. Leave no stone unturned; I want this whole ship searched. If there are any explosives, any humans left behind, anything at all … you let me know."

"Yes, Spectre," said Lurch. And then that dumb drooling idiot went off to do his bloody work.

Spectre waited patiently for it to be done. Taking no chances. Yet, as the future-humans swept through the ship, they found nothing … nothing but an empty ship, devoid of crew and escape pods in equal measure.

He had them check again. And again.

Nothing.

So finally, Spectre stepped through the door in the armored casement, and onto the bridge.

Everything was calm. Quiet. The machines hummed silently, reporting everything as normal. Spectre scanned over them briefly, checking each one. He was half-expecting a computer voice to be softly counting down a self-destruct sequence, *ten, nine, eight* … such that he'd have to make a desperate escape. But no. Nothing. Everything was normal.

Odd. He would have expected Mattis to try *something*.

Slowly, carefully, Spectre lowered himself down into the command chair, smiling to himself as he slid comfortably into the soft seat. The material creaked faintly as he adjusted himself. What was this stuff? Some kind of synthetic leather, perhaps? It felt firm but comfortable, smooth and yet gave plenty of friction.

"Lurch," he said into his radio, as much to himself as to the creature. "I'll have to get myself one of these when I'm done with this ship. Maybe I'll take it with me."

Lurch didn't answer. Given its nature, that made sense, but Spectre checked the readouts again, just to be sure.

And then he saw it. An excess of heat in the hangar bay. The glow drew him in, snatched his attention as something that was distinctly out of place.

The image looked so grainy and unclear to him; so lacking in the finer details. Going back to this level of technology was frustrating. He swept the camera over the hangar bay, left and right, and then found the source.

The glowing outline of his shuttle—the one he'd originally used to travel to the *Midway*, its engines and reactors powered up.

So simple, and yet, so effective. The old bastard Mattis … that was his trick; using the very ship Spectre had sailed in on as a bomb, no doubt. Overloading its reactors. Obviously flooding it with coolant to try and keep the secret hidden until it was too late, keep the heat levels at roughly that which would be expected for a ship that size.

Clever. Spectre appreciated the effort.

But a simple tap on his console jettisoned the ship out of the hangar bay, shooting it off into space, the tiny ship tumbling end over end as it shrank away.

His ship. The ship he had come aboard the USS *Midway* on. There was a certain poetic symmetry to it; they had traded ships, although, of course, Spectre had absolutely no affection for that tiny vessel. It was just a lump of reactor strapped to some engines. Spectre double checked everything, just in case, waiting for its reactor to explode or its weapons to activate....

The ship just continued to lazily turn over and over. It became a blip on their close range radar; still within range to damage the *Midway*'s paint job if it blew, but hardly any more than that. He watched idly as the *Midway*'s computers identified it based on its transponder signal, flagging it as *US Navy Vessel 57014.*

Odd. Hadn't his shuttle's transponder originally squawked a civilian code? Spectre flopped back into the strangely comfortable seat, watching the ship's tiny blinking dot on the radar screen.

And all the other grey dots closing in toward it.

Frowning, he sat up again, watching the swarm of dots get closer and closer. Were they fighters? No, unlikely. Where would they have launched from? Long range sensors were clear. Were they munitions of some sort? No. Why would anyone target his little ship?

Slowly, slowly, the truth dawned on him. The grey dots were mines. The mines that were programmed to destroy any military ship that came close without an approved transponder code.

The shuttle wasn't the weapon at all.

It was bait.

"Mattis, you son of a bitch," he muttered to himself, unable to keep a respectful, almost admiring, smile off his face as a dozen heavy gravity mines slammed into the shuttle. With a surge of energy and a white flash, the shuttle's hull imploded, crushed to oblivion. The resulting surge of gravity, barely a stones throw off the bow, tore the *Midway* across space, peeling off its hull plating and snapping its bones like twigs. Air howled as it rushed out of thick cracks in the armored casement that surrounded the bridge, a thousand spider-web fractures crawling all over it, the force sending tiny spears of metal in all directions, the armor spalling and shredding the inner heart of the *Midway*.

Yet the ship managed to survive even that. Bloody, battered, Spectre watched through one eye—the other taken by a whizzing shard of metal—as the gravity surge pulled the ship and the surrounding cloud of debris in closer. The forward section of the ship cracked and broke off, spiraling lazily toward the gravimetric surge as more of the dastardly mines activated, the powerful forces nearly yanking him from his chair.

For a brief moment, everything went quiet. Too badly damaged to even whimper out an alarm, the bridge computers fell eerily silent, their lights dying as the damage broke their internals.

Then a brief moment of tranquility, where the loss of gravity caused him to drift slightly out of his chair, floating in the bridge's rapidly escaping air.

Lovely, almost.

A dull roar heralded a series of powerful secondary explosions as the terrible damage done to every part of the *Midway* spread to the massive pile of freshly loaded ammunition nestled deep within its hull, the freshly overstocked reserve of explosive shells detonating all at once, blowing apart the ship from within.

And everything after that was white nothingness.

CHAPTER SEVENTY

Chrysalis, Low Orbit
Shuttle Zulu-1

"Mattis, you son of a bitch...."

More satisfying words he'd never heard. Mattis let the corner of his mouth turn up, a fleeting moment of joy that was stolen away as the hangar bay filled with flame, secondary explosions tore through the USS *Midway* from within, and the whole ship detonated as the explosions took out her reactors, breaching them and blasting her into a billion pieces. The fragments slowly spiraled out toward the gravity surge, forming a flat, disk-like shape.

Mattis, Modi, and Lynch watched as the ship burned, pieces drifting away as the former ship became nothing more than a slowly expanding cloud of debris, burning gas, and occasional secondary explosions. The future-human fleet, clustered around the *Midway*, slowly exploded or broke apart one by one, as shrapnel and secondary explosions tore each ship to pieces, their flaming swan songs joining with that of their former enemy.

It was beautiful, in a way, like watching the last firework show on Earth.

"All of the crew definitely got off okay, yeah?" asked Mattis, for what seemed like the four hundred-thousandth time.

"Yes," said Lynch. "Sure as shooting. I checked the computer myself."

Mattis turned away from the porthole on the shuttle, unable to look at the raging inferno any longer. "Good," he said, although the words sounded hollow in his throat, like he knew he'd made some kind of error. "My god … what have I done?"

"You blew up our home, you jackass," said Modi, although the words did not carry an accusation's tone … it instead, sounded something like his attempt at a joke.

"It's just a ship," said Lynch, echoing Mattis's earlier statement, as the shuttle touched down on Chrysalis. "It's just a ship."

It's not just a ship. She was far more than that.
She was their home.

The loading ramp unsealed and lowered, revealing the surface of Chrysalis, dotted with escape pods, each one opening like seeds, the dazed, surprised crew climbing out, or helping those who had yet to pry open the doors.

Pieces of the *Midway* and the future-human fleet fell into Chrysalis's artificial atmosphere, slowing down and burning up as they encountered the thick air, an artificial meteor shower to match the firework display.

A thousand brilliant lights in the sky turned darkness into daylight, bathing the surface of Chrysalis in strange, lurid lights and shadows, adding a serene, almost surreal, quality to the deep, sinking pain Mattis felt in his gut.

The shuttle banked slightly, and out of the window, Mattis could see a series of bright flashes; the stark white burst of a ship exiting Z-space translation, so bright and harsh on the eyes from this side, and so beautiful and multihued on the other. He squinted as another came in, and another, and another.

A whole US fleet, complete with heavy cruisers and carriers. In amongst the fleet he saw other ships—a pink-colored civilian craft he recognized as Harry Reardon's ship, pulling in just behind Yim's cruiser, the Chinese-flagged vessel leading the pack, weapons charged and ready.

You're just a little bit too late, friend.

His communicator buzzed and, almost in a daze, he hit the talk key. "Mattis here."

"Good evening, Admiral," came Yim's voice, a curious edge to it. "What happened to your ship?"

He didn't even have the heart to say. "Doesn't matter," he said, taking a low, deep breath and letting it out slowly. "She's gone. It's just a ship."

Silence on the line.

"I'm sorry," said Yim, with all the sincerity in the world.

"I know." Mattis closed his eyes, letting the soothing darkness keep him from thinking about what he'd done. "Why … *how* are you here?"

"Your friend, Harry Reardon." Yim's voice was gentle but beneath that was a layer of concern that struggled, obviously,

against the weight of other conflicting emotions. "He's …
come into possession of something you need to see. One of
the future-humans. *Alive*. He tried to deliver it to you, but once
he realized you were engaged with the enemy, he came to me."

Mattis should have cared. He really, really should have
cared; he should have ordered the pilot of *Zulu-1* to turn
toward Reardon's ship and complete the original mission he
was given, to meet up with the smuggler and take his story,
then find out what this … living future-human was, and pry
out all the mysteries from its mind he could. He knew that he
should do all these things and more, and yet…

And yet he was so tired. He simply couldn't do it.

"Why don't we get coffee first," said Yim, in a way which
suggested some level of understanding. "Take a victory lap
around Chrysalis. I have to debrief Mister Reardon and his
brother, and see what we can find out. I'll meet you on the
surface."

"Agreed," said Mattis, and then, slowly and deliberately,
closed the commlink.

It was just a ship, he told himself, allowing himself to use
the past tense for the first time.

And they knew things. They knew how the future-humans
were getting there, and that with the gravimetric technology
they could close the rifts through which they came. If Spectre
hadn't been lying they might even begin to understand how to
open them, too.

Either way, it was a problem for Modi, and a problem for
someone else. Without a ship he was just a man.

And for the first time, he almost felt okay with that.

Everything was going to be okay.

THE LAST DAWN

CHAPTER SEVENTY-ONE

Chrysalis, High Orbit
The Aerostar

Reardon squirmed uncomfortably in his seat as he stared out the cockpit window at the massive, expanding debris field which his computer had helpfully identified was largely the former USS *Midway*.

"Kind of glad we didn't meet up with them when we were supposed to, huh," said Sammy, similarly transfixed.

"Pretty much." Reardon grimaced. "We would have likely have been aboard when she blew."

Although, well, there would have been so many other different possibilities that might have played out that, potentially, the ship wouldn't have been destroyed at all, or wouldn't have even come to Chrysalis. A thousand possibilities swarmed in his head; some better, some worse, but all irrelevant because they never happened.

Sammy glanced over to him. "How did you know Admiral

Yim, anyway?" he asked.

Reardon cocked a little smile. "I don't," he said. "But I saw him on the news once. Something about a friend of Mattis. Seemed close enough."

"Bro," said Sammy, sounding half disappointed, half angry. "You can't just sail up to a Chinese warship like you did and just … you know, *expect* that they won't destroy us simply for getting too close to them. You risked both our lives on a lucky guess."

Reardon just smiled. "So, business as usual, then."

"Business as usual," echoed Sammy.

He sat there, watching the spinning debris field, and then his computer chirped. Reardon sat up, blinking in surprise.

"What's that?" asked Sammy, leaning over to look at his console curiously.

"That," said Reardon, "is a signal from the listening device I put on the cat. Way back on that station above Ganymede. I programmed it to alert me if certain words were said. Most notably, Spectre."

"I'd honestly forgotten about that," said Sammy, wide-eyed. He stared at Reardon. "Can I listen?"

There was something in his tone that caught Reardon off guard. A strong desire to be … useful, perhaps? He knew better than to try and steal away something Sammy could do. Especially since opportunities for him to help out, beyond piloting and gunnery, were so limited. "Go for it," he said, waving his hand. "Lemme know what they're saying."

Sammy clipped on an earpiece and listened. His face contorted, first in confusion, fading to bewilderment, then something vaguely resembling dull surprise. "It's hard to tell because of all the purring, it's making it hard to be certain, but…"

"What?" asked Reardon, curious.

"It's … Spectre," said Sammy, his tone skeptical. "And … Spectre. But both *aren't* Spectre."

That made absolutely no sense at all. "Uhh, okay … try again."

"It is," said Sammy, insistently. "There's like, two different people talking. Near the cat. And they're both referring to each other Spectre." His eyes widened. "It's … really weird."

"Like…" Reardon struggled to process it. "They're twins or something?"

"No, not twins," said Sammy, grimacing. "Seriously? Why would twins have the same name, dumbass."

"Yeah, my bad."

"No, it's like, they're both calling each other Spectre. And others. But they add stuff after the Spectre, like there's *Spectre-Logistics*, and *Spectre-Intel*, and … more." He looked up, ashen-faced. "I think there's a *lot* more."

"What like it's just a nickname? For different people?"

Sammy shook his head. "No. I don't think so. I … think it's a lot worse than that."

CHAPTER SEVENTY-TWO

Earth
United States
Georgetown, Maryland
Presbyterian Hospital

The door finally opened, and in walked a nurse holding a happy baby Jack, followed by the doc, who looked equally happy.

"Mr. Mattis. I'm happy to report that your child is perfectly fine."

Jack was smiling. A lot. He sure did look … fine.

"Really? But didn't you just say an hour ago that he'd developed a new heart murmur? Worse than bef—"

"I was wrong, and I apologize. Little Jack is *fine*."

Chuck looked from the smiling nurse, to the smiling doctor, down to the smiling baby Jack.

The hair stood up on the back of his neck. Something was wrong. Very, very wrong. He couldn't explain it, but it just felt … off. He took Jack out of the nurse's arms and looked skeptically at the doctor. "So, how can you go from a diagnosis of *strange and disturbing new heart murmur*, to *perfectly fine*, in the space of less than an hour?"

The doctor heaved a sigh and held out his hands in what his father Admiral Mattis would often call *the penguin salute*— something his enlisted men would do when they were trying to say *Sorry, boss, no idea how that canister of high explosives fell into the barbeque pit*. "Mr. Mattis, sometimes these things just happen. A kid comes in, looks sick, we come up with a theory as to what's wrong, and in the meantime, the kid just gets better." He snapped a finger for effect. "Just like that."

Chuck wasn't buying it. Though Jack *did* look very happy.

"All right." He stood up and carried Jack to the door of the exam room. "All right, uh, I'll follow up with you if, uh, … things change. Ok?"

The doctor smiled broadly again. "Absolutely. But I wouldn't worry about a thing."

Chuck left the room. Left the hospital. Left downtown and finally made it home to their apartment in the suburb. And by the time he walked through the front door, he was sure: he was *very* worried. That doc was talking out his ass. And he was going to get to the bottom of it.

Epilogue

Chrysalis
Surface

Guano pressed the *open* button on her escape pod, and once again, the screen flashed up in front of her.

ERROR: POD DOOR JAMMED
ATMOSPHERIC INTEGRITY COMPROMISED

She was far from an expert in escape pod maintenance but that didn't sound good at all. Guano hammered on the door of the escape pod, worry growing within her. What if she had landed in an unpressurised zone? If the door opened, she would just, you know, die. Which would not be ideal. The whole *point* of escape pods was to avoid death. Not bring her to it.

Taking off her flight suit had not been a great idea.

"Hey!" she shouted. "Someone help me here! Galaxy's best pilot, suffocating in a box right here!"

Someone knocked on the top of her pod—*rap-tap-tap-tap*—and then it was pried open. She squinted as the light and, most importantly, fresh air rushed in.

"Patricia," said Doctor Brooks, offering her his hand. "What a surprise seeing you here."

Huffing to catch her breath, Guano took the hand and eased out of the pod with a groan. "Where's Flatline?" she asked. "Where's Roadie?" She went to stand, but her knees felt weak.

Doctor Brooks caught her before she fell. "Hey, easy," he said. "You okay?"

"I don't feel good," she said, and she meant it. Maybe there hadn't been enough oxygen in that escape pod thingie … she felt vaguely lightheaded as she looked around, trying to sort out where she was. There were buildings, but her pod was way, way out from all the others. "Where are we?"

"We're on Chrysalis," said Doctor Brooks, reassuringly. "Just on the outskirts. The industrial sector."

Industrial sector … that didn't sound good. "We gotta get back to the main settlement … area … place … thing." She blinked as her eyes swam. "I'm real dizzy."

"Don't worry. You're mildly hypoxic and it looks like you just need a moment to recover."

Fair enough. "Stupid oxygen," said Guano. Brooks began to lead her toward a nearby building, short and squat and painted a mundane grey, with no windows and a single door. "And stupid escape pods. Coffins. Space coffins. They can't maneuver for *shit*." She let out a hacking cough that burned her throat. "And they … and they choke me to death apparently."

"That's fine, just come in here."

It was … *odd* that he was being so specific, but Guano couldn't really think about it. She gulped down air as Doctor Brooks pushed open the door with his foot, and then half walked, half carried her through the threshold into some kind of unmanned, unstaffed reception area. A steel pressure door, similar to the internal doors on a starship, stood against the far wall.

What was this place? "Is this a water treatment plant?"

Without stopping to take in the sights. Brooks led her toward the steel door and waved his wrist in front of the sensor to the right. The door opened with a faint hiss. Beyond was a room lit with a series of green lights, and full of large tanks filled with fluid. Purposefully, Brooks walked past the tanks.

She was full of adrenaline and gulping down air like it was pills at a rock concert, but she *swore* that inside the tanks were people. People of a myriad of forms; tall, short, male, female, some she couldn't even tell. They were all sleeping … peaceful, eyes closed, relaxed.

There was no way this was real. Her head swam. She sat down on a nearby seat. There were rows of them, nearly a dozen, each placed before one of the strange vats.

"What is this place?" she asked, squinting as she looked around. The tanks were huge … and the glow seemed to be coming from within, shrouding the faces in light and harsh shadows.

"What are those things?" asked Guano, her eyes slowly widening. Some of the faces were identical. The same person, multiple times. "Are those … clones?"

"Something like that," said Doctor Brooks, as he reached

over and injected her in the arm with a syringe. "And so much more."

"Ow!" Guano yelped, rubbing her arm ruefully. "What the fuck was that?"

"Just something to help you sleep," said Doctor Brooks, smiling reassuringly at her. "Now. Close your eyes."

She definitely did *not* want to sleep. Guano went to stand but her legs didn't work. A creeping numbness spread up her body, from her knees to her hips to her waist, enveloping her and stealing away her motor control. Her arms flopped weakly down by her side and she could only gurgle.

She stared, wide eyed, at the tanks further down the corridor. Through the thick, almost opaque glass she could see a dozen of them with Doctor Brooks's face. All of them pale white, eyes closed, almost as if sleeping. Or dead. Or….

Oh. Shit.

"Who are you?" she asked, her voice slurring. "*What* are you?"

"I am the man who will defeat Admiral Jack Mattis," said Doctor Brooks, a slow smile creeping across his face. "And the man who will save humanity. Make it better. Oh, so very much better. I have many names."

"Nah," said Guano, spots dancing in front of her eyes. "You're … you're Doctor Brooks." It was getting really hard to think….

"That is one name I've used," he said. "One face. One identity. I have others; other versions of me, like reflections in a mirror. Many of them. Mattis knew but one of them … and the best part is, now he believes that person is dead."

It was babble. Bullshit. Guano tried to suck it up, force

herself back to consciousness, but whatever she'd been injected with was powerful. She couldn't move. Just lay there, drooling, on the floor.

Doctor Brooks observed her with a cautious nod, and then replaced the syringe on his belt. With careful deliberation, he unhooked a communicator from his belt, dialed a few numbers, and then spoke into the line.

"Yes," he said, "this is Spectre. The escape pod went right where you programmed it to go." There was a long pause, and then Doctor Brooks smiled in a way very much unlike him, and very much like someone else she'd seen wandering around the ship. "You can come get her whenever you like. Tell Spectre-Intel to start operation Ad Infinitum. We're ready."

And then the sedative finally took hold, and there was only darkness.

Thank you for reading *The Last Dawn*.

Sign up to find out when *The Last Champion*, book 4 of *The Last War Series*, is released: smarturl.it/peterbostrom

Contact information:
www.authorpeterbostrom.com
facebook.com/authorpeterbostrom
peterdbostrom@gmail.com

80497151R10240

Made in the USA
Lexington, KY
03 February 2018